Bear Witness

BEAR WITNESS

J.&D. BURGES

Naaltsoos Press

Published by Naaltsoos Press

ISBN 979-8-4884-8032-2

Typesetting services by BOOKOW.COM

ACKNOWLEDGMENTS

We wish to give high praise to graphic artist Paul Burges for his spot-on cover design. Thanks to Dr. Lynn Stevenson, Paul Burges, and Audrey Burges for their excellent suggestions and encouragement. Special praise goes to professional voice actor Renee Dodd for her performance of the audio book.

CHAPTER ONE

SCAMPERING toward a barroom brawl wasn't in my plan for the evening. I'm a mother of two with a good reputation. I don't hang out at bars. I really don't, and I don't like seeing fistfights, not even in movies. I'd classify this situation as a knitting circle that went terribly wrong.

My Stitch and Bitch group—we usually call it S&B—was in the bar that Saturday night because of the band. Not even the band—one guy *in* the band who used to go out with S&B member Laura Dumfries in the wild days of her youth. To hear her tell it, he'd been the sexiest thing in sideburns back in the early 1970s, when she waited tables at a beach café near her hometown of Pasadena and watched him surf. That was fifteen years ago. She hadn't seen him since then, but when a friend from high school called to let her know that the guy's country band was playing in Sage Landing, she couldn't resist the chance to check him out. The small-town rumor mill being what it is, though, she didn't want to be seen at Wranglers by herself on a Saturday night, so she proposed a last-minute S&B field trip. Only five of us could be there, but the rest of the group would be expecting a full report at S&B on Monday.

It was as simple as that, really. The band would start playing at 8:00, and we got there at about 7:30. We were lucky to get a table at all because the place was packed with strangers—not because of the band, but because of the movie crew that had been straggling into town over the past couple of days. It hadn't taken the outsiders long to discover Wranglers, with its "rustic" atmosphere featuring unfinished plywood walls, jumbles of mismatched tables and chairs, and dim ceiling fixtures with a few bare lightbulbs.

The band appeared on the cramped platform that Wranglers called "the stage" as our pitcher of beer arrived. Laura squinted past the crowded dance floor, saying, "He's the drummer, I think." She searched all the faces on the stage as the members of the band milled around before taking their places. Then she said, "Oh…oh my god." We all looked over at the guy sitting behind the pearl-white drum kit, glowing in a greenish spotlight, and—well, let's just say that the years had not been kind to him. We watched as he energetically clacked his sticks together overhead to launch the band into a Creedence cover. I couldn't tell if Laura was disappointed or relieved.

Sitting directly across from Laura, Dee Moreno was the first to recover. She quickly said, "Boy, this music takes you back, doesn't it?" As president of the local community college, she was used to steering conversations into safe territory.

We all nodded, settling back to listen. The band wasn't bad, and the tunes reminded me of high school dances, but without sweaty palms and acne anxiety. I was about halfway through my first beer when my friend Wanda nudged me and said, "Naomi, a guy is staring at you. Don't look!"

"Where?" I asked, keeping my eyes obediently focused on the table in front of me.

"Clear across the room. In the corner. He's with two other people, a guy and a girl. But I'm pretty sure he's been scoping you out. Wait— some skinny bottle-blonde is standing in the way." Under her breath, she muttered, "That's right, lady, just stand there trying to see through those big sunglasses." Wanda hummed along with the band for a chorus or two before giving me the go-ahead. "Okay. Over there."

I glanced around the room like I was marveling at the size of the crowd. Sure enough, a man was sitting in the shadows who might have been gazing in my direction. He suddenly turned away. I took a quick gulp of my beer, which went straight into my windpipe. *Real smooth, Naomi,* I told myself as I coughed and sputtered. *Way to draw attention to yourself.*

"He's doing it again," Wanda said, pounding my back. "He's staring right at you."

I looked at him again, more directly this time, and again he turned away to talk to one of his friends. I risked a little longer appraisal of him. Unfortunately, the air was already thick with cigarette smoke, and none of the lightbulbs in his vicinity seemed to be working, so peering in his direction didn't help me much.

"I think... I don't know, there's something familiar about him," I said.

"Is there? He's not ringing any bells for me." Wanda glanced his way. "Is he Navajo?"

I laughed. "You mean, does he seem familiar because I'm Navajo, too?"

Wanda shook her head. "Nope. I'm trying to figure out if he's from around here. I don't think he is."

By now everyone at our table had taken at least one turn at staring across the room to see who Wanda was talking about. Each of us quietly agreed that he was not a local.

"Hollywood maybe," Dee said. "Actor? He's pretty cute."

"Ruggedly handsome, more like," said Laura. "Definitely hot enough to be an actor."

"Sort of lean and rangy," added Wanda. "Thirty-five? Forty? What do you think, Sue?"

"Great hair," said Sue, who should know, since she does hair for a living.

I snuck another peek, this time noticing his glossy black hair. "If he's an actor, that would explain why he seems familiar."

After a while, it was clear that, whoever the guy was, he wasn't interested enough to walk over to our table. I wasn't going to walk over there, either, so we all turned our attention back to the music, such as it was. When it was time for another pitcher, Dee said that it was her turn to buy. It was about nine o'clock, I guess. She picked up the empty pitcher and made her way to the bar, where the lone bartender was swamped.

While Dee stood patiently at the end of the bar by the back door to wait her turn, I watched a couple of guys oozing closer to her along the bar. One of them was a strikingly gorgeous fellow, maybe in his early twenties. The other was a chubby specimen who could easily have been sixty, at least from where I sat. I wondered which one would be first at trying to buy her a drink, but she hadn't noticed them at all. Instead, she was tapping her toe and enjoying the music, smiling at the people dancing wherever there wasn't a table. In her flashy cowboy boots and curvy jeans, she would've passed for thirty. Twenty-nine, even. Still, she was, by my reckoning, about twenty years older than the hunk and about an equal number of years younger than the senior citizen.

I saw the younger guy step up close to Dee and drape his arm around her shoulders, putting his face close to hers. He was wearing jeans, too, but his were black and stone-washed. His boots, shirt, and cowboy hat were also black. His shirt was open most of the way to his big belt buckle, all the better to show off three or four gold chains draped against his chest. The song "Rhinestone Cowboy" came to mind.

That was when things kind of exploded. The guy pivoted suddenly so that he was almost in profile to me. Dee's right arm shot out and her fist connected squarely in the middle of his face. A split second later her left connected with his belly. As he doubled over, losing his hat, her right came up again and clipped him on the chin. That drove his head up against the underside of the bar's tile counter, whacking it pretty hard.

Slowly the guy sat down on the floor, and it was clear to me that he wouldn't be jumping right up again. He slumped over to his left and sort of rested against the bar.

I was surprised—impressed, really—that Dee had put the guy down so effectively.

It seemed like everybody else in the place was too busy drinking, dancing, and shout-talking to notice the goings-on in a dark corner, and that included the others at my table. I grabbed Wanda's arm. Scowling, she looked sharply in my direction and then followed my gaze. We scrambled out of our chairs and headed over to help, but navigating the crowd slowed us down.

Meanwhile, the chubby guy made the mistake of stepping aggressively toward Dee. He said something that I couldn't hear and quickly learned the same lesson as his buddy, earning himself a straight-on right jab in the nose. Blood followed. He put his hands on his face, spun around, and hurried out the open front door to a big, shiny sedan parked illegally right outside. He didn't even get the car door closed before burning rubber out of the parking lot.

Dee stood over the man sitting on the floor, poised as if she thought he might spring to his feet and do again whatever he'd done to get himself whupped. He raised his hands in surrender. She turned on her heel, marched to the back door, and walked out. By the time Wanda and I got to the exit, she'd already reached her truck and was climbing behind the wheel.

"Dee." Wanda grabbed the door handle. "What happened?"

"I lost my temper."

I said, "No, you didn't. You defended yourself. I'm calling the cops."

Dee froze. She said, "Naomi, don't. Please. I just overreacted. End-of-semester stress and all."

Wanda said, "But they—"

"Guys, I'm fine." Dee glanced toward the back exit of the bar. "I need you to do something for me. Please go back in there and smooth things over."

"Smooth what things over?" I asked. "You didn't do anything wrong."

She gave a small shrug. "Just make sure that the jackass is ambulatory, okay? And tell Laura I'm sorry for derailing the field trip. I'll buy the first round next time. But right now, I'm heading home."

Wanda and I stared at her. Then we both shrugged, too, and walked back into Wranglers.

The place was just as we'd left it a few minutes before. No one was paying any attention to the stranger who was using the rungs of a bar stool to help himself stand up. I noticed that he'd already jammed the black hat back onto his head.

"Did you learn your lesson, cowboy?" I asked, putting as much snark into my voice as I could, given that I had to lean over and holler close to his ear so he could hear me.

"Yeah," he said, "she was a pretty good teacher." He started peering through the crowd as best he could in the dim light.

Turning back to me, he asked, "Did you see where…?"

"Your buddy left," I said. "Drove off."

He shook his head and frowned.

"Was he your ride?" Wanda asked.

"Yeah."

"Bummer," I said. "Know anyone else here?"

He checked again and said, "Not anyone I can see in this light."

"I hope you weren't going to Flagstaff," said Wanda. "That'd be a long walk."

"No, back to the hotel later."

"Which hotel?" I asked.

"The one out by the marina. On the lake, you know."

Wanda, who works for the Park Service and spends many of her days out on that very lake, said, "Yes, I know. Closer than Flagstaff, but still too far to walk—it's about ten miles out. We'll find someone to take you."

He let go of the barstool he'd been hanging on to and said, "Hell no." Then he remembered the lesson in manners that he'd just been taught and added, "Um, no thank you. I'll go check the parking lot and see if I recognize any cars. I need some fresh air anyway." He turned toward the front door.

As he started to swagger away, I said, "If you can't find anybody, come on back."

Wanda added, "Yeah, we can get you that ride." She gazed after him, admiring his rear view as he disappeared through the door. She waggled her eyebrows like Groucho Marx.

"I don't want to interrupt whatever cradle-robbing fantasy you've got going there," I said, "but I'm heading home, too. I'll call Dee when I get there."

Wanda's expression changed immediately. "Don't do that. She said she's fine. Trust her."

I drew back and looked at her in disbelief. "Of course she said that. But—"

"There's no *but*, Naomi. Take her at her word. She'll call when she's ready." Wanda signaled the bartender for a pitcher of beer to take back to the table.

I hated to admit it, but I knew she was right.

"Fine," I said. The band finished a pretty terrible rendition of Proud Mary. As the raucous cheering died down, I said, "Wanda, did you know Dee could do that? Clean a guy's clock without breaking a sweat?"

"Not a clue. Our girl Dee contains multitudes." She nodded her thanks as the harried bartender handed her a pitcher that was just a little too full.

I said, "Let's hope the board of trustees doesn't hear about it."

Wanda grasped the slippery pitcher with both hands. "Who knows, maybe those boxing skills are at the top of her résumé. Maybe the trustees were looking to hire a college president who can hold her own when a couple of drunk idiots get in her face." Holding the pitcher steady, she stepped carefully away from the bar and added, "I mean, it's not like she killed somebody, right?"

CHAPTER TWO

As I walked the quarter-mile to work on Monday morning, I had strangers on my mind. Hordes of people were arriving in earnest. An area as isolated as Sage Landing doesn't often host a cast and crew big enough for a full-length feature film like *A Desert Place*, but it wasn't unusual to have film crews around—the stark scenery in the area offers memorable settings for commercials and television episodes. Magic hour —that brief time just after sunset or just before sunrise—really is magic among the rusty-red sandstone cliffs that jut above the huge lake and the white froth of the river. At other times of day, the bluffs cast dramatic shadows through the dry high-desert air. Sage Landing itself doesn't cover more than about a square mile or so, but it's bland enough to show up in exterior shots as a "typical small town" that could be located just about anywhere. All in all, it was easy to see what the attraction was.

"A desert place." That phrase kept nagging at me. I couldn't quite put my finger on where it came from, but it certainly suited this place where Arizona meets Utah, where the Navajo Nation meets the larger nation, and where the mighty Colorado River meets the first of a humiliating string of barriers. Some years, the dams and the canals combine to reduce the big river to a salty trickle before it reaches the sea.

By the time I got to the office, I'd moved on to wondering what kind of movie *A Desert Place* would be. With a name like that, it could be anything—biblical epic, futuristic alien saga, silly rom-com, battle block-buster, anything. My job gives me plenty of questions to ponder, and I was still pondering that random one as I unlocked the office door to the sound of a phone ringing. I didn't hurry to answer it, but it kept on ringing. I gave in and picked up the receiver, breaking my unwritten rule about staying away from the phone till I'd had my coffee.

"Carson Law," I said. I had lately been experimenting with snappy new business greetings, but this plain-vanilla version was all I could manage under the circumstances.

"Naomi, I can't get hold of Carson, and this is important." The caller sounded like Dee Moreno: community college president, knitter, and surprisingly agile boxing champ. Also one of my boss's occasional girl-friends. But my boss's girlfriends usually didn't dial his business line, and nobody who knew him would think they could catch him at work so early in the morning, especially on a Monday.

Dee's voice continued, "Mike Rodriguez is on his way over here to arrest me, I think." She hung up.

"Arrest?" I asked the silent phone receiver in my hand. It had nothing to say, so I put it back in its place.

Grant Carson is the only "Carson" in Carson Law. He's also its only lawyer. And he's my boss. We're just a simple little practice in the middle of nowhere, and we don't usually do criminal law.

Back when we did have a few criminal cases that brought in some fat checks, I sent away for printed business cards that called our firm simply, "Grant Carson," with a second line that reads, "Attorney at Law." Under that, I had them put my name, "Naomi Manymules," in a slightly smaller font. I hadn't shown them to Carson, because I wasn't sure what his reaction would be. My paralegal *bona fides* are pretty thin, but I'm probably the only thing that keeps the law firm going, and sometimes he says so. Not in so many words, maybe, but it's easy to read between the lines.

When it comes right down to it, I'm the one who needs the office to have a healthy caseload anyway. Carson would be happy to bring in barely enough to keep up the costs of his aging yacht, the *Deep Inn*. Other than that, he doesn't need much money. He lives in an old mobile home, drives a battered little pickup, and doesn't seem to have more than three or four changes of clothes, only one of which is presentable enough for the courtroom. But the fact is that he couldn't keep organized enough on his own to manage even that much legal work, so here I am. The office has to support us both.

To that end, I tried to shake myself out of my early-morning fog. If I'd heard correctly, Dee thought that Mike—Chief of Police Mike Rodriguez —was on his way to arrest her, which meant that one of Carson's best friends was about to arrest one of Carson's girlfriends.

I rummaged through my desk and found our tiny local phone book. It listed only a main number for the college, so I dialed it. Dee's secretary answered and put me through.

"This is Naomi," I said. "Did you call me and hang up?"

"Naomi, thank God. I got interrupted. Listen, can you find Carson for me?"

"Not at this time of the morning."

This was not what she wanted to hear. She said, "That's ridiculous. It's almost 8:30. He has to be somewhere."

"Sure, he's somewhere," I said. "Do you think of him as an early riser, Dee? Even if he's at home he's conked out. If he's not home, he's conked out anyway. I usually don't see him until about ten o'clock."

"How do you run a law office?"

"Like this," I said. "*I* run the law office until around ten o'clock." I shouldn't have said it, and normally I wouldn't have. But this was Dee, and while she was too upset to remember it at the moment, Carson's casual work schedule was the main reason she'd recommended me for this paralegal job in the first place. "Anyway, don't change the subject. You said they were going to arrest you? Who told you that?"

"Peggy Thomas called me from the police station. She only had time to tell me that Mike was on his way and why."

That was interesting. Peggy was a Sage Landing cop who also went out with Carson. While it seemed remarkably friendly for her to tip off another of Carson's girlfriends, it wasn't all that surprising. They both come to the regular Monday S&B gathering whenever their schedules allow, so they've bonded over wine and yarn and annual S&B holiday cookie exchanges.

Besides, Sage Landing's a very small one-traffic-light town. There aren't many options for male companionship. We have lots of guys drifting through town seasonally, working at the power plant in the winter or on the river in the summer, but they're way too young to be interesting. My boss, on the other hand, is pretty handsome for a guy at the doorstep of middle age, faintly resembling a chunkier Clint Eastwood if you squint and the light is dim. He's "eligible" if that means that he's unmarried, undemanding, and unlikely to settle down. Cooperation between rivals for his attention didn't seem unusual. Everyone in a place like this has to get along as best they can.

Dee continued. "If you can't locate Carson before 9:30, can you head over here yourself?"

I stood up and immediately got tangled in the phone cord. Twisting my way out of the tangle, I said, "What? Why?"

"Naomi…please." The line went dead again.

I called Carson's home line and left a detailed message on the answering machine that I was trying to train him to use. Both the office and his trailer have answering machines—the new ones with the tiny cassette tapes. He was starting to get used to the technology, so I had some hope that he would actually listen to the message once he woke up.

Not for the first time, I wished that Carson could use one of those new radio phones. But they were pricey and clunky, and our landscape was too jagged for the phones to work very well. Leaving messages on the answering machine was the best I could do.

I looked down at my watch and saw that I had less than an hour. I needed to go home and spruce up a bit if I was going to show up at the college office as some sort of legal presence. The morning had been hectic. My two teenagers dashed around getting ready for the last week of school before summer, leaving me short on time for primping. Naturally, my hair had been in a bad mood, looking more frizzy than wavy, so it was stuffed into a faded bandana. I had to do something about that at least.

The telephone rang again before I could get to the door. This time the call was from Maggie Thornton, an assistant principal at the high school. Maggie is a personal friend and another member of S&B. I assumed that she was calling about that evening's meeting, where those of us who'd been on the Saturday night field trip to Wranglers would be expected to provide details about Laura's ex. But I was wrong.

"Naomi, you'd better get over here. Kai's in big trouble."

I tried to respond but couldn't seem to make my lips move. Kai, my daughter, was nearing the end of her freshman year. She'd recently turned fifteen and had never been in any trouble at school or anywhere else. She seemed more focused on keeping *me* out of trouble than on enjoying any for herself.

Maggie spoke again. "Naomi? Are you there?"

"Kai?" My daughter's name was all I could manage to say in answer to her question.

"Arthur Donnegan says he's gonna call the police."

"Maggie, what the hell? What happened?"

"I have no idea, Naomi. You know how Arthur gets. He brought Elle Highsmith and Kai to the principal's office."

"You mean Elle Nakai," I said—a sudden departure from the topic, I admit, but my mind was going numb from the sheer volume of impending police activity.

"What?"

"Elle and her brother changed their names back to Nakai at the same time their mom did, after... after Willard died." *Damn,* I thought, *pull yourself together, Naomi.* Mentioning that rat-bastard Willard Highsmith did nothing but stir up past events that were best forgotten. He'd been shot dead a few months before, and his wife—Elle's mom, my friend Ellen —had been a prime suspect at first. But she was far from the only one. In fact, I was on that list myself for about a minute and a half. Several of the other suspects became Carson's clients at the same time he was representing Ellen, which seemed ethically questionable. That said, I hadn't hesitated to order those new business cards after the murder was solved and the checks cleared.

Now I kicked myself for bringing up Ellen's brief stint as a murder suspect, so when Maggie didn't respond right away, I went on, "You know, like I did when I went back to using Manymules after my divorce."

Before I could continue my nervous rambling, Maggie said, "Highsmith...Nakai. What I'm telling you is you better get over here. Now."

"On my way." I knew that she wouldn't be able to reach Ellen, who was spending the day working at her family's sheep ranch on the reservation instead of at her furniture store in town, so I'd need to speak up for Elle as well as for Kai. "You said they're in the office?"

"Yes."

"Got it. And don't call the police—they've got enough on their hands this morning." I hung up before Maggie could ask what I meant. Whatever ended up happening between Chief Rodriguez and Dee Moreno at 9:30 would probably come out at tonight's S&B anyway. It was too juicy not to. In our hierarchy of topics, arrests took priority over everything except newly discovered infidelities.

Normally I would've debated whether to walk or drive to the high school because I was trying to avoid the use of my car or, rather, the use of gasoline. Gas prices were high, and my income wasn't great, so every rumble of the engine felt like a drop of lost blood or something. Besides, I was just plain cheap by nature. But at that moment it looked like I needed to be in three places at practically the same time, so I ran straight home to my car and jumped in. Like a regular spendthrift, I gunned it without any regard for fuel economy.

I reminded myself to be calm and professional despite having to deal with two police situations before I'd even had my first cup of coffee, assuming that luck was with me and I could get to both of them. Since my luck so far that day had been cruddy, it was one of those times when it would've been nice to have a boss who showed up a little earlier in the workday.

Maggie was waiting for me in the high school parking lot. She walked me directly to the principal's office, which wasn't necessary. I'd been to the principal's office a few times when I was a student in this same building, but the police hadn't ever been involved, so maybe my daughter would be one up on me.

I opened the door and walked in without knocking.

The principal, Gail Banner, was standing at her desk. She was a very attractive forty-something blond. The expression on her face warned me that this wasn't going to be easy, which unsettled me even more. I reminded myself that she owed me some favors. Carson and I had recently helped her out when her whole family got entangled in that murder investigation.

Arthur Donnegan was also standing near the desk. Short and slight, with a wispy mustache and a flat-top haircut, he was the school's assistant principal for athletics. From what I'd heard, he spent most of his time on the job glaring at the students, and I was seeing some of that now.

My daughter and her friend Elle sat in straight-backed wooden chairs facing the principal's desk. They were both staring at the floor.

"Good morning, Ms. Manymules," said Gail. "I'm glad you could come by. Mr. Donnegan, you know Ms. Manymules, Kai's mother, don't you? Please, let's all take a seat." Once that was accomplished, she continued. "Kai, why don't you tell your mother why you're in here?"

Kai was hunched in her chair with her arms crossed, still looking at the floor, and said nothing. Elle Nakai spoke up instead. "Driving."

"What do you mean, *driving*? Driving where? Who was driving?"

"They were driving in the parking lot," said Donnegan. "Your daughter was driving at the time that I caught them, but Elle says that she was driving first. They were trading off."

"Trading off?" I said. "Neither one of them has a license or a permit."

"Neither one of them has a car, either," he said.

"They stole a car?" I asked in a near shriek.

Gail Banner spoke up. "No, no. Another student loaned them the car. He said he didn't know that they didn't have licenses. They'd told him they wanted to learn how to use a stick shift."

"It is a *crime* to *drive* without a *license*," said Donnegan, facing me to speak with the exaggerated patience that a person uses when explaining something obvious to the dim-witted. "It sets a bad example. That's why we need to involve the police."

My paralegal mind kicked into operating mode. "Where were they driving—were they out on the street?"

"The parking lot is public property," Donnegan said. "Just like the street is." Now he sounded defensive.

"I know that you see it that way, and I'm not trying to minimize the situation," I said, trying to sound respectful while absolutely intending to minimize the situation. I fished around in my purse and extended one of my cards, the one with my name on a line right under the words "Attorney at Law." To some, that could imply that I was an attorney. However, it didn't say so, and neither did I. The assistant principal examined the card and laid it on the principal's desk. Gail slid it closer to her side of the desk so that she could read it. She raised an eyebrow but didn't give me away.

I continued, "But how would it be seen in a court of law?" I did a neat little turn to face the guy directly. "Mr. Donnegan, what we're after here most of all is to avoid embarrassment for the school district. If you were to try charging these girls with illegal driving, it would come to light that they were in the school parking lot, not on a public street. That could be embarrassing for the school district. You see what I mean?" That verbal ploy is called *deflection*. I learned it from watching Carson.

All I got from Donnegan was another frown. To tell the truth, I was thinking that I'd handled that argument well and wished that my boss could've seen it. I was pretty sure that the principal would back me up.

She did, sort of, shifting her attention away from Arthur Donnegan to the girls sitting mutely in front of her. "Kai's mother has a point. However, I don't think we can let these girls off the hook entirely. They may not have committed a traffic violation, technically, but the high school parking lot is not a practice track for unlicensed drivers, especially at this busy time of the morning."

The assistant principal didn't want to give up. He tried again. "There could be other charges," he said. "Reckless endangerment, for one."

He was reaching, and everyone in the room knew it now. Kai's mouth opened to protest, but I held up a hand, warning her to stay quiet. Miraculously, she heeded the signal and went back to staring sullenly at the floor. Again, I made the effort to talk like a dignified legal professional addressing a respected school official, saying, "I understand your concern, but that doesn't seem to fit the situation. In my experience, a charge like reckless endangerment would require injury or dangerous intent, or both. Neither seems to be present here."

Before he could come back with alternative "other charges" that he could press, the principal stood up. "Thank you, Mr. Donnegan. I will take the matter from here. I don't believe the district administration would appreciate getting the police involved at this point." He opened his mouth to speak, but something in the expression on her face made him leave the office without replying.

I glanced at the girls. They both flinched as the door closed a little too loudly behind the assistant principal, but the floor still had all their attention.

The principal didn't say anything to them at first. Slowly she walked toward them until she towered almost directly above Kai's chair. "Kai," she said quietly, "listen up."

She waited until Kai leaned back a little and reluctantly looked upward. Gail Banner continued, "Tell me the truth. Was this another gonzo journalism stunt?"

I had not seen that coming. Not at all. Gonzo journalism? She'd been working on the school paper since the beginning of the school year, and she'd shown me a few of her humorous articles—one about trying out to be a cheerleader for the wrestling team, another about experimenting in the Home Economics kitchen. Now, though, Kai's face relaxed into a broad grin. Who was this girl, and what had she done with my demure, bookish daughter?

"Another stunt?" I was finally able to ask. "Kai? There were *others?"*

Kai faced me now, her sulky expression transformed into outright excitement. "Not stunts, Mom. Experiences. And we weren't trying to get caught, it just happened."

Staring directly down at Kai, the principal said, "You can catch your mom up later. Stunt or not, I'm telling you right now that you will not be writing about this."

Elle and Kai blurted in unison, "But…" and Ms. Banner's voice sliced right through their protests. Forcefully, she went on, "Driving without a license is not amusing. Fun is not to be made of Mr. Donnegan, either. Am I understood?"

Sullen again, they didn't answer.

I snapped, "Kai! Elle! Do you understand?"

They said nothing. I stood up with my arms crossed over my chest. Without speaking, I willed my heartbeat to slow down as I waited. It took a few seconds, but they eventually caught on and looked back up at the principal's face. Kai said, "Yes, ma'am," and Elle said, "I understand, Ms. Banner."

Apparently satisfied, Gail sat back down before turning to me. She said, "So, Naomi, what are we going to do?"

A little surprised to be included in her decision process, I went back to my chair and sat down as well. "What, you mean besides grounding these girls for the foreseeable future?"

"Yes, besides that—" here she cut a look over at Kai— "and the loss of one juicy topic for a humorous feature article."

Although her punishment had landed pretty well, I agreed that more was required. I didn't want to discourage Kai's desire to write, but her judgment was less developed than I'd thought. I knew from experience that ethics took a while to learn, and that gave me an idea. "Ms. Banner, what they need is an editor. Let's have them show me any work they plan to publish before they submit it."

Gail smiled. "That could work. Okay, girls, I'll designate Ms. Many-mules as the editor of record for your work until further notice. She has to give the okay before you can show anything you've written to anyone else. That will set my mind at ease, and I won't feel the need to involve the police and say anything about possible reckless endangerment." She said this with a straight face. "Elle, I will call your mother to let her know what happened and ask her to help you stick to the plan. Now, you are both late for class. Get a pass from Attendance."

The girls left the room quickly, making no eye contact with each other or with me.

After the door closed, I faced the principal again. "One more thing. *Was* she driving recklessly?"

"No," Gail said firmly. "Not at all. Arthur said they were going about five miles per hour out at the edge of the lot. They couldn't handle the clutch and were jerking the car and stalling. That's what caught his attention."

"You think he was serious about the police?"

She shrugged. "Could be. He's used to bigger schools with more exciting problems. It's pretty boring for him around here."

I had my own thoughts about employing the kind of guy who makes his work more interesting by treating high school students like that, but for once I kept them to myself. "Well, *I* was serious about grounding her, and I'm sure that Ellen Nakai will do the same for Elle." I had another thought. "And I'll add a month to Kai's waiting time for her learning permit."

She shook her head with the authority of one who's been there. "Naomi, she'll make your life miserable if you do that. She won't like having you screen her writing, and she sure won't like being grounded, but she'll see the logic. She'll take it as justice. More than that will seem unreasonable to her. It would do more harm than good." She smiled self-consciously. "Some free advice."

I was tempted to ignore Gail's advice because of her son's troubles. But since my kids had entered teenager territory, I'd been reminded again and again that parenting involves at least as much luck as skill. And a whole lot of humility. So I nodded my thanks before sneaking a peek at my watch and saying, "I'm sorry, but I have to go. I have another crisis to attend this morning."

All she said was, "I won't ask."

~ ~ ~

I probably would've made it to the community college with plenty of time to spare if I hadn't seen my renegade dog running around in the grocery store parking lot on the way. I pulled over and stopped the car, grumbling to no one in particular that I'd never actually agreed to adopt any dog, much less a dog raised by a criminal who was now doing time in federal prison. Larry Sabano, better known as Three-Steps Larry due to an embarrassing incident in his past, had named her Princess and loved her dearly. Like Three-Steps himself, the little mutt was scruffy and sneaky and appealing and not very smart. My kids and I were looking after her while the guy served his sentence. The way she ended up with us was a long story, and my son, Len, changed the dog's name to Three-Steps so that he'd have an excuse to tell it often.

We kept the dog in the house and a fenced backyard. That was the theory. In practice, Three-Steps got out of the back yard just about any time she wanted to. Sage Landing had a leash law, and the fine for letting a dog run loose was twenty-five dollars. That's why I chased the dog around the parking lot, yelling, "Here, Three-Steps. Here girl!" I even tried hollering her old name, even though Len had forbidden its use. But desperate times call for desperate measures, so I pleaded, "Princess, please come here! *Please, Princess!* Aw, Three-Steps, come *on.*" I did this for ten minutes before I glanced at my watch again and gave it up.

The next obstacle was traffic on Main Street. Main was the most direct route from the high school to the community college, and it never had any traffic. In fact, no street in Sage Landing ever had any traffic to speak of, but this morning, naturally, the road was clogged with vehicles. There was a caravan of at least fifteen motorhomes and cargo trailers stretched out along the curb all along Main, and all the other cars slowed down so the drivers could gape at each one of them.

The full cast and crew for *A Desert Place*, it seemed, had arrived. The big, blocky vehicles were not moving. They'd generously pulled over to the right curb, leaving the rest of the northbound traffic about half a lane to navigate. I knew the back streets, so I was able to turn between a couple of the monster trucks and detour through the east side of town all the way to the community college campus.

As the clock reached 9:00 a.m., I had a friend who was about to be arrested, a daughter who would kind of like to be arrested, and a dog who probably ought to be arrested. And since my first life-giving cup of coffee still hadn't appeared, I wasn't feeling all that law-abiding myself.

CHAPTER THREE

A NASAZI Community College seemed calm when I pulled into the parking lot. A lot of cars were parked there, but no police car was in sight. Inside, students were sitting at tables in the central study commons. Things appeared quite ordinary as I walked toward the president's office.

When I entered the main office, the level of sound in the room changed from the normal noise of two or three conversations at once to dead silence as the staff all glanced at me and then quickly away. When the conversations resumed, they were quieter, choppier, as if each person in the room suddenly had her mind on more than one thing. Dee's assistant, slightly red-faced, headed over to the president's office door and opened it for me. I walked in and reached back to close the door, but it had already been pulled shut behind me without making a sound.

Inside, Dee was not sitting at her desk. Instead, she was leaning in a doorway on the other side of her office with her arms folded across the trim waist of her size-eight designer suit. That made me even more self-conscious about my frayed bandana and untamed hair. Not to mention the ten sweaty minutes I'd spent chasing a disrespectful dog around a dusty parking lot.

Dee gestured toward a chair in the corner behind her desk, and I sat down. She glanced toward the door where I'd entered, giving only a casual shrug to indicate that she realized Carson was not with me.

"Thanks for coming, Naomi. I was afraid you wouldn't get here before —"

"Sorry. I ran into a traffic jam if you can believe that. Big rigs are parked all along Main."

"The movie people are here," she said. "They've been parked on Main all night—some paperwork holdup with the Park Service is keeping them out of the location until they get clearance. Something about sanitary facilities."

That was more than I needed to know. "Yeah, they're all here, all right. I forgot that this was the week," I said. "What's up?"

"Thanks for coming over so quickly. I don't want to say anything that will get the college in trouble."

I smiled and said, "I'm not a lawyer, even if I play one on TV." But the look on her face told me that she had no interest in keeping things light. I sat up a little straighter and added, "Seriously, Dee, Chief Rodriguez knows that I'm not a lawyer. I'm barely a paralegal."

"Oh, I know, but I've learned over the years to include a neutral third party in any situation that promises to be adversarial. This time I would prefer not to have any college personnel serve in that role. Besides—" she hesitated, stepping toward the desk to sift through some of the papers on the blotter, "—if you're here you'll be able to fill Carson in."

I glanced at the door to the outer office and lowered my voice. "Dee, you're probably not supposed to know that this is going to happen. It's going to seem funny that I'm here."

She picked up one of the papers and tucked it into a folder. She said, "That's true, but it'll just have to look funny."

Lifting my chin toward the door, I asked, "Do the people out there know?"

"Of course not."

I'm pretty sure that most office personnel know everything the boss knows before the boss knows it, but I said, "Okay," not wanting to pursue the subject any further. "Do you think this is about the guy you decked at Wranglers Saturday night?"

Dee pulled out her desk chair and sat down near me. She shook her head. "I don't see how. Good lord, scuffles like that happen there all the time, and nothing ever comes of it. That's what I hear from the students, anyway."

She had a point, but what I'd seen that night wasn't exactly a typical scuffle. "Can you tell me what actually happened with the rhinestone cowboy? Or what his pudgy friend said before—before his nose started bleeding?"

Dee sighed. "We don't have time to go into all that now. Anyway, guys like that would want to forget about the whole thing as soon as they can."

I couldn't help smiling. "Yeah, they wouldn't want to admit that a girl mopped up the floor with them. But can't you at least tell me what Mr. Black Hat said?"

Before she could answer, the office door opened, and Grant Carson stood there staring at both of us. He came in and closed the door. "Just got your message," he said. "I was out jogging."

He'd been on a health and fitness kick lately—ever since his fistfight with a young thug a few months earlier—and some of the flab *was* disappearing. He had a serious wardrobe problem that morning, though. His only suit was probably still crumpled on the floor of his closet, awaiting its next trip to the dry cleaners. He did have on a freshly laundered pair of jeans and a reasonably smooth chambray shirt. A braided leather bolo tie with a big turquoise-nugget clasp was sitting where a traditional tie should've been. I gathered that his dress shoes were hiding somewhere, too, but they wouldn't work with the denim anyway. He wore brown leather sandals on his bare feet—probably couldn't find clean socks. Why he thought those sandals would be a better choice than his running shoes was a mystery to me. But then, I'd never seen his running shoes. He'd also apparently been unable to find any of his belts.

There'd been no time to do anything dressy with his longish salt-and-pepper hair, so it was combed straight back, achieving a sort of movie-mafia impression with his two-day beard. He smelled like bug repellant and sunscreen, which could've been what was holding his hair in place.

If you asked me, the overall impression was more ex-con than ex-prosecutor.

After glancing at him, Dee looked back at me, picked up a pencil, and wove it through her fingers. "She used the word 'felony.' She said it was a felony."

Carson asked, "Peggy said it was a felony?"

Dee frowned. "*The person who called me* said it might be a felony and didn't provide further details." Frowning again at Carson's sandals, she added, "Don't you have a suit?"

"It's at the cleaners."

"With your shoes?"

Carson said, "You want me to suggest another attorney?"

"No, I don't." She smiled. "Thanks for coming over. It was short notice. You're the lawyer I want here."

Carson shrugged. "Sorry about the shoes."

Dee's assistant opened the door after rapping on it quietly. She sent a halfhearted smile in Carson's direction before announcing, "Dr. Moreno, Chief Rodriguez would like a word with you if you have a minute." She added, "Mayor Buckmaster is with him."

"Thanks, Jennifer. Show them in." Noticing the assistant's hesitation, she added, "Ms. Manymules and Mr. Carson will be staying."

When Jennifer started back toward the outer office to escort the guys in, Carson said quietly, "Dee, listen, I'm serious. Don't answer *any* questions. Refer everything to me until we know what they've got."

Carson and I both stood up.

Once Rodriguez and Buckmaster were in the room it was time for ritual introductions even though we all knew each other, at least casually. Dee introduced Rodriguez to Carson even though the two men knew each other well. Mike Rodriguez brought his six-foot-four-inch frame a step forward and shook hands. He, in turn, introduced Mayor Buckmaster. I knew who Herman Buckmaster was, but I'd never met him personally. He'd been a few years ahead of me in high school. I'd seen him around in the years since, and I often ate at one of the fast-food places he owned.

In almost every way, the police chief and the mayor couldn't have been more different. Where Mike was athletic, tanned, and broad-shouldered, Buckmaster was paunchy and pale, with the narrow chest of someone who avoids physical exertion at all costs. Mike's crisp uniform contrasted with Buckmaster's flashy madras sport coat.

Continuing the introductions, Rodriguez nodded in our direction as he said to Buckmaster, "President Moreno and Ms. Manymules."

Buckmaster sucked in his gut as his eyes traveled up and down Dee and me. Men can be a real hoot, doing stuff like that and pretending it isn't happening. But any woman knows the truth—stuff like that is *always* happening. Which is why I didn't feel bad at all about staring pointedly at his bad comb-over. He was famous for it.

"Please, everyone calls me Buck," the mayor said, reaching out to shake Carson's hand.

As far as I knew, *no one* called him Buck. The kind of guy who got called Buck around here could light a campfire in the rain or judge a county livestock competition. Not to put too fine a point on it, there's never been anyone less Buck-like than Herman Buckmaster. I suppressed a smirk.

Carson shook his hand and said, "Pleased to meet you."

Dee said, "Good morning, gentlemen. What can Anasazi Community College do for you?"

Instead of answering, Rodriguez surveyed the room. "I'm a little surprised to see... well, never mind. Dr. Moreno, I wonder if you could spare a little time to talk with us?" He looked again at Carson and me but didn't say anything to us.

Dee went out to the front office briefly, said something to her assistant, and rejoined the rest of us. There was an awkward minute while everyone found a place to sit down.

Rodriguez cleared his throat before saying, "Early this morning I ran into Mayor Buckmaster in the hallway."

That shouldn't have been unusual, I thought, since the city offices shared a building with the police station. Also the public library, but that was beside the point.

Mike glanced over at the mayor before going on. "Mr. Buckmaster took the opportunity to describe a... a forthcoming complaint against Dr. Moreno. After hearing him out, I'm sure this is all a misunderstanding, but for now, he is under the impression that a serious assault complaint is about to be filed."

If he was expecting to shock Dee with this news, he was sorely disappointed. At first, she didn't say anything at all. While Mike waited, she turned her head toward the wall of windows and gazed at a small slice of the lake that sparkled in the distance. I would've bet that she was mentally throwing someone into it.

I opened my mouth to object to what Mike had said. Carson looked my way, the bland expression on his face reminding me silently to listen and observe instead of reacting. I pressed my lips together.

Dee turned away from the view and faced Mike. "What's really going on?" she asked.

It didn't seem to me that Chief Rodriguez knew the full answer to that question. He glanced at Buckmaster's smug expression.

"You tell me," Rodriguez answered. "We'll go sort it out down at the station."

"Right now?" Dee asked, "I can't leave campus at the drop of a hat, Mike."

"Dr. Moreno," Rodriguez said apologetically, "this could be serious."

Dee stood up and leaned forward, her hands spread on the top of her desk. "I am well aware that a felony charge would be serious. Let's do this, right here, right now, so I can get back to work."

Carson, startled, looked up at her sharply. But before he could say anything, Rodriguez cut in. "No, President Moreno. This is not a college issue, and the college is not the place for this conversation." He paused. "As I said, I'm sure this is a misunderstanding that will be cleared up soon."

Sitting down in her chair again, she made a tent of her hands like a criminal mastermind in a movie and said, "No charges have actually been filed?"

"Yet," said Buckmaster.

Mike Rodriguez scowled at the mayor, who wouldn't meet his eyes, and said to Dee, "You've already made some arrangements—notified an attorney?"

Sounding defiant, she said, "Sure, Mike. Who wouldn't?"

Mike had no intention of arguing with her about that. "And you said 'felony.' Who said anything about a felony?"

She said nothing.

He waited, and when it was clear that she wasn't going to answer him, he shifted his attention to Grant Carson. "And you. What, exactly, is your role here? You're here to represent the college?"

"I'm here as Desiree's attorney. Dr. Moreno's, I mean. If she needs one."

Rodriguez seemed to think this over. Then he said, "Damn," flopping back in his chair with exaggerated frustration. "Somebody down at my office has got some explaining to do." He said this in the mayor's general direction, and I realized that it was entirely for Buckmaster's benefit. Mike probably *had* expected Peggy to give some kind of heads-up to Dee. Maybe he even told her to do it.

For her part, though, Dee didn't seem interested in playing that game. She said, "So now what?"

Rodriguez gestured toward the door. "Now you'll come with me."

Feeling like I was in a scene from The Twilight Zone, I blurted, "Do you think there's anything to this... this... to whatever this is? Are you seriously taking her into custody, Mike?" Everyone looked at me, and my boss shook his head and frowned. I scowled back at him. "You can't drag the president of the college out of here like this. You need to find out more before you take her anywhere."

The mayor jumped in, "Chief Rodriguez, we have received a very serious charge. Grievous injuries are involved. A man was assaulted and battered. Saturday night. *In Sage Landing.* I told you that."

Saturday night? Grievous injuries? Not from what I saw. I was there. *Buck* wasn't.

"I understand that, Herman," Rodriguez said, very quietly, "but we won't make a scene here on campus. We don't even have a written complaint yet. And while it may not be any of Naomi's business,"—here he glanced in my direction—"she's right. I need more information before doing anything official."

Buckmaster began to gather steam for another protest, but Mike calmly cut him off, saying, "I'll respectfully remind you that I'm Chief of Police, and I will follow the law as I see it."

The mayor opened his mouth again, but Mike wasn't done. He went on, "We don't work for the movie company."

Carson spoke up, "Mayor Buckmaster, you're not an officer of the law. I'd advise you to let Chief Rodriguez make the decisions."

"And I'd remind Chief Rodriguez that he works for me," Buckmaster said.

Rodriguez stood up. "Well, then. I'll commend myself for exercising caution in response to political pressure," he said with a smile I could hear, though it didn't show on his face, "later on today."

Buckmaster didn't want to let it go. "Chief Rodriguez," he said, "I'm not trying to be hard-headed here, but my neck is on the line for the city's behavior. We've got a serious injury to one of the film stars. I would think …" His voice trailed off.

An injury to a film star? I wondered. *Was that Mr. Black Hat or Mr. Bloody Nose?*

Rodriguez smiled down at the mayor. "Herman, I'm not going to make a scene on this campus by marching Dr. Moreno out in handcuffs or anything," he said. "In *my* judgment, there's nothing in this situation to justify that."

Buckmaster looked at Dee before trying again. "Chief, there could be a flight risk," he said.

That made me laugh out loud, and even Carson sounded amused when he said, "Think about it…Buck. There are only three roads out of Sage Landing. All three are narrow two-lane highways, mostly across rock and barren sand. The closest real town in any direction is seventy-five miles away in Utah. If you were trying to run away from here, how would you do it?"

Before the mayor could think of an answer, Mike Rodriguez lost the rest of his patience. "In the absence of a written complaint, all I have is your story. It has not been corroborated, and I have no way of knowing if you have your facts straight. Normally, *Herman*, you wouldn't even be here with me." Rodriguez was warming to his subject. He got louder, his voice more resonant, his words more crisply bitten off. "Now that I think about it, any interference from you would be entirely inappropriate."

He said, "Dr. Moreno, how'd you like to come over to my office to talk for a little while? Maybe Naomi and Grant could join us there."

"Sure," she said.

"You'll be over there in a few minutes, right, Grant?"

Carson's eyes were on Dee, who was looking out at the lake again and seemed to be taking some deep, calming breaths. He said, "Well, my client and I would like to have breakfast first so that she can bring me up to speed. If she rides with us, we could stop somewhere and grab a bite."

With a glance toward Buckmaster, who was kind of turning purple with frustration, Rodriguez said, "Carson, please let Dr. Moreno ride with me. I promise not to ask her any questions. We won't even chat. Mayor Buckmaster will be driving his car. You and Naomi will be right behind us."

Dee said, "It's fine, Carson. We'll crank up the radio. No talking at all."

Rodriguez smiled. "Bon Jovi's in the cassette deck, ready to go."

She smiled back at him, "That'll work."

Buckmaster opened his mouth but decided against saying whatever he'd been about to say. Rodriguez seemed pleased by the mayor's discomfort. I know I sure was.

Buckmaster walked out first, followed by Mike Rodriguez and Dee. Carson and I followed along. Conversation and activity came to a halt in the school office as we passed through, but almost no one else took any notice. We all crossed the lawn at a leisurely pace toward the visitor parking lot. One man standing by the parking lot raised a small camera to take a snapshot of a young woman as we walked by. She was smiling and posing next to the college's entry sign, gesturing like a game-show hostess. Were they a proud father and daughter, maybe, commemorating her upcoming graduation?

Chief Rodriguez continued to talk to Buckmaster while Carson followed Dee to the unmarked police sedan and opened the front passenger door for her.

"You did fine," Carson said. "See you in a few minutes."

She raised her voice. "You are such a jerk. You know I hate to be called Desiree, but you couldn't pass up the chance." More quietly, she asked, "What's going to happen now?"

Carson was all business now. He said, "Who am I representing here? Are you retaining me personally or on behalf of the college?"

"Just me. If I retained you for the college, you couldn't defend me personally because if charges are brought, the college will probably suspend me."

That didn't make sense to me— wasn't she innocent until proven guilty? How could they suspend her while she was legally innocent? So I asked, "Why would they do that?"

Dee said, "Because it's Board policy to suspend anyone under investigation for a felony."

News travels fast in Sage Landing, true, but it isn't instantaneous. I was sure that Mike would keep everything as quiet as he could. "They wouldn't know, would they?" I said.

Dr. Moreno opened her purse and took out a compact mirror. She used it to watch Mike and Buckmaster as they stood talking behind her. "They already do," she said. "Herman Buckmaster is married to the newest trustee on the Board."

Carson said, "Okay, retain me as your personal attorney. If I can make the right moves quickly, I can get you out of this."

"How?" she asked. "We don't even know exactly what this is yet."

He grinned for the first time since he'd entered the office. "Doesn't matter. I used to be an assistant district attorney. I've learned a few things."

Dee snapped the compact shut and dropped it into her bag. "I knew that. And I'm sorry," she said.

"I know."

"I mean for before—last month. It was something I said in anger. I don't think you're…."

I didn't want to be anywhere near that conversation, so I clumsily patted a couple of my pockets and walked out of earshot as if I'd forgotten something and needed to go back into the building. Dee and Carson were on the outs again. Everyone knew that, but the details were none of my business.

CHAPTER FOUR

CARSON and I left Dee standing next to the chief's car, saying that we'd see her at the police station. We both got in my car, because Carson didn't have his. Instead of driving over, he had run the half-mile or so to the college, and in sandals, no less. God only knows why. As I navigated past the big rigs that were still parked along the road, he was too preoccupied to notice that I didn't head directly to the station. Instead, I drove to his place and pulled up in the gravel driveway behind his little truck.

"Shoes," I said, pointing toward his front door with my chin and pursed lips.

"Naomi, we don't have time for—"

Gesturing at the door again, I went on. "And socks that match. Each other."

He got out of the car.

When he returned after a few minutes, his hair was better, and he had on decent socks with presentable shoes. He carried a navy-blue blazer over his shoulder. I would have described him as almost spiffy, but the expression on his face kept me from saying so.

As we passed the grocery store parking lot on the way to the station, I glanced over in case the dog was waiting for a ride. No luck. No dog in sight.

I wasn't surprised to see that Peggy was still the officer on duty when we walked into the station. Even if she hadn't been, she would've been nearby to see what happened. Sitting behind the front desk, she announced our arrival over the station's little-used intercom before standing up to lock eyes with Carson. Tall and willowy in her crisp uniform, she gave him a quick nod. He smiled faintly and started to say something, but Rodriguez came out of his office at the end of the hall, motioning us to join him.

Three chairs had been squeezed into the tiny room. Mike worked his way behind the desk and sat in the biggest chair. Dee sat facing the desk in an armless chair that was wedged in next to a tall, battered file cabinet. Her posture was flawless, completely out of place in that cramped gray room. Mayor Buckmaster, on the other hand, fit right in. He'd taken off his plaid sport coat, revealing a rumpled white short-sleeve shirt, and he was making himself comfortable in the other guest chair. Unlike Dee's, it had arms, but it sat where it would be scraped by the metal door whenever someone opened it.

Carson put his hands in his pockets, leaned against the wall, and said nothing.

"I'll wait out here," I said, pulling the door closed and relishing the metal-on-metal sound when it hit the mayor's chair.

Fortunately, from the hallway, I could hear everything in the crowded office anyway.

Rodriguez started things off. He said, "Thanks for getting over here promptly. What we're going to do here, Dr. Moreno, is we're going to have kind of an informal conversation. Mayor Buckmaster is going to explain the complaint he heard, and we're going to see if we can clear the matter up right here."

I heard Carson say, "This should be interesting." *Yes*, I thought. *It really should.*

Peggy silently materialized beside me. I thought she would shoo me away from the door, but she put a finger to her lips and stood there listening with me.

Rodriguez answered, "Please keep the commentary to yourself, counselor. I'm trying to get a clear understanding of what happened, since I haven't *seen* any charges yet."

Mayor Buckmaster spoke up. "Someone's filing the paperwork this morning. That's what I heard he was going to do."

Sounding impatient, Carson asked, "Who's doing this paperwork, an alleged *victim*? And who would that be?"

Instead of letting Buckmaster answer Carson's question, Rodriguez got on with having Dee tell her side of the story. He said, "Please tell us what happened Saturday night, starting at nine p.m., as you remember it."

She answered, "Pretty typical Saturday night stuff, I imagine. Some guys drank too much, wouldn't take no for an answer, and needed some …convincing."

Buckmaster couldn't contradict her fast enough. "Needed some convincing? *Convincing!* Is that what you call it? Hardly!"

Ignoring Herman's interruption, Mike said to Dee, "But you didn't attack anybody?"

"Of course not." She sounded dismissive.

Carson said. "My client has nothing more to say at this time. I, however, do have a few questions."

The chief said, "Go ahead, Carson."

Carson said, "So, what were you getting at, Buck, about a film star being seriously injured?"

Now it was Dee who interrupted. "I have no idea what he's talking about. What happened is, I was at Wranglers with some friends Saturday night to watch a set or two of music."

"You simply went to the bar with friends?" Carson asked. I guess he realized that since he couldn't keep her from talking, he might as well get the story out in the best light.

"That's right. Naomi, for one," Dee said. "Five of us. Knitters. We usually meet on Mondays, but this was a special outing."

"At the bar?" Rodriguez asked.

"We're all over twenty-one. It's a free country, last I heard," Dee answered.

"We're only trying to get the picture," Rodriguez said. "Please continue, Dr. Moreno."

"I was standing at the bar, waiting for a pitcher of beer to take back to our table, minding my own business and singing along. They were doing

Creedence, songs that everybody knows. Anyway, this stranger comes over and says he'll buy me a drink. 'No thank you,' I say, very politely, 'I'm with my friends.' Then he makes a very inappropriate comment about unsnapping my shirt. I keep my eyes on the band and try to ignore him. Now he's getting louder, calling me 'sweetheart' and saying I'd kick myself later if I missed my chance to spend some time with him."

Out in the hall, I raised my eyebrows at Peggy. She showed me an exaggerated expression of disgust.

"Naomi and the others heard this?" Rodriguez asked.

"I don't know how much they heard," Dee said. "It was noisy. Anyway, things escalated after that—his choice, not mine."

Carson said. "How long did this little scene continue?"

"Not long. The guy was young and stupid. He was pretty wasted. He got louder, and he moved closer, and then he made a big mistake."

Rodriguez asked, "Did he make a move on you?"

Dee took a few seconds before answering. "He grabbed me."

No one said a word.

"In a sensitive area," Dee said. "He grabbed my… jeans."

No wonder she slugged him, I thought, wishing I could see the faces of the three guys in the room as they listened to her.

"Oh, that's not good," Carson said. "Then what?"

"I tried to knee him where, you know, it would hurt. But he saw that coming and messed up my aim, so I gave him a roundhouse to the jaw."

Rodriguez asked, "Just the one punch put him down on the floor?"

By my count, it took three to get the job done, and I was wondering how much detail Dee would give them when I heard her say, "I don't think so, no. I think it was more than one, but my adrenaline level was so elevated that I honestly don't remember."

The chief asked, "Was the man unconscious?"

"No, he sat up right away—leaned his back against the bar and stayed down," Dee said.

"Was he a big man?" Rodriguez asked.

"Not really. Under six feet, I'd say. He'd weigh in at about one-seventy-five, one-eighty. Light-heavyweight—he had maybe fifty pounds on me, but he was no fighter."

"That's a funny way to describe him," Buckmaster said.

Dee said, "I used to watch a lot of boxing at the gym."

"Dr. Moreno, there must have been many witnesses, right?" Carson asked.

"I'm not sure," she said. "We were at the end of the bar near the back door. A couple of people noticed him sitting on the floor, but I don't know who all saw what happened before that."

There was silence as everyone waited for her to say more. After a while, Carson said, "And that's it?"

"And that's it," she said. "Almost all of it."

"Almost?" the chief said.

"Well, he had a wingman. Or maybe the guy I decked was the wingman since he was the one talking to me. I don't know how these things work. But after the first guy dropped, this other drunk guy, older guy, stomped over to me and called me some unpleasant names."

"And what did *you* do?" Carson said.

"Oh, I bopped him one on the nose," Dee said.

Rodriguez asked her, "Did this second guy drop like a pallet of bricks, too?"

Dee said, "Nope. He grabbed his nose and headed out the door."

Out in our hallway listening post, Peggy grinned at me.

"Did you have any idea who these two assholes were?" Carson asked Dee.

"According to what the mayor was saying this morning," she said, "at least one of them was an actor, but on Saturday night they were just a couple of the unfamiliar faces that are everywhere now."

For my part, I couldn't see what felony the mayor was accusing Dee of committing.

Dee added, "I walked out the back door right after that."

"Did you go home, Dr. Moreno?" the chief asked.

She laughed. "Good lord, no. I went for a long drive to cool off before I went home."

"Well, there we are," Carson said. "This sounds simple enough."

Mayor Buckmaster spoke up loud and clear. "Well, my information is that Dr. Moreno's irresponsible actions have resulted in serious injuries."

"That isn't possible," Dee said.

Buckmaster continued, "So maybe it isn't so simple as you make it sound."

More silence, probably to give Dee the chance to add anything she'd left out. When she didn't say anything more, Rodriguez prompted, "So nothing serious? No loose teeth, nobody knocked unconscious, nothing like that?"

Dee must've only shaken her head, because when Mike Rodriguez spoke again, it was to the mayor. "What was the story they told you, Herman?"

The mayor's voice crackled with indignation. He said, "I heard from a reliable source that a major Hollywood star was merely trying to be friendly. She should've been flattered, but instead, she tore into the poor guy and beat him up. She slammed his head against the bar and left him lying on the floor."

"That is complete and utter nonsense," Dee said. "From beginning to end. Herman, would you call that kind of harassment 'being friendly'? I sure don't. Anyway, the asshole was fine when I walked away."

Carson said, "All right. Against the advice of counsel, Dr. Moreno has told you what happened. She will have nothing more to say at this time. All questions come to me."

The mayor piped up again. "Contrary to your client's claims, I am telling you that the *victim* was seriously injured."

Rodriguez said, "Let's get him in here, Herman. Let's hear what he has to say."

"And just how do you propose we do that?" Buckmaster's voice was getting squeakier. "I told you this morning, he didn't show up for today's cast meeting. How do you expect him to show up here?"

Carson said, "Mayor Buckmaster, I'm still not clear on how you heard this story. When did you hear it?"

The mayor ignored Carson and went on, loudly. "Her *victim* is in *serious condition*." He paused to let that sink in before saying, "This could kill the movie project! Do you realize that? Do you have any idea what the city stands to lose if that happens?"

"Again," Carson said, "what is your source of information?"

"Never you mind," Buckmaster said, "This is serious, and it's all your fault."

I figured that he was yelling at Dee. He sounded as smug as he'd seemed while pitching his fit in Dee's office. As far as I could tell, that seemed to be his natural state these days.

"Bullshit," Carson said. "Mike, what do *you* know about this?"

Rodriguez answered, "I'm pretty much hearing about it at the same time you are. Coming to see Dr. Moreno is all I've had time to do since the mayor brought it up this morning. I did call the county attorney's office, trying to find out about any complaints. They'll call me back."

Buckmaster said, "I already told you. Now do your job." I heard his chair scrape as he added, "I've got work to do." He opened the door and walked out past me and Peggy in the hallway, slamming the door behind him.

The phone on the desk rang, and I heard Rodriguez answer it. After a lengthy silence, he said, "Understood."

He banged the phone down, and no one made a sound for a few seconds. The chief cleared his throat and spoke again in a softer tone. "One of the names is Shawn Gordon. He *is* a movie star."

I glanced over at Peggy, whose eyes opened very wide.

We heard a chair squeak, and I pictured Rodriguez standing up and towering over everyone else as he said, "I'm sorry, Dr. Moreno. That was a call from the assistant county attorney in Flagstaff. A formal complaint *has* been filed charging you with assault."

"Is there an arrest warrant?" Carson asked.

After a pause, the chief answered, "He says there will be. The judge down there will probably issue it by noon. One delay is that one of the victims hasn't been around to tell his story. The one who showed up there is the producer, Benjamin Pressfield. He has a broken nose and says that Shawn Gordon was seriously hurt."

"All this is happening down in Flagstaff?" Carson said. "That's odd. Why not here in Sage Landing? I mean, the injured parties could've come in here Saturday night or Sunday morning. Why would they wait till today? Why Flagstaff?"

My fellow eavesdropper, Officer Thomas, raised an eyebrow—*why indeed?*—and I nodded to indicate that I had the same questions, too. At the same time, I was glad that no one could see us, two grown women standing side by side in front of a blank steel door, gesturing and making faces.

We heard Rodriguez answer, "Yeah, well, I assume that there's some big juice coming down from somewhere higher up. Maybe much higher up."

"For a sock to the jaw and a bop on the nose?" Carson asked.

"Apparently, but we keep hearing that the injuries are serious."

"Felony assault requires more than that," Carson said. "Intent, for one thing."

I'd heard more than enough. I opened the office door and asked, "Is it okay if I say something?"

"No," Carson said.

"Sure, Naomi," the chief said. "What's on your mind?"

"Well, first," I said, "I was there. Buckmaster wasn't. I don't know where he got his story, but it isn't what happened. Second, how do they know that Mr. Black Hat has serious injuries if he hasn't shown up himself? Are they taking Mr. Bloody Nose's word for that? And where's the damn warrant, anyway? I've heard enough about how it's coming. The fact is, it isn't here." I stood there staring daggers at Mike Rodriguez.

I don't know if what followed was stunned silence or some plain old regular silence, but it lasted a while.

Carson spoke up. "As my associate points out, it seems that there is no legal basis for detaining our client. Or did I miss something?"

The chief was silent.

Carson said, "We've seen no complaint. No warrant has been issued." Still facing Rodriguez, he said, "Naomi, let's take Dr. Moreno out to your car."

I backed out of the doorway into the hall. Dee stood up, smoothing the front of her tailored skirt, and headed toward me. As Carson followed her, Mike Rodriguez leaned back so that he could see Dee and said, "You'll be staying in town, correct?"

Carson said, "Well, Mike, I haven't finalized my plans for the week yet."

"Oh, now that *is* funny," said Mike. "Ha. Ha. Ha."

Without turning around, Dee said, "You guys are a riot. You should take your comedy routine on the road," and she walked on down the hall.

CHAPTER FIVE

"Back to the college, right?" I asked as Dee climbed into the back seat of my Datsun and brushed aside the scatterings of papers, snack wrappers, and sports equipment that accumulate in a mom's car during the school year. "Sorry about the mess back there."

"Hey, no problem," she said, "Yes, I do need to go to the college first, but let's meet after that so I can fill you both in."

"I think it's pretty clear for now," Carson said, scooting into shotgun position and buckling his seatbelt. "At least until the county attorney does something."

"Still, there are some details I want to go over," she said, "and I want to write you a check."

I adjusted the rearview mirror so that I could see her face. "I don't think you have a legal problem," I said, "After we talked to you outside the Wrangler that night, Wanda and I had a little chat with Mr. Black Hat. He said the guy with the bloody nose left him stranded. We offered to find him a ride, but he declined politely. Last we saw, he was headed out to the parking lot."

"Under his own power?" Carson asked.

I nodded. "And probably planning to find someplace to go on drinking, too."

"That's interesting," Carson said, "and very helpful if there's another interview with Rodriguez."

"Nevertheless," Dee said, "we do need to meet in your office later, okay?"

"The afternoon is clear," Carson said. Then he added, "I think. Is there anything else on the agenda, Naomi?" Suddenly he'd remembered that he had only a vague idea of what was going on in his law firm. He happened to be right about the schedule, though.

Still, I should try to keep up appearances. "What time did you have in mind?" I asked Dee, as if it mattered.

"I have things on my desk that I have to finish and some that'll take a little time to delegate. My lunch is in the workroom refrigerator. So, after lunch—say one o'clock."

We dropped her off in the Anasazi parking lot and headed back toward our office. We hadn't gone more than a couple of blocks down Main when I noticed that we were driving behind a convertible with its top and all its windows down. It was full of teenage girls who were laughing as their hair whipped around in the wind. Unfortunately, I saw that the two girls in the back seat were my daughter and Elle. Since I was under the distinct impression that both of them were grounded, I said something that I'd never had the chance to say before: "Follow that car!"

"You're the driver, Naomi, so you can't say that." Glancing again at the car in front of us, he grinned. "Give them a little space so they won't know they're being tailed."

The convertible turned in at McDonald's. I pulled in next to it as the driver got out and headed for the entrance. That was when I noticed that not only were the two girls openly defying their restriction, but they were also harboring a third transgressor—my dog, Three-Steps. Despite the seriousness of her offense, the dog seemed a lot happier to see me than the two girls in the back seat did.

I got out of my car and leaned over, resting my arms on the back door of the convertible. Carson also got out of my car, but he headed straight into McDonald's.

"Where are you supposed to be right now, Kai?" I asked.

"It's lunchtime," Kai answered.

"But you and Elle are grounded."

"You mean *now*?"

"What do *you* think?"

Kai lifted her chin a little and shot back, "You didn't specify," going all attorney on me.

I stood up straight, belatedly realizing that I was making a scene in front of my boss, my daughter's friends, and the whole lunchtime crowd at McDonald's, some of whom were openly watching me through the glass walls. It was not my finest hour. "You're right," I said, "I didn't."

Kai waited—she's half-Navajo herself, and can outwait even a grown-up Navajo like me when she wants to—so I went on, "Where did you find Three-Steps?" I asked.

"I saw her sitting outside Safeway on the sidewalk when we drove by." She stroked the dog's head and said, "Poor thing, you were tired and thirsty, weren't you?" before looking up at me to say, "I was going to take her home and lock her in the house after lunch."

I reached over and scratched the dog's ears. "Maybe she'll make better choices next time she's tempted to make a break for it." I caught my daughter's eye. "Thank you, Kai, that's very responsible. I'll see you at home. You'll be there as soon as your last class finishes up, right?"

Kai sighed deeply. "Fine, yes, I get it, Mom. I'm grounded."

Having made my point, I smiled and got back into my car. I put my hands on the steering wheel and waited for Carson. In the meantime, the girls' getaway driver came out with the food. She glanced at me, then at the girls. If she had any questions, she kept them to herself. After carefully setting the food on the passenger side of the front seat, she got behind the wheel, inched slowly out of the space, and drove back toward the school.

A few minutes later Carson emerged with a couple of white bags with familiar golden arches printed on them. He noticed the empty parking space next to my car and wisely said nothing as he got back into the car. We maintained silence all the way to the office.

Carson's desk was too heaped with paper to serve as a lunch table, so we unbagged burgers and shakes on my desk in the outer office and settled in to eat, right in full view of the public. Anyone walking by would get an eyeful of the expense-account lunches that make the practice of law so glamorous.

Once he'd gotten a good start on his burger, Carson said, "So, Dee says she needs an attorney. What do you think?"

"Besides the fact that we need her retainer?"

"Besides that." He took another bite.

"I have no idea. Buckmaster was sure being strange, though."

The front door opened, and a man walked in. A handsome guy with short black hair. Clean-shaven, brown-eyed, cheekbones worthy of a United Colors of Benetton model. I realized that it was the guy who'd been looking at me in Wranglers on Saturday night. I also realized—holy hell, it was Lew Nez, but looking maybe twice as hunky as he did in high school.

He smiled down at me. "*Yá' áte' ééh, shideezhí,*" he said.

I answered, "*Yá' áte' ééh, shínaaí.*"

Carson was glancing back and forth between me and Lew.

"Grant Carson, meet Llewellyn Nez," I said.

Carson asked, "Llewellyn?"

Our new guest reached over to shake Carson's hand, saying, "Lew. Nobody calls me Llewellyn." He smiled at me again. "Nobody nice, anyway."

It took me a second to think of a witty reply. "Haven't seen you in a while," I said. "How's it going?" So much for wit.

"Good, very good, and you?" There it was again, that heart-stopping grin. Not to mention those soulful brown eyes. Some women would've gone weak in the knees, but I was tempered by many years and a couple of kids. And I was sitting down.

Wait, he'd asked me a question. "Um…good, good," I stammered. "Yes, good."

Lew sat down in the remaining chair and scooted it around so that the three of us were facing each other. He said, "I saw the thing Saturday night with Dr. Moreno."

This was a surprise. I mean, it didn't surprise me that he saw the 'thing' happen Saturday night, now that I knew that he was there when it happened. What surprised me was that he would know by lunchtime on Monday that he should come into the law offices of Grant Carson to tell us about it.

Carson must've been thinking the same thing, because he said, "Oh? And what brings you *here?*"

Now it was Lew's turn to be a little surprised. "Well, you're President Moreno's attorney, right?"

I was pretty sure that Carson wouldn't answer, and he didn't. He simply waited for Lew to explain.

Lew glanced over at me first and said, "I was delivering a computer to the main college office this morning, and I overheard some talk."

I asked, "A computer?"

"I do computers," Lew said. "Build, sell, fix, troubleshoot—pretty much everything."

Not only had I not seen Lewellen Nez for several years, but I also had no idea what he did these days. To tell the truth, I'd avoided asking anyone about him. "I didn't realize," I said. "I haven't seen you around."

"I've only been back in town a few months," he said.

Did he sound defensive? Wistful, maybe? Nostalgic? I couldn't tell. I was thinking of a song, "Save The Last Dance for Me." The Drifters. Lew and I had finished a few high school dances with that one.

Our little catch-up session was interrupted when Carson said, "You delivered the computer, and…"

Lew said, "…and while I was there, the office staff was—well, they were speculating," Lew said. "People pretty much ignore the computer guy when they have something interesting to talk about. I was setting up a computer on a desk, and they talked quietly among themselves."

I said, "Apparently they weren't talking all that quietly."

"As I said, I was invisible. Anyway, it was clear that they thought Dr. Moreno had been arrested for assault. That made me realize that I probably knew what they were talking about because of what I saw Saturday night at Wranglers."

Carson stood up and said, "Okay. Great. Hang on." He walked into his office and came back with a pencil and legal pad. Plopping back down on the chair, he adjusted the pad on the desk. "Tell us what you saw."

"I saw an assault all right. A guy wearing a stupid black cowboy hat assaulted Dr. Moreno and got what he deserved."

Carson said, "Back up a bit. What's the first thing you noticed? What made you think something was going on?"

Lew said, "I noticed Dr. Moreno was standing at the end of the bar with an empty pitcher. She caught my eye because—well, because Naomi was looking at her and I was watching Naomi." He glanced at me, grinning, and I felt a blush spread across my face.

Carson stopped taking the notes he'd started scribbling. His eyes flicked from Lew to me and back to Lew, letting me know that he'd be expecting the rest of *that* particular story after Lew left.

For now, though, he had a different story to fill in, so he said, "And then?"

Lew's grin disappeared. "So, anyway, she's standing at the end of the bar. The guy in the black hat closes in on her, kind of leans against her, no daylight between them at all, and kind of throws his arm around her. She shoves it off. It looks like he's talking in her ear and, he puts his hand …you know."

Carson waited for him to go on. When he didn't, Carson prompted, "Puts his hand where?"

Lew glanced at me again, this time without the grin. I could almost see a thought bubble over his head saying *ahem—there are ladies present.* As uncomfortable as he was, though, he forged on. "He grabbed her… where no decent guy would. Naomi probably couldn't see from where she was sitting, but he put his hand—"

I said, "You're telling us that he grabbed her crotch, right?"

He said, "Well, yes. That's what he did." Poor guy was relieved that he hadn't had to say the actual word. My first thought was that this was the same Lew Nez that I'd known years ago. The guy had always been a gentleman. My next thought was that the guy Dee hit was no gentleman.

Carson said, "What did Dr. Moreno do?"

"First, she tried to knee the guy, you know, where it would do some good. But he saw that coming and shifted a little, so she missed. Then she doubled up her fist and punched his face. I saw that as clear as day. It was great."

"And what did he do?" Carson asked.

"Wait, there's more," Lew said. "So, the right to the face, then a left to the midsection and a right to the chin as he doubled over. She didn't seem mad, and she didn't hit him all that hard, but, man, was it fast. Efficient, like here was a task she had to do, and she didn't waste any—"

Carson had stopped writing notes about halfway into Lew's admiring account of Dee's skills, and at this point, he asked, "So what did the guy do?"

"He dropped to the floor."

"Try to describe that to me as if you were a slow-motion camera," Carson said.

"Let me think," Lew said. "The uppercut to the chin made the back of his head bump up under the bar counter. *Under* it. And then he sat down on the floor. He just sat there and scooted around so that he could rest his back against the bar, and he stayed there like that."

"There was another man," Carson said. "Tell us about him."

"Yeah, older guy, heavy set. He stepped in really close to Dr. Moreno. I think he was pretty drunk, too. He was swearing at her, calling her names, really offensive, you know? So, I wasn't surprised when she hit *him*, too."

"How? How did she hit him?" Carson asked.

"Punched him in the nose," Lew said. "Slugged him right in the face. He sure as hell had it coming." Lew faced me and said, "Pardon my French."

A gentleman, and still old-fashioned as well. Though my ears are far from delicate—and my vocabulary at times would probably make him blush—I couldn't help smiling at him.

Carson asked, "Would you have hit him in the face if he'd spoken to you like that?"

Lew shrugged, "Maybe not me. Most guys would, though."

Carson made a few notes and said, "But *you* wouldn't have hit him?"

"Not in *that* bar," Lew said quietly.

"'Not in *that* bar'?" Carson repeated. "What does that mean?"

Lew's expression gave nothing away.

I explained, "Most of the regulars are white guys. *They* might hit each other in there, but Lew wouldn't."

Carson shook his head—he understood, and he didn't like it. "Why do you think those guys acted the way they did?"

"Who knows what goes through men's minds at times like that?" Lew said. "Men do a lot of stupid things in bars when they've been drinking. No telling what they thought they were doing, or who they thought they were, or who they thought Dr. Moreno was. They were strangers. They didn't know who she was."

Carson said, "They thought she was an available woman alone in a bar."

"A Mexican woman," I said. "A sexy Chicana. Let's be honest, that's what they thought."

Carson stayed quiet. I couldn't tell what he was thinking.

"What?" I said. "Two white guys? From out of town? And she's standing at the bar by herself? You know what they were thinking."

Lew said, "Naomi's probably right, but I'm telling you what I saw. Dr. Moreno got assaulted. She did what any white guy would've done."

I thought, *damn straight she did*. Right then, I was ready to go back in time and place a few well-aimed kicks myself.

After a minute of silence, while Carson finished his notes, Lew said, "I'm sorry, but I've got to run. I've got a business call to make at one." He stood and laid a card on my desk. "That's my shop number." He took a pen out of his shirt pocket, flipped the card over, and wrote on the back. "That's my home number here in Sage Landing." He scribbled something else on the card. "Those phones have answering machines on them, but here's my main office number in Gallup. They usually know where I am."

He shook hands with Carson and walked out.

"Why didn't we take him right over to the police station?" I asked after the front door closed behind Lew.

"We may not need to involve him." I could tell that he was choosing his words carefully before he went on, "He's a good witness, Naomi, but it would still be two locals against famous outsiders. And there's Buckmaster. We still don't have a clue about what the hell he's up to."

I'd just stood up to gather the lunch trash when Carson said, "Naomi, can I ask a question?"

I tossed the wrappers and crumpled napkins into the wastebasket and sat back down. "You mean besides that one? When have you ever needed permission to ask me questions?"

"Well, Mr. Nez spoke to you in Navajo, and you answered him, also in Navajo."

"Right, a simple greeting."

"And I could tell that you two knew each other pretty well."

I thought, *what was your first clue?* but instead asked, "Is there a question coming here, Carson?"

He shrugged. "I'm just curious. You know me, always curious."

"What's the question?" I asked.

"Well... what's the story? Go ahead and tell me it's none of my business if it's too personal."

It was pretty personal, but he wasn't going to stop being curious until I filled him in. I leaned back in my desk chair and said, "It's a pretty short story."

To show that he intended to pay close attention, he pulled his chair over so that he was sitting next to me, facing the same direction I was. He'd learned a few things about Navajo customs for showing respect by now, so he didn't face me directly. Growing up, it felt natural to avoid staring into someone's face, and even now that can feel confrontational. Sometimes it's best to listen only with the ears, letting a person's words and silences speak for themselves. "Okay," he said. "I'm good with that."

I took a deep breath. "Lew and I went to grade school, middle school, and high school together. We were buddies. My junior year, his senior, we were in some of the same classes and we got to liking each other more. You know, *like* like. We started dating in a we're-not-dating sort of way. Meeting each other for a soda after school, walking around together in the park, holding hands sometimes, trying out a few kisses. Both of us took a sudden interest in going to football games so that we could sit together. Dating without dating, you know?"

When I didn't go on, Carson said, "Sounds nice."

"It was. It was very nice. But...well, what Lew said to me when he got here was, 'It is good, my little sister.'"

"I understood the 'it is good' part," Carson said. "*Yá' áte' ééh.* That's like 'hello' or 'aloha,' right?"

"Right, but 'my little sister' is the important part," I said. "*Shideezhí.* And I answered, 'It is good, my elder brother.'" I quickly glanced at Carson. "That's the problem."

"He's your brother?"

"He may as well be."

"As in a blood relative?"

I could see that this explanation was going to take a little longer than I'd intended, but I wanted to keep it short and simple if I could. "The thing is, we belong to the same clan. My mother and Lew Nez's mother are both born of the Bear People Clan, so Lew and I are, too."

"So, your mothers' clans make you related, kind of?"

I shook my head. "According to tradition, we're not merely *kind of* related. We're brother and sister. No romance allowed, same as for first cousins under Arizona law. It isn't a government-type law. It's stronger than that."

I'd been a little worried that Carson would think this was silly or strange, but when I glanced over, his face was serious. He waited for me to go on, and when I didn't, he said, "I see. Then how did you and Lew get to running around together in the first place?"

"Neither of us paid any real attention to our clan kinships. Back when we were teenagers' older people usually asked someone's clan when they first met them, but kids like us didn't give it much thought."

"How did you find out?"

"Well, now we come to the bump in the road. Lew asked me to the prom. I said yes. I was happy and excited. But when Lou's mother heard about it, she asked my mom what her clan was, and that was that."

After a short silence, Carson said, "That must've been rough."

"It was. I wanted to ignore the whole thing. We both argued endlessly with our moms. We weren't asking to get married, for crying out loud. I wanted to dress up in a poufy formal. I wanted to go see my friends in their Cinderella outfits and laugh at the guys in their rented tuxes. I wanted to pose for a cheesy prom photo with Lew."

Carson's face showed nothing but sympathy. He said, "But your moms thought that going to prom could lead to something serious."

"Yeah. That's what they kept saying. His mom especially, and she won in the end. No prom for us, and no dates. There weren't even many conversations after that. Lew graduated and left town. Now he's back. I wonder if he's single."

Carson said, "Oh? Do you?"

"What's that supposed to mean?"

"Those events happened years ago, but you guys have stayed away from each other ever since, right?"

"So?"

"Maybe it means that it wasn't just your moms who didn't want to step over that line."

"What? No. Not after all the high school drama, anyway. It was just …we just lost track of each other. That's all."

"Sure. I get it. So now what?"

"Beats me. I'd just as soon not think about it."

We sat without saying anything for a little while. Then Carson stood up. "I need to head over to the station to see if those movie assholes have come to their senses and dropped the charges. That would be better than relying on a witness. But Desiree will be back here soon."

"Don't call her Desiree, Carson. She doesn't like it, and you shouldn't do it."

Carson held up his hands in surrender, like Mr. Black Hat did when he was sitting on the floor in Wranglers. "Yeah, I know. I won't. *Dee* should be back soon."

I gave him a look. "That's a little better. Now try 'Our client, *Dr. Moreno*, will be here soon.'"

He said, "Okay, that. And will you stay here to wait for *Dr. Moreno* to get back from the college, where she is the *president*?"

I chuckled. "It will be my pleasure."

After he left, I called the high school to make sure that the girls were back in class. As I waited for our client to return, I sat there thinking about what I'd told my boss I didn't want to think about.

CHAPTER SIX

DEE didn't get to our office till about one-thirty. Good thing, because Carson had only just gotten back, with barely enough time to dash past me into his office and scrape some of the stacks from the top of his desk into a deep drawer underneath. When she walked in, we all sorted ourselves into chairs around that desk.

"So, you still think you need legal counsel?" Carson said as he rummaged through the deep desk drawer to find the legal pad that was now buried under random paperwork.

"Yep," Dee said. She got a checkbook out of her purse and tore out a check that she'd already filled in. It was made out to Carson, but she handed it to me.

The amount was five thousand dollars, an amount so large that it worried me. "Dee, this business about Saturday night may not go any further," I said.

"But it could," she said.

Carson sat back and fiddled with his pencil. "Let me outline where we are with the situation as I understand it. We can take it from there."

"Okay."

"I heard your description of the scuffle in the bar. I've also heard from another witness who tells the same story. With maybe a little more gusto than you did."

"Right. Naomi was there," Dee said, glancing my way.

"Besides Naomi—another witness who was in the bar and who saw the whole thing from a different angle."

"Okay, good," she said.

"From all reports, you didn't injure him as seriously as Buckmaster said."

I added, "The guy was fine when he walked out of the bar."

Dee said, "Well, good. I'm glad it's not only me saying so."

Carson didn't comment on that. "And you say you got into your car and drove around for a while before going home. Where did you go?"

Dee said, "Out along the lakeshore."

"How long would you say that took?"

"I don't know. Say two hours."

"So, you left the bar, drove around a couple of hours to calm your nerv—"

Dee interrupted, "That's what I said, yes. A couple of hours, give or take."

Carson continued. "And, Dee, you didn't see him, this movie star, again."

Dee shuffled her feet around in front of her chair before answering. "Well, *that's* the question that never came up this morning."

Carson dropped his pencil. "You saw him again?"

"Calm down, Carson," she said. "Jeez Louise, we don't even know if a warrant will show up. Like Naomi was saying, this may all go away."

"*Jeez Louise?* Who says that?" I asked, and at the same time, Carson said, "You didn't answer my question."

There was another long silence before Dee answered, "Yeah, well, let's wait—I'd rather wait."

Carson said nothing. I was bursting with questions. Wasn't Dee the one who wanted to open up, tell us more, fill us in? One tantalizing little hint hardly qualified as "filling us in." It was in her best interest to tell us everything, and now I was wondering why she wouldn't. Still, she was the client, Carson was the attorney. I was merely the paralegal. Also, a witness, a friend, a protégé, an interested bystander.

Dee stood up. "I've got to get back to campus. Commencement and all. Busy week."

With that, she left our office.

After a few seconds, Carson asked, "How much is that retainer?"

"A lot," I said, "five thousand."

Carson said, "So, Dee thinks she could be in some serious trouble."

"Yeah," I said. "You need to talk to Mr. Black Hat."

"Yeah."

"Should I check with Peggy?"

"Maybe," Carson said. "She wasn't at the station when I went back, and Mike wasn't inclined to share."

"I might be seeing Peggy tonight anyway. It's our knitting night, but she doesn't always come."

"It's worth a shot, but we'll probably have to wait till Mr. Black Hat— Shawn Gordon, I mean—decides to show up."

~ ~ ~

Since this was a Monday, I knew that Kai would already be fixing dinner. Sure enough, when I got home, she was in the middle of chopping lettuce while singing along with Kenny Loggins about the Danger Zone. As I walked into the kitchen, she muted the radio, appearing a lot happier than she had at noon in the McDonald's parking lot. She practically bounced when she faced me and said, "Hey, mom, I've got something great to tell you."

"Wonderful, I'm totally in the mood to hear something great." I put my purse down on the kitchen counter and switched gears so that I could listen. "What's the news?"

"I've got a summer job!"

That took me by surprise because she hadn't said anything before about a job, summer or otherwise. Kai was fifteen years old, and not many local businesses would hire someone her age. I didn't have any real objections, but I was a little wary.

"That's interesting," I said. "Where are you thinking of going to work?"

"Well, it's not a paying job. It's an internship."

"An internship where?"

Kai finished chopping the lettuce and put it in the salad bowl. Before answering me, she went to the kitchen windowsill for a fresh tomato. She returned, knife in hand, and said, "The movie company is giving summer internships to high school students if they have a recommendation from the school."

"And their parent's permission, I assume," I said.

Kai gestured with her kitchen knife, making a circular motion in the air. "Yeah, in fact, you have to come to a parent meeting for the orientation."

"Oh? When will that be?"

"Some night this week," Kai said as she began to slice the tomato. "I brought home a form for you to sign. When they see how many students they have, they'll set it up and let us know."

From what I'd heard today about some of the people involved in the movie production, I was less than enthusiastic about this news but told myself to keep an open mind. I asked, "What kind of work will students be doing?" and sat down on a wooden barstool at the kitchen island.

Len and I had made the island together. We assembled it from a cute cabinet and a length of forest green Formica countertop that we salvaged from a friend's kitchen remodel. Neither the countertop nor the cabinet matched those in the rest of the room, but it had become our favorite part of the kitchen. I was happy sitting at that counter.

Kai diced up the tomato slices and opened the refrigerator for more ingredients. "That's the coolest part," she said, leaning over to reach deep into the bottom shelf. "There's a good chance that I'll get to work with the scriptwriters." She straightened up and bumped the refrigerator door shut with her hip, stepping up to the island with a bell pepper in one hand, the knife in the other, and a face filled with teenage enthusiasm. "One of the internships listed was something they called 'script assistant,' and I put that down on my application."

"Wow!" I had no idea what a script assistant was, but Kai seemed to think it was fabulous.

"My counselor told me that a script assistant needed the recommendation of an English teacher. Nobody else on the list was particularly interested in English. At least that's what I thought. Almost all of the kids were from the drama club."

"Anyone I know?"

"Elle."

"That'll be fun," I said. "What's she interested in?"

"Props and set decoration. There are probably a few other kids who are interested in that one, too. She'll have more competition than me."

I got up to get the percolator started, mostly to give myself something to do in the kitchen that wouldn't interfere with Kai's finely tuned meal prep process while we talked. Lately, she'd entered another touchy phase of teenhood, and we communicated best when each of us had something to do in the same room.

"Do you have any idea what they want a script assistant to do?" I asked.

"Well, it might not involve any actual writing. But at least I'd be working with the writers."

"I'd imagine that most of the writing is already done," I said as I filled the coffee pot with water.

Kai continued her vegetable chopping in silence for a little while and said, "Yeah, sure, it would have to be, wouldn't it?"

I didn't want to discourage her, so I added, "But they probably have to make script revisions as they go along, wouldn't you think?"

"Right. I mean, I hope so, but there's other writing I can do. I'm going to write some articles."

"Articles?"

"A column—for the paper," Kai said. "I'll be able to write about what's going on during the filming. I figure everyone'll be curious, but most people won't be able to take off work to watch any of the action. Not much of it, anyway."

I said, "Sounds like you've got a good idea there." It wouldn't be the first time that Kai had written small articles for the local paper. She started when she was six years old and won a contest to get a story about Christmas published in the paper. She'd been set on becoming a professional writer ever since, and she even got the paper to print a few articles she wrote about high school sports.

"But first I have to get the internship," Kai said.

I added, "And you'll need to get permission from the movie company." I wanted to remind her about the deal she'd made with the principal, promising to have me look over her articles before publishing them, but that could wait. "Do you know where the scriptwriters will be working?"

"Yeah, everyone is working on location. They've got a ton of trailers set up near Red Cliffs Beach. I heard that they were trying to shoot mostly on location to save money."

That seemed odd. I would've guessed that working on location was more expensive than working in a Hollywood studio. But what did I know? "Bringing everybody a thousand miles from Los Angeles doesn't seem too thrifty to me," I said.

"I wondered about that," Kai said. "It doesn't, does it?"

Our conversation was interrupted when Len said, "It's not fair." We both turned to see that he'd been standing in the doorway to the living room, listening to Kai's exciting news.

"What's not fair?" I asked.

"The high school kids get all the breaks. Guys my age aren't even allowed to work in the summer."

There wasn't any way to argue with that. Len would turn fourteen toward the end of the summer, but nobody would hire him until then. That left lawn mowing in the desert heat as pretty much the only option if he wanted summer work.

He continued, "I'd be able to learn a lot working for the movie."

"About photography, you mean?" I said, knowing that Len's current plan was to be a photographer. Kai and I had pooled our resources a year earlier and bought him a used 35mm single-lens reflex camera. Since then, he used most of his allowance to buy black and white film to shoot. Now, all kinds of guys who made their living with cameras would be out on that location, and he wouldn't get to meet any of them.

Finished now with her salad preparations, Kai put the knife in the sink. She rinsed her hands and was drying them on the linen towel draped over her shoulder when she smiled at her brother. Tilting her head to one side, she said, "I've got a job for you, Len. A photography job."

"How's that?" he asked.

"You can take photos for my newspaper column," she said.

Listening to all this teen enthusiasm, I hoped that there *would* be a movie production. With one of the stars AWOL as of this morning, not to mention a producer with a broken nose and a great big chip on his shoulder, it didn't seem promising. But maybe this kind of kerfuffle was typical at the beginning of a production, so I didn't rain on the kids' parade. I'd jump off that bridge when I came to it.

~ ~ ~

Going to S&B on Monday nights was usually the highlight of my week. This week, though, was one of those times when I'd have to keep my eyes on my knitting and my lips mostly sealed.

The thing about that group is that membership is casual—no one's able to attend all the time—but it's also inclusive. We all come from different worlds: school, police department, public library, offices both public and private, beauty parlors, retail stores, and so on. That means that on Monday nights we can usually get updates on everything happening in and around Sage Landing because we strictly follow some unspoken rules: 1) anyone can ask anything, but 2) there's no pressure if you can't answer, and 3) what's said at S&B stays at S&B. Violators with big mouths aren't invited back. This time I'd be relying on Rule #2 because I couldn't divulge anything, even to them, about any case.

Anyway, there I was, walking up to Alice Yazzie's house on Elm Drive, balancing my knitting basket and a tray of Wheat Thins with Rondele pepper cheese to share. Alice's windows were all open, letting out the sounds of pop music and laughter. As I shifted the stuff in my hands, trying to open the screen door without dropping anything, I could hear Marybeth Wilson say, "… that's hilarious. Buckmaster with that kind of money?" Marybeth was a city employee who did side work for Buckmaster's businesses, so I quit juggling and stood still to listen while she finished. What money was she talking about?

Someone else—Laura or Sue, maybe—said, "Well, Wayne said Herman bragged at the Elks Club about being an investor in the movie."

Marybeth said, "Herman Buckmaster, bragging? Why am I not surprised? What happened is he got a big catering contract from the movie guy, so he took out another mortgage on his house to buy a second truck. Maybe that's what he meant by *being an investor?*" She laughed again.

I managed to get the cracker tray balanced on my knitting-basket arm, freeing up my other hand to open the screen door. I walked on into the house.

Eight women sat in the living room. Two perched on the couch, two in armchairs, and the rest sat cross-legged on the carpet. Most had some kind of yarn project in front of them, though Sue Gallo seemed to be balancing her checkbook. They all stopped talking and looked expectantly at me.

"Hi, guys," I said, scooting a platter of nachos out of the way to make room on the coffee table for my tray.

From the far end of the couch, Alice said, "Hey, Naomi," and patted the empty space next to her. "We saved you a place."

Yeah, I was in the hot seat. All anyone wanted to talk about now was the Saturday Night Scuffle and Dee's run-in with the authorities. As I expected, Dee wasn't there to field questions. Peggy wasn't there, either, not that she would've spilled any beans, what with the ongoing investigation and all. The other knitters who'd been there at Wranglers on Saturday night had a lot to say, but they'd been watching the band and didn't have eyes on Dee till Mr. Bloody Nose had fled and Mr. Black Hat was on the floor. When I grabbed another nacho instead of filling in any details, the group was disappointed, but they weren't surprised. No pressure.

"Anyone want more wine?" Alice asked as she stood up. I jumped up, too, and stepped around the floor-sitters to follow her to the kitchen.

Reaching into the fridge, Alice said, "Go ahead and grab a wine glass from the counter over there." She poured me some white zinfandel and moved back toward the living room with the bottle.

I said, "Wait. Can I ask you something?"

"Shoot."

"I saw Lew Nez this afternoon. Did you know he was back?"

Alice tilted her head. "Well, sure. Didn't you?"

I said, "Not till today. He said he's been here for months."

Smiling, Alice said, "You think he's been avoiding you?" When we were in high school, she'd listened sympathetically as Lew and I ranted about the unfairness of it all. Now that she ran the parish office at St. Gerome's, she was still listening sympathetically to people with problems, which has made her very people-smart. Sometimes, like now, she seems clairvoyant.

My cheeks flushed. "No, of course not. We had a perfectly friendly conversation when he was—when I saw him today. No, I think he's been busy getting his Sage Landing shop set up. Our paths never happened to cross, that's all."

"Right, that's all," said Alice. She headed out to the living room. Over her shoulder, she stage-whispered, "Looking fine, isn't he?"

~ ~ ~

I'd barely come through my front door at home when the telephone rang. I made a face at Kai because telephone calls weren't allowed after 8 o'clock, and here it was almost two hours past the cutoff. She scowled back and picked up the phone. She smirked as she handed it over to me and said, "It's for you. It's Mr. Carson." She covered the receiver with her hand and added, "A little late, isn't it?"

I took the phone, mildly embarrassed.

"Turn on your television, Naomi," Carson said. "Channel 12."

"What's going on?" I said. Although I didn't normally watch television at that time of night, I knew that the only thing on at ten o'clock would be the news. Sage Landing didn't have a television station, so everything came through feeds from Phoenix.

"The news teaser a few minutes ago mentioned Sage Landing," he said.

"That can't be good," I said. "Any details?"

"It said, and I quote, 'Hollywood trouble in Sage Landing, Arizona. News at ten.'"

"Shit!" I said before I could catch myself.

Len said, "That's going to cost you twenty-five cents," while Kai giggled and Three-Steps looked at me disapprovingly.

We had a no-swearing house rule that was supposed to be reinforced by fines paid into a jar. To be clear, I wasn't the only offender. I was, however, the leading contributor to the jar.

I told Carson to hold on, and I leaned over to turn on the television while still holding the phone. The TV happened to be on Channel 12 already. Both kids sat down on the couch, taking full advantage of having the set on that late on a school night, and Three-Steps jumped up to sit between them. She wasn't usually allowed on the furniture, but she acted like she really wanted to see the news, and I honestly didn't have the energy to scold her.

Predictably, Sage Landing didn't appear at the beginning of the newscast, so we all had to wait through a bunch of other stuff before the item about our little corner of the world came up. When it did, though, it was a zinger.

The piece began with a candid photo of Dee walking in front of the community college. It was followed by a photo of Rodriguez and Buckmaster, also in front of Anasazi. They cut to a shot of Grant Carson and Dee walking into the police station. All the photos had been taken that very morning. I remembered the "dad" taking pictures of the girl by the college sign. He must've followed our cars to the police station.

Next was a publicity headshot of Shawn Gordon, followed by a black and white photo of Benjamin Pressfield with a bandage on his face.

Meanwhile, a dramatic off-camera voice was saying, "The men were on location, working on a groundbreaking film project. Both were criminally attacked on Saturday in Sage Landing by one Desiree Moreno, who is affiliated with the local community college. No motive has been uncovered."

The dramatic voice went on at length. Quite a bit of airtime was devoted to describing how ambitious the movie was going to be, and what a visionary the producer was, and how popular and beloved the handsome actor was. I concluded that it must've been a slow news day.

The voice went on, "The alleged attacker is represented by a rural attorney named Grant Carson, who was once under investigation by the district attorney's office in Maricopa County."

Though I'm ashamed to admit it, I was relieved that there was no mention of Grant Carson's employee.

But the coverage didn't end there. The next part was shot in a television studio. Two guys wearing tweedy blazers, one of them having paired his with a black turtleneck sweater for the full cliché, sat in club chairs like Masterpiece Theatre hosts. They argued with each other about "the Scottish play" and its bad luck across the centuries—near-misses, onstage injuries, and gory deaths. Good grief. It must've been a *very* slow news day.

One of the pundits said, "A bad situation can only get worse when Benjamin Pressfield is the producer." The other pundit nodded. On this, at least, they agreed.

"And—" The guy wearing the turtleneck paused for effect and studied his notes. "Moments ago, we were informed by authorities that Shawn Gordon is, in fact, missing."

"Shit!" Carson shouted through the phone so loudly that my kids heard it across the room.

I shrugged at the kids, gesturing with the phone—*he's the one who swore, not me*— as the other pundit clasped his hands under his chin and added, "His whereabouts are unknown."

"Shit shit shit," Carson muttered.

I summoned my most calming voice. "Carson, those guys don't know anything. They're sitting in L.A. They're sensationalizing."

When the news moved on to a flood elsewhere in the country, I clicked the television off and said goodnight to Carson.

I turned back to my kids. "Scottish play?"

"Mom!" Kai said, "*Macbeth*."

"Okay, right. I remember now." I said. "What's that got to do with the movie in Sage Landing?"

"Mom!" Kai felt compelled to say again, "A desert place."

"I know that," I said. "*That's* the title of the movie they're making out at Red Cliffs Beach. *A Desert Place*. Not *Macbeth*."

"That's the first line of *Macbeth*. 'A desert place' – those three words."

"I don't think so. The first line is some witch talking about a recipe for newt soup."

Kai got up from the couch and started toward her room. "No, it's not. I'll prove it."

She returned with her British Lit book. She opened it and promptly proved that she *was* right.

I said, "Okay, unfair advantage. You've been discussing this in class, haven't you?"

She grinned and said, "Maybe." Then it hit her. "Oh my god!" she said. "He's missing, they said!" She looked at me and her brother. "They could cancel the movie!"

She was most likely correct, but there was no point in saying so now.

The phone rang, and I avoided meeting three pairs of eyes that watched as I answered.

"We're going to need Lew in the morning," Carson said. "I'll try to call him. Be at the office by eight." As I reached out to hang up, I faintly heard him add, "um, please."

CHAPTER SEVEN

L EW Nez was standing on the sidewalk outside our office when I walked up shortly before eight o'clock on Tuesday morning. He was wearing a tie and a white shirt, like either a credible witness or a Mormon missionary. Carson arrived before I could unlock the front door, so I put my keys away, and the three of us piled into Lew's new minivan to drive the short distance to the police station.

Settling behind the wheel, Lew said, "I heard that Shawn Gordon's missing."

"Let's not discuss the case until after you've talked to the investigators," said Carson, "but I do have a request. When we get in there, I'd like you to begin by formally introducing yourself. It's important that your account be taken as seriously as possible."

Lew glanced at him and gave a slight nod.

By 8:30, Carson, Lew, and I were seated in a small conference room with Mayor Buckmaster and an assistant county attorney named George Bliss. Chief Rodriguez and Peggy Thomas joined us. On the table were two tape recorders, already turning.

Carson reminded everyone that a new witness to the events of Saturday night had come forward. He turned to Lew, waiting respectfully for him to speak.

Lew folded his hands on the table and made eye contact with each person in the room, which I thought was a nice touch. He said, "I am Llewellyn Nez. I'm Bear People Clan, born for One-Walks-Around clan."

I had to admit that it did sound impressive—his name, his mother's clan, his father's clan—a formal Navajo introduction, but in English.

Nobody spoke, so Lew went on, "Sage Landing is where I grew up. I recently came back here to open an additional branch of my Gallup, New Mexico business."

Herman Buckmaster snickered. When we all glared at him, he said, "Am I the only one who appreciates a good pun?"

Carson leaned forward. "What *pun* are you talking about?"

"Your *witness* is a *bear* person. Get it? He's here to *bear…witness*." Very pleased with himself, he chuckled again.

George Bliss dropped his pen on the legal pad in front of him. He said, "Mr. Buckmaster."

Buckmaster showed no embarrassment. "Oh, come on! Lew and I went to high school together. We always used to joke like that, didn't we, Lew?"

What an idiot.

Lew said, "Shall we get on with it?"

Carson was staring at Buckmaster, shaking his head in amazement. He shifted his attention back to Lew and said, "Yes, thank you, Mr. Nez. Please describe exactly what you saw Saturday night."

As Lew repeated everything he'd told us the previous afternoon, Bliss made notes on the legal pad. I kept my eyes on his face, but it revealed nothing. Buckmaster's face, on the other hand, showed every idiotic thought that went through his balding head. He rolled his eyes—not very original—and went on to scowl and snort dismissively every time Lew finished a sentence. It was quite a show, but he must have been warned not to interrupt because he didn't argue out loud till Lew finished. Then he made up for it with a torrent of words and arm-waving.

"That doesn't change a thing," Buckmaster said, waving a hand in the air to reject everything Lew had said. "It was criminal assault. A textbook case. Maybe even worse, because Mr. Gordon is still missing."

"Bull. Shit." I said. Oddly enough, nobody in the room reacted except the mayor.

"Young lady," he said to me, a grown woman nearly as old as he was, "you can't speak to me like that."

Carson cut in. "Naomi can speak to you any way she wants to, Buckmaster," he said. "And she's right. We're doing our best to persuade Dr. Moreno not to file assault charges against both of those men. She'd have every right to."

The assistant county attorney smiled slightly, though his eyes stayed on his notes.

"Nonsense," Mayor Buckmaster blustered. "Sheer and utter nonsense. Two gentlemen from a *major* production studio are doing *substantial* business in Sage Landing. When they go to a local establishment to *relax* after a long day's work, that...*woman*...assaults them *both*. One of them maybe *critically!*" Now quite red in the face, he launched his dramatic finish. "That *Moreno* woman has threatened the success of a *huge* movie production. It was going to be a *game-changer* for Sage Landing."

His performance made George Bliss pause his notes, but before he or Carson could think of anything to say in response, Lew spoke up.

"You were not there, Herman," he said, his voice sharp. "What you're saying is completely wrong. It is not what I saw, nor does it bear any resemblance at all to the description I just gave."

Buckmaster sputtered, no longer reluctant to interrupt, but Lew held up a hand, saying, "No. I'm not finished. I do not know the two men involved, and I've only met Dr. Moreno a couple of times. I don't have a dog in this fight. But I will not have my honesty questioned."

All eyes in the room were on Buckmaster. We waited a long fifteen seconds before he said anything. When he did, it was with exaggerated patience. "Oh, are you finished *now*? Yes? Well, then, *Llewellyn*, I apologize if you think I was calling your honesty into question. The simple fact is that the same event looks different to different people."

Carson said, "Herman, are you hearing yourself at all? We're talking about Dr. Moreno, president of the college. She's been part of this community for years. Her reputation is beyond reproach. Why on earth would you take this charge seriously?"

Buckmaster tapped the file folder resting on the table in front of him. "Right here's your answer. This evidence answers that very question." With a sly smile, he slid the file folder across the table to Carson. "It seems that this isn't the first time that Dr. Moreno has committed assault."

Carson opened the folder and did a quick read of the top page. He turned to the county's lawyer and asked, "Have you seen this?"

Bliss replied, "As near as I can tell, a public relations outfit in L.A. hired a private investigator early Sunday morning. By the next day—yesterday—the PR folks already had a photographer and a staff writer on the ground here, and they'd collected all the stuff in that file. They've been in high gear ever since."

"I'm betting they're using all this to get their movie in the news," Carson said. "Isn't it possible that Gordon's disappearance is just more of the same?"

"Frankly, I think that's a strong possibility," Bliss said, glancing at the mayor, "considering what we saw on TV last night."

Buckmaster didn't seem to hear what Carson and Bliss were saying about the motives behind all the fuss. He reached across the table and tapped the file folder in front of Carson, practically shouting, "She's a trained fighter!"

Carson continued leafing through the folder's few pages. "What do you mean? I don't see it, Herman."

"It's right there, third page. Moreno did fight training at a boxing club in Tucson. That was before her previous assault case."

"Where did you get this file, Buckmaster?" Carson barked. He glanced toward George Bliss.

"Not from us," Bliss said quickly. "He didn't get that from us. We got ours by courier from Phoenix. Chief Rodriguez saw our copy a few minutes ago."

Rodriguez spoke up, "Calm down, Buckmaster. And please resist the temptation to exaggerate." He explained, "When Dr. Moreno was a college student in Tucson, she was mugged one night as she walked across the campus. After that, she enrolled in a women's self-defense class offered by a local gymnasium."

"For fighters," Buckmaster said. "A gym for fighters. The private investigators found out that professional fighters sparred there all the time. She trained with them. And then she was convicted of assault."

"*Boxing* is a sport. The gym trained *boxers*. And no, she was not," the chief said, clearly exasperated. "I'm warning you, Herman. One more word out of you and I'm booting you from the room."

The room stayed quiet as the chief's threat hung in the air and Herman Buckmaster held his tongue for once. Then George Bliss went on with the story. "It was actually kind of like this incident. After her training, Moreno was accosted again on the Tucson campus, but *that* time she defended herself using what she'd learned in the class. She decked a guy, and he filed a charge."

"Was Dr. Moreno held over for trial?" Carson asked.

"No," Bliss answered. "Charges were dropped."

"No trial, no conviction?" I asked.

"No," Bliss repeated. "I'm surprised they were able to find any record of it."

Carson closed the file folder and said, "So, George, what are we going to do here?"

The assistant county attorney laid his pen down on his legal pad, sat back, and laced his fingers together behind his head. "In light of what Mr. Nez told us, I'll advise against going any further, at least till we've interviewed Pressfield. He seems to be behind all this, and it's sure sounding like a publicity move to me."

Without another word, Herman Buckmaster stood and left the room.

Carson closed the file. "Okay. Let us know. We have a right to hear whatever he has to say."

"Especially since the victim hasn't seen fit to show up," I added.

George Bliss smiled at me. "Well, Mr. Pressfield could file a valid complaint on his own. His nose did get broken. You and Mr. Nez both saw how that happened, so this isn't over yet."

When we got outside the police station, Lew headed to his van. Before we joined him, I asked Carson, "What's next for Dee?"

"Mike is a good cop, and he has a lot of unanswered questions on his hands. He'll probably question her some more, maybe check her car or ask to go through her house."

"Why would he do that? Like, maybe Dee's got Shawn Gordon tied up in her laundry room or something?" I said.

Carson gave me a sharp look before glancing at Lew, who was on the other side of his van unlocking the passenger doors. Gruffly he said, "Jesus, Naomi. Don't say stuff like that. We have enough to handle without putting ideas in anyone's head."

"Okay, sorry." I remembered what George Bliss told us. "What about charges for assaulting the producer?"

"That could happen, but come on! He'll drop those charges once he's gotten enough movie publicity for getting a bloody nose from a girl and then keeping an embarrassed actor under wraps for a few days."

After we got into the van, Carson said to Lew, "That was great, man. You made a big difference to Dr. Moreno's case."

Lew said, "Thanks. To be fair, it didn't hurt that Buckmaster was being a total—was behaving so badly."

Carson laughed. "You could say that, sure, but I'm serious. You're a first-class witness, and I've interviewed a *lot* of witnesses."

In about two minutes we were back at our office. Lew let us out, saying that he was off to catch up on the work that had piled up while he'd been fighting for truth and justice. Carson told me to take the rest of the day off. He said he would go talk to Dee and maybe take her to lunch. None of that was especially worrying, except that it meant that I'd be missing too many hours of work.

All I could do was walk home, thinking about my finances. Carson paid me a fair rate for a paralegal, but I needed a minimum of twenty hours a week to keep my household going.

Working on a part-time hourly basis meant I didn't have health insurance, or paid vacation days, or sick leave. Carson didn't either. He didn't even get an hourly rate. I knew because I was the bookkeeper and payroll clerk. I wrote my paychecks out of the law firm's account. Carson paid no attention to the balance. When funds got too low, as they did sometimes, I had to ask him to transfer money from his personal funds. He had a couple of small pensions from previous careers, and it didn't seem to bother him any to share those funds with our law firm when he had to. The retainer that we'd gotten from Dee would tide us over for a while, but her case might not end up taking much legal work. As her friend, I hoped it wouldn't. But still.

Business was pretty slow at small-but-spunky Carson and Associates, and I'd been putting in short weeks for a while. Having to take the afternoon off today brought me uncomfortably close to dipping below that twenty-hour mark for the week, and I couldn't ask to be paid for hours I didn't work. What we needed were more clients.

I was in my kitchen getting ready to slap together a peanut butter-and-banana sandwich for lunch when Lew called and asked me to meet him at Pedro's Hideaway. I put the peanut butter back in the fridge and said, "I'll be there in ten."

Pedro's was my favorite Mexican food restaurant. It was also Sage Landing's only Mexican food restaurant. Pedro's Hideaway did not belong to a man named Pedro nor was it in any sense a hideaway. Its dozen or so tables were arranged in a large, square room with all of the ambiance of a bus station waiting room. The lighting was unflatteringly bright, thanks to fluorescent ceiling fixtures and huge front windows. If you tried, you could stand in the middle of the parking lot and see who was sitting anywhere in the place.

So, when Lew and I sat down, the two of us together in a restaurant for the first time in our lives, it was in full view of anyone who wanted to see us. That didn't bother me a bit. It was good to see him across the table, really good, like he was fitting into a place that I hadn't noticed was empty.

Though the place was usually as noisy as a school cafeteria, that day it was short of lunch customers and, therefore, reasonably quiet. I took it as a good sign.

"You joined the Navy after you graduated, I heard." That was my way of picking up a conversation after more than sixteen years of not seeing each other.

There was that smile again. It hadn't changed at all. He said, "Yeah, it was that or get drafted into the Army. No one in his right mind wanted that in those days."

"I remember. Did you like the Navy?" I asked.

"I did. I got training from them that I've been using one way or another ever since."

"Computers?"

"Yeah, computer operations at first, then programming. All the computers were huge mainframes, but they were changing fast. I stuck with it after I got out, did a few years with GE and a couple with IBM."

"I guess these little machines that you're selling now must seem like a step down," I said.

Lew laughed. "Not at all. These desktop models are about as powerful as the mainframes I worked on at the beginning."

"No kidding?" I tried to think of something else I could say to make him laugh that laugh of his again.

A waitress came over to take our orders. It turned out that we both knew her because we were both regulars in Pedro's, even though we'd never run into each other there. We both ordered the same thing—Number 3, enchilada-style burrito with rice and beans—and got back to the subject of our lives.

"I hear you've got a couple of kids," Lew said. "You married Don Chaka?"

"About a year after graduation," I said. "You didn't know him. He was from Tuba City."

Lew's beer arrived, and he took a sip before speaking. "Chaka is a Hopi name."

Ah, now we were getting to it. Back when I got married it *was* kind of unusual for a Navajo to marry a Hopi. It got even more unusual a few years later when land disputes between the two tribes caused a lot of bad feelings between Navajos and Hopis for quite a while. But by then Don and I were divorced, and I'd changed my name back to Manymules. School still registered the kids under the name Chaka, but otherwise, they seemed to use Manymules most of the time, too.

Still, none of this seemed like any of Lew's business, so I asked, "And your point is?"

"No point," he said, carefully putting his glass down in the exact middle of the soggy cocktail napkin that served as a coaster, "but I'm pretty sure I know why you married… outside."

I bristled. "You mean because I *loved Don*?"

Lew didn't seem to care about the steam coming out of my ears. Or maybe he couldn't see it. Either way, he went on, "I'm not saying you didn't love Chaka. But marrying him was a good way to solve the problem, too, wasn't it?"

I had to admit that he was right about that, at least partly, but I was annoyed that he'd said so out loud. The truth was that after the struggle about our clan relationship, I got super-aware of the whole clan kinship issue for a while. Other kids did, too, once word got out about why we'd broken up. After Lew graduated and left town, I spent my senior year finding out that practically every guy I thought about dating was either born in my mom's clan or born for my dad's. Yes, I had a school full of brothers. Lucky me.

After I graduated and started to work out at the marina resort, Don Chaka showed up in town to work for one of the river-running companies that operated in the summers. He was cute, strong, sweet, and a little bit wild. He was Hopi, sure, but that seemed kind of exotic to me, and he sure as heck wasn't my brother.

"Did you ever marry?" I asked, not quite changing the subject.

"Not yet," Lew said, "I'm still hoping."

Our lunches arrived. We ate in silence, and I appreciated the chance to collect my thoughts before I got back to what was on our minds.

"I guess the problem of finding the right wife is still as difficult as ever," I said. I guessed that he was still trying to follow all the traditional rules. In the end, I'd ducked them. Maybe Lew had, too, by joining the Navy.

"Sometimes it seems impossible," he said. "You meet a woman who seems right—but she turns out to be in your clan. You meet a woman who isn't in your clan—and it doesn't work out for any of a dozen other reasons." He dipped a tortilla chip into the enchilada sauce on his plate and ate it thoughtfully before continuing. "It's enough to make a guy channel all his energy into building his business."

I spotted the opportunity to change the subject and grabbed it with both hands. "The computer business is yours?"

"Sure is. I sell them, and I also do the repairs, tackle the software problems, train the staff. My shop is over on the other side of Main, but it's tucked in behind the Chinese restaurant. Would you like to see it? If you have time, I mean."

I did have time, and I did want to see his shop. Lew had always been a good friend, and I saw no reason why he couldn't be one now. "That'd be great," I said.

After lunch, when we walked into Lou's shop, I discovered that it was no small operation. Near the front of the store was a long table holding five or six computers. A young woman was busy demonstrating one of them to a potential customer. Behind the counter in the back, a young man was staring at a computer screen and making notes. Lew gestured with a sweeping motion and said, "Commodore, Texas Instruments, and IBM – a pretty broad price range."

"Impressive," I said, and I meant it. "You mentioned that you have a store in Gallup. Are there others besides the one here in Sage Landing?"

"One other. Gallup was first, Farmington was next, and Sage Landing is the newest. This one is where I'm doing most of my work these days. The market in Sage Landing is a little small, so I worried that this shop might not make it. But business is growing fast, even here."

He walked toward the back of the store and opened the door, gesturing for me to follow. He flipped on the light in an equipment-filled room at the back of the building. All around the room were shelves holding computers, tools, and supplies. "This is my workstation," he said. "My technician is still learning, so I do most of the troubleshooting and debugging. Sal out there mostly works on hardware. That's where you start when you're learning this stuff."

"So if I screw something up, you're the guy I'd come to see?"

"Yep. That would be me."

"I'm asking because I think I may have done just that."

"Really?" He asked. "What've you done?"

"It'll sound stupid," I said. "It involves coffee."

"Classic," he said, "with cream and sugar?"

"Yes."

"Into the computer, onto the keyboard, or all over a floppy?"

I laughed as I realized that he'd heard all this before, and I was happy to hear him laugh, too. "On the keyboard and on a disc. The keyboard still works, but the disc doesn't. It's got quite a few documents on it."

Lew shook his head and walked over to his workbench. He picked up a plastic-clad disc like the ones I used every day in the office. "One of these newer ones like you use with your IBM, or one of the big paper ones?"

"A new plastic one like that," I said.

He nodded and walked over to a clear plastic tray on a shelf. Inside it were lots of plastic discs. He pulled out a handful, walked back to me, and spread them out on a table. They were covered with gunk, if that's the correct word for what I was seeing.

"Is your disc as bad as these?" he asked.

"Ick. Did someone try to stash them in a beehive or something?" I said. "They're disgusting. No, nothing like that. Mine is just bad enough to stop working."

"These are from the city office," he said, "and their data wasn't saved anywhere else. They're originals."

"Wow. Are they toast, or is there some hope for them?"

"Hard to say, but I'll give it my best. Yours should be pretty easy—easier than these anyway. Bring it over when you have a chance and I'll show you how."

"Thanks, Lew. You'll save me a couple of bucks."

"Not after I charge you for my time," he said, but he was laughing.

~ ~ ~

Kai came home full of excitement, and Len was not far behind her. Kai reported that the meeting for parents about the summer internships would be the next evening. She was thrilled that it hadn't been canceled, even though Shawn Gordon was still missing.

I didn't want to dampen anybody's enthusiasm, but I had to mention a few things before we got any further, so I had them sit down in the kitchen. Using my serious-parent voice, I said, "I want to talk to you guys about the movie a little. I don't mean the movie, but the people making the movie...the people...Hollywood."

Kai and Len exchanged glances. "I heard a lot about that today," Kai said. "Everybody was talking about it—the guys in the bar. Mom, that was the producer and a movie star. They won't have anything to do with us."

"Well, *one* of them sure won't," Len said. Apparently, a missing person could be the subject of humor if you were in middle school.

I tried to maintain a stern and disapproving expression. "I know," I said, "but I want to talk about Hollywood people in general, some movie people." It occurred to me that I hadn't thought through exactly what I wanted to say about movie people.

"What about them?" Len asked.

"Well, these movie people," I said, "they're adults, and they live in Hollywood."

Patiently, Len said, "We know that, Mom. That's why you call them 'Hollywood people.'"

"Don't be a smarta— smarty-pants." I didn't seem to be getting anywhere, but I kept trying. "The point is that Hollywood—Los Angeles and around there—is not like Sage Landing."

"It isn't? Really?" Kai said. "I had no idea." She leaned forward, her elbows on the countertop and her chin in her hands before going on, "Please, tell me more."

I thought it best to overlook the sarcasm. Staying on message, I said, "There's a whole different way of life that goes on there." Damn, that was lame, but I didn't want to go into specifics.

Len and Kai, though, had no such qualms. Kai said, "You mean hitting on someone at the bar?"

Len indicated that, yes, like his sister, he knew exactly what I was talking about.

I said, "Well, yes. That probably doesn't seem so bad in Hollywood. But it was, and not just in Sage Landing. It's…"

"It's bad," Len said. "We understand that."

"I think we all know what I'm trying to say," I said. "Hollywood people act…"

"Badly," said Kai, patting my back sympathetically. "We get it, Mom."

I gave up, relieved. They were way ahead of me. "Be careful, is what I'm saying. This crew has a lot of people in it, and they don't come from a small town in northern Arizona."

Kai smiled. "Hardly anyone does, you know."

Len nudged her with an elbow and said, "Stranger danger."

She giggled and repeated, "Stranger danger."

They were smarta—smartypants. Both of them.

CHAPTER EIGHT

In a moment of madness way back at the beginning of the school year, I had let Len sign me up to help at the middle school's year-end track and field events. To be clear, there is nothing about the track or the field that I like. But I wanted to do my bit, parent-wise, and filling little paper cups with tepid water while Len and his fellow middle-schoolers ran off some of their annoying springtime energy sure beat chaperoning one of their school dances. I'd done that once. It gave me déjà vu, and not in a good way, so sweating for a couple of hours on the windy field seemed like a pretty good bargain by comparison. At least it did until it threw my Wednesday morning out of whack.

Which is to say that it was almost ten o'clock by the time I could get away and walk to the office. When I got there, I was surprised to see Carson's truck already parked out front, with a shiny new Cadillac sedan parked next to it. Since the movie crowd seemed to be driving around in luxury cars like that one, I expected to find some of them in the office when I walked in.

No such luck. There wasn't anyone in the front office, but when I went back to Carson's inner sanctum, I was shocked to see John Rice, an attorney from Albuquerque. Maybe "attorney" is too dignified a word to apply to Mr. Rice. It would be more accurate to call him a mob lawyer. We'd dealt with him before, and the experience had not been a pleasant one. In fact, the last time he came to town, he brought a muscled-up thug with him. Over the course of a few days, the thug helped Rice scare the crap out of me and threaten my kids. He also duked it out with Carson in a parking-lot brawl that left them both very much the worse for wear.

In fairness to John Rice, we did see him all by himself once after that. That time he behaved like a perfect gentleman. Nevertheless, I couldn't help hearing faint alarm bells at seeing him now.

He was sitting across the desk from Carson, and he didn't rise as I came into the room. "Good morning, Naomi," he said, smiling. "Nice to see you."

"Mr. Rice," I said without returning his smile. "What brings you out our way?" As if I cared.

Carson spoke up. "John is bringing us a little business, Naomi. It seems he needs some legal representation on a matter involving our Hollywood friends."

I raised an eyebrow at Carson before sitting down in the remaining chair. "It's always good to see business coming in. We've already got some Hollywood people on our radar."

Rice's face twitched with the tiniest hint of impatience. "Carson was filling me in on that. Crude behavior isn't surprising, considering the source, but it sounds like they've met their comeuppance this time."

"Well, it's probably all over now," I said.

"I wish I could say it was, but Benjamin Pressfield is kind of a litigious son of a bitch, if you'll pardon my language. That's why I'm here today."

I wondered why John Rice would need to retain Carson since he was an attorney himself, but he was based in Albuquerque so maybe he couldn't do legal work in Arizona. "You think Pressfield is going to sue you?"

Rice smiled broadly—kind of like a hungry lizard. "No, it isn't his litigiousness that brings me. It's other behaviors befitting a son of a bitch. I expect that we may have the opportunity to bring legal action against him as a result."

The list of possible son-of-a-bitch behaviors that might justify bringing an action—legal or otherwise—was pretty long, and I wondered which ones Rice was talking about.

Before I could figure out how to ask, Carson spoke up in my direction. "Pressfield is apparently in violation of a contract, and we may need to encourage his compliance."

Rice asked me, "Are you familiar with the work of the actress Kathy Roberson?"

I hereby admit to being a sucker for a romantic comedy. Kathy Roberson was in several that I'd seen recently, cast as the best friend, or maid of honor, or quirky neighbor. "I've seen a few of her films," I said.

"Did you know she was in town?" Carson asked. "She's starring in the movie."

"She's in *A Desert Place*?" I said. She wasn't someone I'd imagine in a Shakespearean role, "cute" and "perky" being more her style, but maybe she was branching out. "She's here in Sage Landing?"

Carson said, "Sure is. She'll be right here in this office in a few minutes."

"Oh, that's… nice." I stood up and said, "Excuse me." I stepped back out into my office and made a quick survey of the clutter. I opened the center drawer of my desk and swept every little thing that was sitting on the desk's surface into the drawer.

I opened my purse and hunted in vain for a mirror. There wasn't time to put on makeup, but it would've been nice to check on my hair, having spent most of the morning out in the wind. While I was worrying about that, though, there she was, walking through the front door.

As I said, Kathy Roberson looked more like a best friend than a glamour girl. Like a regular person, but a little better in almost every way. She was dressed in khaki shorts and a pastel shirt, both of which fit like they'd been made for her. Her dark hair curled around her soft and dewy face. Her blue, blue eyes were shining like she'd been waiting all week to meet me. I was dazzled.

"Grant Carson?" she asked, and her voice sounded as bouncy as it did in her films.

"We're back here, Kathy," Rice called from the other room. By the time she started to move toward Carson's office, John Rice had appeared in the doorway with Carson right behind him. "Come on in and meet Grant," he said. Then he added, waving vaguely in my direction, "and this is Naomi, his associate."

The actress rotated back toward me and extended her perfectly manicured hand. "Naomi," she said with a beautiful smile. "I'm Kathy Roberson."

"Naomi Manymules," I said, taking her hand lightly in mine. "I know. You're—" and that's as far as I got. The two men were retreating into Carson's office, and she gave my hand a friendly squeeze before following them. There weren't enough chairs in that room for me to sit in there, too, much as I wanted to, so I'd listen from my desk out front. The wall between Carson's desk and mine didn't muffle sound at all, even when the door to Carson's office was closed, and this time it stayed open. I didn't have to pretend I couldn't hear.

John Rice was the first to speak. "As I said, Grant, Kathy is a major investor in this production. Through her, one of the companies I represent is also a major investor. We insisted on a solid contract when she accepted this role. Her investment—our investment—was contingent on Pressfield's acceptance of that contract. Unfortunately, he's already in violation, and production hasn't even started yet."

I leaned back in my chair. Benjamin Pressfield—or Mr. Bloody Nose, as I liked to think of him—was in more trouble, and I was getting to help go after him. More to the point, John Rice was about to give us a retainer. I hoped it would stretch to cover full-time hours for me, at least for a while.

"So, this film is an independent production?" Carson asked.

Kathy Roberson's voice spoke up, "Entirely."

"Yes," Rice said, "there is no studio money in this. Pressfield tried to get major studios on board, but he was unsuccessful. Pressfield himself isn't under contract to any studio, so he was able to take his project anywhere he wanted to."

"I brought it to my uncle," Roberson said.

"Kathy is Carlos Deguerra's niece," Rice said.

Well, that was quite a news flash. Carlos Deguerra was Rice's boss. He had quite a reputation—word was that he used his family's grocery wholesale business in Albuquerque as a cover for a pretty big crime operation. Rice continued as if he hadn't revealed that Sage Landing was the setting for a mob-funded film and that Kathy Roberson was related to a mob boss. *Connected* would be a better way to put it.

Kathy said, "The film is a good investment. Benjamin's won two Academy Awards. He's never made a flop. And I wanted the role."

"I know his reputation," Carson said, "but it amazes me that this isn't a studio production. They've rolled into town here with a major crew and a huge amount of equipment. Movie crews are pretty common here, I gather, but usually not on this scale."

"Benjamin hasn't made a film in five years. He spent all that time planning this film," Kathy Roberson said. "Since he doesn't own a studio, it'll be cheaper to shoot on location. We'll shoot everything we can outdoors. For some of it, we'll move to a prairie up in Utah, but we can do most of the production here."

John Rice added, "*The Godfather* was filmed on location. Coppola saved a ton of money and came in under budget."

More mobsters.

Carson said, "I guess it's hard to argue with a precedent like that. What is Pressfield doing that violates your contract?"

Rice answered, "Kathy is an associate producer on this film. She is supposed to approve all major casting and any substantial changes in the script."

"And that's not happening?" Carson asked.

"No, not where it counts the most," Kathy Roberson said. "I specifically told him back in Los Angeles that I wanted Hamilton O'Neill as my co-star, but he cast Shawn Gordon behind my back and left Hamilton out."

John Rice's squeaky chair made noise as he shifted weight. "Gordon's barely beginning to move up to major roles."

"And he's not a *dramatic* actor," Kathy said.

Well, if that wasn't the pot calling the kettle black, I didn't know what was.

Carson cleared his throat. "I wonder how his disappearance figures into all this."

Rice said, "I'm sure you've heard speculation that Shawn's absence is a publicity stunt, but one way or the other, Pressfield made a point of informing Kathy that he is absolutely opposed to casting Hamilton in the lead."

"And he's doing it for spite," Kathy said. "Everyone in the industry knows about my choice of Hamilton for the film, and Benjamin thinks that doing what I want would make him lose face. He won't show respect for me as an experienced professional."

"Entirely inappropriate," Rice added.

I heard Kathy Roberson rummaging around in her purse. "You won't mind if I smoke?" she said, the implication being *…because you wouldn't begrudge me this comfort in my hour of stress.*

Carson didn't reply. I minded, but that wouldn't matter with some clients. Besides, we tried not to say "no" to clients.

After the sounds of lighting, inhaling, and exhaling, Kathy continued. "Benjamin's stalling to stir up publicity. He's been kicking up as much drama as he can about how they got beat up by a local gal—what, Saturday night? By Sunday morning, he had a PR firm churning stuff out."

I thought it was crude of her to call Dee a "local gal" and to say she beat them up, but Carson didn't argue.

"And that was before Shawn was missing," Rice added.

Carson said, "If we're going to make a case for enforcing the contract, Ms. Roberson, I'll need a few more details."

"Okay, where do I begin?" she said before pausing to take a long draw on her cigarette. Then came the dramatic exhale, the sound of tapping the ash, and the smell of smoke permeating the whole office. I tried to picture what Carson had in there to use as an ashtray. *Focus, Naomi.* Having taken her own sweet time, she went on, "The first thing is he's too young."

"Shawn Gordon? He's too young to play the role?"

"To play opposite me in a serious role," she said. "I've trained with major figures in the drama pantheon. Shawn's still playing macho action stuff—he has no dramatic weight." She paused again, perhaps waiting for some affirmation from one of the men. They must've shown agreement because she continued, "We'd be ridiculous on the screen together, playing royalty. Audiences wouldn't buy that. It'd undermine the credibility of the whole film."

"Gordon is barely past the teen idol stage," said Rice. "That would be fine if the film had explosions and car chases, but I agree with Kathy that he's completely wrong for a role like this."

Kathy said, "I've worked opposite Hamilton O'Neill before. We'd look right together. That's why I insisted on casting him."

"He has gravitas," Rice said.

I thought that was kind of an overstatement because my own impression was that O'Neill seemed more like a has-been to me.

Kathy chimed in, "Hamilton O'Neill is an award-winning leading man. I made it clear that he would be my co-star when I agreed to invest in the project."

"Was O'Neill specified in your investment contract?" Carson asked.

"No," Kathy answered, "but the contract makes very clear that I have to approve casting decisions. Pressfield knew I wanted O'Neill instead of little boy Shawn."

Carson said, "Wouldn't Shawn's disappearance void *his* contract anyway?"

"If he's really missing, you mean? It *should*," John Rice said. "But we can't rely on that. What we're telling you is that Pressfield isn't to be trusted."

It seemed to me that Pressfield wasn't the only one, but Carson asked, "Do you know if Hamilton O'Neil is available now?"

Kathy answered, "I got in touch this morning. He's available. In fact, he's vacationing right now at the Grand Canyon."

"How do the other investors feel?" Carson asked. "Have you checked with any of them?"

"Well, no," Roberson said. "As far as I know, none of the other investors have film production experience. Except for Pressfield. He's investing his own money, and maybe he's attracted some other people in the industry. I don't know."

"Most of the money is from outside the industry," Rice said, "with a substantial amount coming in from sources here in northern Arizona. In any case, I drafted the investment contract myself, with the assistance of Los Angeles entertainment counsel. I don't think Pressfield has a leg to stand on."

Carson asked, "Do you think that Pressfield's prepared to fight you? Financially prepared, I mean. Can he afford it? And can you?"

The room was silent for quite a while. I could hear feet shuffling, chairs squeaking, a sigh or two, and the tamping out of Kathy's cigarette on whatever she was using as an ashtray.

"Honestly," she finally said, "everyone is stretched a little thin on this one, including me. I sweet-talked Uncle Carl into investing a chunk of cash, even though he doesn't usually make this kind of investment, and I don't know how he'd feel about putting in more. But we're still better off than Benjamin. He definitely can't afford a legal fight. It would eat up too much of the money he's gonna need for production."

His voice sounding silky, John Rice agreed. "We can afford to apply more pressure to Pressfield than he can afford to defend."

Carson asked, "Okay, but couldn't he shut down production before it starts? Pack up and caravan on out of here?"

Kathy said, "Well, yes. He could do that. There's insurance involved. But he wouldn't want to."

"Insurance?" Carson asked.

Rice said, "Production insurance. Carlos insisted that the production be protected against catastrophic events."

I heard Kathy light another cigarette—I was getting less dazzled by the minute—and make a sound that was more like a snort than a laugh. "Like it would be a catastrophic event for Shawn to leave."

Neither guy had anything to say to that. Eventually Carson cleared his throat and asked, "How would the insurance policy work?"

Rice said, "The production is insured against specific circumstances that would prevent its successful completion. If production shuts down due to one of those circumstances, the policy pays a percentage of the money already spent. If Pressfield were to shut down now, before filming begins, insurance would pay out seventy-five percent of expenditures to date. The returned money would be distributed to the investors *pro rata*."

"How much do you think has been spent?" Carson asked.

Kathy exhaled loudly again. Smoke was visibly curling out of the small inner office. I wondered how many days it would take to get rid of that smell.

Rice answered, "Probably a couple hundred thousand. Little enough that the investors would get most of their funds back."

"Is that what you and Mr. Deguerra want?"

"Carlos would go for stopping, but Kathy is determined to continue."

"And who decides whether to go forward with production?"

"It's up to Pressfield," Rice answered.

"He wants to follow through with this movie," Kathy said. "All we have to do is help him make the right decisions along the way. So, Mr. Carson, what's our next step?"

Carson rustled some papers and answered, "First, I'll review this copy of the contract and draft a demand letter. Let me work on that so that we can have it in his hands by the end of the day."

I heard everyone get up from their chairs, and Carson said, "I'll be in touch."

In my mind's eye, I could see them shaking hands all around. As they emerged from his office, Carson asked, "So, this film has something to do with *Macbeth*?"

"Right," Kathy Roberson said, turning that dazzling smile in his direction. "It's a stylized version of the Scottish play—sandstone pillars instead of forests, witch doctors instead of witches."

Witch doctors? I thought. She'd said it was *stylized*, but that sounded more like *grossly stereotyped*. I could picture a 1950's-era movie "witch doctor"—some barefoot white guy in brown makeup wearing buffalo horns on his head, shaking a rattle, and chanting gibberish. Maybe I could sneak something into the demand letter Carson was writing, like "In addition, you are hereby instructed to avoid any stereotyped, uninformed, or stupid representations of Native American culture." I'd be doing them a favor.

Kathy was still talking. "Benjamin is hard to work with, but he's also brilliant. That's why I wanted to be in on his project. It'll bring me an Oscar unless he keeps that idiot kid in the lead."

"Well, let's leave it at that for now," Rice said. He opened the door for Kathy, and she smiled warmly at us again before she walked out. Rice followed her without a backward glance.

Carson stood there grinning at me.

"What?" I asked.

"Nice turn of events," he said.

"You forgot to ask for a retainer," I said, "but we'll be okay for a while since we got Dee's check yesterday."

"Rice wrote me a check before you got here."

"Oh? How much?"

"Twenty thousand dollars," he said, grinning even more broadly, and rubbing his hands together with—there's no other word for it—glee.

I wanted to say something about movie people and mob money but held my tongue for once.

"Movie people are a different breed," Carson said.

"And mob people," I blurted. "That sort of brings up another thing I have to ask you about."

"What's that?"

"As it turns out, Kai and a few of the other high school kids have landed summer internships on the movie location. They'll be out there all the time. It's a great opportunity for them, but I can't say it doesn't worry me. Because movie people are a different breed—like you said."

Carson stopped grinning. "I can see how that would be on your mind after what happened Saturday night,"

"Right, so I was thinking—I was kind of hoping to spend some time out there while this is going on. Kai won't like it if she thinks her mom is hanging around spying on her, but…."

"…but I'll be sending you out there on official business," Carson said. "It's not your fault that we have a client who demands that we keep an eye on everything. The biggest client we've ever had wants us to watch things closely."

I laughed. "I couldn't say that with a straight face," I said, "but it sounds plausible."

"Oh, it's better than that. It's profitable. We can bill John Rice for every minute you spend out there."

~ ~ ~

The parent meeting at the high school that night didn't involve very many students and parents, but what it lacked in size it made up for in refreshments and celebrities. We had Benjamin Pressfield, with two black eyes and his nose still decorated with a white bandage. Along with Kathy Roberson and a handful of other movie people, we had a few out-of-town members of the press. Shawn Gordon wasn't there. My guess was that Pressfield was keeping him out of view in order to build the buzz around the movie. Or Shawn didn't want the public to see his face till the swelling subsided. Maybe both.

Pressfield acted as master of ceremonies, pointing out a few crew members and staff before calling on each one to speak to the group. I was hoping to see someone from the writing staff so that I could ask about witch doctors and other travesties, but that didn't happen. Instead, he introduced script supervisor Molly Murphy, who made it clear that she didn't do any of the writing. Pressfield added, "Molly here will have her hands full. The scripts for my films are not one-and-done lumps of inert text, like they are for other films. No. The scripts for a Pressfield film are alive. They breathe. They evolve. The writers are part of the team here on location, where these magnificent surroundings are already inspiring a new directions for the script. We will depend on Molly to keep us on track with all the script improvements." He gestured grandly in Molly's direction, prompting a smattering of applause, but she just looked uncomfortable.

When Kathy Roberson spoke, she made a point of telling parents that they were welcome to visit the movie site any time. She also gave my status in Sage Landing a boost when she recognized me in the audience. She raised her hand in a wave and said, "Hi, Naomi!" When everyone looked at me, she added, "I'm sure you all know Naomi Manymules. Her law firm will be helping *me* out during the filming."

This last bit was aimed at Pressfield, who was getting the stink-eye from her at that point. But I have to admit that what she said about "my" law firm made it sound like I had important Hollywood friends. Kai grinned broadly. Len, who'd come with us even though he wouldn't be an official intern, ducked his head, embarrassed at having a mom in the spotlight.

Each of the other speakers assured parents that this would be a great learning experience for our kids. No one said anything about Saturday night's incident, but the movie people knew that every parent in the room had concerns. I could tell because all the speakers told us—several times—that everyone on set understood how to behave in the presence of children. I was pretty sure they were right, but I was still glad to have a reason to be out there myself, whether my kids liked it or not.

One of the parents asked about Shawn Gordon. Pressfield was vague, saying that filming would begin with scenes that didn't include Shawn but that he couldn't talk about the star's "current whereabouts or condition." Another parent asked why this location was chosen for filming a version of *Macbeth*, and Pressfield was vague about that, too. Glancing at the reporters sitting near the back, he said that he had to keep quiet about details because of people trying to "give everything away." Nothing was further from the truth, as far as I could tell. He'd already demonstrated that he wanted every shred of publicity he could get.

One of the staff handed out schedules. The kids would have an orientation day on location the following Tuesday, and parents would be welcome to join the tours of the set. Starting the day after that, a bus would pick up the kids in front of the high school at 4:30 in the morning and bring them back in the afternoon. I was skeptical—I mean, 4:30 a.m.? But I was surprised to see that they all seemed thrilled with the prospect of a predawn bus just for them. Plus, they'd get breakfast, lunch, and snacks on location. I made a mental note to check with someone to be sure it was okay for Len to tag along with Kai, at least sometimes.

While we were going over the schedule, Pressfield ducked out. Kathy Roberson stayed to mingle as the crowd drifted to the buffet table, which featured platters of the biggest chocolate-chip cookies I'd ever seen. A couple of the production company's photographers took a bunch of pictures. They passed around a sign-up sheet so we could request photos of ourselves with the celebrities, who were more than happy to accommodate us. Len even got a chance to practice taking the kind of insider candids that Kai wanted for her columns.

The evening was friendly, well-organized, and delicious. There wasn't even a hint that all hell was about to break loose.

CHAPTER NINE

Nᴏᴛ long after Len and Kai left the house the next morning, full of plans for the second-to-last day of school, Carson called. He said, "Is there anything in particular to keep us in the office all day?"

I did a quick mental inventory. Appointments? None. Filings to submit? None. Letters to send? Nope, we'd already sent the demand letter on Kathy's behalf. "No, nothing in particular," I said. "Not unless Pressfield storms into the office after he gets your letter."

Carson laughed. "Reason enough to make ourselves scarce for a little while. I'll pick you up at the office about a quarter past eleven. We'll have an early lunch at the Lunker Room."

Carson didn't say much on our drive out to the marina. When I told him about the parents' meeting, he nodded. I began to think that he was just bored and didn't want to eat lunch alone.

The Lunker Room at the marina resort was one of Carson's favorite hangouts. Attached to the hotel, it was a large bar with comfortable seating, a good menu, and excellent service. Its walls were festooned with stuffed fish that were big enough to justify the name "lunker." Its north wall was mostly made up of large windows overlooking the beach. That early on a Thursday we pretty much had the place to ourselves.

The east end of the Lunker Room opened out onto the hotel's main dining room, by far the most picturesque place to eat in the Sage Landing area. For one thing, it was gigantic, capable of seating hundreds. It was high ceilinged, with huge chandeliers and a long, curved glass wall to the east. Through that glass, diners were treated to the best views of red cliffs and blue water that could be found anywhere in the country. The wall facing north was also glass, with another beautiful view and a permanent stage and dance floor. It was surprising how many top-name bands vacationed at the resort from time to time, stopping here for a brief rest during a tour. When they did, diners here sometimes got a free, if brief, spontaneous concert.

Once we were seated in our booth and he'd ordered a pitcher of beer, he said, "I wonder what Pressfield will do."

"You mean will he hire that other guy like Kathy wants?" I asked.

"Exactly."

"Here's a touchy question," I said. "What happens to the retainer we got yesterday if Shawn decides not to come back and Pressfield shuts down the production?"

Our menus and pitcher arrived, so he waited before answering until we were alone again. "That would be unfortunate. So far, we haven't done anything except meet with them and read over the contract."

"We wrote the demand letter."

Quickly pouring beer into the two chilled glasses, he said, "The retainer check hasn't even cleared yet. I'd probably return it and bill them for, what, two hours? Three, max?"

"Bummer."

"You can say that again."

"Okay, bummer. I had visions of buying things."

He sipped his beer, and then sipped again. "Me too. The *Deep Inn* could use some maintenance, for one thing. Chuck won't work on her anymore until I settle up." Chuck Margolin was the most expensive boat mechanic on the lake, and that's saying something.

With visions of the firm's fat bank account shrinking to nothing, I asked, "What's your guess about Dee's situation? What'll Pressfield do about that?"

"If I were a person who guessed, which I'm not, I'd guess it depends on whether he continues production. If he doesn't, there wouldn't be any point in trying to stay in the news with that silly story."

"Yesterday Kathy said he wasn't going to put the brakes on production."
Carson shrugged. I'd get no more predictions from him.

I noticed a small group of people being seated in the main dining room,
about a hundred feet from our table. I recognized two of them easily:
Herman Buckmaster was having lunch with Benjamin Pressfield.

I told Carson not to turn around while I filled him in on this little
development, opening the menu so I could pretend to be studying it
while covertly keeping an eye on Herman and his companions. There
was no chance that I could overhear anything, so I watched carefully as
their drinks were served. Hiding behind my menu, I said, "Cocktails at
lunch? How fancy."

"Why do we care?" Carson said.

"We don't. I mean, we don't care about the drinks, but the meeting
piques my interest."

"*Piques your interest*, does it? Talk about fancy!"

"That's how we spies talk, Carson. Don't be jealous."

Carson said, "There's a rumor going around that Buckmaster may be
an investor in the movie. That would explain why he's so riled up about
anything hurting the movie project. But I don't think he's in that league,
money-wise."

This was old news to me, having heard it all Monday night, and I briefly
wondered what his sources were before continuing my play-by-play commentary. "Pressfield sure isn't down in the dumps. Now he's patting
Herman's arm and grinning at him. Herman is leaning away from him,
and if looks could kill, Pressfield would likely be maimed, at least."

"You told me that Sage Landing's had other productions almost as big
as this one's supposed to be. Did they bring in a lot of money for the
town?" Carson asked.

"Not as much as you'd think." To tell the truth, the excitement of a
Hollywood production tended to make us forget—for a little while, anyway—that the driving force of Sage Landing's economy was, and always
had been, the big coal-burning power plant that dominated the skyline.
It paid for everything. The lake's tourism was a distant second, and movie
productions were a momentary bump at best.

We were interrupted again by our waitress, so Carson ordered some lunch. I was too intent on watching the unlikely business meeting in the next room to notice what. I'd finished my first beer at approximately the same time as Carson finished his, which was unusual for me. Doing surveillance out in the open was proving to be thirsty work. I needed to keep my wits about me, so I set the empty beer glass aside and pulled my glass of water closer.

Two additional men arrived at Pressfield's table and sat down. They were wearing business suits like Buckmaster was. Pressfield was dressed for golf, probably absent the spiked shoes. "Now *this* is a business meeting," I said, with maybe a little too much enthusiasm. "Two new guys at the table. They didn't shake anyone's hands. They're frowning and shaking their heads, and they're wearing suits."

"Fascinating," said Carson. "Three suits and a sport."

"I know, right?" I looked back at the group in question. "Any idea who those bozos could be?" I asked.

"No idea," Carson said. "They could be public relations people talking about how they plan to ruin Dee's reputation. Or maybe they're Los Angeles lawyers here to help Pressfield cheat Kathy Roberson."

"I'm betting they're PR guys, but, yeah, they could be lawyers."

"You said they were wearing suits. If they're L.A. attorneys, their suits are tailored. Are the suits tailored?"

I laughed. "Do you make up stuff like that as you go along, Carson?"

"Pretty much."

I appraised Carson's usual motley attire, taking in his worn chinos and wrinkled camp shirt. He must've felt like my glance in his direction was kind of judgy, because he sounded a little defensive when he said, "I'm driving to Flagstaff this weekend to buy a new suit. Maybe two new suits."

"Oh? There's a tailor in Flagstaff?" I asked, as if I thought he'd stand still long enough to be fitted for anything.

"Off-the-rack is good enough for a simple country lawyer like me," he said. "Even when I was in Phoenix, you didn't see many lawyers in tailored suits—just the big-time corporate guys."

I craned my neck to peer at his feet under the table. Yep, he was wearing sandals with no socks, so I said, "Don't forget new shoes. And socks that match. Each other."

He muttered something under his breath, but I ignored it and got up from the table. "Okay, I'm done wondering about the bozos. Watch this," I said as I walked away. My first stop was at the hostess desk at the entrance to the main dining room, where a friend of mine was standing at the podium.

"Hey, Frankie."

"Hey yourself, kiddo. What's up? You and Carson are over in the bar, aren't you?"

"Having lunch, yeah. Listen, who were those guys you seated at Buckmaster's table?" I was careful to keep my back to them so they couldn't read my lips. Just in case they were looking.

"I haven't seen them before today," Frankie said, "but I served them breakfast in the coffee shop this morning."

"Well, Carson says they might be a couple of lawyers he knew in Phoenix. If they are, he doesn't want to snub them, but he isn't sure. I told him that if they're staying here, maybe I could find out who they are for him before he maybe interrupts a meeting to say hello to perfect strangers."

She leaned a little closer to me and said, "At breakfast, they paid with a company credit card. It was an insurance company, I remember. One of them ordered a Bloody Mary. He paid for that with cash instead of putting it on the card."

"Insurance company?"

"Pacific something or other. I don't remember. They are guests here at the hotel, though, if you want me to see what I can find out."

"No need, Frankie," I said as an older couple dressed for vacationing walked up to the podium. "I can tell Carson he's off the hook, but maybe I'll help the mayor welcome those newcomers."

My next stop was at the table in question. I walked right over and, in my heartiest outdoor voice, boomed, "Mayor Buckmaster. How nice to see you again so soon."

He seemed confused, and all the men sitting around the table stood up, as befits a gentleman when a lady approaches. Herman had no choice but to stand up, too. I stuck out my hand, but he was too flustered to shake it.

Shoving my hands into my pockets to avoid further awkwardness, I addressed the movie producer. "Mr. Pressfield. We met at the summer internship parent orientation last night. I'm Naomi Manymules."

His face told me that the name was familiar, but he wasn't sure from where and wasn't inclined to spend much time thinking about it.

I glanced back at Buckmaster before offering my hand to the taller of the newcomers. "Buck, you and your guests sure outclass the rest of the lunch crowd. Naomi Manymules," I said, reminding myself to grasp hands firmly, like an Anglo, instead of lightly touching fingers as I'd been taught from childhood. "What brings you to Sage Landing?"

"We are discussing project logistics, Ms. Manymules," Pressfield answered smoothly. He wasn't giving the insurance guys a chance to speak for themselves. "Now, if you'll please excuse us, we must get back to our planning session."

I went back into the Lunker Room, where Carson and my lunch awaited. "They're insurance guys from California," I said, "but Pressfield won't admit it."

"Why did you do that?" Carson asked.

"You've gotta know the territory, Carson."

~ ~ ~

When we got back to the office, Dee was sitting in her car, windows rolled up and engine running. She didn't appear to be moving. While Carson unlocked the office, I ran over to make sure she didn't have a hose from the tailpipe stuck into a window.

I quickly figured out that she was just running her air conditioning while she waited. Since the AC wasn't working in my own car, that hadn't occurred to me at first. She was mad as hell, though. Apparently, she thought that an attorney should be on-premises in the middle of a weekday, which only proved that she didn't know Carson as well as I thought she did. I mean, it was Thursday. For Carson, that was practically the weekend.

She didn't waste time on pleasantries. She didn't even wait to sit down in a chair. Standing inside the front door, she said, "Peggy called me at home about an hour ago. She said Mike wanted her to let me know he'll 'touch base' with me later this afternoon, so I got out of there."

"Sitting here in your car isn't a very good way to hide out," Carson said.

"I wasn't hiding out, you jackass! I thought I was going to get counsel from my lawyer about a legal crisis. Turns out jackasses don't keep office hours." She nodded toward me. "And neither do their associates."

Dee knew that I was part-time, but that was kind of beside the point, so I let it go.

Carson said, "We were taking lunch to discuss your case without interruption. And we were rewarded with an opportunity to spy on Mr. Pressfield."

Dee looked at me for confirmation.

Carson asked, "Did Peggy give any details about what Mike meant by 'touching base' with you?"

"No. She said that the assistant district attorney called this morning. He and Mike were on the phone for a while. When he hung up, he told her to call me. Then he left and hadn't come back."

Carson started pacing, not that our front office gave him much room to move. "Rodriguez and Bliss. At this stage of the game, that's not good news."

He walked on into his inner office, but when I saw a car pull up outside the window, I said, "You better get back out here, Carson. We're about to get some company."

Chief Rodriguez and George Bliss walked through the front door. "Glad I caught you all," said the chief as he closed the door behind George.

"That's a lousy choice of words, Mike," Carson said. "I hope you meant to say 'found' rather than 'caught.'" He was smiling. The chief was not.

George Bliss cleared his throat. "Mr. Carson. We examined the body of Shawn Gordon."

Carson frowned. "The body of—you're telling us he's—when? What happened? Where was the body?"

Dee sat down slowly in one of the guest chairs. I leaned against the desk. This was what Mike meant by *touching base*?

The chief was shaking his head. Instead of answering Carson's questions, he said, "We'll get to that. But first, we need to know where several people were after Dr. Moreno's…encounter in the bar."

Carson shot a warning glance at Dee, silently reminding her not to say anything, as he said, "Is that a question?"

Mike said, "No, we're merely sharing our thinking. But we *would* like to ask Dr. Moreno where she was after she left the Wranglers."

In spite of Carson's many warnings, repeated advice, and dire predictions about talking to the police instead of letting him do it, Dee spoke up. "I already told you. And Naomi told you that he was fine after I left."

Mike put his hands on his hips and rocked forward a little. "That doesn't answer my question, Dr. Moreno. We're not asking for your medical opinion, or Naomi's, either. We're trying to fill in some gaps."

"Meaning what?" Carson said.

"When we examined the body, we found a bump on the back of the head, some discoloration on the face, an abrasion on the chin." As he spoke, he gestured at each of those places on his own face and head. Then he looked at Dee. "Those are all consistent with the accounts of what happened that night, and they were fairly superficial. This doesn't put you in the clear, exactly, but those punches you landed in the bar probably weren't what killed him."

"*Probably* weren't what killed him?" Carson asked.

George Bliss looked at Mike rather sternly, I thought, and said, "We'd prefer not to say more at this point." He turned to Dee, saying, "With all due respect, Dr. Moreno, we need you to recount the events that followed your leaving the scene of the incident Saturday night."

Carson cut in, "Don't answer that, Dr. Moreno." To the assistant district attorney, he said, "*With all due respect*, Mr. Bliss, I need to consult with my client before she can provide any more information."

Bliss sighed. "Fine, Mr. Carson. And I assume that you, too, would prefer to consult with counsel before telling us where you were that evening?"

"You're kidding," I said. "What on earth does Carson have to do with it?"

Carson said, "You assume correctly, Mr. Bliss. What else can you tell us?"

Rodriguez said, "We're not here to tell you anything. We're investigating what happened between 10:30 p.m. and 2:00 a.m. Where did Gordon go after he spoke with Naomi? Where was Benjamin Pressfield? Where was Desiree Moreno? Where were *you*, Carson? And god knows who else —the list is as long as—well, we're just getting started."

Dee sat in stony silence, her only reaction a wince when Mike used her full name. Carson opened the front door and said, "Thanks for the update, gentlemen. I'm sure you'll be checking in with us as the investigation continues."

Rodriguez gestured at Bliss and said he had to get back to the station anyway. They walked out, leaving the three of us in uncomfortable silence.

Carson was the first to speak. He said, "Dee? Can you fill me in?"

She watched through the front window as Rodriguez and Bliss drove out of the parking lot. After a while, she said, "No."

Carson pulled the other guest chair closer to Dee and sat down. Quietly, he said, "I'd say that now would be a good time to tell me whatever you almost told me on Monday."

"I have nothing more to say," she answered, and set her jaw stubbornly.

I had a more important question. "Why are they asking *your* whereabouts, Carson? You weren't at Wranglers."

"No." His eyes were still on Dee.

"Where were you?" I added, "It was a Saturday night, so I'm betting you were on the *Deep Inn* with Peggy or somebody."

Carson still seemed deep in thought and didn't answer me right away. When he finally did, again he just said, "No."

"And you're not telling?" I said.

"Under advice of counsel, which is me, nobody's telling anyone anything yet."

After that, we settled into a rather uneasy silence. I sat still and wondered what Carson and Dee were thinking, but I didn't ask. Generally speaking—and I say this mostly as a mom—it's better to leave people alone when they're wandering around inside their own heads.

Suddenly Carson jumped up and marched to the door. He pulled the key to his truck out of a pocket and said, "Let's go. We're heading to the marina."

CHAPTER TEN

I stared at him. "What?"

Dee stared at him, too. "We're heading where?"

He opened the door and stood halfway out on the sidewalk. "Here's what I figure. Sage Landing's small, right? Not many places to find a body, so we would've heard way before this if Gordon was found anywhere in town. On the other hand, the desert is enormous. If he was discovered out on the desert somewhere, nobody would've been examining the body yet. They'd still be staking out a crime scene. That leaves the lake. I'm betting they found him in the lake. We can take the *Deep Inn* to wherever that was and learn something. At this point, we *need* to learn something."

I said, "That is the most ridiculous reasoning I've ever heard. You want to hop on your boat and sail into the middle of a police investigation?"

Carson didn't take issue with my point about his reasoning. Instead, he quibbled about details. "First, don't call it a boat. It's a yacht. And it doesn't sail, it cruises."

I said, "Fine, your yacht cruises rather than sails, but, Carson, I've got kids who'll be coming home from school. If you want me to go out to the lake, I'll have to go home first. I'll meet you there in an hour."

Before he could weigh in on that, Dee stood up and stepped toward the door. "I'm going home. I'll talk to you guys later."

"Hold on, Dee," Carson said as she slipped past him in the doorway.

She stopped and turned around slowly. "Yes?" Her voice was strained.

"Listen, don't be doing any recreational driving. Go home and stay there."

The look on her face said that she was biting back any number of comebacks, none of them friendly. She turned back around, even more slowly, and left without giving voice to any of them.

Carson didn't seem to realize how close he'd come to getting his ass handed to him. I thought maybe I should tell him but decided against it. Instead, I grabbed my bag and ducked out through the door that he was still holding open.

"Need a lift?" he asked.

I shook my head, managed a vague smile in his direction, and kept walking. I needed a few minutes by myself to think things through.

He called after me, "Okay, I'll see you at the dock when you get there."

As I walked home, I tried to organize everything I had on my mind. Topping the list was the question of Carson's whereabouts last Saturday night. Then there was the question of whether the movie would get shut down, leaving my kids at loose ends for the summer and taking the retainer money back from Carson and me. Plus, what was going to happen to Dee? Would she still need an attorney? Would she need an even better one? It wasn't a very loyal thought, that last one. And now, on top of all that, I had to wonder where Shawn Gordon's body was.

When I opened my front door, Kai and Len were jumping up and down in the living room, chanting, "One more day to go!" over and over again. The dog formerly known as Princess was jumping right along with them as she helpfully added barking to the joyful noise. I half-heartedly joined in for a few hops myself before sprinting into the kitchen to check the fridge. Eggs, cheddar cheese, a little ham. Tomatoes and cucumber. Good.

By the time I got back to the living room, the kids had settled down a smidgen. "Okay, guys," I told them, "I have to go out to the lake on legal business. I won't be late, but you're probably on your own for dinner."

Len flopped down on the couch, all elbows and knees. Three-Steps jumped up on his lap, and Len hugged her against his chest. "Excellent. We'll order pizza from Rico's."

Kai reached for my purse, which I'd dropped on the coffee table on my way in. "Have you got a twenty, Mom? I'll give you the change when you get back."

"Um, no." I picked up the purse and slung it over my shoulder. "I don't have a twenty, and, no, you won't be ordering pizza. You can scramble some eggs or make an omelet when it's time for dinner." I ignored the mutinous look on their faces and went on, "Both of you are to stay in the house."

They sat in silence. Then Len said to Kai, "Shawn Gordon's still missing, isn't he?"

Kai nodded slowly and sat on the arm of the couch. "Yeah, and Mom's confining us to quarters."

Len straightened up, turning his face in my direction. "While she goes out to work on a case." Three-Steps, annoyed, hopped down and went over to sit next to Kai's feet.

Kai looked back at me, too. "After hours."

Len added, "At the lake."

Still looking at me, Kai said, "Is he dead, Mom? Shawn Gordon, I mean. Did they find him at the lake?"

Total denial would be futile, not to mention dishonest, so I said, "We don't know where, but, yes, Mr. Gordon's body has been found. Mr. Carson thinks it might be somewhere on the lake. We're going out there to see what we can find out."

"How did he die?" Len said.

"What about Dr. Moreno? Is she in trouble?" Kai said.

Those were very good questions, and I wanted the answers as much as they did. I said, "We don't know. There are several clients who may need our advice. That's why we need to find out whatever we can." I added, "No phone calls to anyone…and I mean *anyone*, guys."

They drifted away to their rooms, grumbling, as the dog followed me into mine and hopped up on the bed. She settled into the exact middle, falling asleep in the time it took me to change into cutoffs. I grabbed my purse, checking inside for my car keys. At the last minute, I wondered if I should take my gun. That little pistol and I had some history. I'd gotten it from a friend the last time there'd been a killer at large in Sage Landing.

Damn. Once *that* thought entered my mind, I couldn't leave my children home alone. Tucking the pistol into my bag, I hollered, "Kai! Len! Put your shoes on. You get to come along." I used my *don't ask questions* voice, so they didn't.

~ ~ ~

When we pulled into the parking lot at the marina, the docks were blocked off with police tape. Uniformed cops of all kinds were everywhere, even on the *Deep Inn*—city cops, state cops, park rangers, and maybe some Utah officers, too. With that variety of jurisdictions already in place, I knew that if the FBI weren't here already, they soon would be.

I wanted to see if any press had shown up yet, but the only one I spotted was Barnaby Riggs, the retired school bus driver who wrote the "Police Blotter" roundup for the weekly *Gazette*. He always listened to the police scanner while working on one of the rusty cars in his front yard, so it wasn't surprising that he'd heard about the body. What *was* surprising, though, was the absence of any other reporters. No photographers, either. Benjamin Pressfield's public relations folks didn't seem to be keeping up.

Carson was standing on the service dock with Chuck Margolin, the boat mechanic who leased the dock facilities from the Park Service, renting out boats and slips and mooring buoys. Peggy stood with them in full uniform, complete with sidearm. From where we were, it appeared she was telling them something. I couldn't think of a safer place to be, so I headed toward them and herded the kids along with me. Nobody paid any attention when we ducked under the yellow police tape.

There was news to be had, all right. Peggy repeated for me some of what she'd been telling the guys. The gist was that Shawn Gordon's body was on the *Deep Inn*. That prompted a yelp from Kai, but Len maintained a manly silence. Margolin added that a tourist had been loading a rental houseboat near Carson's prized yacht and later came into the service center to complain about an odor "coming from that old tub at the end of the dock."

That brought more reaction from Kai and a peeved expression from Carson. Margolin said he called the park rangers rather than going aboard himself. The rangers called the Sage Landing police station. Once a deputy arrived, it took less than a minute to establish that they had a murder scene on their hands.

I recalled that there'd been maybe three or four murders in Sage Landing in the decades before Carson arrived in town, and that this was the second murder in less than a year. Worse, I'd talked to each of the victims shortly before they died. This was not a habit I intended to keep.

Having moved past shock to thirst and hunger, my kids talked me into letting them do a run to the little convenience store on the dock.

Peggy watched them speed-walk away. Once they ducked inside, she stepped closer to me and spoke quietly. "Naomi. I've got personal stuff on that boat."

"I imagine you do," I said.

"You?" she asked.

I smiled at her. "I don't go out on the *Deep Inn*."

"No?"

I shook my head, with vigor, and added, "I've been aboard a few times. There was that boat chase last year, but it was strictly business. No fun at all."

A moment passed. "Really?" Peggy sounded skeptical.

"Really. I don't have *anything* on that boat." Carson never invited me to visit his yacht in any social way. Peggy, on the other hand, practically lived there on weekends. Well, that might be an exaggeration, but I knew for sure that she'd spent some weekends with Carson on the lake. "There's probably nothing with your name inked on it," I said.

"Right." She looked again at the guys searching the *Deep Inn* and added, "I haven't had name tape in my undershirts since I was twelve."

"Undershirts, that's very funny. Your fingerprints, though. There must be hundreds of those."

Suddenly I had all her attention. I said, "What? I'm joking. The chief knows you hang out with Carson on the boat. Wouldn't he expect to find your fingerprints all over the place?"

"All over the place...sure, but..."

"But what, Peg?"

"Nothing. I… I was remembering how the last time we went out on the lake we made fajitas for dinner. I was trying to teach Carson how to slice peppers like a chef, but his knives were too dull."

Over her shoulder, I saw Chuck Margolin head toward the northern-most of the three docks to talk to a rental customer. The *Deep Inn* was parked at the end of his middle dock, which was draped with police tape. At the shore end of the southern dock to our right, where Chuck's service garage and convenience market were, a crew was filling the tanks of a big cabin cruiser with *Dam Yankee* painted in big spiky letters on the back. Even at some distance, I could hear voices from inside that boat, but it was too far away to make out any words.

Carson ambled over to us. "You've got stuff on my yacht," he said to Peggy. "Including a lovely swimsuit, if memory serves."

She leaned her head closer to him and lowered her voice, "Carson, this is serious. Your boat…"

He interrupted, "Yacht."

"Give it a rest, okay? Whatever you call it, the *Deep Inn* is the scene of a murder, and you won't tell the chief where you were when the victim went missing."

"What are you saying?" Carson said. "Was he shot with a .45 like mine?"

Peggy shrugged. "You think I'm going to answer a question like that?"

Carson said, "Since I'd already be in handcuffs if he was shot with my .45, I'll take that as a *no*."

I glanced around to make sure that no one could hear us. "Was it a .38 like mine? A shotgun? What?"

She shook her head. "No comment. Really, no comment."

I said, "Or maybe it wasn't a gun at all. Bludgeoned with an Oscar? Strangled with an anchor chain? Poisoned with bootleg hooch? Wait—was he stabbed? With a dull knife?"

"No damned comment," Peggy said through clenched teeth. "I should be getting out there—" she took a deep breath, "—and it won't be pretty." Then she walked away.

"Stranger and stranger," Carson said. "How did a dead movie star get on my yacht?"

"What made you ask her if he got shot?"

"Well…people get shot. That's mostly how they become murder victims."

"In your experience," I said.

"I've got plenty of experience," he said. "I was an MP in Saigon. Did I ever tell you that?"

"I don't think so."

"Well, I was. Then a civilian cop, then detective."

"I knew that part," I said.

"Then a prosecutor. That's a lot of murders."

"You win. This is only my second."

He sort of smiled. "Okay, it's not a contest," he said. "but anyway, you learn to expect certain things. You assume. You maybe assume too much."

"Yes, you probably do. Peggy said something about knife skills and fingerprints. What if the guy was stabbed in the—"

We were interrupted by Dee's arrival. She, too, ducked under the police tape to join us. I had to wonder why they'd bothered to put up the tape at all if they didn't expect it to keep people off the dock.

"Surprised to see you here, Dee," I said.

"Yeah, me too." She gazed out across the bay. Her face was pale, but she kept her voice light. "Word on the street is that Gordon was found on your boat, Carson."

"Oh?" he said, "And on what street would that be? I thought you were going home and staying there."

"I stopped by my office first. They told me someone found his body on the *Deep Inn*."

Carson said, "That's what we've heard, too."

"How…when did he…?"

He shook his head. "We don't know anything more than you do. But remember what Mike just told us, back at the office."

She was looking uneasily at the people crowded onto the *Deep Inn* and didn't seem to hear him, so I added, "Mike said what happened in the bar that night isn't what killed Shawn Gordon."

Her eyes were still on the boat. "He said probably. My punches proba-bly didn't kill the guy." She looked at us with a faint smile and said, "You know, I've got things…"

Carson said, "Right, we were just now talking about that."

"About my stuff?" Dee asked.

"No, no," Carson said. "About all kinds of personal items on the yacht."

"My yellow sweater, I think?"

Carson added, "And at least two coffee mugs with the college logo on them, among other things I can think of," Carson said.

"Is he still…aboard?" Dee asked.

"Yeah, he is," I said.

"Probably will be for a while," Carson said. "They have to wait for crime-scene specialists, for one thing."

"FBI, you think?" I asked.

"I don't know. The marina itself isn't in the national park. The lake is, though, so it's FBI territory, but they often leave simple homicide up to local police."

I said, "Why would they hand off a case like this? It'll be pretty high profile, don't you think? Lots of attention?"

Carson thought about it and said, "I don't know. That might be a reason they'd want to stay away. Too much chance of outside meddling."

Dee stood on tiptoe, trying to see into the boat's distant windows, be-fore shifting her gaze back to us. She said, "Well, if I can't get my…my coffee mugs, I'm going home."

"Stay close to your phone," Carson said. "There's no telling what will pop up."

Dee took one last look at the *Deep Inn* and walked back toward the parking lot.

"At least this drops her from the list of suspects," I said, "Now that they know where Gordon is."

"I don't know. Maybe," Carson said. "Let's get your kids and walk up to the resort for a drink."

"You mean, let's take them for an ice cream at that little casual café off the lobby," I said.

"The little café has ice cream, but it doesn't serve what I want," he said.

"They'll bring you a glass of beer on the patio. It's in the shade now, at least. We'll join you there in a few minutes."

"Should I order a pitcher?" he asked.

I shook my head. "Not this time. Sounds perfect, but...you know."

"I can guess."

We converged on a patio table in the shade. Carson already had his beer—just one glass. The kids and I had our ice cream.

Len and Kai sat there exchanging meaningful glances for a minute or so, and Len asked, "Mom, is it okay for us to talk about things we overhear adults saying?"

"Things they don't know you heard?" I asked.

They nodded.

"Things that are none of our business?" Carson asked.

Kai favored him with one of her more withering glares. "Never mind," she said. "We'll just keep it to ourselves."

Len disagreed. "But it *could* be our business. And it could be your and Mom's business, too."

Carson didn't say anything. I looked back at Kai. "Try a little on us," I said. "Who did you overhear?"

Kai glanced around to confirm that we were alone on the patio. "We think it was Ms. Roberson and Mr. Pressfield."

"We're pretty sure," Len said.

"And how is it maybe any of our business?" Carson said.

"It's about the movie, and we work there," Len said.

"You volunteer there," I said.

"The movie is a client of yours, right?" Kai said.

"Sort of," Carson answered. "You think it's in our client's best interest for us to know what you overheard?"

"We don't know," Kai said, looking again at Len. He shrugged.

Carson raised his eyebrows at me like *it's your call*, so I said, "Go ahead."

Len started, "They were at the service dock. Inside that big cruiser, you know."

Kai added, "Its windows were open, and so was the window in the store, back by the magazine rack. We weren't trying to eavesdrop."

"And they were sort of yelling," Len said.

"It's okay," I said. "I heard them a little, even from where I was standing. Go on."

Kai continued, "She, Ms. Roberson, was saying that they had to find some guy. She said they had to get him, and she knew he would come."

Len interrupted. "But Mr. Pressfield said there might not *be* a movie." He started imitating Benjamin Pressfield's mannerisms, saying "*We DON'T have to PROCEED. You HAVE no LEVERAGE, and you HAVE even LESS COMMON SENSE.*" Len was quite a good mimic, and he had Pressfield's exaggerated way of speaking down to a T. He went on, "Stuff like that. Ms. Roberson sort of blew up. She was swearing, like—"

"A lot." Now Kai interrupted. "Like, she'd have to put a five-dollar bill in the jar, and even that wouldn't be enough."

Len laughed, and I had to laugh, too. Carson took a sip of his beer and waited.

"Inside joke," I said.

"I get it," he said. "What else did they say?"

"He mentioned Mayor Buckmaster, too," Len said. "He said that Mr. Buckmaster wanted to shut the movie down."

"Something about insurance," Kai said. "Ms. Roberson said that Herman—she called him Herman—could stick it up his ass."

This last bit was voiced with a bit too much spirit as Kai made the most of this chance to say something like that. I gave her a look. She said, "Mom, Mr. Carson asked what else they said, and that's what she said. That's how she said it." Before I could respond, she continued. "Anyway, they argued about that other man. Ms. Roberson thought he was great, and Mr. Pressfield didn't."

"So, if they shut the movie down, won't that hurt your business?" Len said. "I mean, they're big clients, right?"

Carson ignored Len's question and asked, "How did the argument turn out? Any idea?"

"I think they're gonna keep the movie going and try to get that guy," Len said. He looked over at Kai. "Right?"

"Sounded like it. They stopped yelling, so it was hard to hear them after that."

"Not that we were trying," Len said.

We stopped talking as the sun began to set, and the sky blushed bright coral pink. In front of us was one of the most celebrated views anywhere —the stark cliffs and pillars, the sandstone canyons cradling an enormous body of water, the remote blue mountain in the distance. Every year, something like two million people flocked from all over the world to see it. You could overhear conversations in a dozen languages just by shopping in the grocery store once a week during the summer.

Below us, slightly to the east, was the edge of a particular cliff. It was way under the surface of the lake now, but I'd stood on that cliff dozens of times. First, I stood there watching the construction of the dam. Later I watched the wild river turning into a lake as water slowly began to fill the many canyons extending eastward for a couple of hundred miles. In some of those canyons, my people had lived for centuries, farming and hunting by the river. But my children would never see where our ancestors lived and worked. The canyons and their river were gone.

Instead, we were living on a mesa high above where those farms had been, and I was working in a law firm. How long would that last? Since my early twenties, I'd supported my children mostly by doing whatever job I could find—not that I didn't have help. Jobwise, though, there hadn't been much chance to build stability.

Now I hoped that my job would turn into a career, that Grant Carson, Attorney at Law, might become a viable legal firm, and that Carson would start taking it seriously—that is, if he hadn't murdered Shawn Gordon on his yacht. Which, of course, he hadn't. I was pretty sure he hadn't. No, of course, he hadn't.

Then the silence was broken.

"There you are, Carson," Herman Buckmaster bellowed.

"Jesus save us," Carson said under his breath as the mayor advanced on us from across the patio.

"I called your office. I went by. Don't you people ever work?" Buckmaster said as he barreled toward us.

"We do about anything we want to…Buck," Carson said. "Anyway, it's Friday afternoon, so we're easing into the weekend." He winked at the kids.

Buckmaster said, "It's *Thursday*, Carson."

"Well, it's past closing time. Want a beer?"

"No, I do not want a beer. What I want is an appointment. ASAP," Buckmaster said.

Carson said, "Naomi, do we have any time available tomorrow?"

"Sure do," I said. "I thought today was Friday, so I didn't book anything for tomorrow."

Carson and the kids laughed, but Herman's expression was sour. Carson said, "Hey, whatever you need, Buck, it can wait till ten tomorrow. Right now, you should have a beer. You really need one."

CHAPTER ELEVEN

A FTER the kids left for their last day of school on Friday, I went out to visit the movie location at Red Cliffs Beach for an hour or two. It certainly was "a desert place," a half-mile or so north of the regular campground area, covering about five flat acres of rust-colored sand near the edge of the water.

I was fascinated by the barely controlled chaos. Uniformed crews were moving equipment from place to place, unloading trucks, and laying thick electric cables all over the ground. Trailers and recreational vehicles—some huge, some barely bigger than a minivan—were arranged into a little village near a large tent, like one I saw when a religious revival set up for a week outside of town a couple of years ago. The sound of numerous small generators hummed in the background.

The big tent seemed a good place to start checking things out, so I walked in as if I belonged there. I saw more than a dozen eight-foot folding tables with a bunch of folding chairs scattered around them. More tables were set end-to-end along one wall, ready for a buffet, though I didn't see any actual food yet. Stiff outdoor carpeting covered the sand underfoot. A few sections of the tent wall had been rolled up to admit light and air, but the inside was still gloomy compared with the bright sunlight outdoors. It took a minute for my eyes to adjust enough to see my way around.

I had spotted a large metal urn of coffee on one of the side tables when I heard someone call my name. Kathy Roberson was sitting with another woman at a table at the other end of the tent, and she was waving me over.

I saw that the other woman with Kathy was Molly Malloy, who'd been introduced as the script supervisor at the parent meeting on Wednesday night. As I approached the table, I was pleased to see that their outfits were a lot like mine. All of us were wearing lightweight khaki slacks, cotton shirts, and sturdy lace-up shoes. I wondered if they dressed like that when working in Hollywood. Maybe I'd fit right in if I learned to wear more makeup.

"Good morning Ms. Roberson," I said as I sat down across the table from her.

"Please, call me Kathy," she said. "And you remember Molly." To Molly, she said, "You should take a look at this girl's boss. My, my. I mean, scrumptious." Turning back to me, she went on, "I wouldn't get any work done at all with him around."

I couldn't think of anything to say in answer to that, and it seemed like Molly couldn't, either.

Eventually, Kathy broke the silence. "What brings you out to our little village, Naomi?"

I answered a little too quickly. "Mr. Carson wants me to keep an eye on things and be available if anything comes up." Maybe I shouldn't have said that in front of Molly, but Kathy didn't flinch. "Also," I added, "my children will be out here on internships, and I want to give them the lay of the land before they start next week."

Molly said, "I'm going to go get a refill. Can I get you guys anything?"

"I'm good for now," Kathy said, "What about you, Naomi?"

"No thanks," I said, and Molly walked away toward the coffee urn.

As soon as she was out of earshot, I said, "I'm sorry, I shouldn't have said anything about our business relationship while Molly was sitting here."

"No problem. I don't think she even noticed." She carefully set the cardboard cup of coffee down in front of her. Her warm smile disappeared. "Does Mr. Carson think there's anything you need to do out here? Besides racking up billable hours, I mean."

That might have been a sincere question, but I didn't see any reason for being so rude about it. She wasn't exactly wrong about the billable hours, but she wasn't exactly right, either. I wasn't sure how to respond, because I didn't know her, so I took my time. Keeping my expression as pleasant as I could, I tilted my head to one side as if waiting for the punchline of the joke she must surely be telling.

She didn't say anything else, but her gaze dropped again to the coffee in front of her.

I said, "You mentioned that Benjamin Pressfield is unpredictable, which means that problems could crop up without warning. Since there aren't telephones out here, we figured we'd start this way and see how things develop. Luckily, Mr. Rice's retainer covers my availability." In other words, *you're not actually paying the freight, lady, so you can stuff a sock in it.*

Over at the side of the tent, Molly called out, "Later, guys," as she waved at us before escaping with her coffee. Kathy waved back absently and said to me, "I see. Anyway, I do have some news. Benjamin gave in. We're hiring Hamilton O'Neill."

She gave no hint of the loud argument she'd had with Pressfield the afternoon before. "That's good news," I said. "I mean it's good news contract-wise, not good news about…the circumstances. I'm sorry."

Looking almost amused, Kathy said, "I'm not going to pretend that Shawn and I were pals. I personally never liked him much." Her face quickly shifted to a sorrowful expression, like you'd see on a pretty news anchor describing a tragic car accident. "Not that I'd wish him any harm …I meant…you know?"

It was not an especially convincing performance, but she was still a client, so I asked, "What about Shawn's contract? Does the film still have obligations?"

"The guy's dead, Naomi. What's he going to do, sue us? Benjamin may have to do some wrangling with his agent, yeah, but it won't amount to much."

Someone should tell her not to be so bitchy, I thought. Luckily, it wasn't my job to teach her basic manners, so I kept mum.

Having dismissed the whole contract issue, Kathy went on. "What's the latest news from town? Has anyone been arrested?"

"No. They're still investigating." I saw no reason to tell her that another client of ours was under suspicion, and I sure as hell wasn't going to let on that her attorney was a person of interest, either.

She raised her empty cup and gestured toward the coffee urn. We walked over to the table, where she replenished her coffee and I got a steaming cup for myself. We stepped outside and stood facing the lake. "What about Hamilton O'Neill?" I asked. "When will he get here?"

"He's on his way. Should be here later today." She took a sip of her coffee and made a *yuck* face. "Turns out he's actually in Kanab. That's close, right?"

"Right. Only about seventy miles away." None too hopefully, I tasted my coffee and cringed. If it had been too strong, I could've added water to smooth it out. But there's nothing in the great wide world that can save a weak cup of coffee, and this was dishwater-weak. You'd think movie people would demand better. With an effort, I turned my attention back to Kathy, asking, "Will you need us to put together any paperwork for him?"

"Probably not," Kathy said. "It'll be pretty standard, so the entertainment attorneys in L.A. will handle it. We'll maybe have you guys look it over to be sure Pressfield's people haven't tried to pull a fast one, but that shouldn't take very long."

"Will the change make the movie cost more? I'm thinking about the financing. You mentioned that it was tight."

She laughed. "I'm sure that Pressfield padded his budget. Should be okay, I imagine." She paused to think about it and said, "Based on the price I paid for my piece of the project—well, mine and Uncle Carl's—I'd say Benjamin raised about five million total."

"And that's enough? The budget, I mean?"

"It should be." After a few seconds, she said, "Except he isn't very careful."

"Really?"

"Yeah, like he rented a big stupid boat for the summer after he saw the lake, just because he wanted to."

I asked, "And that's a problem?"

"Just a dumb thing to do. Not worth arguing about. Not now, anyway. There's too much other stuff to keep track of."

I saw a bunch of people moving carts full of artificial foliage. I vaguely remembered that trees were important in *Macbeth*, but nothing at all grew here. During the decade of building the dam, this spot had been a parking and storage area for big equipment. Years of heavy traffic killed every tiny sprig of life that was here before. If they were going to need trees, they'd have to bring them in from somewhere else, and I wondered how expensive that would be.

Two catering trucks pulled up outside the tent. Three guys jumped out and started unloading big trays covered with aluminum foil. They walked past us into the tent. Buckmaster sat behind the wheel of one of the trucks, writing something on a clipboard.

Glancing over at Herman, Kathy said, "Good, he's here. I need to talk to him about this so-called coffee."

That was the first sensible thing I'd heard all day. "I'm with you one hundred percent. Neither of the fast-food places that he owns serves decent coffee. You'd be doing us a big favor if you could get him to level up his java game. But I have to warn you—he's not a guy who listens. To anyone."

She snorted. "That's quite a tone in your voice there, Naomi. Is there anything we should know?"

"No, I simply don't like the guy."

"Well, I'm not a big fan, either. He's an okay caterer, except for this awful coffee." She made the same *yuck* face before going on, "And he's a hard-working guy. But he also invested in the project, and now he wants to throw his weight around."

"Throw his weight around how?"

"Insisting that we stop production, right now. He's been damn near hysterical about it since Shawn first went missing—and you're right about how he doesn't listen. But quitting is *not* an option. Not as far as I'm concerned. No, we're going to bring O'Neill on board. We're going to make movie history. We're going to get me my Oscar."

I couldn't tell if Kathy believed all that, but I needed to steer us back toward more solid ground. "Do you want Carson to look over the insurance stuff? Like, make sure that the change in casting doesn't void the policy?"

"Funny you should ask. No, Benjamin met with a couple of the underwriters yesterday. Recasting doesn't change anything about the coverage. But like that guy over there—" she made another face as she gestured toward Herman, "—they want us to shut down, too."

"Why's that? Why would they *want* to make the payout?"

"It's all about numbers to them." Kathy's face began to redden as her voice got louder. "They contribute nothing. They have no vision. They whine that lightning could strike again later, when the payout would be bigger." She tossed the dregs of her coffee into the sand near one of the plastic shrubs. "Benjamin says they even fussed about the curse. You know, 'The Scottish Play' and all that. But they can't make me stop. They'll never make me fucking stop. It's my goddamn movie, and I'm going ahead."

I stared after her as she stalked off to one of the motor homes, climbed inside, and slammed the door. It was clear to me at that point that movie people—at least, a couple of the movie people—weren't playing with a full deck. Luckily, their personal mobsters recognized the need for an outside referee, which meant that they'd keep Carson busy mediating their squabbles right on through the final curtain, so to speak. We'd earn out our retainer, and I'd be able to work close to full time for the summer.

The smile stayed on my face for the whole drive back into town.

~ ~ ~

I was standing in line at Burger Barn, waiting to grab a quick lunch when someone tapped my shoulder. I stepped to the side, assuming that I was obstructing someone's view of the "Today's Beef" board describing the burger of the day.

Again came the tap, and I whirled around to see Lew grinning at me. He said, "Lost in thought, Naomi?"

I grinned back. Damn, it was great to see him. "I guess so. What's up, Lew?"

"Oh, a little of this, a little of that. I only have a minute, but I saw you from my shop and wondered if I could maybe walk you back to your office."

I finished paying for my lunch and grabbed the bag, which was already showing a satisfying degree of greasiness. "You bet. Let's go."

He took the bag, and if I'd had any books, he'd have carried them for me, too, gentleman that he was. I bumped his shoulder with mine and said, "So?"

He shook his head, steering me across the street and around the corner, getting us off the main drag before answering. Then he said, "What I want to ask about is kind of a gray area."

I laughed. "And how gray is this particular area?"

"Overcast-sky gray. Old-sweatshirt gray."

"You're in luck," I said. "Gray areas are a specialty at Carson and Associates."

There was that grin of his again. He said, "Good to hear, I guess. Well, you know that Marybeth brought me some floppy discs to clean up for the city."

"I remember, yes. I saw them. They were gross and disgusting."

"Yes, they were. The mayor felt bad that he ruined those discs. Anyway, everyone at the city office thought the discs were toast, but Marybeth was hoping the data could be recovered. She said she worked a long time on it, and she was damned if she'd do all that data entry again unless she had to."

"I can relate," I said. "One time—"

He interrupted, "Computers, tools of the devil, yes, I know." He'd heard it all. "Still, I did save some of the data that's on the discs. In the process, I ended up looking closely at quite a bit of it."

"What's gray about that?" I asked. "You kind of *had* to, didn't you?"

"It was accounting stuff. Numbers. And I...well, I kind of...on my calculator and sort of... sort of checked."

"Those numbers are for city accounts, right? Public record."

"Okay, but two things. First, they don't all seem to be city accounts. The accounting categories don't seem like they'd be used for city funds."

"Maybe it's some kind of special project accounting. What's the other thing?"

"The other thing is, it's not so much *examining* the numbers that puts me in that gray area. It's telling *you* about them that makes it gray."

"Telling me what, Lew? What do you think you saw?"

"Funds disappear from some of the regular city accounts. They show up in other accounts. The ones with weird categories."

"So, you think…?"

"Maybe Herman Buckmaster is playing fast and loose with some of the city's funds."

What the hell? "You mean…he's *embezzling*?" Not that I'd put it past him.

Lew said, "Shhh. I didn't say that, Naomi. I only said that money was moving around in strange ways, and I wanted someone besides me to know it."

"Well, I know it now. Shouldn't we go to the police?"

"Probably at some point, but let's keep it to ourselves till we can figure out what's what."

"By 'we' you mean *you*, right? You'll figure it out. Because basic book-keeping is about as far as I can go, and I don't think that'll help."

"But talking it through with you *does* help. Can I ask you something else?"

"It depends. Is this an accounting quiz?"

I was rewarded with that wonderful laugh, and he said, "No, nothing like that. I was wondering how you got into the law."

"It's a funny story," I said. "Walk with me, grasshopper. This'll take a while."

We strolled toward the park, where we sat on one of the few benches that had a little shade at that time of day. I began with the high hopes I'd had, less than two years before, when I entered the college's paralegal training program that folded before I could complete it. I credited Dee for pushing Carson to hire me with only three semesters of training under my belt. I talked about getting our first murder case, getting threatened by a smooth mob lawyer, and getting adopted by a criminal dog.

By the time I finished, he was shaking his head. "Here I thought I was the adventurous one, joining the Navy to see the world."

I said, "After a tame life in the Navy, my friend, Sage Landing will probably be too stressful for you."

~ ~ ~

By three o'clock I was at my desk, eyeing a stack of books from my college paralegal classes and wondering which questions I should research first. Entertainment law? I could sound at least a little bit savvy with clients from that world. Should I track down some forensic accounting, to get an idea of what old Herman may be up to? What if he used city money to invest in the movie but got cold feet—would that be a motive for murder? Should I learn more about—I don't know—felony assault? FBI jurisdictions? I was still weighing the options when Carson arrived and walked straight to his inner office without a word.

He didn't close the door, so I went in and sat down across from him. He was shuffling through some of the scribbled sheets of paper on the desk. I said, "What?"

He dropped the papers he was holding and leaned back. He said, "Gordon had enough alcohol in him to kill a smallish buffalo."

"Where'd you hear that?"

He seemed to consider answering, but he said, "I'd rather not say. I overheard it somewhere while I was talking to someone."

I said, "So you overheard George and Mike in the police station while you were there talking to Peggy. Got it. Hey, I told you before. Last I saw Shawn Gordon at Wranglers, he was drunk enough to be an asshole and sober enough to feel bad about it. Were there other drugs involved?"

"Nope—a major blackout's worth of whiskey, but there'd also been another blow to the head. A bad one."

"Is that what killed him? Or was it a gun, like you thought? What about the knife? There was a knife involved, right? Peggy was nervous about the knife in your galley."

"Slow down, Naomi. The medical examiner's report isn't in yet."

"But Dee's off the hook, isn't she? I mean, they can already tell that she didn't kill him."

"Not during the fight, but she could've gone back to find Gordon later. Beat him up and stabbed him and dumped him on my boat."

"She's our *client*. Jesus, whose side are you on?"

"Hers. But she's got a past that complicates things, and so far, that makes her a pretty tempting suspect. Especially since she won't say much about where she went later that night."

"Neither will you. Doesn't that put you in the same category?"

He smiled, which I found annoying, but he wasn't going to say any more about it.

"I'm serious, Carson. As soon as you men find out that Dee's a woman who can defend herself, right away you're thinking she could be a murderer. Seems like a mighty big leap."

"Hold on, hold on. You're not being—"

"You think I'm not being reasonable. But Buckmaster and you and Mike and George, you're the ones who aren't being reasonable."

His creaky chair snapped upright as he leaned forward and went back to shuffling through the mess on his desk.

Moving on, I said, "Weren't you supposed to meet with Herman Buckmaster this morning?"

"I did. He wasn't here long."

Wondering if Buckmaster's visit had anything to do with the numbers that Lew told me about, I asked, "So what did he want?"

"He wanted to sue Benjamin Pressfield to make him shut the movie down now."

"You told him that we'd have a conflict of interest, right?" I had to ask because Carson and I have very different definitions for *conflict of interest*. One way to describe it is that his definition is quite a bit looser than mine. Another is that Carson's is wrong and mine is right. Potato, potahto.

I waited. Eventually, he said, "I told him he'd have to find another lawyer because we represent Kathy Roberson and her uncle."

"Good."

Carson added, "He seemed to find that very upsetting."

"Even better," I said.

CHAPTER TWELVE

SATURDAY doesn't count as the first day of summer break, since there wouldn't be school anyway. But we were feeling pretty celebratory all the same, so we had a nice family breakfast, the kind the kids and I used to enjoy more often when they were younger. Kai popped open a tube of refrigerator biscuits and doctored them up with butter and cinnamon sugar before sliding them into the oven. Len cooked about half a pound of bacon and scrambled all the eggs we had.

They both had plans for the day, most of which would involve hanging out at the community center swim party and picnic with their respective groups of friends. I know, I know… a few days before, I'd grounded Kai for the foreseeable future, fully intending to make it stick for at least a week, but here's the thing. Not only had she been a model citizen during the chaotic days since, but she was very contrite when she begged to go to the party. More to the point, other vigilant parents would be supervising her and Len there, so I could enjoy some time to myself. In the end, I had no regrets about giving in.

While we were eating, Len said, "Mom, I just remembered something else. Part of the argument on the boat, remember? Mr. Pressfield and Ms. Roberson? Day before yesterday? About getting someone new for the movie?"

Sometimes I'd swear that my kids think I'm sliding into senility already, but I smiled and said, "Yes, Len, I remember that argument."

"Well, Mr. Pressfield said the guy was a drunk, and Ms. Roberson got real mad at that."

Kai added, "She got even madder when Mr. Pressfield said just because she fooled around with the guy, that didn't mean—"

"Except he used a different word," Len said.

"But it *did* start with an F," Kai added.

"Okay, I get it," I said. "Change of subject. Who's going to be at the swimming party?"

The rest of breakfast was profanity-free. The kids helped me clean up the kitchen before gathering the beach balls, snorkels, goggles, and sunscreen they'd need to get them through a long day at the pool. After they left, I sat down with a third cup of coffee.

The peace lasted about fifteen minutes.

When the phone rang, I jinxed myself by praying aloud that it would not be Carson. That meant it wasn't a surprise when I picked up the receiver and heard him say, "Naomi. Can you come to the office?"

"Damn it, Carson. What now?" I winced, mentally adding a quarter to the jar. "Can't it wait?"

Ignoring my questions, both spoken and unspoken, he said, "Bring the clothes you were wearing last Saturday night at the bar."

"What if they're in the washing machine?"

"Are they?"

"Well, no, but why—"

"And bring your little pistol," he added.

"You think I need to be armed?" I asked.

"No. The police want it."

"What, *I'm* a suspect now?"

"It sounds like *we* are," he said. "How soon can you be here?"

"Fifteen or twenty minutes."

"Yeah, well, that wasn't a question. Let me rephrase. Get here now."

"You mean drive over there? I only live two blocks away."

There was no answer because he'd already hung up. I set my mug full of fresh coffee on the counter next to the microwave, hoping I'd soon be back to reheat it and get on with having a Saturday to myself. Less than five minutes later, I arrived at the office with my bar clothes, still smelling of the smoke-filled air at Wranglers, wrapped around my gun in a brown paper bag.

It sounds bad when I say it that way.

A squad car was parked out front beside Carson's truck. Inside, Mike and Peggy were seated in Carson's office. Both were armed and in uniform. I put the crumpled bag on the floor behind the desk and rolled my chair in to join them.

"I brought the stuff," I said as I sat down. Carson's .45 was lying on his desk with the magazine removed. "It's in the other room. What's going on?"

"Just a formality," Rodriguez said.

"A few questions," Peggy added, not very helpfully.

Carson said, "They brought a warrant, Naomi, so no joking around."

That was both rude and totally unfair. He was the one who didn't take things seriously, not me. "Are we under arrest?" I asked, pointedly not joking around.

Peggy suppressed a smile and said, "Nothing like that, Naomi, but now we have some new bases to cover."

"And these new bases involve guns?" I said.

Rodriguez said, "The autopsy found that Shawn Gordon was fatally shot."

Hadn't Peggy hinted there at the boat a couple of days before that the guy was stabbed? And that *maybe* her fingerprints were on the knife?

Peggy knew what I was thinking—as I've said before, I have no poker face at all—and clarified, "Shot, and then he was stabbed more than once. When the body was found, the knife was in the bullet wound, hiding it until the coroner pulled it out."

I began to regret my big breakfast.

Carson said, "If you're finding my prints on the knife—"

Mike interrupted, "Nobody's prints were on the knife. It was wiped clean before it was used on the victim."

He stood up and gestured toward the door. "We need for both of you to come out to the boat with us—well, not come *with* us, but meet us."

"To go over some things," Peggy added as she reached over and picked up Carson's .45 to place it in a plastic bag.

"I want you each to drive your own vehicle," Rodriguez said.

Carson snickered. "Separating the witnesses, right? No chance to co-ordinate our stories? Like we haven't already had ample time to do that?" As she passed my desk, Peggy grabbed the paper bag from the floor and glanced inside. She rolled it closed again and headed out the front door. Mike held the door open for Carson and me. "Like I said, drive your own cars. We'll follow you."

"10-4, Chief," I said. "We got us a convoy. A great big convoy."

"Good one, Naomi. Really funny," said the chief, with no amusement on his face whatsoever.

~ ~ ~

The police tape had been moved down near Carson's boat so that the rest of the middle dock was open for business. Peggy led the way to the *Deep Inn*. "Before you ask, Naomi, yes, you do have to come aboard." She extracted two pairs of rubber gloves from her pocket and handed them to us. She and Rodriguez put on their own. I took my time pulling the gloves over my fingers while I watched Carson and Rodriguez both step onto the boat. Rodriguez ducked his head as he followed Carson into the *Deep Inn*'s cabin, closing the door behind him.

I stepped further away from the boat. "It'll be too crowded," I said to Peggy. "I'll wait right here."

Peggy rested a hand on my arm. "Wait a second. I'll open the cabin door and let it air out first." She went aboard and propped the cabin door open.

Peggy had known me a long time. She knew that the foul air in that cabin wasn't what made it tough for me to step onto the boat. In Navajo tradition, if a person dies indoors, the deceased spirit—especially its shadowy side—lingers. People stay away from such places. Back in the day, if a person died inside a *hogan*, that earthen home would usually be abandoned. For instance, last year, a friend decided against putting in a bid on a nice older home in town because she couldn't be sure that no one ever died there. I'm not all that traditional in some ways, but I find life difficult enough among the living, so I do my best to avoid possible conflicts with the dead.

When Peggy joined me back on the dock, I said, "Thanks. Oh, and I don't know if this is important, but the kids overheard an argument a couple of days ago. Kathy Roberson and Benjamin Pressfield were yelling at each other on that big cabin cruiser over there." I pursed my lips and lifted my chin in the direction of the cruiser, still tied up near the convenience market. "Remember, we heard some shouting from that direction?"

Peggy shook her head. "I was a little busy, Naomi. And I was mostly, you know... working in the boat."

"Right," I said. "Well, the kids were standing inside by the magazine rack, and they couldn't help hearing some interesting stuff through that open window there."

"Interesting how?" Peggy said.

It suddenly occurred to me that attorney-client privilege meant I probably shouldn't say anything about Kathy's contract or the legal tussle or John Rice. "Oh, just kind of movie-stars-interesting, maybe. I don't know." Well, that was lame. I rushed on. "Anyway, the kids heard them yelling at each other about hiring someone Kathy wanted to hire and Pressfield didn't."

"So?"

"So, maybe nothing. Apparently, it was someone that Kathy Roberson fu—fooled around with in the past, if you know what I mean. Someone who's also a drinker. At least, Pressfield said so. Loudly. More than once."

Peggy said nothing. She was waiting for me to talk my nerves out so we could get on with things.

I took a deep breath and let it out slowly. "Okay, we can go aboard now."

"Watch your step," she said, reaching over to steady me as I boarded. "You're right, there isn't a lot of elbow room in that cabin. Let's sit over here till the guys get out of our way." We perched on a couple of folding chairs set up in the stern.

I was grateful for the chance to spend a few minutes getting used to the motion of the water before venturing into the cabin. So far, so good.

Fixing my eyes on the horizon to help me get my bearings, I asked, "*Are* we suspects, Peggy?"

Peggy, too, was gazing into the distance. She said, "Right now, every person of interest is considered a suspect. Those are the orders from higher up. You both have guns. You seem to have some connection to the movie. Your alibis are flimsy. That keeps you guys on the list."

"Orders from higher up? Whose? Who's in charge of the case?"

"State of Arizona is treating it as their case. We're merely assisting them."

"What about the FBI?"

She shrugged. "That's up to the park supervisor. So far, Wanda hasn't requested FBI—doesn't see the need, she says. For now, Arizona's calling the shots."

I said, "Did it happen for sure on the boat? I mean, if he was moved to the boat after getting killed on land, Tribal Police could be in charge, right?"

"As I said, Naomi, the orders are coming from way above my pay grade. Mike's, too. Let's not waste time on hypotheticals."

Carson came up on deck with a can of beer in his hand. He craned his neck to see past Peggy and me to the flat surface behind us, which I knew covered the boat's inboard engines. Over his shoulder, he said, "No, it isn't up here, either."

Rodriguez was right behind him. "Are you sure you left it here on the boat?"

Carson said, "Sure I'm sure. It's been here since I bought her because her plumbing's so fussy."

I asked, "What are you guys talking about?"

Carson said, "My pipe wrench. I thought it was still in the kitchen, but isn't there anymore, so I figured maybe I brought it up here."

Peggy said, "Chief, shouldn't our diver be here by now?"

Rodriguez leaned over the side of the boat so that he could look out toward the parking lot. "He's late."

Carson said, "I've got a swimsuit and a mask. I'll help you out."

Peggy laughed. "We don't let suspects search the crime scene for us, Carson."

"It tends to reduce the conviction rate," the chief said.

"What are you searching for?" I asked.

Carson answered, "If you shot somebody in the middle of a dark night out here, what would you do with the murder weapon?"

Oh. Peering down into the water, I said, "I'd toss it overboard."

Peggy stood up. "Me too." Again she gently put a hand on my arm. "Let's go below, Naomi. It's probably aired out enough now."

"Is there any more beer in the box?" I asked Carson.

"Tons, and we've been plugged in right along, so it's cold."

"Too bad for you cops," I said.

"It's Saturday," Rodriguez said. "Toss one up for mc."

After all my nervousness, walking down the stairs into the cabin didn't bother me much. I didn't know what a room with resident *ch'įįdii*—a dead person's spirit—was supposed to feel like, but I didn't sense anything unusual. Still, I was careful to avoid the chalk outline on the floor as I headed for the galley. I was reaching into the little fridge to grab the drinks when Peggy asked me, "Could Carson have helped someone with this?"

I whirled around and saw that she was staring at the chalk outline. I said, "Help someone with what—killing an actor he'd never met, for no reason at all?"

"Someone he cares about could have found herself in a terrible situation." Peggy took one of the beers I was holding, opened it, and handed it back to me before taking the other one for herself. "I mean, it's his boat. She would've needed help to get Gordon aboard."

No longer in the mood for sharing a friendly beer over a crime scene, I set the opened can on the table. "Of all people, you...for god's sake, Peggy, you know him better than that!"

Peggy said, "My lips are moving, Naomi, but I'm not the one asking the questions. We're under orders from Phoenix to interview you guys here on the boat. We've been told what to ask."

"I don't care who's asking, the answer's *no*. Carson wasn't even here. He was away for the weekend."

"So he says, but no one else has confirmed it. Did you see him at all that weekend?"

"This is nonsense. Is the bullet they got from the body a .45?" I asked. She didn't answer.

"Is it from a .38 like mine?" I asked.

Nothing.

I said, "Peggy, come *on*. Blink twice for no."

Her eyelids didn't even twitch. She said, "So you didn't see him."

"Jesus, Peg." I glanced at the outline. "Dee didn't do it, and Carson didn't help. Next question."

"Okay, here's one. Does Dee ever wear a wig?"

"What kind of question is that—isn't the whole idea of wearing a wig to not *look* like you're wearing a wig?"

Patiently, Peggy said, "Again, it's not my question. I'm the one who's been told to ask it, so here I am asking."

"And here I am, answering. No, if Dee ever wore a wig, I didn't know about it."

"There. Was that so hard?" Peggy smiled. "Next I'm supposed to get you to hunt around the whole boat and tell me if you notice anything out of the ordinary."

I had no idea where this was all going, but it wasn't anyplace good. "Nope, I'm done," I said, heading for the steps up to the deck.

"But we—wait, Naomi."

"Arrest me and call my lawyer," I said as I climbed the stairs. "I'm getting away from this boat."

By the time Peggy reached the deck, I was walking along the dock. I could see Rodriguez and Carson standing near the service dock talking to another guy. Nobody arrested me. As I walked past the trio of men, I said to Carson, "Come by my house when you get through here." I didn't wait for an answer.

~ ~ ~

I stopped at the grocery store on my way home to pick up lunch stuff that I could also feed the kids for supper whenever they dragged themselves home from their day of sun and chlorine. In a burst of hostess-y foresight, I threw in some beer for Carson.

When I got home, I opened the microwave to reheat the untouched cup of coffee that had been waiting for me since Carson's call. Then I closed the microwave, poured the coffee into the sink, and opened a beer.

I couldn't remember the last time I'd had a drink in my own home. Years, probably.

To give the beer some company in my stomach, I made myself a deluxe sandwich—meaning it had meat *and* cheese—and ate it while leaning against the kitchen sink.

Carson rolled up about an hour after I finished. When he walked in, I got some of the sandwich stuff back out and let him build his own. And get his own beer.

"Late lunch," he said while he piled cold cuts on bread. "By the way, Rodriguez said I should tell you to stay in town."

"Me? What about you?"

He shrugged as he took a big bite out of his sandwich.

Taking that to mean that he'd been given the same instructions and didn't feel the need to repeat them, I moved on and asked, "What happened after I left?"

He took his time, chewing slowly before answering me. "The diver found a gun on the lake bottom, about fifty feet up the dock from the yacht. The water's so clear that I think we could've spotted it from the dock if we'd known where to look."

"They think it's the gun that killed Gordon?"

"Well, they quit diving when the diver found it, so, yes, they probably do. It was a pre-war Browning .32." He gulped half of his beer before going on, "Which means that Gordon was killed by a .32."

"That seems logical," I said.

"Now they're combing my yacht again trying to find a shell casing, because the pistol was an automatic. It hadn't been in the water long, but there weren't any fingerprints, and that particular model is very common."

"Does Dee have one?"

"I don't know. I don't know if Dee has a gun at all, but then I didn't know about her boxing prowess, either."

"Dee is full of surprises." I walked to the refrigerator and got out the big jar of sun tea that Kai had made the day before. Switching from beer to tea seemed like a good idea, because who knew what the rest of this strange day would bring. I poured a glass for me and one for Carson, too. "I've never seen a—what was it, a pre-war Browning?"

"I have. Hundreds of them, I guess. They were popular with civilians in Saigon and Phoenix, both. Easy to carry. Ten-round capacity. Dependable." He finished his beer and eyed with suspicion the tall glass of iced tea I put in front of him.

"Drink up. It's going to be a long day," I said cheerfully, going back to the fridge to dig out the queso dip. After nuking it in the microwave, I set it on the table, opened a bag of tortilla chips, and sat down. "I remember Frank Armstrong saying he had a .32. Remember that?"

"Yeah, but Frank died months ago, and he wouldn't have dropped his into the water anyway." He grabbed a few chips. "Hell of a week."

"That's what happens when knitters go to bars," I said.

He laughed. "The college president gets into a bar fight."

"With a movie star."

Carson dunked a chip in the warm queso. "…who then goes missing. And the movie people go nuts."

"The movie people turn out to be mobsters," I said.

"Alleged mobsters."

"Excuse me, *alleged* mobsters."

"That's better. And that movie star turns up dead on the *Deep Inn*."

"Right, so who killed him?" I asked.

"Dee's still in the running, I guess, but I don't see it."

"Me neither, but she's our client, so we probably should feel that way. What about good old Herman Buckmaster?" Carson made a face, but I went on. "Listen, he seems pretty darned keen on stopping the movie. Maybe he was desperate to get his money back."

Carson gulped down his tea like it was medicine. "Gordon was bludgeoned, shot, and stabbed. Desperate or not, that doesn't sound like Herman."

"Okay, what about Kathy Roberson? She didn't want Gordon in the movie—"

"The murder was on my yacht. Dee knows the *Deep Inn*. Kathy Roberson doesn't."

"John Rice does," I said, "doesn't he? After what happened last fall?"

"Maybe not. I don't think he ever figured out that Larry Sabano was hiding on the yacht."

I poured more tea into his empty glass. "You should stop calling that old boat a yacht, Carson. People are laughing behind your back."

Exasperated, Carson said, "Stop right there, Naomi. Let's define our terms."

"You mean the term *boat?*" I asked.

"Yes, *boat.* And *yacht.* We nautical enthusiasts know things."

"And you're willing to share?"

He grinned. "I'm generous like that."

I looked around the kitchen and said, "Wait, maybe I should write this down. Hang on while I find—"

He waved a hand in the air, saying, "No need. No need at all. I'll be happy to cover all this again, any time your memory needs to be refreshed."

I said, "I'd expect nothing less. Please proceed."

"Thank you," he said. "First, any private pleasure watercraft of forty feet or more is, by definition, a yacht."

"That's pretty straightforward. So, the *Deep Inn* is forty feet or more?"

"Almost," he said, quickly adding, "But hear me out. There's a gray area, where a watercraft over thirty-five feet or so is a yacht if she's fitted out as a yacht."

Like I'd told Lew the day before, gray areas were our specialty, and it sounded like this gray area came with tailoring. I asked, "Fitted out?"

"Like the *Deep Inn.* She has a salon, a galley, a stateroom, and a head. At close to forty feet, that makes her a yacht. Definitely."

"Ah. Well, my apologies. I'll be sure to correct whoever calls her a boat the next time it comes up."

Satisfied, he went back to our list of suspects, saying, "There's Hamilton O'Neill. He's getting the lead role in a Pressfield movie. *That's* a motive."

"That reminds me," I said, and proceeded to fill him in on what the kids told me over breakfast. I added, "I'm sure that O'Neill's the guy they were yelling at each other about."

Smiling broadly, Carson said, "So O'Neill's not only a drunk, but he's one of Roberson's exes, too? Oh, that's even better!"

"Sure it is, but he doesn't know the *Deep Inn* any more than Kathy does," I said.

"Details," he said.

"Details, huh? Like Dee not having an alibi? And you not having one either?"

"I was out of town."

"I think you'll have to prove that. Can you?"

He stood up, still holding most of his unfinished sandwich. "Thanks for lunch. See you Monday." And he left.

CHAPTER THIRTEEN

IN the years since the kids outgrew Sesame Street and Electric Company, I've generally avoided turning the television on in the daytime. But on Sunday morning I made an exception, hoping to catch the latest entertainment industry buzz about *A Desert Place* as filming was about to begin. I was not disappointed. Sure enough, one of the Sunday shows spent a few minutes speculating on Pressfield's mysterious movie project.

There was a lot of chatter, all of it without foundation as far as I could tell, about sinister events on location. According to one of the talking heads, Shawn Gordon's murder was an effort to prevent the movie's production. The talking head didn't seem to have any idea about who might be making such an effort, and he was vague when asked where he'd gotten his information.

Kai wasn't having it. "That's bullshit," she said from the doorway where she stood watching.

"That'll cost you a quarter," Len shouted from the other room. "Make sure she puts it in the jar, Mom, because she cheats."

Kai ignored him, making no move toward the jar. I gestured toward the counter. She walked over to a kitchen drawer, took out a scrap of paper and pencil, and wrote an IOU for twenty-five cents. "Nobody is trying to sabotage the movie," she said as she added her promissory note to several others among the coins. "Where do they get that crap?"

Len hollered again. "Another quarter!".

"Crap doesn't count!" Kai said over her shoulder.

"Knock it off, you two. I want to listen to this," I said.

By the time I could hear the TV, a Hollywood-handsome man was gesturing with a big coffee mug while talking to an equally attractive woman, who was holding her equally oversized mug with both hands as she listened attentively. He was saying, "…has been even more secretive than usual about this project, hasn't he, Erica?"

"That's right, Bob," said Erica with a charming smile. "All we know for sure is that *A Desert Place* is based on William Shakespeare's Scottish play."

"Whose name shall not be spoken," said Bob, rather dramatically, I thought. "Haven't productions of that particular play been marred by misfortune, right from the very first one?"

"Well, Bob, it turns out that there is no historical record of the supposed death of an actor during that first production in 1606, but it makes a good story."

"A persistent one," Bob said. "We do know that about seventy years later in Amsterdam, the leading actor substituted a real dagger for the prop and killed a fellow actor, right there on the stage."

"And the stories go on," Erica said, turning her face toward the camera. "As you probably know, the play we're talking about is *Macbeth*. I'm told that it's okay to say its actual title anywhere but the theatre where it's being produced, so I guess you and I are safe." She chuckled musically.

Bob, however, stopped smiling and frowned directly into the camera to end the segment by returning to the current troubles of *A Desert Place*. "But, tragically, Shawn Gordon was far from safe out there in the remote reaches of Arizona."

Kai *tsked* with all the disgust she could muster.

I killed the TV and started organizing Sunday morning chores for the three of us. The kids had finished the lengthy process of reviewing who had done which burdensome jobs the last time. They'd each started making a case for why the other should do work that I'd assigned them when the phone mercifully rang. Kai rushed to pick it up. After saying hello, she listened and said, "Yes, Dr. Moreno. She's right here."

I handed the kids their chore lists, unchanged, and took the phone from Kai. "Dee?" I asked. I heard voices in the background. "What's wrong?"

"Naomi, the police are here with a search warrant."

Where was Carson? He wasn't supposed to leave town, but maybe he was out on a run? Shi—crap. I took a deep breath to calm myself. I knew what Carson would tell her, and, since he wasn't here, it was up to me. "It'll be okay. Don't answer any questions. Don't volunteer anything. I'm on my way."

I hung up and grabbed the pencil that was lying on the counter while gesturing for Kai to give back the list I'd handed her. Writing Carson's phone number on the back, I told her, "Honey, I need you to call Carson's machine at this number and leave a message telling him to meet me at Dr. Moreno's house. Then wait an hour and do it again."

Kai took the list back again. She eyed my house-cleaning outfit of frayed jeans and paint-spattered baseball shirt before saying, "You're wearing that?"

"Yep," I said, heading for the door. "Do your chores, guys. Be nice to each other. Stay put, stay off the phone, and don't let anyone in." And I left before they could give me any more sass.

Dee answered the door in wrinkled pajamas.

"Yeah, I know," she said as if I'd spoken. "I didn't get to sleep till sometime after four this morning, and now this. Thanks for coming over."

"Where are they? Why wouldn't they let you get dressed?" I said as I walked past her into the living room.

"They're searching the bedroom. They told me to stay out here."

"Okay. Have a seat. I'll be right back." I marched myself into Dee's bedroom, where Mike Rodriguez and a young cop I didn't recognize were watching Peggy carefully sort through one of the dresser drawers.

"Excuse me. Dee needs to get dressed. I'll grab—"

All three pairs of eyes turned toward me, and Mike said, "You'll do no such thing, Naomi. Nothing gets touched until we've had a chance to complete our search."

"Peggy can hand me—"

"Nothing. Peggy can't hand you anything. Now please go keep Dr. Moreno company in the living room."

Before getting back to her task, Peggy gave me a very slight shake of the head. There would be no bending of the rules. I spun on my heel and walked back down the hall.

The living room was unoccupied. I heard clattering noises coming from the kitchen and found Dee in there making coffee. I sat down at the counter. "What are they hoping to find?" I asked.

Dee got two mugs from a shelf above the coffeemaker. "I can't tell," she said. "As soon as they got here, I told them where my pistol was, but they didn't seem interested. Peggy went straight to my room while Chief Rodriguez and the other officer nosed around in the living room for a minute. They inspected my fireplace tools and examined my grandmother's silver candlesticks, the ones I keep on the mantle. But they didn't act like those things were important."

"Oh? What do you mean?" I asked, because it sounded to me like they thought those things were plenty important.

"I mean, they didn't…I don't know, dust them for prints or bag them up or do anything forensic like that. They didn't even make notes. They put the things back where they belong." She glared at the carafe, which was filling very slowly, and said, "God, could this stupid thing be taking any longer to brew?"

I tried to think of a way to ask where she'd been till four a.m. without sounding like a cop or a dorm mother. Nothing diplomatic occurred to me, so I went ahead and asked, "What kept you up so late?"

"Gee, let me think…" she tapped her lips with her index finger as if she were deep in thought. Like a lightbulb going on, she said, "Oh yeah… I'm a suspect in the sensational murder of a handsome but clueless young man. I'm on administrative leave from my job. My staff has to handle Commencement, the biggest event of the academic year, without my help. The mayor wants everyone in town—no, wait, everyone *in the country*—to believe that I'm a vicious pugilist. So tell me, Naomi, would *you* be able to sleep if you were me?"

It was a fair question, and the answer wasn't *no*, it was *hell, no*. But instead of saying so, I had to be sure of one more thing. I said, "So you were here at home all night, I take it?"

Before she could answer, Mike walked into the kitchen. The cop I didn't know followed closely behind him.

"Coffee's almost ready," said Dee, reaching for more mugs.

The unknown cop shook his head. Mike said, "None for us, thanks." And there they stood, arms folded across their chests.

Dee said, "What?"

Rodriguez said, "Has anyone called Carson?"

"I asked Kai to leave messages on his machine," I said. "He must be out doing errands or jogging or... well, I don't know. What are we looking for, Chief?"

"We're not—" the young guy started, but Rodriguez waved his hand toward the deputy to shut him up.

I got up, extended my hand toward him, and said, "I'm sorry. I should've introduced myself. I'm Naomi Manymules, and you are...?"

Mike cut in, "Officer Winters is with the state. He drove up here in the wee hours at the request of the attorney general."

I withdrew my hand. "Ah, so this is coming from further up the food chain. Are you guys about done?" I was surprised to see that the clock said it was only a little past ten. It felt a lot later.

"Is your car in the garage?" Rodriguez asked Dee. He lifted his chin, pursing his lips in the direction of the door. Even though he wasn't Navajo, he grew up here and learned, along with the rest of us, how to avoid the extreme rudeness of pointing with his finger.

Dee said, "Where else would it be?"

Winters said, "We'll take a quick peek."

I didn't wait for an invitation. I followed along behind Rodriguez and Winters as they walked through the kitchen to the garage.

Rodriguez pushed a button to open the door of the garage so that its interior was flooded with sunlight. Dee had a double garage but only one vehicle, a three-quarter-ton Ford pickup. It was black and shiny, probably not more than a year old. Winters walked around it in one direction while Rodriguez went the other. Both men were inspecting the truck carefully. They met together at the front of it.

"Looks clean to me," Winters said.

"*Very* clean," Rodriguez said as if that were somehow suspicious.

I said, "So what? My car is clean, too." Mike smiled, but he didn't say a word. In the interest of honesty, I went on. "Well, maybe not right this minute, but it's clean sometimes. Are we through here?"

Rodriguez said, "Not yet." To the state trooper he said, "Your turn."

Officer Winters went out the open garage door and pulled a black case out of the police car. He carried it into the garage, opened the passenger door of Dee's pickup, and laid the case on the seat. He lifted its lid. Over his shoulder, I got a quick glimpse of the jars, brushes, and small bottles strapped inside.

"What's—" I started to ask.

"Naomi, let's go," Rodriguez said. "We'll leave him to it," and before I could get a whole question out, he was escorting me back into the kitchen.

Peggy and Dee were sitting across from each other at the counter. Between them were two mugs of coffee and a revolver.

"It's empty, Chief," Peggy said, gesturing toward the pistol. "A .38 Special. It was right where Dee told us it was."

Barely glancing at the gun, Rodriguez said, "Looks like your truck has recently been washed."

"Last Sunday," Dee said. "A bunch of teenagers at one of the churches had a car wash."

"Oh, yeah," Peggy said, "the Methodist kids. The youth pastor mentioned it to me because he thought there'd probably be water running into the street. They were set up in the parking lot of the bank."

Still talking to Dee, Rodriguez asked, "Last Saturday night after the incident in the bar, where did you go?"

Dee said nothing.

"Did you come straight home, Dee?" Peggy asked.

"Not right away," Dee said. "I went for a drive first to give myself time to calm down." She'd already told him that when he questioned her in his office.

"Heading any place in particular?" Rodriguez asked.

"Up into Utah some, not all the way to Kanab."

This was getting into actual interrogation territory, so I said, "Chief Rodriguez, if you're going to interview our client, shouldn't we go down to the station, set up the tape recorder, et cetera?"

The door from the garage opened. Winters stuck his head in. All he said was "Chief," before disappearing again, leaving the door open.

Rodriguez said, "Okay, sit tight, right where you are. Peggy, please stay here with…everyone." He went through the open door, closing it firmly behind him.

After five minutes ticked away on the kitchen clock, Rodriguez came back in alone. He held out his hand to Dee, palm up, and said, "May we have your car keys?"

Dee waited for me to answer. Carson would've probably wanted me to say "no," but since I wasn't actually a lawyer and therefore had no idea what I'd say after that, I shrugged. She answered Rodriguez, "They're in my purse right there on the counter by the door."

Peggy walked over, retrieved the keys, and handed them to Rodriguez. He said, "We'll have to take the car. It may be unavailable to you for a while."

"How long?" I asked and thought better of it since he probably wouldn't tell me anyway. "Never mind. We can work something out so Dr. Moreno won't be stranded."

"We're through here for now." He pointed toward the revolver on the counter. Peggy reached over with her gloved hand, picked it up, and slipped it into a plastic bag that magically appeared from her hip pocket.

"We'll take this along to show how thorough we are," she said.

"Be my guest," Dee said.

After they left, I refilled Dee's mug and poured one for myself before sitting down. Dee had that far-away look on her face again, and I knew better than to ask what she was thinking. I said, "I wouldn't worry. They're just covering their bases, trying to figure out where Gordon went after he left Wranglers."

Dee wasn't listening. After a while, she asked, "What do you think that young trooper was doing out there in the garage?"

I said, "He was doing some of that forensic stuff you said they didn't do in the living room."

Another long silence. She said, very quietly, "You think he was looking for fingerprints? Blood, maybe?"

I looked at her sharply.

She met my gaze and said, "If he found blood in my truck, it'll be Shawn Gordon's."

Jeez Louise. I sure hadn't seen that coming. I said, "What the—how the hell did Shawn Gordon's blood end up in your truck?"

She shook her head. "Not now, Naomi."

So I asked, "What are you waiting for?"

She shrugged.

And though I didn't want to do it, I finally said, "Dee. Please. Tell me you didn't kill Shawn Gordon."

She studied my face, like she was trying to decide what to say. Finally, she smiled. "A little bit ago you asked if I was here all night, since I was up so late." She stood up and reached over to open the refrigerator door. Her arm made a graceful arc that would've done Vanna White proud, directing my attention to the top shelf. It was neatly stacked with Ziploc bags of tamales.

"Three dozen," she said. "Nothing like the twenty dozen my sisters and I can make in one of our marathon tamale sessions during the holidays, but not bad. When I couldn't sleep last night, I took some machaca from the freezer. Then I got out the tamale pot and the masa and just cooked the night away."

I'll admit that my next question wasn't the most appropriate one to be asking at that point, but I couldn't help myself. Dee's pork tamales were delicious, but her green corn tamales were legendary. "Is…are some of them green corn?" My mouth was watering.

She nodded. "Some." She took one of the bags out of the refrigerator and reached into a drawer for a container.

"I didn't kill Shawn Gordon," she said, pulling a tamale out of the bag and putting it in the little plastic box. She paused to face me. "The rest of the story will have to wait till Carson shows up."

~ ~ ~

I headed for home after tenderly placing the container holding three green corn tamales on the passenger seat. I was supposed to share them with Kai and Len, and I probably would.

On a Sunday morning in Sage Landing, the church parking lots were full, the stores were closed, and the hangovers, rumor had it, were fierce. A few people like me were out and about, mostly trying to catch up after a busy week.

The news was playing on my car radio, letting me catch the end of an update about the turmoil surrounding the movie production. Like the story I'd seen earlier on Sunday morning TV, this one was heavy on rumor, but there was some actual news as well. The reporter said that, oh, by the way, prominent producer Benjamin Pressfield had been convicted on a drug charge some years ago, and, more recently, so had leading lady Kathy Roberson. I wondered if Carson was hearing all this, wherever he was.

When I passed the post office, I stopped to pick up the mail that had probably piled up in my PO box during the week. Sage Landing didn't have home delivery of mail, so we all had to go inside the post office and retrieve our own. On the one hand, that could be pretty inconvenient sometimes. On the other hand, you almost always ran into someone you knew, and those chance conversations could be great.

As I walked across the parking lot, another car pulled up. When I saw who stepped out of the driver's side, I knew that I wasn't going to be having one of the great conversations.

Back in high school, Ursula Curley—Ursula Begay then—was a queen bee if ever there was one. She was a cheerleader, while I was a typical band nerd. I was mostly beneath her notice, but when she did say anything to me, it was mean and deadly accurate. Like, "Cute shoes, Naomi. Are they your mom's?" Well, the shoes *weren't* cute, and they *were* my mom's. They'd been the only ones by the door when I had to rush out to the school bus with no time to grab shoes from my room. My witty reply at the time was, "Um…," which was all I had the chance to say as she swept past me with her giggling buddies.

After high school, she went away to Flagstaff and almost finished a degree in education. When she came back to town, she married her high school sweetheart, whose family owned the town's only pharmacy. Over the years she'd had lots of chances to be catty. As a master of the back-handed compliment, she was what my mom would call "a piece of work."

Unfortunately, she was also Lew Nez's cousin.

I waved half-heartedly when she looked my way and noticed my outfit. Kai was right, I shouldn't have worn it out in public, but now it was too late.

Ursula wasted no time on pleasantries. She said, "I already called Lew's mom, over in Gallup."

Trying to show polite interest, I said, "Oh? How is she?"

She put her hands on her hips and planted her feet like Wonder Woman on a bad day. "I told her that you've been hanging out with Lew all over town."

I said, "Don't you think that's between Lew and me?"

Clearly, she did not. "You won't get your hooks into him now, any more than you did in high school. He's got a girlfriend in Gallup. Did you know that? Nice girl. Bitter Water clan. You can be sure that Aunt Annie's going to set him straight. Do I need to call your mom, too? Because I will if I have to."

Ursula was turning slightly purple, and I wondered why she was so wound up. Was it still a cheerleader vs. band nerd thing? That would be pretty immature. Was she now super-conservative about clan relationships, like her aunt was? I didn't know. But it didn't matter what her problem was. Because this time, I knew exactly the right thing to say.

Without getting my mail, I walked back to my car and stood beside it to wait for her to pause for breath. When she did, I calmly said, "Ursula, mind your own fucking business."

She stood with her mouth open as I got in the car, gently pulled the door closed, and eased out of the parking lot. She was still standing there when I turned the corner.

When I got home, I put a quarter in the jar.

CHAPTER FOURTEEN

O N Tuesday morning my kids and I arrived "on location," as they say, bright and early, but it wasn't nearly as exciting as we expected. I couldn't even describe it as interesting. Sure, the backdrop was a gorgeous view of the lake and red cliffs. We saw some acting activity, along with cameras that were probably rolling, but it was so far away that we couldn't tell for sure,

We headed downhill toward the action on the beach, but we didn't get far. Yellow caution tape draped across metal stands kept most everyone a hundred feet or more from the actual acting. I could make out two or three actors with speaking parts in the scene and three others who were probably extras. They were surrounded by camera operators, sound-boom guys, and people holding up reflectors that looked like aluminum foil glued to cardboard.

Kai joined a few other high-school students who were milling around near the tape. Len started talking with one of the off-duty camera guys. At loose ends, I headed over to the tent.

This time, the brew I got out of the coffee urn was surprisingly good. Herman Buckmaster, dressed in sort of a white lab coat, was working in the tent with his whole crew, busily putting out breakfast foods and drinks. He and I ignored each other.

After a while, Kathy Roberson came into the tent. She surveyed the tempting variety of sweets on the buffet table before picking up a pitcher of ice water and pouring some into a tall plastic cup. Spotting me at the table, she walked over and said, "Is this more like you thought the movie business would look? All the activity outside, I mean?"

"A little bit," I said. "What I could see from behind the yellow tape."

"This first few days we'll be doing minor scenes, mostly extras and small parts. Gives us a chance to warm up the crew, adjust the equipment and lighting, iron out a lot of things."

"When do the real scenes start?"

"Probably early next week, or on the weekend."

"You'll shoot on the weekend?"

"Usually every day, but only as long as there is good light because we're doing everything outdoors."

"You're in luck," I said. "This time of year, there's plenty of light for at least fourteen hours."

Kathy shook her head. "There's light, maybe, but not good light. The light will only be good this morning for a couple more hours—after that, it'll be way too bright and way too hot. We start as early as we can, shut down mid-day, and pick up again when it cools off."

"Oh? Where will… everyone be able to wait out the heat of the day?" Having a bunch of teenagers hanging out in someone's trailer for a few hours every day seemed like a terrible idea.

She sipped her cool water and said, "The interns will go home after lunch. Their bus starts running tomorrow, and I think we've sent out schedules so the parents will know the times." She smiled suddenly, her eyes focused somewhere behind me. "Well, well, well," she said, "What brings *you* out to Hollywood-on-the-Desert today?"

Turning toward the entrance, I was surprised to see Carson walk in. I was also surprised to see that he'd spent some time getting himself neatly dressed and tidied up from whatever he'd been doing all weekend. He was wearing new leather oxfords, already dusted with the fine pink sand he'd walked across to get to the tent.

"Early for you," I said as he pulled up a chair next to me. "Nice shoes. Did you get the messages on your machine?"

Ignoring my question, he smiled at Kathy. "I have to run things single-handedly these days," he said, "My associate has gone Hollywood."

"Watch out," she said. "Once they get a taste of the bright lights, they never come back."

He turned to me. "Naomi, when I stopped by the office this morning, there was a message for you on the office machine." His slight emphasis on *office* let me know that he didn't want to talk about the messages that Kai left on his home machine—the ones about Dee and the police search. That discussion would have to wait.

"From who?" I asked

"From Lew Nez. He said to call him back."

Well, that was quick, I thought. *Ursula didn't waste a minute, so now Lew's mom has laid down the law.*

Carson went on, "As important as the revival of your high school romance might be, I also got a call this morning from Window Rock."

I said, "Who in Window Rock?"

"Nelson Benally, an attorney with the Navajo Nation Department of Justice." Carson turned to Kathy and went on, "He said they got an anonymous complaint about some of your costumes."

I interrupted, "Wait, what? Why did he call us—I mean, you?"

Carson said, "Funny story. He couldn't get hold of production staff—no phones out here where they're filming—and there wasn't a studio to call, since it's an independent film. So he checked with the Park Service to get contact info from their location permit application. Guess who answered when he called that number?"

Kathy flashed him a smile again. "Uncle Carl's executive assistant. She did the paperwork. She told them that you'd handle any complaints, right?"

Carson didn't answer for what seemed like a long time, even to me, before saying, "Right."

"Billable hours, Mr. Carson," Kathy said brightly. "Anyway, what was the complaint?"

Again, Carson was quiet for quite a while before he said, "Do some of the film's characters have to wear animal skins?"

Kathy frowned.

I prompted, "What are the costumes like?"

Kathy said, "I don't know for sure. I haven't been to the wardrobe trailer yet. What would I be looking for?"

Carson looked at me.

I hesitated. For one thing, I'm no expert on our history or traditions. For another, I know that anyone's traditions can sound strange to outsiders, and I couldn't imagine anyone being more of an outsider than Kathy Roberson was. Still, it seemed like she wanted to know, so I'd do my best to explain.

I said, "Anything resembling the skin of a bear or cougar or wolf. Any predator. That would be a problem."

Kathy said, "Why's that?"

I asked Carson, "You've heard about Skinwalkers?"

He nodded. "A little, sure." He asked Kathy, "Did the topic of Skinwalkers come up in the course of your research for the film?"

"Never heard of them," she said.

That was kind of a relief to hear. I hated to imagine the mess that Hollywood could make of those shadowy figures.

Choosing my words carefully, I said, "The Skinwalker stories are about people who can transform themselves into animals when they want to. Putting on animal skins or skulls and such helps them become the predator whose skin they're wearing."

Kathy asked, "And?"

I said, "In the stories, they… prey on their enemies. And then take their human shape again."

"People believe this?" Kathy asked.

Carson scowled at her. She quickly tried to take it back. "What I mean —I respect—what people believe has to be—we have to—no one should —"

I cut in. "Okay, maybe think of it as a way to explain evil. People do awful things sometimes. Regular people. There isn't any sense to it."

Kathy said, "Like in *The Exorcist*. Demons."

I said, "Sort of. Anyway, it isn't something we talk about, but almost anyone would be uncomfortable wearing skins like that."

Carson said, "The attorney said there'd been protests."

"Not that I've heard about, and I think I would have," Kathy said, sounding annoyed. "Who in the hell called the Navajo government instead of telling Benjamin or me?"

"I don't know," said Carson. "It was second-hand. Benally said that the complaint went to him through the Sage Landing city office. He didn't seem too concerned, but I told him we'd check it out."

That reminded me to ask about Kathy's witch-doctor comment. I said, "As long as we're checking things—cultural things, I mean—I'm wondering about something you mentioned last week."

"Oh? What's that?"

"When you talked about how the movie's a version of *Macbeth*, you said something about using 'witch doctors instead of witches.' Am I remembering that correctly?"

Frowning, she said, "Maybe. I'm too busy to keep track of everything."

"Well, I thought you'd want to know how offensive that would be."

Kathy blinked. "Come again?" She shifted her weight in the chair, swiveling so that she faced Carson directly. "What does she mean, 'offensive'?"

Carson shrugged instead of answering. He looked over at me. Kathy reluctantly shifted her gaze to me, too.

I spoke so quietly that Kathy had to lean over to hear me. "What *she* means—what *I* mean—is that there's no such thing as witch doctors around here. 'Witch doctor' is just a stupid label that white people use. That's what makes it offensive."

She said, "But—"

I held my hand up to get her to stop talking so that I could finish. "Look, you guys are making a big deal about filming way out here on the edge of the Navajo Nation, so it's a safe bet that your audience expects to see some actual Navajo culture."

Kathy's face began to flush, but before she could say anything, Carson added, "If that's not what they'll be seeing, it won't take long for word to get out. Then people will just be looking for the silly stereotypes to laugh at."

I said, "You don't want that, especially if the problems would be pretty easy to fix. Think about hiring someone to advise you."

Kathy sneered. "You, I suppose?"

I forced a laugh. "No, Kathy, I already have a job. But I can help you find someone."

"Christ on a cracker, Naomi. It's art, not a documentary. A little poetic license isn't going to hurt anybody."

Carson let that response hang in the air for a little while. Then, with an edge in his voice, he said, "Unfortunately, that doesn't seem to be the case. That kind of misstep could hurt your project quite a bit."

Steering us back to the question from Window Rock, I said, "Like, using animal pelts in the costumes could cause serious problems with locals in the cast and crew."

Carson took the cue, saying, "Yes, as Naomi said, you don't want that. Please examine the costumes carefully, so that I can assure the Navajo Nation that you aren't forcing people to wear dead predators."

Kathy stood up, leaving her cup on the table. Sighing dramatically, she said, "Fine. What's one more item added to the never-ending list of things I have to do? It'll take a few days. I suppose I'd better get at it." She treated Carson to a strained smile as she headed outside.

Carson said, "I'd better get at it, too." He carefully untangled himself from the flimsy folding chair.

I followed him to the tent's doorway, intending to check on my kids. Instead, I saw Kathy standing very close to a remarkably handsome man a few yards away. After a few seconds, I recognized him.

My daughter broke away from her group and joined us. "Mom, that's Hamilton O'Neill talking to Ms. Roberson," she whispered.

"We noticed," I said.

"Mr. Pressfield told us about him this morning," she said. "Where's Len? He should get a shot of the two of them together for the piece I'm writing." She spotted her brother among the camera operators at the far reaches of the set.

I reached out and took her arm before she could shout to get his attention. "Len 's too far away to hear you, and you shouldn't be yelling while they're trying to film."

She seemed disappointed, so I said, "Let's go meet the star."

Her face lit up. Carson's didn't. "You can't interrupt like that," he said.

"Watch me," I said over my shoulder.

Kathy saw us coming and leaned over to say something to O'Neill. By the time we got over to them, she and the distinguished actor were both facing us. In full view of the interns clustered near the yellow tape, she introduced Kai first, which meant that Kai would be a high-school celebrity before sunset.

We managed to refrain from asking for autographs and instead acted like we belonged there. After agreeing that yes, the lake sure was beautiful, and damn, the desert sure was blazing hot, we excused ourselves. I rejoined Carson and watched Kai taking her time to stroll back to her admiring friends.

As he headed for his truck, Carson said, "If you don't mind, I'd like you to spend some time over here tomorrow morning."

I said, "That suits me fine. I like being able to keep an eye on the kids. What do you want me to do while I'm here?"

Carson gazed over at Kathy and her new co-star as they entertained the people gathered around them. "I don't need you to do anything in particular, just hang out here for a while. We need to figure out what's going on."

～ ～ ～

The kids and I stayed at the location till it got too hot for filming to continue. When we got back to town, I dropped them off at the community pool and headed to the office, where the phone rang before I even had a chance to sit down.

"Is Carson there?" Peggy asked.

"Hello to you, too," I said. "No, he isn't—wait, there's a note here on my computer screen. He'll be—it says he'll be here in a half-hour or so. Want me to have him call you?"

"You're the one I want to talk to. I wanted to do it when he wasn't around."

"Well, okay. What's up?"

"I have a personal question. Mostly personal. I mean it could turn out to be police business, I guess."

Sitting down slowly behind the desk, I cautiously said, "That sounds a little scary, but go ahead."

"Did Carson ever tell you where he was that weekend?"

I didn't have to ask which weekend she meant. "No, he didn't. Not a word." I also didn't know where he'd been this past weekend, but I kept that to myself.

"We know where his credit card was," she said. "It was used in a motel in Flagstaff for both Saturday and Sunday night." She sounded peeved.

"How do you know that?"

"I made computer inquiries to the Flagstaff police, among others."

"Computer inquiries? Computers can talk to other computers?" I asked. I was sure that my computer couldn't do that.

"Police computers can," she said. "We have a Hayes modem. Most of the departments in the state have them now. It lets our computers exchange information over regular telephone lines. Like Telex, but for words. We can type questions to each other, send files and documents."

"That should speed things up," I said.

"Yeah, maybe. Anyway, Carson is a person of interest in this murder, so that gave me a reason to ask for help from Flagstaff."

Not a very good reason, I thought, but I could see where she was coming from. I said, "And they told you he was in a motel?"

"Yeah, and they did some follow-up."

"What kind of follow-up?" I asked, as if her tone of voice hadn't already given me the answer.

"They found out he wasn't alone."

I said, "How do you feel about that?" which made me sound like a psychologist in a TV sitcom.

Peggy said, "It's none of my business," which had nothing at all to do with her feelings.

Trying to be funny, I said, "Well, it wasn't me."

"Don't think I didn't check on that," she said. "But you don't know anything about what he was doing that weekend?"

"I don't," I said. "Sorry."

"Yeah, me too. I hoped—well, never mind. Thanks anyway."

Hanging up after finishing the call with Peggy reminded me that I was supposed to call Lew, and my heart sank. Then I got mad. Was his mom still telling him who he could hang out with? Whom, I mean?

I fished around in my pencil drawer for his business card and called the shop, telling myself that whatever he said, I wouldn't let it get me down. Life's too short to get upset about meddling old ladies who listen to their mean nieces and interfere with their sons' social lives.

After my third try with no answer, I left a note for Carson, locked up, and walked over to Lew's shop. *Might as well get it over with*, I thought. When I got there, I could see why he wasn't answering the phone. Several people were working at computers, and Lew moved from one to the other, answering questions as fast as one person could manage. I spun around to leave, but he saw me through the glass door. His face lit up so sweetly that I blushed, and he motioned me in.

"Naomi, hello!" he said, taking both my hands in his. Speaking to the room in general, he said, "I'll be a minute," as he dropped my right hand and gestured toward the little office in the back. He kept hold of my left hand.

"Lew…" I started, as soon as he closed the door behind us.

"Hey, how about a hike?" he said.

"A hike? Now?"

"I wish, but we're swamped here in the shop. And it's too hot out there anyway. No, I was thinking tomorrow, in the morning while it's still cool."

"Um, okay. Listen, your mom—"

"I know. We'll talk. But right now I have to get back to those folks out there. Pick you up at five o'clock tomorrow morning?"

"Looking forward to it," I said.

He squeezed my hand, which he'd been holding the whole time, and said, "Not as much as I am." He kissed me on the cheek, opened the door, and ushered me out.

~ ~ ~

When I got back to the office, Carson's truck was in the parking lot. There was also a new silver Mercedes sedan parked beside it. I walked in and saw that the door to Carson's inner office was open, revealing an attractive woman sitting in one of the guest chairs. Both the upmarket car outside and the cut of her navy-blue suit suggested that she was too classy to be seeking our legal services, so I wondered what she was doing there.

Before I could sit down at my desk, I heard Carson call out, "Is that you, Naomi?"

"Yes, Mr. Carson."

He lowered his voice and spoke to his guest. "She never really calls me that."

I walked on back and stood in the doorway so I could see him.

He said, "I want you to meet someone." I couldn't tell if he was saying that to me or to the smiling woman who was now looking up at me with great interest.

The woman stood up, stepping toward me and extending her hand. I shook it softly, and she said, "Very happy to meet you. I'm Eleanor Carson."

The name certainly had my attention. "Pleased to meet you," I said. "I'm Naomi Manymules, Mr. Carson's paralegal."

"She's being too modest," Carson said. "She actually runs the place." He went on, "Naomi, Eleanor is a lawyer from Phoenix. We've known each other for a long time. If you ever need—"

Eleanor interrupted, "I can't let the old goat keep you in suspense— I'm Grant's ex-wife."

I laughed. "Well, thanks for that. I would've been wondering about that until I had the chance to worm it out of him. What kind of law are you in?"

"She's in private practice like us," Carson said. "But corporate law, none of this tawdry criminal stuff."

"True, but I used to be a prosecutor," Eleanor said.

"That's how we met. We worked together, quite the scandal for a while." Carson was obviously enjoying himself.

I was studying our guest as we spoke. A woman of maybe mid-forties who looked younger at first. Auburn hair, expensive cut. Her suit was tailored to her figure, proving Carson right about the suits that corporate lawyers wear.

My train of thought was interrupted when the front door opened and Peggy walked in, sidearm and all. Under the circumstances, I sort of wished that she weren't armed, but if one's employer *will* date officers of the law.... "Hello, Peggy!" I said a little loudly, since Carson couldn't see her from where he sat.

"Carson here?" she said while staring past me at Eleanor through the inner door. I was sure she'd seen his little truck outside. And the shiny Mercedes. And she sure as hell was seeing the striking woman in front of her.

"I'm here, Peggy. Come on in," Carson called out.

Eleanor's expression registered a little surprise, along with maybe a little embarrassment. She was cool, though. "Naomi, let's go over that contract out in your office," she said. She stepped past me and then past Peggy, giving her a quick smile as she exited Carson's office. I was impressed.

Peggy walked into Carson's office and closed the door. I put my finger up to my lips and gestured at the walls and ceiling. Eleanor glanced up at the ceiling, placed a hand on our flimsy wall, and winked. She was one quick-thinking lawyer. I started my computer.

From inside Carson's office, we heard Peggy say, "You're not easy to find these days."

My computer warmed up and gave me a blank blue screen. I called up a document that I had in there so that when Peggy came back through it would appear that Eleanor and I had been consulting instead of eavesdropping.

We heard Peggy go on, "Where were you that night—the night when Shawn Gordon was murdered?"

That was certainly direct, and I wondered how my boss would answer as the silence stretched out longer than I imagined it could. Were they having a stare-down? Had they started writing back and forth to avoid being overheard?

Finally, I heard Carson say, "Who's asking? A friend or a police officer?"

Good question, I thought.

Peggy snapped, "Why would that make a difference? The answer should be the same, shouldn't it? You were where you were, no matter who's asking."

So, not a friend asking.

I knocked on Carson's door and opened it. "Eleanor and I are going out to the Lunker Room. Maybe you could join us later?" See, I wanted to give Carson a chance to make introductions and get everyone on the same page. I thought I was helping.

"Eleanor?" Peggy said, staring at me and then at my boss. "Eleanor Carson?"

I saw that I may have made a mistake. Apparently, Peggy knew more about Eleanor Carson than I did.

CHAPTER FIFTEEN

Here's a remarkable thing about waking kids up in the morning. On a school day, you can't drag them from their beds, and when they do crawl out of their rooms, the air crackles with their bitter complaints. But when they have their non-school reasons to rise and shine at four in the morning, they'll sleep in their clothes so that they can jump up and dash out the door in time to catch the intern bus, with nary a word and no foot-dragging at all. Naturally, that means that their mother has to get up at dark o'clock, too, but that was fine with me on this particular day. I had my own reason for rising and shining extra early.

By the time Lew came to pick me up, I'd been ready for half an hour. I even had two canteens filled with ice cubes and water. When he pulled up into the driveway right after sunrise, I dashed out so that he didn't have to come to the door.

"Good morning," I said as I hopped in.

"Good morning to you, too," he said, "Your house hasn't changed at all."

I took that as a compliment because I'd been taking care of it myself since my folks moved out and the kids and I moved in, about ten years before. "I'm glad, thanks," I said.

"I thought we'd go down the ropes this morning, if that's okay with you," he said as he backed out of my driveway.

"Wonderful," I said. "I haven't been out there for a couple of years." Navigating the trail along the ropes down to the river was more like mountain climbing than hiking, but it was something we all used to do pretty regularly. I was probably about five years old when my dad took me the first time. We caught a huge rainbow trout that day, and I laughed at him because he had to carry it up the ropes. I took my kids, too, when they were old enough to pay attention to the trail. It wasn't dangerous if you were careful, but it wasn't a place to goof around, either. The shale surface was slippery underfoot, and the ropes were spiked into the cliffside for a reason.

Lew and I were both quiet as he drove, shielding our eyes from the bright sun sitting at the horizon and shining directly through the windshield. He turned the car northward, getting the sun out of our eyes, and continued the conversation. "So, where are they living now? Your folks, I mean?"

"In the Middle East. They moved from Turkey to Saudi." My dad had worked construction on big commercial projects all my life. He started out right here in Sage Landing, working on the dam and then on the power plant. Once those were done, he stayed with the international contractor, moving all over the world. He and my mom were the most adventurous people I knew.

"Your dad's still doing high-iron work?"

"Not as much as he'd like. Right now he's stuck working on roads." My dad loved working up in the air with iron and concrete like he did for years when the dam was going up here in Sage Landing, but my mom was happier when he worked closer to the ground.

Lew grinned. "I don't think it matters where people are. It seems like we always want to be somewhere else."

"Not me," I said. "Sage Landing suits me."

"Better than Gallup suits me, I imagine."

I was about to ask how Gallup suited his mom when he pulled the car over and parked.

"Is it still okay to park the car here?" he asked.

"As far as I know," I said. The trail we were heading for wasn't approved by the Park Service, and they didn't like how people went down the ropes, but they didn't have anyone towed or arrested or anything. They did cut the ropes down occasionally to discourage the use of the trail, but within a day or two new ones would take their place.

I grabbed the canteens and handed one to Lew as we walked across the sandy mesa to where the trail started.

When we got there, Lew stood back and said, "You lead the way, okay?"

"Okay," I said. "While we're walking, you can tell me about your girlfriend. Bitter Water clan, I hear."

"Yeah, I heard that you got an earful from Ursula," he said, sounding exasperated. "Sorry about that. My cousin is not a happy person."

"I won't argue with that, but you didn't answer my question."

"Anita's not my girlfriend. She's a good friend, and my mom likes her a lot, but we're not... romantically involved." He was still walking behind me, so I couldn't see his face, but he was speaking very carefully.

"*Yet?*" I asked.

"What do you mean?" he said.

"I mean, I'm hearing 'yet' in your voice when you say she's not your girlfriend and so on. She's not your girlfriend *yet*, and you're not romantically involved *yet*."

Lew surprised me by laughing. I stopped.

"What?" I said.

"You. And Mom. And Ursula. You all think you can see my thoughts, but you can't. Hey, let's get going or we'll roast by the time we climb back up."

I started walking again. "Okay. No more mind reading. Seen any good movies lately?"

"Come on, Naomi. I didn't mean that we couldn't...you know, *talk*."

"Okay, let's talk about that gray area you told me about. Have you found out any more?"

"I haven't been able to find any more numbers. Everything was hidden pretty well."

"Lew, we're not talking about some criminal mastermind here, some... accounting genius. No. We're talking about Herman Effing Buckmaster. He's a jerk, and I wouldn't put lawbreaking past him, but I don't think he's that smart."

His answer was quick and firm. "I saw what I saw. And it's obvious to me that Buckmaster deliberately tried to destroy those discs before Marybeth could catch on to what he was doing."

I took a sip from my canteen. Looking back at Lew, I said, "Marybeth would've smacked him silly if she found out he was messing with her numbers."

He unscrewed the lid from his own canteen. After he took a long drink, he said, "Yeah, the police would be the least of his worries."

We headed on down the trail, and Lew continued, "He didn't realize that the discs could be repaired. He doesn't know that Marybeth gave them to me to fix. If I'm right, I'm the only one who's seen the real accounts."

I thought about that. I said, "If you *are* right, how much crime are we talking about?"

"You mean in dollars?"

"Yeah, how bad? How much money?"

By now we were reaching the bottom of the canyon. The river was running high, leaving almost no beach, so we stood side by side on a narrow spit of sand right next to the river.

Lew peered down into deep, clear water. "Remember how badly we wanted to jump in after hiking down on a hot day?"

"Oh, I sure do." My parents always warned me to stay out of the water, every time I took this hike. *It's too cold,* they'd say, *the current's too fast.* I was sure I could handle it, but I figured someone would tell my mom if I so much as dipped a toe into the water. I fussed about it during most of every hike, right up until the day that Steve Sunderland jumped in to grab his hat when it blew off, and I saw with my own eyes how the forty-degree water seized all his muscles into one big body cramp. Almost helpless in the current, he barely made it back to where we could drag him back up on shore. We covered him with sun-warmed sand till he stopped shaking. Lesson learned.

Lew was still watching the water, probably remembering the same thing.

I repeated my question. "Um, Lew? How bad? How much money?"

He glanced over at me. "About half a million dollars."

"Shit!" I said. "Of Sage Landing's money?"

"That's what I think."

I leaned back against the rough sandstone of the canyon wall. "So, what do we do now?"

"We?" he asked.

"Well, yeah. We're gonna do something about it, aren't we?" I punched him lightly on the arm. "I can't have Herman Effing Buckmaster ripping off my city. What can we do?"

He sloshed the water around in his canteen, now about half-full, and made sure the lid was on tight. "I need to check some other records to figure that out."

"Records on Sage Landing city computers?" I asked.

He shook his head. "There wouldn't still be anything on the computers themselves."

"Where, then?"

"In paper files, maybe. Physical ledgers. Something non-electronic."

"Paper files where? In Herman's desk?"

"There's a secure room in the city building that they call 'the vault,' but it isn't a vault. I heard Marybeth mention it to one of her co-workers."

I pushed myself away from the wall and stood up straight. "I know the room," I said, nodding. "It's not all that secure." One of my jobs in my pre-professional life was with a local cleaning service. The city of Sage Landing was one of the clients. I remembered when an area in the city building had been fitted with extra locks for security. "And you think that what you're looking for is probably in there."

"I think it'll be like Sherlock Holmes's dog in the nighttime—I'd be looking for what *isn't* there. If Buckmaster tried to destroy the records on the discs, he probably also got rid of the paper records. All I need to do is see if there's anything like that in the room."

I laughed. "We need to pull a caper but not a heist, is that it?"

He laughed, too. "Right. *Ocean's Eleven* we are not. Ready to hike back up to the car?"

I headed up the trail. It was still shady down there in the shadow of the canyon wall, but the sun was climbing higher and it was getting warm. We walked in silence for a few minutes.

The trail was getting steep when, from behind me, Lew said, "You were saying that the secure room wasn't actually secure?"

"Yes…no…it isn't very secure."

"How do you know?"

"I worked as a cleaner in those buildings during the time that they closed off that room."

"It wasn't always there?"

"No, remember? Back when you lived here? The police station, city offices, and library were all close together, but they were separate buildings. A few years ago, they filled in the spaces between them by building new rooms. Then they ran a new hallway across the back of all three."

By now I'd reached the first of the ropes tacked into the rock, stretching over one hundred feet up the face. I rested my hand on it, just in case, as I navigated a steeper part of the trail.

I looked behind me, and Lew was doing the same. He said, "That's when they added the secure room?"

I faced forward again and resumed my climb. "Not exactly," I said. "The room was already there. It was a wide hallway that they enclosed."

"I'm not sure I get the picture."

"The short version is that I know how to get into the room. Theoretically. I've never had a reason to try it."

"Until now," Lew said.

We climbed on in silence till we got to the top of the trail and walked side-by-side toward the car.

Still thinking about the caper, I said, "I'll need to double-check a few things tomorrow. Can you meet me super early Friday morning?"

"How early is super early?"

"Four-thirty in the morning. We can meet at your shop."

Lew unlocked and opened the passenger door with a flourish. "Can't wait."

~ ~ ~

When I got to the film location later that morning, things were bustling. There was no yellow tape up to hold people back today, so I was able to get a little closer to the camera set-up than the day before. Len was standing with his camera a few feet from the official camera operator. Kathy and Pressfield were nowhere in sight, and neither was Kai.

Hamilton O'Neill was in a costume made of burlap or something like that. The fabric was rough, but the garment was carefully tailored to make him resemble an oversized action figure. He was carrying a spear and a short ax. His feet were shod with high-top moccasins without any decoration. He'd been clean-shaven when I met him the day before, but now a full beard was entirely convincing as it covered a lot of that handsome face.

The scene they were shooting involved some sort of dialogue between O'Neill and another actor. I was too far away to hear the lines very well, but I sure heard the director as he kept shouting "cut" every minute or so and barking orders about restarting the scene. Watching all that got tedious after a few minutes, so I walked back up to the big tent.

Once inside, it took only half a minute to realize that something wasn't right in the room. It sounded like the various small groups of crew and extras were whispering rather than talking normally. Kai and Molly were part of one small group, probably the writers. The faces I could see were all uncomfortable. I began to listen to the other sounds in the tent and realized that a very loud argument was going on outside, between the big tent and the trailers next to it. John Rice and his minion were seated near that side of the tent, and they were giving the voices outside their full attention.

The loudest voice was Kathy Roberson's. She was ranting, and she wasn't letting whoever she was talking to say very much. The other voice, not as loud and not nearly as frequent, could've been Pressfield's. From where I stood, I couldn't understand more than an occasional word. The other listeners in the tent were closer to the argument than I was and probably had a much better idea of what her problem was.

Eventually, Kathy stopped yelling, and the people inside started speaking at a more normal volume. I went back outside and saw Benjamin

Pressfield walking briskly through the spectators toward the action that was being filmed. He waved his arms, and the actors all turned to face him. The director watched as the producer continued to gesture wildly. The cameraman tilted the camera up and put a lens cover on it. Len was still standing next to him, watching as the rest of the crew started packing up. Then he walked uphill toward me.

"They're shutting down for the day," he said glumly. "Mr. Pressfield's orders."

Poor Len was disappointed, but I was bursting with curiosity. I said, "Let's go get you a soda."

As we went back toward the big tent, Len said, "It's a stupid business."

"What business?"

"The movie business. They never really get anything done. Everything is in little short pieces, and they do them over and over. It's so boring."

"They're just getting started," I said. "I'm sure it'll get better."

"I don't think so." Len stopped walking and touched my arm so that I would stop, too. "Like, they were never going to get it right today, not that scene anyway."

"Really? What was the problem?"

Len lowered his voice. "Mr. O'Neill couldn't remember his lines, and when he did, he slurred. Mom, I think he was drunk."

Len was no fool. I was pretty sure he'd be able to tell when someone was under the influence. But he probably shouldn't be saying so where other people could hear him. "Well, let's not jump to conclusions," I said.

"It's not only me. The cameraman said it when he was packing up the equipment. The sound guy on the boom mic said so, too."

We entered the tent, which was filling up by then. I motioned Len over to an empty table as far from others as I could manage. After we sat down, I glanced toward John Rice and saw Kathy sitting there with him and Fred. The three of them were leaning in close to each other in what looked like a quiet but intense conversation. Everyone else seemed to be ignoring them. I didn't blame them, because I didn't want to make eye contact with Kathy, either. Even that brief glimpse had given me the impression that she was off-center somehow.

"I don't know, Len," I said when he'd opened his soda. "Seems to me that the movie business is the exact opposite of boring."

"No," he sighed, world-weary and jaded. "It isn't." I was pretty sure that I was hearing the voices of the camera operators and grips and boom-mic guys that he'd been listening to for a couple of days by then.

I laughed. "Are you kidding? There's nothing but drama going on, whether the cameras are rolling or not."

He took a long gulp of the soda and set the can down firmly, looking for all the world like a cowboy who had just come in off the dusty trail. Patiently, he explained, "Maybe the movie is exciting when it's done, sure. But making films is a real pain in the you-know-what."

He saved himself a quarter there.

At the tent's other end, the group at the writers' table all got up, and Kai came over to join Len and me.

"Wow! That got a little spicy, didn't it?" she said.

"What did?" Len asked.

"Oh yeah, you were out watching the shoot. Well, right behind the tent there was a loud fight between Ms. Roberson and Mr. Pressfield. Ms. Roberson was literally shrieking. *Literally*. It was embarrassing as…as anything," Kai said, also carefully sidestepping a language fine, making me suspect that my teens were not so careful when I wasn't around. "She was mad about a script change, but Molly said changes like that happen over and over on a Pressfield film."

"What's the problem?" Len asked.

"Molly said he cut most of Kathy's lines for today's scenes, making everything about Mr. O'Neill's character instead of being about Ms. Roberson's like they were in *Macbeth*. Oops! I mean the Scottish play." She looked around to make sure no one had heard her.

"Ah," I said, "I can see how that would cause hard feelings."

"It wasn't just hard feelings, Mom. She yelled that she would sue him. And then she screamed that she'd get him beat up or something. She was, like, out of control."

"Cool," Len said.

Kai lowered her voice. "That's not all."

"What else?" Len asked, eager to be in the know.

"Kathy stormed back in here and got into it with those guys." She gestured with her chin, pursing her lips in the direction of John Rice and Fred. "We overheard that too."

I interrupted her. "First, I think you should stick to calling her Ms. Roberson." Kai knew better than to argue, and I went on. "Second, you should be careful about eavesdropping." *No matter how useful it can be*, I silently added, knowing that sometimes half of my job depended on my overhearing something or other.

"We weren't eavesdropping, Mom. Believe me, we weren't trying to listen. Maybe she thought she was talking low enough, but she wasn't."

"Anyway," Len said, "what did Ms. Roberson say?"

Before I could intervene, Kai said, "She told them, she said, 'Let's make the fucker an offer he can't refuse!'" She looked at me quickly, hand to her heart, opening her eyes wide. The very picture of innocence, she said, "That's not *me* swearing, Mom. I'm reporting."

"Still going to cost you," Len said.

"And you know where you can stick *that*, Len."

"Enough," I said.

"And then," Kai continued, "The older guy reached over and took hold of Ms. Roberson's arm and shook his head. Mr.—"

"Mr. Rice," I said.

"Mr. Rice said something real quiet while he was shaking his head, and she pulled her arm away. Then she tried to hit him, but the other guy stopped her."

"Cool," Len said again.

"And Molly and everybody got up and kind of drifted away."

I raised my eyebrows at Len, thinking that Kai's stories had just made my point about the drama of filmmaking. He shrugged and went to get another soda. When he sat back down, I said, "Well, that's a lot to take in. Remember what we said about—"

"Hollywood people," they said in unison. Kai said, "Mom, it's fine. We're fine. We'll remember, won't we, Len?"

Len nodded, looking toward the long table that was now being loaded with food for lunch. "We remember about Hollywood people. Don't worry."

I tapped my watch and said, "I have to go. Want a ride home?"

They didn't even pretend to think about it, and I couldn't blame them, given the options. On one hand, a catered lunch among cast and crew on a movie location, followed by a boisterous trip on the intern bus with their friends. On the other, a car ride with their mother. It was no contest at all.

~ ~ ~

I got to the office a little after one. Carson wasn't there. As far as I could tell, he hadn't been in. The phone tape was full of messages from Peggy, all demanding that Carson call her at the station.

Before I could figure out what to do about that, Peggy walked in the door.

"Where the hell is Carson?" she demanded.

"No idea. What's wrong?"

"Well, he's got a problem. We've got Dr. Moreno in custody at the station."

I thought back to the search they'd done on Sunday—was that just three days ago? Time sure flies when you're trying to fend off a client's murder charge while planning a pre-dawn caper with an old flame. "Is this about... about what they found in Dee's truck?"

"I can't answer that, Naomi. Find Carson. Don't bother with his place or the motels. I've checked."

"Did you check—"

Peggy cut me off. "Eleanor Carson's whereabouts was the first thing I checked. I couldn't find her, either."

"Oh," I said.

"FYI," Peggy said, "She hasn't checked in to any motel in town. Ever."

Since that wasn't police business—or mine, for that matter—I said, "I'll check with Abe Bingham. He's between construction projects, so maybe they've been out fishing or something." Abe ran a construction company, doing commercial jobs all over the area. He was also a plig, which was the local term for someone who practices polygamy. There was a community of such folks barely over the state line, and they were among the most interesting people I knew. Abe and Carson had bonded over boats and fishing, not to mention a tendency to make their own rules.

After Peggy left, I didn't have any trouble getting in touch with Abe's head wife, Henrietta. She said that Abe hadn't seen Carson, and she was in a position to know— she ran an organized household, as Abe had told us before she joined his other two wives in the family. Rather than making more calls all over town, I left a note on Carson's desk, locked up, and went over to the police station myself.

When I parked in front of the police station, Carson's pickup was already there. Inside, he and Chief Rodriguez were talking in the lobby.

Rodriguez led us to a room at the end of the hall. He opened the door, and we went in to join Peggy and Dee, along with two plain-clothes cops I didn't know. Rodriguez followed us in as well, so that made seven people at the table, along with two tape recorders.

Centered on the table was one plastic bag with a turquoise bandana inside. Even from several feet away, I could see that the cloth had blood on it. A lot of blood.

CHAPTER SIXTEEN

W ITH the push of some buttons, Mike got the tapes rolling. These weren't cassette tapes, but big ones—reel to reel, and they were turning slowly. That seemed like bad news. We'd be here for hours.

Or maybe not. Carson shut it down by saying, "I haven't had an opportunity to consult with my client today. She will answer no questions until we have spoken with her in private."

Without comment, Mike punched the buttons again and picked up the bag with the bandana. Everyone but Dee, Carson, and me headed for the door. I looked around for a two-way mirror. There wasn't one, but I still wondered if our conversation would be "overheard" from a nearby room.

Peggy could tell what I was thinking and said, "It's a secure room," on her way out. She stopped next to my boss and added, "As you are well aware, *Mr. Carson*." Her voice was loaded with stuff that she wasn't saying. I was curious about what she meant, but I wasn't going to ask. Neither of them would've told me anyway.

When we were alone and the door was closed, Carson said, "What have they got, Dee?"

She waited until the sounds from the hall faded. Then she said, "I don't know, but I can tell you what was in that bag."

I rummaged around in my purse and got out a spiral notepad and a pen.

"Okay," Carson said. "The bloody bandana."

Dee went on. "It was crumpled, so you couldn't see it well, but it's printed with college logos. I had it in my truck and remember giving it to the actor that night."

"That's a start. What else?" Carson asked. "Don't leave anything out. They can't hear us."

Dee glanced up at the ugly acoustic ceiling. "It's going to look bad to them."

Carson said, "Everything does when they're zeroing in on you. They ignore everything and everybody else. We can decide later what to tell them, but I can't operate if I don't know everything."

She clasped her hands together tightly on the tabletop.

"Dee?" Carson said, more gently than I thought possible.

"Yes, okay. Well, Naomi said she offered him a ride, and he didn't take it. That would've been a few minutes before I saw him walking across the parking lot."

Writing quickly, I asked, "This was after you talked to Wanda and me outside at your truck?"

"Right. After you and Wanda went back inside, I sat there in my truck, trying to calm down. I was mad at myself for overreacting inside—we talked about that, remember? It wasn't very smart behavior for a person in my position."

Carson said nothing, waiting for her to go on. I studied my notes.

Dee spread her hands on the tabletop and drummed her fingers for a little while before continuing the story. Finally, she said, "The guy was wandering around the parking lot like he was looking for someone. He looked about twelve years old, especially when he took off that silly hat and I could see that he was bleeding—you know how a scalp cut bleeds all over the place."

Carson said, "Boxing first-aid 101, I suppose?"

She went on. "Anyway, I knew that he was bleeding because of our scuffle. The bandana was on the front seat of the truck—they sell them at the college bookstore, you know. I handed it to him through the window. He held it to the back of his head. I asked him if he needed a ride, and he said yes."

All I could think was, *what a foolish thing for a smart woman to do.* Carson seemed to be thinking the same thing, because he said, "That explains why you wouldn't say where you went after leaving the bar, I guess, but why in the world would you do that?"

Moments passed. Then Dee said, "I didn't think first. It was just what popped into my mind. I'd hurt the guy, he needed a ride, it seemed like the thing to do."

There was another long silence. Carson prompted, "It didn't seem dangerous to you?"

She gave a short laugh. "No. Strangely enough, it didn't. Like, when I told him to go ahead and get in, he started to climb into the back of the truck." Her eyes went from Carson to me. "The back of the truck is not for passengers. I cringe whenever I see someone riding like that, especially kids. That's the worst. Or a dog."

I nodded, agreeing with her, but Carson just waited.

Eventually she went on. "Anyway, I scooted over to unlock the passenger door for him, and he waited till I got settled back into the driver's seat before he got in. He stuck to his side of the cab. He said he was staying at the marina resort, so I headed that way. But when we were about halfway there, he said no, he shouldn't go back there because he'd be in big trouble with his boss—that's what he said, no name. He said he'd made a fool of himself and his boss was pissed and left the bar without him."

I flipped a page and hurried to catch up as she started speaking faster.

"He asked if I knew anyplace else he could maybe spend the night without anyone seeing him. I didn't like the sound of that. Too much like a certain kind of line I'd heard before, more than once. It struck me as funny that the guy might still be trying to pick me up."

Carson cut in, "But then you thought of *another* place where he could spend the night."

Dee looked embarrassed. "Sorry, yes, I didn't want him at my place, because he'd get the wrong idea. The boat was someplace where he wouldn't have to walk far when he was ready to go back to the resort."

"Naomi's been known to use my boat for much the same purpose in the past."

I smacked my notebook shut. "Damn it, Carson. That wasn't my idea. And it was only a few days. Besides, it worked out okay," I said. A few months before, I'd stumbled across a scruffy but appealing criminal on Carson's boat. It was Three-Steps—the man, not the dog. He'd broken into the *Deep Inn* to hide from the mob for several days. True, I hadn't told Carson about it right away, but that was totally different from this situation.

"It must've worked out better than this," Dee said. "I haven't heard of any dead bodies turning up on the *Deep Inn* before."

"Came close to being our own dead bodies at one point," Carson said. "But that's a story for another time."

"Bygones," I said. I reopened the notebook, holding my pen at the ready. "Then what?"

Dee watched my pen as I took notes, speaking slowly enough that I could write down what she said, almost word for word. "I drove the guy to the dock and walked him out to the boat and helped him aboard, bandana and all. I remembered where you kept the key to the cabin door. Before I let him in, I pointed out the lights of the resort so he'd know where to go the next day. I didn't go in myself. I got off the boat right after that and drove home."

"That's it?" I asked.

"That's it. I never saw him again."

"Did you happen to see a wrench?" Carson asked.

Dee's face was blank. "A wrench?"

"A pipe wrench. It's a wrench with...."

"I know what a *pipe wrench* is," she said, getting impatient. "Was he killed with a wrench?"

Carson said, "Maybe."

"No, Carson. No, I did not see a pipe wrench. Nor a pipe. Nor a wrench of any other description. That's not to say that they weren't there, but I didn't notice them. Good enough?"

"Fine," he said. "But you'll want to phrase that a little differently."

"*Fine,*" Dee said. "So now what?"

"My advice is to tell them everything. Tell them what happened that night. If you withhold anything, they'll figure it out. They've probably pieced most of it together already."

"Will the pieces add up to my luring him to your boat and killing him?" Dee said.

"No. You gave him your bandana, drove him out to the boat, and let him inside. That's all they've got. Sure, they'll try to make more out of it. I won't let them. I'll be with you every time they question you. Starting now." He stood up and went to the door to call the others back in.

"Carson," I said. "I need to get home."

"Right," he said. "You should leave after they've come back into the room but before they have the chance to sit down. Then walk on out of the station and don't get into any conversations."

That's exactly what I did. For me, the workday was over.

～ ～ ～

On Thursday morning, the kids jumped out of bed in the early hours again. They said that filming would resume, even though it got shut down suddenly the day before. I wasn't so sure, so I pulled on some sweats, slipped on my old Keds, and clipped a leash to the dog's collar. I was darned if she was going to keep on snoring while I walked the kids over to the bus by myself. Sure enough, all the other intern kids were waiting there in the parking lot as the bus pulled in. After seeing them off, the dog and I headed home to sleep a little bit more.

Fully refreshed, I opened the office at nine. Carson wasn't in yet, naturally, so I called Lew's shop and verified that I'd meet him the next morning unless he'd changed his mind. He was still determined to break into the not-so-secure room, but he said he had an important question.

"Shoot," I said.

"Not funny," he said. "Okay, this sounds silly, but take it seriously. What do you think we should wear?"

"That's a pretty good question. Let me think." Here I'll admit that until he asked me about it, I'd been picturing us moving silently through the predawn streets, dressed in something like...ninja outfits, for goodness sake. In my mind's eye, we were even wearing black hoods and gloves. Sadly, I had to give all that up in favor of something more ordinary.

I said, "Regular summer clothes, I guess. Shorts and a t-shirt or something like that. Jeans, maybe. So we don't raise any more suspicions than we need to."

"Got it. Leave the black turtleneck at home?"

I had to laugh. He really did know me pretty well.

The smile was still on my face when Carson came into the office at a little past ten.

"So?" I asked as he lowered himself into the visitor chair next to my desk. He hadn't shaved, and he'd probably fished the polo shirt and rumpled chinos off his closet floor. As my dad would've said, he looked like he'd been "rode hard and put away wet." I don't know if my dad has ever ridden an actual horse, but he loves using folksy sayings.

It turns out that after I left Dee's interrogation the day before, it took a very unexpected turn. She wasn't asked to describe the events of that Saturday night as we expected. Instead, Mike tried to question her about a previous arrest in Tucson.

"A *what*?" I yelped. "*What* previous arrest? For *what*?"

Carson leaned back in the chair, exasperation written all over his face. "Naomi. Jesus. Calm the hell down and listen, would you?"

I folded my hands in my lap.

He waited a good long while before going on, "We already knew that Dee defended herself from an assault on campus, right?"

I nodded silently.

"Well, Mike said after that happened, Dee organized a group of women and men to accompany each other after dark, so there'd always be a group of at least three. So nobody had to go out by themselves at night."

I interrupted, "Typical Dee, isn't it? Organizing something like that?"

Carson said, "You're not wrong, but that does raise the question of whether you want to provide commentary or hear the story."

I clammed up and gestured for him to continue.

"Dee told us that the whole point of the group was for the students to *find safety in numbers*. They weren't vigilantes. She emphasized that. Several times."

The way he said that made it sound like someone might think that they were. Vigilantes, I mean. I kept my eyes on Carson's face but didn't say anything.

He could see what I was thinking and went on quickly. "One night a bunch of them were clowning around off-campus, singing together while walking along the sidewalk. They were stopped by city police, who thought they might be drunk."

"And maybe vigilantes?" I asked.

"No," he said, giving me a strange look. "No, he thought they might be drunk while also being Mexican. Most of them, anyway. Then the cops found a concealed pistol on one guy in the group and took them all in."

I said, "Oh. Oh, no."

Carson said, "Oh, yes, and then Dee argued with the officers. That got her citations for disorderly conduct and resisting arrest. It was a big story on campus and in Tucson papers, so it wasn't hard to dig it up."

"Not when a big Hollywood PR machine is doing the digging," I said. "What happened after she was cited?"

"Suspended fines. Over and done with."

Unless, I thought, years later you're a college president. And a guy grabs you. And you defend yourself. And later the guy turns up dead on your sometime-boyfriend's boat. I knew how that story would go. There was already an article about Dee in the weekly newspaper, complete with a nasty quote from Buckmaster saying she'd been "in a gang." What a jerk. No, I corrected myself—what a dishonest, moneygrubbing, double-dealing, reputation-ruining, dorky-looking jerk.

Carson stood up slowly, scratching the stubble on his chin and heading to the door. With his hand on the doorknob, he said, "Can you go out to the location again today? The wardrobe department is supposed to have a written statement ready for us."

"Sure. I want to check in on the kids anyway. Are we getting the statement about animal skins? Something like, no part of any animal is being harmed—or worn—in the making of the movie, etc.?"

"Let's hope so." He opened the door and left. I had no idea where he was going, and he had no intention of telling me.

~ ~ ~

By the time I got to the movie location, everyone was finishing lunch. I sat down with the kids, who happened to be sitting at the same table, so that they could catch me up before I went over toward the wardrobe trailer. They told me that the morning had been humdrum (my word, not theirs), but the afternoon would be better because the interns all had appointments to talk one-on-one with a crew member. Kai would be talking with one of the experienced scriptwriters. She already had Molly's permission to write the interview up for the *Sage Landing Gazette*. And since, so far, Len was getting away with being treated as if he were one of the interns, he'd be sitting down with a camera operator. I guess no one was checking any roll sheets.

I didn't see Kathy during lunch, but after the kids left the table, she came into the tent and found me. No one else came near us. I figured that anyone who could avoid her was giving her a wide berth.

"Hey, Naomi," she said, "I need your help on something."

Her face was pleasant enough, but she was practically vibrating with a strange sort of energy. I wondered what kinds of things she might ask me for help with. Hook her up with a good-looking guy, maybe? Give her tips on hair products that could cope with the dry, dusty wind here? I was pretty sure she wouldn't be looking for a place to get whatever drugs were making her so squirrely, because it seemed like she had plenty of those. Whatever it was, I also wondered what would happen if I refused. Would she scream at me like she seemed to be doing with everyone else? I didn't want to find out. Besides, she was still a client. And she could help me get that statement from the wardrobe department. I smiled and gestured toward the chair across the table from me. "Happy to help, Kathy. I need something from you, too."

Kathy perched on the very edge of the chair. She gave me a brief but practiced smile, leaning in like she was confessing a deep secret. "We want to host an intimate little party for a few local friends and supporters. Saturday."

"Won't there be filming on Saturday?"

"Well, yes. Some, anyway. Second-unit stuff. The party won't involve many people from the company, so we want to keep it low-key. Under the radar. You understand."

I couldn't tell what help she was asking for. I said, "Sounds nice. Are you looking for a place to have it?"

"Oh, no," Kathy said. "We're going to have it on the big cabin cruiser that Benjamin rented."

That was interesting. I said, "What do you need me to do?"

Kathy sat back in her folding chair and rummaged around in the boxy safari vest that covered most of her outfit. The vest struck me as an odd thing to wear on a hot day, but I didn't pretend to understand Hollywood fashion. She found her cigarettes and lighter in one of its many pockets.

Seeing how I was kind of eyeing the vest, she patted a couple of its pockets again. "You should get one of these, Naomi. It holds everything I need. Now if I can remember what's in which pocket." She laughed and lit her cigarette. After tucking the lighter and cigarettes into a different pocket than the one she'd gotten them out of, she continued. "I need you to help me invite some people in confidence. We don't want to offend anyone who isn't invited."

"Do you want me to tell them the invitation is coming from you, or …" I asked.

"Me and Benjamin, yes."

"Together?" After everything I'd heard the day before, this was kind of a shock.

"Together!" Kathy said brightly. "We're the co-producers, remember?"

I'm sure I showed my skepticism. She waved a perfectly manicured hand in the air, dismissing any suggestion that all was not well in movieland.

"Don't be taken in by our little dramas around here, Naomi. Benjamin and I are working together now. In fact, this little celebration is all about that very thing."

I tried to smile as if I believed her. "Who do you want me to invite?"

"You, of course. And Carson, in case we don't see him between now and then. We'd hate for him to miss it."

"He may not be in town this weekend," I said. "I don't know what his plans are yet." The truth was that I rarely knew much about Carson's plans or whereabouts these days, except that the police expected him to stay in town, but she didn't need to hear about that.

She asked me if I would please try to persuade him.

While she was talking to me, I noticed that Rice's companion, dear old Fred, had taken up a position at a nearby table. The big lug was hard to miss. If the dictionary had an entry for "mob thug," it would feature Fred's picture as a cross between Arnold Schwarzenegger and, I don't know, Bill Murray, maybe. Big and broad, with slick hair and a bad attitude. He seemed to be keeping a close eye on Kathy, or maybe on me. I wondered if he thought I was any kind of threat to her. I glanced around and saw Rice across the tent. He, too, was watching us.

I tuned in again to what Kathy was saying. "And that policewoman, Officer Thomas. She's been very nice to me during all this turmoil."

I dug the notebook and pen out of my purse, in case the list got too long to keep in my head.

Kathy went on, "And Mayor Buckmaster, please. He's in and out around here, and I may not get a chance to talk to him in private."

I wrote that down but crossed Herman Buckmaster off my mental list. I didn't want to talk to him, and I sure didn't want to socialize with him. But I knew that he would be there anyway, because he'd be doing the catering. "Anyone else?" I asked.

She pondered that for a few seconds. "Maybe I'll think of some others for you later. Thanks, though. If you could help me with those, I'd appreciate it."

Well, who doesn't want to help a famous movie star? More to the point, though, who wouldn't be a little afraid to say no to this one?

"No problem," I told her. "And can you maybe get the wardrobe supervisor's statement for me? I'm sure you don't want me crashing around and interrupting important stuff."

"Oh, right," she said, vaguely, "It's probably in the wardrobe trailer. I need to talk to John for a minute. Hold on." She walked over to John Rice's table.

A sneaky idea occurred to me. Saying a silent apology to my kids for fixing to do exactly what I'd warned them not to do, I got up and drifted to the food table. After pouring myself a plastic cup of lemonade, I ambled on out of the tent and circled around to stand on the west side between the tent and the trailers.

Having noted where the poles supporting the tent were placed, I knew exactly where Rice was sitting on the other side of the canvas. I had to pay close attention to my own shadow because the sun, like me, was now to the west of the tent. Still, I got plenty close enough to hear several conversations inside. What I most wanted to hear was anything Rice had to say, either to Kathy or about her. Did he think she was as nuts as I did?

Right away I heard Kathy excuse herself, saying that she had to go over to the wardrobe tent. I hoped that was where she was really going, because I didn't want her coming around to where I was standing. I kept a watchful eye out for her while I listened.

As soon as I stopped hearing Kathy's voice, I heard John Rice's voice clearly. His chair was probably only about five feet away from where I stood.

"What do you think, Fred?" he asked his bodyguard, or whatever Fred's job title was.

"I agree, John, I think she's using them—that'd be my guess, anyway."

"Yeah," Rice said, "me too. What about the other?"

"I'd guess probably she does, but it's not in the vest. I've had a good look at it from several angles."

Rice was quiet for a few seconds; then he continued, "Well, you'd know if anyone would. Keep watching. I'm going to drive over to the marina and call Carl." I heard Rice's chair as he got up. That was my cue to get away from the tent. I headed north before turning downhill past the big tent and walking to the beach with my lemonade. I stood down there by the water, while my mind was churning thoughts around like the Bingo tumbler in the church gym. *What the hell?* I wondered. What were they talking about? What did John Rice and Fred guess Kathy was "using" now? What did Fred think she "does" with something that probably *wasn't* in her vest? And what was up with that bulky vest anyway?

A few minutes later I saw Kathy come out of the wardrobe tent with a manila folder under her arm, and I waved till she saw me.

~ ~ ~

At dinner that evening, the kids talked about the conversations they'd had with their experts that afternoon. Len said that his cameraman kept complaining that they'd put zero feet of usable film in the can. Kai added that the scriptwriter she interviewed was weary of Benjamin Pressfield's script changes, which (here she checked some notes she'd taken) the writer said were "spontaneous and irrational." Len added that O'Neill wouldn't be able to say any lines they gave him anyway. Kai agreed, one-upping her brother's cynicism by lamenting that actors made life difficult for writers, the true creative force in film.

All in all, Hollywood had lost much of its glitter. While I was relieved that they no longer seemed to want to run off to Los Angeles at the first opportunity, I was also a little sad. It would probably be a long time before they would let themselves enjoy a movie the way they used to.

Len added that he'd heard rumors that Mr. Rice, who was there, like, *a lot*, was a mobster and that his bodyguard carried a gun all the time. Not to be outdone, Kai said that one of the crew saw a gun in Kathy Roberson's purse.

It seemed like a good time to remind her that the piece she was writing about the interview had to get my okay before she submitted it to the paper. The last thing we needed was to be putting wild rumors and theories in the newspaper. There was too much of that going around anyway. Predictably, she got up from the table in a huff, saying that she had an article to write and that "her editor" had better not mess with her journalistic rights.

Still, just because I didn't want Kai to be putting rumors into the paper, that didn't mean I wasn't paying attention to them. I was making a mental note to mention the possible gun in Kathy's purse to Carson when the phone rang. Still scowling, Kai answered it.

Naturally, it would be Carson. Who else called me at night? Smiling sweetly, I accepted the receiver and said, "Why, thank you, Kai." She stomped to her room and closed the door rather firmly. I put the phone to my ear, saying "Yes?"

"It's Dee," Carson said.

I wanted to make a joke that it obviously wasn't Dee who was calling, but he sounded serious. "Okay," I said. "Are they letting her go?"

"Well, no," Carson said. "They found my wrench."

"Crap!" I said, saving myself a household language fine. From his place on the couch, Len grinned at me. I looked meaningfully toward the kitchen. He slowly stood up and shuffled through to clear the table.

Carson asked, "Want to know where?"

"Isn't it obvious?" I said. "Dee's house."

"The very place."

"How convenient. Where did they find it?"

"Buried, most of it, in her back yard behind the garden shed."

"Crap," I repeated. Instantly, Len was at the doorway with a dinner plate in each hand. I covered the telephone receiver and stage-whispered, "Crap doesn't count." He disappeared. I heard water running into the sink.

When I put the receiver back to my ear, Carson was still talking about the wrench. "—blood on it."

I picked up the base of the phone and walked as far away from the kitchen as the cord poking out of the wall would let me. I kept my voice low so that Len wouldn't overhear. "Of course they found blood on it," I said. "But how do you know that?"

"They have to tell me about evidence." He sounded distracted, like he was having two conversations at the same time. I wondered if someone was there with him. After a pause, he added, "Disclosure."

"Oh, yeah. When did they tell you?"

"Right now, ten minutes ago."

I looked at the clock. It wasn't late, but it wasn't business hours, either. "Lucky they could find you," I said, thinking maybe I could get away with asking where he was.

"I'm at home," he said, as if he'd heard what I was thinking.

"Alone?" I don't know why I asked that. It was none of my business.

"No. Peggy came over here to tell me about it."

"Anyone else?" Now I was really pushing it, but I couldn't help picturing Peggy, Eleanor, and Carson hanging out together in his dinky kitchen.

"No, only Officer Thomas."

Officer Thomas, huh? How formal. But all I said was, "Do you want me to do anything?"

"Nope, just keeping you informed," he said. "I'll be in the office tomorrow."

"See you at ten," I said.

He faltered a bit. "Oh. Well. How about nine?"

I hesitated, thinking about my plans for the next morning, but said, "Okay."

Lew and I would need to wrap up our burgling extra early.

CHAPTER SEVENTEEN

L EN and Kai weren't quite so chipper about rising and shining in the dark anymore. By Friday, the appeal was already wearing thin, and they griped none too quietly as they lurched around getting ready. I ignored the change in their mood, and they perked up a little when I bid them goodbye at the door instead of tagging along to the bus like I had the day before. It's hard to be cool when your mom's walking you to the bus.

As soon as the kids were out of sight, I slipped on old jeans and one of my dad's big button-down shirts that had a little paint on it. I tied a paisley scarf around my unruly hair. Looking in the mirror, I hesitated. Seriously, was I going to take the lead on a break-in? Planning it had been kind of a game, but now it was real, and I was having some misgivings. Then I reminded myself that we weren't going to take anything. We just needed to find out if Buckmaster was doing bad things with a big chunk of city funds. I took a deep breath and grabbed the plastic tote of cleaning supplies that I'd assembled the night before.

It was 4:20 in the morning when I started my walk to Lew's shop in the gray pre-dawn. Fifteen minutes later, I spotted him waiting for me in front of his place. He was wearing a tattered gray Sage Landing High School Athletic Department t-shirt, frayed sweats, and scuffed-up running shoes. Perfect.

"Okay, how do we do this?" he said as we walked toward the city building.

"We'll go in through the back door to the police station, the one that goes to the rear parking lot. They never used to lock it when I worked there."

"What if they lock it nowadays?"

"That could be trickier. The front door to the police end of the building is never locked, but there's often a cop at the lobby desk—not always, though. We'd have to play it by ear."

"Oh."

"Lew, we don't look suspicious. If someone sees us, they'll think you were out on a run, saw me walking to my early cleaning job, and didn't want me to be walking alone in the mostly dark. That'll be the story if anyone asks, anyway."

Lew laughed. "Sure, while we're still outside, but after that…."

I hefted my tote full of assorted cleaning products and said, "If someone sees us after we're inside, we'll both grab a rag and get to work."

"That's kind of… far-fetched," he said.

"Yeah, but it would work. There aren't any windows into the secure room, not even in its doors. In the unlikely event that someone unlocks one and walks in, we'll be cleaning. It probably wouldn't even cross their minds that we were in there to snoop on the mayor. See?"

"I hope you're right," Lew said. "Now, how are *we* going to unlock the room, assuming we get that far?"

I lifted a pile of sponges to show him the tools hidden underneath. "Sometimes there are things that a janitor notices, things no one else pays attention to."

"Aha! You *said* the other day that the secure room wasn't so secure." He grinned at me. "Do I get to crawl through any air conditioning ducts?"

"Sadly, no. We're not in a movie," I said. "What we're going to do is walk into an unlocked women's restroom."

The sun hadn't come up yet when we waltzed through the back door to the police station. I led Lew into the "new" hallway that was built five or six years before, along the back of what had once been three smaller buildings. We didn't see anyone. About fifty feet down the hall we came to one of the building's several restrooms.

Once inside the restroom, we made sure we were alone in there. In a near whisper, I said, "See that other door back there?"

The door in question was a plain flat steel-clad door. It didn't have a doorknob. It didn't even have a deadbolt mounted in it. Originally, it had been a push-in entry to this restroom.

Lew walked over and examined it. "This goes into the secure room?"

"Yes. The secure room used to be a wide hallway leading to this restroom. After the new back hallway was built, they cut the new entrance we walked through. Then they built the new wall blocking off the other end of the old hallway. That's where they installed the security door with deadbolt and all."

"But they never put locks on this old door?" Lew tapped on the steel in front of him.

"They did, but they didn't," I said. "They wanted to prevent entry into the new secure room from *this side*."

"The lock is on the other side," he said.

"Two locks. But this was end-of-project stuff. Minor details, low budget. So, they bolted two heavy-duty slide locks to the other side of the existing door."

Lew looked at me. "There's no way to get to those locks?"

"Look again," I said.

It took thirty seconds for him to find the flaw. Our side of the door had two sets of four steel washers and nuts each—one high up, the other down low.

"If we remove these nuts—"

"And push the bolts through—"

"The slide locks will fall into that room."

"After a bit of jiggling, yes." I reached under the sponges in my plastic tote and pulled out a socket. It was one size too small, but I had the next one, too. And I had a small ratchet that fit the sockets. Lew went to work on the lower lock, handing me each nut and washer as he went along. The lock fell to the floor, making a solid *cha-clink* sound as its two ends landed a split-second apart. We flinched, then stayed completely still for thirty seconds or so, but all was quiet. Less than two minutes later, the second of the slide locks hit the floor, sounding louder than the first one because it was falling farther. Again we held perfectly still, listening for any reaction to the unusual sound coming from the secure room, and again there wasn't any.

We nudged the door open slowly and slipped in. The room was completely dark, so we couldn't close the door behind us until we switched on the light. As I remembered it, the light switch was at the other end of the room. I found it by feeling along the wall, but before I switched it on, I noticed another problem. There was a gap of at least a half-inch between the bottom of the secure door and the floor below it. If I turned the light on, anyone walking down that hall would notice the light under the door and figure out that someone was in the room. I searched around for some boxes or something to scoot in front of the door to block the light, but it was too dark to see anything. Walking back over next to Lew, I whispered, "Do you have an undershirt on?"

"Huh? No. Why do you ask?" I heard the smile in his lowered voice.

Under cover of darkness, I rolled my eyes. "We need to plug a gap under the door at the other end, or we'll give ourselves away."

"It isn't even five o'clock in the morning yet."

"There are offices on both sides of this room. Cops walk along that hall any time of day or night. They might notice if—"

"Do *you* have an undershirt on?" he asked, the smile even stronger in his voice.

"No," I said. I didn't think I needed to provide further details.

Lew walked past me to the other door as he pulled his shirt off. He knelt down to stuff the shirt against the gap under the door. He stood up and found the light switch.

What a surprise. The guy obviously worked out and watched his diet. I let out a little sound—let's call it a murmur of approval. He was charmingly embarrassed. I closed the restroom door behind me and quietly moved a steel chair against it. When I looked at Lew again, I couldn't help imagining us on the cover of a paperback romance. Sort of took the wind out of me for a few seconds.

"Now, what are we trying to find?" I asked.

"First thing is to figure out which file cabinet he's using." About a minute later, Lew said, "This one."

"Can I help?" I asked while staring at the muscles that were flexing in his back.

"Listen for sounds outside," he said.

I touched his shoulder. He faced me as I lifted my chin toward the ceiling. He looked upward. There, at the top of the wall, was a small vent. It connected this room directly to one where people were working. We couldn't be sure how far any sound we made would carry.

Lew smiled, putting his finger to his lips to indicate that he understood. He leaned toward my ear to whisper, "Here's the thing. I know which records I want. If they're in here, it'll take a few minutes to skim over the figures."

I whispered back, "And if they aren't in here?"

"That would confirm my suspicions."

He turned back to the filing cabinet. I drifted around, examining the miscellaneous junk crammed into shelves and boxes along the walls. I was wondering why a stack of weekly *Sage Landing Gazette*s from 1982 was locked in the secure room when I heard something that froze me where I stood.

Someone pushed the restroom's outer door open.

Lew and I stared at each other, not breathing. We both looked at the gap under the door to the restroom. There wasn't time to stuff anything into that space, even if we could find something that would work. It was probably too late anyway.

I remembered that the restroom light had already been on when we walked in. It was still on when whoever it was walked in there, too. That probably meant that she—Peggy, maybe?—wouldn't notice the light under the door to the secure room.

Next, a toilet flushed, right next to the wall where I was standing.

I heard water running in the sink. I heard a paper towel being ripped from the roll. I heard my heart beat loudly enough to alarm whoever was taking forever to dry her hands on rough brown paper. Finally, finally, I heard the door on the other side of the restroom swish open and thump closed.

Lew went back to work while I concentrated on remembering how to breathe. Less than five minutes later, he said, "Let's get out of here."

"Okay," I said. "Now we cover our tracks on the way out. Don't move your shirt until we don't need the light."

"I've been wondering how you think we are going to put those slide locks back."

"That's easy," I said. "You'll hold the lock in place and shove the bolts through to the restroom side. I'll replace the washers and nuts on that side and tighten them up."

"Got it."

Ten minutes later, washers and nuts restored, Lew killed the light. He retrieved his shirt, slipped it on, and joined me in the restroom. We pulled the door shut. Since we couldn't slide the bolts from our side, I wedged a plastic Bic pen fragment between the jamb and the door to keep it from opening.

We walked out into the "new" hallway. The sun was coming up as we left the building and strolled casually through the parking lot toward Lew's shop.

I waited till we were half a block away from the city building to ask, "What'd you find out?"

He shook his head. "The dog didn't bark in the night."

"Okay, what does that mean, exactly?

"The ledger is gone."

I looked at him, mildly annoyed. "Can you explain what that tells you?"

He said, "Marybeth told me that Buckmaster kept his business ledgers locked in the secure room. She was supposed to do updates in the paper ledger after the discs got trashed, but now nobody can find the key to get in."

"How convenient," I said.

"Quite the coincidence, I know. Anyway, when I checked the file cabinet labeled 'Buckmaster' just now, the current ledger was missing. It should be there, but it isn't. He doesn't want Marybeth to see those numbers."

That did sound kind of suspicious. I said, "And he doesn't want her to know that he's keeping her from seeing them, right?"

"That's it exactly." He grinned and took the cleaning tote from me. Then he asked, "Do you think anyone will notice that the slide bolts aren't locked?"

I said, "No one will even see them till they find the key. When someone goes in after that, they won't be looking at the old door at the other end of the room."

"But if someone does—"

"They won't find anything missing except Buckmaster's ledger. That's Buckmaster's problem, not ours. Besides, as far as they know, it could've happened years ago. They'd probably think someone accidentally left it unlocked at some point. Like maybe after giving the room a good cleaning."

Laughing, he handed the tote back to me and headed toward his shop. I walked home, eager for coffee and a shower before work.

~ ~ ~

Carson had already unlocked the office and was sitting at his desk waiting for me when I got there at nine. I was amazed.

"Are we going to see Dee at the station?" I asked as I walked back to where I could see him.

He said, "I already tried, about half an hour ago. They moved her in the middle of the night," Carson said.

"Moved her where? Why?"

"Probably to Phoenix. The state cops took her. The 'why' part is to make things more difficult for her defense counsel. It puts us over five hours away from her."

"That isn't right," I said. "She's probably scared to death."

"Yeah, well, that helps them too. It's a perfectly legal maneuver. We used to do variations of it when I was a prosecutor. If defense files a complaint, prosecution makes up some smoke-and-mirrors reason for the move."

"What do we do next?"

"I can't do anything," Carson said, "until I find out where she is. Depending on what kind of game they're playing, that could take hours."

"Who can we call?" I asked.

"It wouldn't do any good to call anyone yet. They're possibly still moving her around among different facilities so that no one really knows where she is."

I noticed that Carson was dressed very well, for him. He was wearing a pressed dress shirt and a clean tie. A suit coat in a plastic wrapper was draped over one of the client chairs. I had to assume that his slacks matched the coat. "You're dressed up," I said. "What's the occasion?"

"Attorneys dress a little better down in Phoenix."

"Aren't you supposed to stay in town?" I asked him, surprised. "Person of interest and all that?"

"Mike never actually said that to me."

"But—" I started.

"Personal business," he said. "Don't concern yourself." His face warned me not to ask any questions as he went on, "You'll run things here. I'll probably be down there all weekend. Stay as close as you can to the phones here and at home."

"Sure," I said, "Don't get caught fleeing the area."

Carson stood up. "Take a seat, Naomi." He gestured toward the chair closest to me. As I sat down, he moved the suit coat to the chair behind his desk and settled into the other client chair, on the same side of the desk as I was. I realized that he was sitting by my side because whatever he had to say—or ask—was going to be upsetting, and he was trying to make it easier for me to answer.

I waited. It felt like some kind of bomb was going to drop.

His eyes on the suit coat in its plastic wrapper, he asked, "Were you and Lew taking a sunrise stroll this morning?"

I tried to figure out what he thought was going on. Cautiously I said, "Well, yes, we were. What makes you ask?"

"Just wondering," he said.

"Who…" I stopped. I started again, "Who…" and then changed direction. "That's kind of a weird thing for you to be wondering about, isn't it?"

He leaned forward with his forearms on his knees. He clasped his hands together loosely, and his eyes were still focused on a space behind his desk. He said, "I'm pretty sure the two of you didn't spend a night of wild passion together. It's a *very* small town, as you keep telling me, and you have two smart kids at home. Even if you wanted to, you couldn't get away with an overnight tryst. So that makes me wonder what's up."

I said, "That's funny. Overnight tryst. No, Lew was out on a run before the heat of the day, and I—"

He interrupted. "Cut the crap, Naomi. I'm not buying it." Now he was looking down at the floor. Waiting.

Damn him and his damn skills. I ran a few possible explanations through my head. Lew and I'd been walking in the middle of town, so I couldn't say we were hiking. Besides, I'd been carrying a bunch of cleaning supplies. Whoever ratted us out would've surely told Carson that, too.

Figuring that I might as well get it over with, I said, "We were breaking into the secure room at City Hall."

I think he was stunned. It was probably ten seconds before he reacted. He sat up straight, then he swiveled his whole body sideways in the chair to face me. He seemed to be searching for words. Finally he said, "Why. On *earth*. Would you. And Lew. Do that." When I didn't answer, he added, "At, what, the crack of dawn?"

"Best time to break into a secure room, if you ask me," I said.

That got the laugh I was hoping for, but it ended abruptly. He said, "This is serious, Naomi. What's in the secure room?"

"Evidence that Herman Effing Buckmaster is an embezzler," I said. "Probably."

Carson thought about that. He leaned back in the chair, looking again at the wall behind his desk. "Okay…and is he probably embezzling from Lew?"

"No."

"From a client, then?"

"Client?"

He crossed his arms over his chest and cleared his throat. "Surely you had some good reason to take on this sleuthing mission—some reason connected to cases for which we are on a retainer?"

"We had a good reason," I said. "Really good. Buckmaster's stealing from the city. Probably."

"And has the *city* retained Grant Carson, Attorney at Law?" He already knew the answer to that, so I didn't have to say anything.

He stood up and walked to his I'm-the-boss chair, grabbing the plastic-wrapped suit coat and tossing it back across the desk. It hit the chair he'd just vacated and slithered to the floor, but he didn't seem to notice. Instead, he jabbed his finger in my direction, even though he knew how incredibly rude that was, and said, "Have *you* taken out a license as a private investigator?"

"Is one required?" I asked, leaning down to pick up the jacket.

"Beats me," he said, "but that's kind of beside the point, don't you think?" He plopped down in the big chair.

I carefully draped the jacket over the back of the chair next to me, so that I wouldn't have to look Carson in the eye. "Lew stumbled across some suspicious information."

"Oh? And how did that happen?"

I smoothed the flimsy plastic covering the suit coat. "He was… helping out someone who works for the city and for Buckmaster. Some floppy discs looked totally trashed, but the person asked him to try saving their data if he could. He got some of them running, and that's when he saw the numbers that didn't look right."

"And *you* got involved *why*?"

"As a favor to Lew."

"Your big brother, didn't you say? Why would he need this favor from you?"

I was still looking at the three-button jacket lying on the chair, thinking that it was a good thing he'd finally gotten a new suit. Then I looked him in the eye and said, "I'm the one who knows how to break into the secure room."

That made him sputter again. "Naomi. I'm trying to come up with a defense for you. I'm having a hard time. You're not helping. What did you guys take?"

"We didn't take anything. Lew just needed to check some financial records. It was a caper. It wasn't a heist."

"That sounds adorable, but it's hardly a defense. Did anyone see you in the building?"

"No, but I had a cover story ready in case they did. I carried cleaning supplies so I could say I was picking up a cleaning shift for Nolan. He has the contract to clean the city complex a couple of times a week."

"And what if they called this Nolan to confirm?"

"They wouldn't. They already know I worked for him. They also know —um, Peggy knows—that sometimes I need more hours than I can get here at the office. Doing a shift for Nolan is totally believable. But, yeah, if they called him he would've backed me up, for sure."

"So you'd ask a friend to lie for you?"

"I wouldn't have to ask, but I take your point, Carson, and I'll resign right now. I'll make sure you're not involved in all this. I'm sorry."

Leaning forward, he put his elbows on the desk and pinched the bridge of his nose between thumb and index finger, looking just like a disappointed dad. After a long pause, he quietly said, "No, Naomi, I need you here. In case you haven't noticed, we have a lot going on."

"It was a stupid thing for me to do," I said. In my own head, though, I added, *but somebody had to do it.*

"You have no idea." He opened a file, shuffling idly through some sheets of paper.

Again, I adjusted the jacket on the back of the chair next to me. No point in having it wrinkled before it was even out of its plastic bag.

Without looking up, Carson asked, "How much is Buck stealing?"

"Lew thinks around a half million."

He said, "Well, we can probably think of a way to turn that into being hired by *somebody*. Herman Buckmaster, maybe."

"You would defend Buckmaster? Knowing that he stole from the city?"

"We represent defendants. I'm a defense attorney," Carson said, his voice harsh. "We defend people who are accused of committing crimes.

We make sure their legal rights are protected. Besides, we don't even know for sure that a crime has been committed."

"Oh, I do. I know for sure," I said.

"Brave words," he said, grabbing another file and flipping it open.

"And it isn't only that." I rushed on. "I've been thinking about why Herman would've plundered the city accounts. I mean, nobody could figure out where he got enough money to be a big-shot investor in the film, right? I bet most of it was the city's money. At first he was desperate to keep the movie going. He'd do anything, even destroy Dee's reputation, to keep the movie people happy. But after Shawn Gordon was killed, he lost his nerve, and he wanted to get the money back. He had lunch with the insurance guys. We saw him, remember?"

Carson's eyes stayed on the documents in front of him. I didn't let that stop me. "And the call to Window Rock about the costumes and the predator skins and the so-called protests? Do you remember where that call came from?"

There was still no response, but I was on a roll. "It came from Sage Landing City Hall, that's where. Herman Buckmaster made that call, you can bet, or else he made someone on his crew do it. Because he thought the tribe would shut the movie down, and then the insurance would have to cash him out."

Looking at me like he'd just noticed that I was still sitting there, Carson said, "None of that justifies your shenanigans this morning. None of it."

I couldn't believe that he wasn't getting it. Buckmaster was the real criminal, not Lew and me, so I had to state the obvious. "Well, what if that…that *crook* also killed Shawn, to sink the film so that he could get the city's money back in a hurry? What then?"

Carson reached into his desk drawer. He slid two of his business cards across the desk toward me, saying, "Give one of these to Lew. Give the other to Nolan. They'll need to know who to call when you all get arrested, which is what'll happen if you try something like that again."

CHAPTER EIGHTEEN

Having finished cross-examining me, Carson left the office to go pack a few things for Phoenix. He asked me to stay by the phone in case someone called. No one did, and he was back, hovering over my desk, in less than an hour.

"No calls," I said.

"I was afraid of that. They're stonewalling us."

"Is your…is Eleanor still up here, or is she down there?" I asked.

"She's back in Phoenix."

"Carson, you told me that you're pretty much persona non grata with the prosecutor's office there, right?"

He said, "Persona non grata?"

"What, I can't throw around a little Latin? Fine. You told me that you didn't leave your position there on the best of terms, correct?"

"Correct, but I don't see what—"

"Well, Eleanor worked there, too. Is she still in their good graces? Maybe she has connections that could give her some inside information."

"Maybe," Carson said.

"It's Friday. Wouldn't she be in her office by now?"

"Probably. I'll try to get her." He walked into his office.

I was at a loss as to what to do. The night before, I'd been thinking about Carson's bloody wrench in Dee's back yard, wondering how the new "evidence" changed her chances. I'd started the day by committing an early-morning crime and later ended up confessing all to Carson. At some point along the way, our client was whisked away to foil our defense efforts. I'd been awake since three-thirty, so I'd practically put in a full day already and wasn't exactly firing on all cylinders at that point.

Carson walked back out and stood next to my desk again. "She'll call around. She still hangs out with a few prosecutors who aren't bad guys."

"Were you a bad guy when you were down there?" I asked.

"I was fired…well, I negotiated out, but it was because I resisted being a bad guy too often. Like, I kept trying to prevent the department from doing what was just done to us."

I didn't ask for more details about his prosecutorial past—*all in good time*, I thought—but something more recent was nagging at me. He might not answer, but what the hell. I said, "So, Carson. Can I ask about something—something kind of dicey?"

He gave me the side-eye but said, "You can ask, sure. I don't promise an answer."

"Why was Eleanor in Sage Landing this week?"

He sat down in the chair next to the window. Looking out at the parking lot, he said, "We ran into each other in Flagstaff the weekend Shawn was killed."

"Ran into each other? What does that mean?"

"Well, it would be more accurate to say that we *met* in Flagstaff. We're dealing with a…legal action…something involving a house we still own together. We met to go over some documents, and that made us kind of remember that we liked each other a little bit, now that the whole marriage thing was behind us."

"Oh." I don't know what I was expecting him to say, but it wasn't this. "Is that why you wouldn't give Mike your alibi?"

"Things were already tangled up enough without bringing my ex into the mix."

I raised an eyebrow. "*Things* were tangled up?"

He shrugged. "I'd have said something if the authorities got anywhere close to being serious about me as a suspect. Eleanor would've corroborated."

"Was that why she came to Sage Landing?"

"Not really. Eleanor said she'd never been here and wanted to see it so that she could picture me in my new surroundings."

I could think of nothing to say to that.

"She's very visual, Eleanor is. I'm not. It was one of the things that made us a good team—she could visualize a crime scene, that's for sure."

He had a dreamy, nostalgic look on his face, which seemed so out of character that I hated to say anything that would bring him back to Dee's crisis. So I didn't.

Instead, I said, "Oh, I forgot. I'm supposed to get you to accept an invitation to a movie party on Pressfield's boat, tomorrow. Kathy says it's mandatory. And get this—Kathy and Pressfield are co-hosting. Like they're best friends or something."

"Mandatory? What, she'll put it on my permanent record if I don't show up? I have other plans."

I gave him my best you-know-better-than-that look. "Oh, really? You have plans? Well, change them. Kathy's the client and she's telling you to be there. Besides, Mike Rodriguez would not be okay with your leaving town."

Ignoring the police interest in his whereabouts, he went on. "You can represent the firm fine without me."

"That's a bit of a stretch," I said, "the firm represented by a part-time paralegal."

"Please, Naomi. To people in Sage Landing, you're practically a partner."

"Now you're just trying to flatter me so that I'll stop nagging you not to leave town."

He managed to look sincerely offended. "No, I'm not. I'm delegating. Look, we are big minnows, both of us, because our puddle is so damned small."

"And that's the way you like it."

"Exactly," he said, with great satisfaction.

I could tell that there would be no further discussion of his plans and no talking him out of going to Phoenix if that was what he wanted to do. I sighed. "Then it's a good thing our small pond has at least a little crime."

"And it's a good thing we know some gangsters," Carson said.

The jury was still out on that, so to speak, but at least it jogged my memory. "Speaking of which," I said, "I did some eavesdropping on those guys yesterday. John Rice and Fred, out at the movie location. It sounded to me like they were trying to figure something out about Kathy."

"Like what?"

"I couldn't tell—didn't hear enough of it."

"You do realize, don't you, that we are neither private investigators nor cops?"

"I'm not—"

He went on, "Because you seem a little confused about that. Investigating guys like John Rice can be dangerous. He hired us to deal with Pressfield. Nobody hired us to watch John and Fred."

"Yes, I know. And nobody hired us to babysit Kathy, either, but I don't trust her. I heard that she's carrying a gun."

"So? I have a gun. You have a gun. From what you've told me, half the population of Sage Landing might have a gun on them at any time."

"Don't exaggerate. Just because we own them, that doesn't mean we make a habit of carrying them around. Besides, Kai heard Kathy telling Fred to make Pressfield *an offer he couldn't refuse*, like she was the Godfather or something."

"Didn't you just tell me that Kathy and Pressfield are supposed to be best friends now?"

The phone rang, and Carson jumped up to answer it at my desk. After listening for a minute, he said, "I'll probably come down anyway. Keep trying to find out. I'll want to be close by in case there's a chance to contact her." He was quiet again before going on, "The retainer was only five thousand so I don't think there's much room for additional counsel, but I may need someone down there to take this over. Dr. Moreno has a house. I don't know how much equity."

Sadly, I thought, it always comes down to money. Public defenders were available, true, but no one seemed to have much confidence in them. People need money when they have trouble with the law.

Carson signed off and hung up the phone. "That was Eleanor. She hasn't broken through the wall yet." He went back to the chair, sat down, and surveyed the parking lot through the window again. "Dee could be held in Maricopa County's system, even the state corrections system. We probably won't find out until Monday. The movie coverage has made this a high-profile case."

"National publicity," I said. "The *Deep Inn* will be famous. Maybe you could sell her."

"Never." He got up and headed to his inner office. "I'll grab a couple of things in here and take off."

Too late. I heard a car pull up out front. In walked Kathy Roberson, alone, ignoring me completely and heading straight for Carson's office. She was still wearing that silly vest instead of carrying the designer bag I'd seen on her arm the first time she came to the office. I followed her and stood in Carson's doorway as she leaned over his desk.

"I'm glad I caught you in," she said. "I saw a suitcase in the cab of your truck out there. Didn't Naomi tell you about the party on the ship we rented?"

I wondered how Carson was going to answer that one.

Carson said, "She did, and I *hate* to miss it, but I've got to go to Phoenix. I'm running a little late, so—"

"Oh no," she said, loudly enough to be just short of shouting. "No, no, no. This party is especially important to Benjamin and me. You can't miss it!"

"I feel bad about it, but we have a client who is in serious trouble. She's been moved down there, and I can't give her vital legal advice over the phone."

"That teacher-woman who murdered Shawn?"

"The respected president of the community college, who is innocent," I corrected from the doorway.

Kathy said, "Well. That is not what *I* hear. The news on the radio said something about *new* evidence. Anyway, you can advise her next week. She's in jail, for god's sake. You can advise her any time. It's not like she's going anywhere."

Now I was mad. I said, "That's the point, Kathy, Dr. Moreno *has* gone somewhere. They're deliberately moving her around in the jail system. Carson needs to find her."

Carson cleared his throat, a gentle reminder that he generally doesn't want me to contradict a client. He'd rather do that himself.

"My uncle Carl has advanced you a lot of money," she said, her voice sounding even more piercing. "I know that this schoolteacher woman is a client, and she's in trouble. I get it. But my project is in peril. You've got to get your priorities straight here."

Carson spoke very quietly. "Ms. Roberson. Kathy. I fail to see how my attendance at a party could have any effect at all on the success of your film."

"We're at a critical juncture. I'm dealing with a delicate balance of power, and I have to have your full support."

"You do. You have my full support—*as your attorney*. In fact, we are consulting with a top-shelf Los Angeles entertainment law firm next week."

This was the first I'd heard of that particular consultation, so that might have been a minor exaggeration.

"In the meantime, though," Carson said, "in her current situation my other client might say things she shouldn't—inadvertently weakening our case. Without me there to protect her interests, she could compromise her defense."

"I don't care! I mean no, she won't. It's already past noon on Friday. You wouldn't be able to see her until Monday. At the earliest. I really must insist, Carson. I need you on board with me right now."

Carson laughed.

Kathy laughed, too, but it sounded forced. A little creepy. She said, "No pun intended, but we have to show a united front to Pressfield, and to O'Neill—what a disappointment *that* idiot's been. I'll have to deal with that mistake, too, which will probably mean more legal work for you. Win-win."

I was looking around for something to hit her with, but Carson held his hands up in surrender.

"Okay…okay, Kathy. I see your point and you're right. There's nothing down in Phoenix that can't wait a few days."

Kathy smiled warmly. "So, you'll come to the party! Great!"

Carson said, "I'll be there. Thank you for the invitation." He sounded very reassuring.

Kathy's smile got downright scary, and her eyes glittered. "Promise me, Grant Carson. Pinky promise?" She actually crooked her little finger at him so that he could link his pinky with hers.

He didn't do that, being more than eight years old, but he did say, "Sure, pinky promise, Kathy. Sounds great. Can we bring anything?"

"That's the team spirit," she said. "No need to bring anything. Herman Buckmaster is catering."

"Well, tell old Herman to bring plenty of beer." Carson chuckled as he said, "I'm not much of a champagne man."

"Will do," she said before turning a creepy smile my way. "Naomi, any requests?"

"Soft drinks for my kids," I said. "They're coming with me."

"No," Kathy said, her smile melting like an ice cream cone dropped on a hot sidewalk. "They can't come. It's an adult party."

"I don't have a choice, Kathy. I'm not leaving my kids home alone. Not with Shawn Gordon's killer still at large."

"I'm sure the killer's already in custody, but your faith in your client is very touching." She seemed to give it deep thought before saying, "Well, okay. If that's what it'll take to get you to my party, go ahead and bring them. There's plenty of room, but there won't be any other kids, I'm afraid."

"They keep each other company," I said.

The smile was back. "Good, it'll be so much fun. Service dock at one o'clock. Plenty of food and drink."

"See you then," Carson said.

Kathy practically skipped past me to continue on her appointed rounds, whatever they were.

After we heard Kathy's car pull away, Carson said, "I'm going to try to catch Eleanor again. Maybe she's heard something by now."

"You'll have to tell her you aren't coming down like you said you would."

"What do you mean?" he asked.

"The party—"

Carson interrupted, "I'm not going to the damn party, Naomi! What gave you that idea?"

"*You* did! You just now swore you would! You pinky-promised our biggest client that you'd definitely be there."

"And I told you earlier that you'd be representing the firm at that party on the 'ship.'" He smirked. "Ship, indeed."

I stepped into his office to perch on a client chair. "Help me out here, boss. I'm not following you."

"How long do you think that woman would've argued if I kept saying that I couldn't attend her soiree?"

"I don't think she ever would've stopped."

"Right. I get the impression that Kathy Roberson hasn't heard the word 'no' enough times in her life."

"Including now," I said. "You didn't say 'no' to her either."

"My 'no' will be evident to her soon enough."

"And I'll be the one facing the music," I said.

Carson shrugged. "Don't go, then. I don't give a damn." He picked up the phone but didn't start dialing. "No, wait. You should go. We need to keep an eye on whatever the hell she thinks she's doing. But don't face any music. Just be oblivious."

"Oblivious how?"

"If she asks, say that you're sure I'm on my way, I'll be there any minute, you can't imagine what's holding me up, things like that."

"Now you want me to lie to our biggest client?"

"Actually, Naomi, what I really want is for you to steal some evidence from the city building, but you already did that."

I jumped up off the chair. "I did not. We didn't take anything. I told you, it was a *caper*, not a *heist*."

"Well, then what you tell Kathy can be a *creative evasion*, not a *lie*," he said as he dialed the phone.

I went out to my desk to pretend he had some privacy. Overhearing his end of the short conversation didn't tell me anything anyway. He came back out of his office.

"I'm not going to Phoenix yet," he said. "We still have no idea where Dee is. Eleanor reminded me about the prisons all over the state, including one at Winslow. If Dee's in that one, I'd drive right past her if I go to Phoenix."

Plus, staying in town also meant that he'd be staying out of trouble with Mike Rodriguez, but I let that go unsaid. I looked at my watch instead and asked Carson whether he wanted burgers or barbeque for lunch.

~ ~ ~

I hated contributing to Buckmaster's bottom line, but he owned the closest place to pick up good barbeque. Standing at the counter, waiting for our sandwiches, I thought about our crooked mayor and his delusions of grandeur. He was still on my mind when I got back to the office.

Handing the bag to Carson, I said, "Now, about Buckmaster—"

"Don't go there," he said, reaching into the bag. "Mmm. Pulled pork. Coleslaw, too. Where are my curly fries?"

"They were out," I said. "And why should we not discuss Buckmaster?"

"Damn," he said. "I was expecting those fries." He took the top bun off his sandwich, opened the container of coleslaw, and slathered the pork with a generous layer of creamy cabbage. Carefully setting the top bun back in its place, he cut the sandwich in quarters with a plastic knife.

Impatiently, I said, "I hate to interrupt, but you haven't answered my question. Why not go there? I mean, why not talk about Buckmaster?"

"Many reasons. First and foremost is that you and Lew don't *know* anything. You suspect something, or Lew does. That isn't how the law works."

"But if you see a crime, shouldn't you report it?"

"Lew didn't see a crime. He saw an irregularity in some bookkeeping."

"Related to public funds."

"Lew *suspects*, and you suspect, and now even I suspect. None of us is an accountant."

I had to think about that for a while. I said, "Okay, so how would *you* explain Herman's big investment in the movie?"

"I'll concede, because of you and Lew, I'm beginning to wonder if he maybe got the money from the city."

"Stole the money from the city, you mean."

"Or borrowed it, maybe even legally."

"Come on, Carson. Half a million dollars?"

Carson raised a "not so fast" palm toward me. "Half a million in funds that no one has reported missing. About which no one has complained, as far as we know."

I laid my smoked chicken sandwich down on its wrapper. "Don't we have an obligation—"

"As a legal firm? Yes, we have a plethora of obligations. One is to avoid drumming up business by stating our suspicions to possible victims."

"Lew has suspicions, and he wouldn't be drumming up business. He could say something."

"You know better than that, Naomi. Anything he, or you—or I, for that matter—said would be tainted, for several reasons."

I knew what was coming.

Carson leaned forward. Raising his voice the tiniest bit, trying in vain to get me to meet his gaze, he said, "Among them is your involvement in a criminal fishing expedition in City Hall. Frankly, if it came to an arrest warrant for Herman Buckmaster on Lew's say-so, I'd be able to suppress almost all the evidence. I'd successfully defend him and get a big fee."

I winced. "And Lew and I would go to jail."

He snorted. "You think you'd get off that easy? Hell, no, you wouldn't. No, you'd get maybe a suspended sentence, and that would be the fun part. Things wouldn't get really serious until Herman Buckmaster sued the ever-living daylights out of you both."

CHAPTER NINETEEN

SATURDAY started with arguments. Neither of my children wanted to go to the "stupid party" and be "trapped on the stupid boat." So much for the allure of glamorous Hollywood. Reminding them that their favorite crew members would be there didn't persuade them, especially since I hadn't seen the guest list. They pointed out that none of the other interns were invited, which they knew because none of their friends had mentioned it.

First, they trotted out all variations of "we're not babies, Mom, we can take care of ourselves." I pointed out that a murderer was still at large—because didn't we all agree that Dr. Moreno, the only suspect in police custody, *wasn't* actually the murderer? But they dismissed that concern, on the grounds that I was only a mom and therefore didn't know anything. Not a single, solitary thing. I'm kind of reading between the lines here, but that's what it boiled down to.

Next, Len claimed that our dog, Three-Steps, was "not feeling good," so he should stay home to take care of her. I secretly agreed that the mutt seemed a little listless. God knows what she may have gotten into. Still, I told him that Three-Steps would be fine, just fine.

Kai argued that canceling the plans she'd made to hang out with her best friend, Elle, would ruin their friendship forever. I told her that Elle could probably find forgiveness in her heart once she learned how little I cared about ruining Kai's life.

Then each of them complained that they had no idea what to wear and probably didn't own the right clothes anyway. I was in the same predicament myself and said so, but that didn't change anything. The bottom line was (1) both my boss and our biggest client insisted that I attend, and (2) I refused to leave my kids to their own devices while I was gone. No more arguments.

In the end, they sulked, moped, and grumbled their way to the car. During the glum but mercifully silent trip to the marina, I remembered something my mom used to say when the kids were little: "You told them to do it, Naomi. You didn't tell them to like it." Fair enough.

When we arrived at the docks a little early, Chuck Margolin intercepted us before we headed toward the *Dam Yankee*.

"She's not ready yet," he said, "Everybody is supposed to hang back a few minutes."

"You mean the *Yankee* isn't ready?" I asked.

"No, the movie star isn't ready. She's doing last-minute stuff, she says. Probably tacking up bunting and streamers and goddamn balloons for the party, messing up the finishes on my biggest boat. Anyway, you're the first ones here. I hope everyone else gets here soon. I'm not supposed to park that cruiser there."

It occurred to me that the *Dam Yankee* qualified as a yacht, if I'd eyeballed its measurements accurately. I said, "It's your dock, Chuck, and it's your *yacht*, too. Who'd give you a bad time about parking it there?"

He flashed me a worried smile. "It *is* my…yacht, but that end spot on the pier is leased out. I moved the other cruiser to a mooring buoy temporarily to give that boss lady the passenger access she wanted for a couple of hours."

"Kathy paid extra for that, I guess."

"Well, sure, but if the other guy shows up before his boat's back at the dock, I'll have some explaining to do."

"You could've told her no," I said.

"Have you tried doing that?" Chuck asked.

I laughed. "Not personally, but I've watched others, Carson included."

"Is he coming to the party, too?"

"I'm sure he's on his way," I lied.

Next to arrive on the dock was an assistant director I'd talked to a few times. I had him pegged as someone who didn't much like either of the co-hosts. Hamilton O'Neill didn't seem to be one of his favorite people, either. He and I shook hands as he greeted Len and Kai each by name.

Herman Buckmaster showed up with an assistant and a couple of gigantic ice chests. Margolin didn't stop them, so they rolled the ice chests down to the yacht and hauled them aboard.

Hamilton O'Neill himself arrived a few minutes later. He seemed sober, but I wondered how long that would last at the party.

At a few minutes past one, Kathy walked up the dock wearing her explorer outfit, complete with multi-pocketed vest. She said, "Sorry for the delay, everyone. I wanted it to be perfect, and now we're all set. Let the party begin!" We all followed her back to the *Dam Yankee* and trooped aboard.

After what Chuck told me, I was expecting to see a bunch of festive decorations plastered all over, but I didn't. I thought maybe the decorations were below decks, where the food and drinks were, but before I could head down there I heard someone call, "Looking good, Billy Ray!"

I looked around to see who was quoting my favorite movie, *Trading Places,* to get my attention. It was Peggy, wearing a lime green swimsuit under a lightweight pink beach jacket and waving from the dock to get my attention. I remembered the previous morning, when I'd held my breath so as not to get caught inside the city's secure room by someone —probably her—on the other side of a very thin wall, and I felt relieved all over again. Channeling my inner Eddy Murphy, I raised an imaginary glass of champagne and answered, "Feeling good, Louis!" as she climbed aboard. We both laughed way too hard.

Kathy bustled by, asking as she passed me, "When's Carson getting here?"

I called after her, "Any minute now."

Len went below to get a soft drink and came back up to tell me that he couldn't find any. There was "just booze and a buffet." He said proudly that Mr. O'Neill offered him a beer, which meant that now Mr. O'Neill wasn't one of *my* favorite people, either. I gave the kids some cash and told them to run up to the little store on the dock and get whatever they wanted. I hoped they wouldn't make a clean getaway while they were at it.

As Kai and Len were setting off on their mission, one of the gaffers boarded with a member of the sound crew. They both greeted Len, who introduced me to them. They explained that they were there to pilot the "ship" while we enjoyed the party. Len said he'd be back to help them steer in a little while. They smiled and gave him a thumbs-up, bless them.

When Benjamin Pressfield came down the dock, he was accompanied by a young woman I thought I recognized. I was almost sure that she was a member of the polygamous community in High Creek, several miles north of Sage Landing—Abe Bingham's group, but not his family. At least, I didn't think she was related to Abe himself. Pressfield was dressed for golf, I guess—white leather shoes, plaid Bermuda shorts, and a loose-fitting polo shirt, while his companion was dressed to impress, in her white bikini with pink polka dots.

Before my children returned to the boat, Kathy brought me a beer in a large plastic cup. I asked, "Who is that girl with Pressfield?"

Glancing Pressfield's way with a sour expression, she said, "Someone local. He hired her as a personal assistant, a gopher. I don't think she's from Sage Landing, though."

I said, "Around here, he needs to be careful about hiring younger women."

Kathy barked a high-pitched laugh. "A lot of producers see hiring young women as one of the perks of the position."

I took a sip of my beer. "Okay, but out here the fathers and older brothers aren't from Hollywood. It can get ugly."

Kathy's eyes narrowed as she raised her drink. "Let's hope!"

Feeling a little unsettled, I looked away and was mildly relieved to see Len and Kai heading back along the dock with a couple of paper bags. I hadn't thought that they'd ditch me, but still.

"That's almost everybody," Kathy said. "Where the hell is Carson?"

I stood on tiptoe and made a big show of straining to see way up into the parking lot. "Gosh, I can't imagine," I said. "What time is it?"

"Damn it! I'm sure it's close to two by now." She stormed off, climbing up to bark at the designated pilot. The kids came aboard and went down into the salon to put their sodas on ice. A minute later, the pilot cast off the lines. The engines roared to life.

The party had officially begun. We were a motley bunch of people who scarcely knew each other, entirely different in background and social status. Even our connections to the movie project were as different as could be. I wondered what the rationale was for this particular guest list, reasonably sure I shared that question with almost everyone aboard.

~ ~ ~

It's a big, big lake, and a cruiser like the one we were on burns through gasoline fast when it's running full speed. Even if we were going to drop anchor in some cove and stay put for most of the party, we couldn't go much more than a couple of hours out, or else we wouldn't have enough gas to get us back to the marina. I hoped that Kathy and her pilots knew all that.

We made the long half-hour trek across the first big bay at about half-throttle and went eastward through the "narrows." Fifteen minutes later, we opened out into another giant bay. The big cruiser turned northeast for a long diagonal crossing, heading straight toward the distant dome of Navajo Mountain. I always knew where I was when it was in my view, and I preferred its real name: *Naatsis'áán*, Head of the Earth Woman, because it made me feel like she watched over me.

We'd been running a little over an hour when the engines slowed for a little and then stopped, placing us nearly a quarter-mile offshore, near Cookie Jar Butte. The beach that we could see from the deck was smooth and level, and we probably could've dropped anchor closer to it. But at the lake's current water level, that beach was long and shallow, so the pilot was being cautious by anchoring this far out.

At least cruising through the spectacular scenery had kept everyone occupied so far, but now we sat, becalmed in the middle of nowhere, on a hot afternoon. No roads came down to the lakeshore we were pointed at, not for many miles in either direction. We were way off the main channel and hadn't passed another boat for quite a while. It was mercifully quiet once the cruiser cut its engines, until the music blasted from the sound system. At least it was Motown.

Kai and Len chatted with film crew members they knew. Hardly anyone else was talking, which wasn't surprising, given that it was hard to tell what this assortment of people might have in common. Most of them sure were drinking, though, and maybe that would improve conversation after a little while. That wouldn't help me any, because I was being cautious with the beer. Social awkwardness and beer serve each other too well, especially when the weather is hot, and I had my kids to look after.

Pressfield's personal assistant announced that she was ready to swim. Pressfield said he didn't know how, so she dived into the crystal-clear water and swam around alone. The pilot took off his shirt and jumped in wearing shorts. He immediately swam toward the young woman.

Peggy joined me beside the deck rail. "That could get him shot," she said.

"By Pressfield?" I said. "Nah. I wouldn't worry."

"Dear lord, no. Not Pressfield. By, you know, her father. Elders. Brothers." She gestured vaguely northward, indicating the settlement where Abe Bingham and his wives lived among other polygamists.

"Oh, right. Yeah, I *thought* she was from High Creek," I said. "He probably has no idea." We watched in fascination as the pilot and the girl frisked in the water, like dolphins at play. I asked Peggy, "Are you going to swim, too?"

"Probably," she said, "nothing else to do but drink." She glanced around the deck and sipped a little more before asking, "What's with this group? I hardly recognize anyone."

"I was wondering that myself," I said. "I keep expecting Hercule Poirot to show up and say that he supposes we're all wondering why he gathered us here."

That made Peggy laugh. "It does seem like a guest list put together by Agatha Christie. Where's the hostess?"

I said, "Maybe I'll run into her below while I'm hunting for the head."

"The fanciest one is off the corridor forward. Take a right when you get to the bottom of the stairs."

Following Peggy's directions, I passed a door with a hand-lettered "closed for repair" sign at the bottom of the stairs. Waiting in the hallway —there's always a line for the restrooms when more than two people are on a boat—I wondered if Margolin was giving Hollywood a discount due to the off-limits bathroom. That reminded me of his concern about decorations, so I checked out the buffet and bar on my way back out —no streamers, no bunting, no balloons. There wasn't even a flower arrangement on the table.

By the time I reached topside, the pilot was back aboard. So was the assistant, and now that her white suit was dripping wet from the swim, she may as well have been buck naked with the bright pink polka dots painted right on her skin. She didn't seem to notice.

Settling into a lounge chair, I watched lazily as assorted swimmers jumped in, splashed around, and climbed back up on board to drink some more.

Kai perched on a folding chair next to me and pulled a notebook from her pocket to make notes for an article about the party that she planned to write for the paper. It wouldn't include any photos, because I hadn't let Len bring his camera. I told him that there was too much risk of losing it on the lake, and that was certainly true. But the real reason was that photos of a party involving scantily-clad people drinking way too much would surely be embarrassing. The girl in the see-through swimming suit was a case in point.

It was past four o'clock when I saw Kathy again. Wherever she'd been hiding, she still hadn't changed into a swimsuit. Not that I blamed her —I wasn't wearing a swimsuit, either. She stood at the rail and peered southward for a few minutes. I hoped that she was about ready to pull up anchor and shove off for the marina.

She watched as Peggy dived into the water, neatly entering the surface without any splashing at all. Hamilton O'Neill sort of fell in after Peggy. He was swimming pretty well, so he wasn't as drunk as I thought. Off in the middle distance, a boat was turning north and heading in our direction. Kathy turned her attention to that for a while and then went below again. It occurred to me that she might be feeling a little seasick.

The approaching boat was moving faster than I would've thought. I leaned on the rail to see it better. It was a long-nosed ski boat carrying two people and at least one set of water skis. As it got closer and slowed its pace, I recognized John Rice and Fred.

When they pulled alongside and tied up to a cleat, Kathy emerged from the salon again. Stepping up to the rail, she shouted, "Ahoy there! Permission to board granted!"

Fred jumped onto the sport ladder bolted to the side of the yacht and climbed aboard, brushing Kathy aside none too gently, and Rice climbed up right behind him.

As soon as they stepped on deck, Kathy said, "What a beautiful boat!" Smiling, she turned to Rice and said, "I bet it's been a hot, bumpy ride for you guys, though. You need to sit in the shade for a while and have yourselves a beer or two."

Before they could say anything, she scrambled down the ladder and dropped behind the wheel of the ski boat. She looked up to face the cruiser and smiled. "I've always wanted to drive one of these!" she shouted up at us, "I'll be back in a couple of minutes!" She untied the rope and started the engines, a pair of large outboard motors.

As she cleared the side of the cruiser and picked up speed, everyone on deck watched in amazement. She waved happily. Seconds later, the speedboat gunned it loudly.

I turned to John Rice. "What was *that* all about?"

"Beats the hell out of me," he said, staring at the boat he'd just climbed out of. "What a spoiled brat." I must've looked surprised, because he went on, "What? Do you think I didn't know? Jesus."

"I've gotta hit the head," Fred said as he moved away from the rail.

"I'm next," Rice said. "Hurry up."

As I said, there's always a line for the bathroom on a party boat.

Kai joined the crowd that had gathered near the ladder. After things calmed down, she rested her notebook on the railing, writing notes as fast as she could. I went back to watching the swimmers, who were all treading water near the bow as they watched the speed boat race away. Then I heard Len call, "Hey, Mom!" and I twisted around to see him sitting up on the top deck behind the controls, pretending to drive the big cruiser.

Out of the corner of my eye, I saw Herman's assistant stumble up the stairs from the salon. He was followed by Herman, who was clearly being shoved from behind.

Fred was the one doing the shoving as he ran up the stairs shouting, "Jump! Jump, everybody!" When he got to the rail, he grabbed Kai around her waist and threw her overboard, notebook and all.

"Everybody!" he shouted again. "Jump overboard! The boat is going to explode!" With that, he plunged into the lake himself.

First, I looked to see if Kai had righted in the water and was swimming okay. She was. I saw Len jump into the water from the top deck. Neither of them had a life vest on. No one did, but that didn't stop them from jumping.

As I stood there worrying about life vests, John Rice threw me overboard. I surfaced, coughing and blinking water out of my eyes before getting my bearings.

Fred was still shouting. "Swim, damn it! Get the hell away from the boat, go!" He started swimming east to clear the bow by a good distance and then turned north. My kids followed him.

Pressfield was still standing at the rail. He yelled, "I can't swim!"

"Jump anyway," I shouted up at him. "We'll help you."

He hadn't moved when I heard my kids yelling, "Mom! Mom!" The lake had enough wave action to make it difficult to see them in the water, but I moved toward the sound of their voices.

As I swam, I tried to count noses. Those nearest to me were still staring at the boat. "Let's go!" I shouted. "Swim away from the boat!"

Within a few minutes, we were all strung out depending on our various amounts of clothing and swimming abilities. The beach to the north of us was a long way off, hundreds of yards. I'm not a great swimmer, but I knew that we would find sand beneath our feet long before we got to dry land.

My kids were treading water, waiting for me to get closer. Len swam over behind me like a border collie rounding up sheep.

"Can you guys see everybody?" I asked, glancing back toward the boat.

"No," Kai said, "but I can see the beach. Somebody is already standing in the water to his knees."

"Yeah," Len said. "We're going in the right—"

Behind him, the yacht exploded.

I covered my face. Had Pressfield made it into the water? When I opened my eyes, pieces of the boat were still tumbling down from the sky. It wouldn't be safe to get any closer to the wreck.

Suddenly I remembered Buckmaster and the enormous coolers he rolled onto the boat before we boarded. Holy hell, did Buckmaster bring a bomb to the party? Did Fred catch him setting it up? Did Herman Effing Buckmaster try—

"Mom! Mom, can you see anyone else?" Kai asked.

All I could see between us and the smoldering boat was debris floating on the water. I shook my head.

Len looked toward shore. "I think somebody's swimming back to us."

Black smoke was spiraling upward to the south. Poor Chuck Margolin had more to worry about than tape and thumbtacks messing up the finishes on his yacht.

There was a second explosion, and we saw flames rising into the black smoke above them.

CHAPTER TWENTY

IT was Fred who was swimming back to help us. By the time he reached us, though, our feet had already touched the sandy bottom, and we were resting, chest-deep in the water.

"Have you seen anyone else?" he asked when he got close enough.

"I couldn't see anyone behind us," I said.

When Fred stood up, his head was considerably higher than mine. He looked toward the burning cruiser and scanned the water for a while. "I can't, either," he said.

"Do you know how many made it to shore?" I asked.

"I haven't counted, but I could see you three still had quite a way to go." He reached out and nudged Kai. "Sorry about, you know, throwing you—"

She considered the smoke billowing out of the wreck before turning to him. "Don't be," she said and lifted her left hand out of the water. I was amazed to see that she was still holding her notebook. "No harm done," she said, grinning. "Good thing I use a pencil."

I looked at the dripping notebook as she held it up above the surface. "Won't the water… I don't know, dissolve the paper? Wash away your notes?"

"Not hardly," she said happily. "I'll let the notebook dry out before opening it, and then the notes'll be perfect. I lost my pencil, though."

After the kids and I caught our breath, we found swimming toward shore a little easier. Fred stayed behind to keep scanning the water for anyone else who needed help.

When we straggled ashore, everyone else was standing in a group, gaping at the fire and smoke. I knew that other boats in the channel would be turning north by now. Lots of help would arrive soon. In the meantime, I stood next to Peggy and joined the others in silently watching the remaining pieces of yacht burn and sink.

After a while, Peggy turned to me and said, "Pressfield," answering the question I hadn't asked yet. "I've counted, and I think he's the only one missing. Did you see him jump?"

"No, I was swimming toward the kids. Last I saw, he was still at the rail. Then the explosion."

Nobody seemed interested in talking, so I walked over to where John Rice was standing a little distance from the others. He was watching Fred, who was still in the water.

"What happened, Mr. Rice?"

"Please, Naomi. Call me John. I think the situation in which we find ourselves precludes formalities."

"I guess it does. So, what happened, John?"

He faced me and shook his head. Standing there in a dripping silk shirt and bedraggled linen trousers, he looked almost vulnerable. He ran a hand over the top of his head before crossing his arms. Then he said, "All I know is that Kathy arranged for the ski boat and asked me to bring it out. She said she wanted to let the party guests waterski."

"And that made sense to you?" I said.

Peering out at Fred again, he said, "I've long since given up making sense of anything Kathy says. Or does. Fred and I think she's been… self-medicating. Especially recently. Pills. But she's always thought she was a law unto herself." That seemed almost funny, coming from a mob attorney, but I let it go.

I glanced over at Herman, who was shivering at the other end of the group. I pursed my lips and pointed at him with my chin. "He does, too. I bet he had something to do with it."

Rice raised one shoulder, like he had no opinion on the matter and didn't want to talk about it anymore. He walked over to where Fred was trudging up out of the water, and they sat down on the sand.

I joined them. Sitting down next to Fred, I asked, "How did you know the boat was going to explode?"

Fred leaned back on his elbows and stretched his legs out, like a sunbather perfecting his tan. "I'd like to say that my keen professional instincts kicked in. But the truth is that I really, really had to use the head. The one that was closest to the stairs had an "out of order" sign, but I managed to push the door open anyway."

I said, "Ew, Fred."

"I had to see—I mean, who knew what 'out of order' meant? Maybe the shower was broken, or the sink was missing. Besides, I was desperate, so I peeked inside."

John said, "And?"

"Well, like I said, I had to shove the door open because something was wedged under the door, sealing the room. The first thing that happened was that the smell of propane practically knocked me out."

"Yikes," I said.

"Yikes is right. I saw the propane tank on the floor, with the valve wide open. I figured someone must've opened it right before John and I tied up to the cruiser."

"Did you turn off the valve?"

"Did I—hell no, I didn't touch the damn thing. The room was already full of propane. There was no telling what was in there to ignite it."

I remembered the setup on the buffet table. "The chafing dishes all had little burners under them to keep the food warm. Maybe that's what did it, once the propane got out."

"Maybe. I didn't wait around to find out. I grabbed the waiters and ran up the stairs to get everyone the hell off the boat."

I glanced over at Herman Buckmaster, whose eyes stayed on the flaming debris that used to be a yacht. I checked on my kids, who were sitting near the edge of the shallow water as if it were an ordinary day at the beach. I turned to Fred, wanting to thank him for saving the day, but my voice failed me. I stood up, brushed off the sand, patted him awkwardly on the back, and went to see if anyone needed help.

Twenty minutes later the first Good Samaritan boat arrived, quickly followed by two more. All were runabouts that slid right up onto the beach. A couple of larger cruisers were holding about fifty yards offshore.

I was shocked when the fourth boat that beached was occupied by Lew Nez and his mother. Lew jumped out into the shallow water and helped his mom out. As they waded ashore, he spotted me and let go of his mother's hand.

He looked worried as he ran over and grabbed my shoulders. "Naomi! Thank God! Where are your kids? Are they okay?" I remembered telling him about the party and how I'd be forcing my children to go along for the ride. Lew's face relaxed into a smile when I told him we were fine, just a little waterlogged. He squeezed my shoulders, and that made me smile, too. His mother, on the other hand, was *not* smiling. Her face was doing the opposite of smiling.

She walked to us quickly. Urgently, even. "Well, Naomi Manymules," she said, "*Yá'át'ééh.*"

"*Yá'át'ééh shik'is,*" I said. It seemed okay for me to say hello, my friend instead of saying hello, my mother, the way a polite young person is supposed to greet an older woman. I was no longer a child.

"I didn't know that you still lived in Sage Landing," Ms. Nez said with a sharp sideways scowl at her son.

Lew let go of me. "That fire is bad, Naomi. Was anyone hurt?"

My kids were watching us. I motioned them over while answering, "We think one man was still on the boat when it exploded."

Lew said, "I see Herman over there. So this is the movie party?"

As Kai joined us, she answered, "It *was* a movie party. Len and I weren't *invited,* but Mom made us come *anyway* so that we *wouldn't be in danger.*" Then a grin spread over her face and she added, "You'll be able to read about it in the paper next week." She waved her soggy notebook in the air for emphasis.

Lew seemed at a loss for a response, so I asked, "What are you doing out on the lake today?"

Mrs. Nez edged herself in front of Lew and answered for him. "Lew was going to show me Rainbow Bridge now that the water is high enough to take a boat in close to it, but we got a late start." She regarded my kids. "What lovely children," she said.

I knew that Kai was trying to think of a way to protest that she wasn't a child, but she politely kept her mouth shut. Len looked down at the sand. I was sure I'd hear later how "not lovely" he was.

Before I could do any formal introductions, Peggy pulled me aside. "The Park Service needs to know about the explosion, and the chief needs to find Kathy," she said quietly. "I'd ask for a lift to the marina so that I could call in, but I have a crime scene to secure and a bunch of witnesses to sort out."

"I'm on it," I said. "Kids, stay here with Peggy for a minute. I'll be right back." Nodding my apologies to Lew and Mrs. Nez, I headed straight to where John Rice and Fred were still sitting.

"Hey, guys," I said, "I have to get to the marina to alert the authorities. This may sound like a stupid question, Fred, but are you carrying a gun?"

Fred looked over at Rice and got a permission-to-answer smile. "Yes," he said.

"You didn't lose it in the lake?"

"No," he said.

"Will it still work?" I asked, thinking of his long stay in the water.

"Of course it'll still work. Why?"

"I need to borrow it," I said.

Again, he deferred to his boss.

Rice said, "No. You can't."

"Look, I won't tell anybody," I said. "I can get Lew to take me back to the marina, but I don't know what we'll run into."

"Naomi," Rice said, "I'm a lawyer. Fred is a licensed security employee. We can't be handing over—" he glanced at Fred. "We can't hand you a weapon. But Fred can go with you."

Fred's eyes were on the people who were milling around the boats on the beach while Peggy tried to line them up in some sort of order, but he was listening to his boss. "Fred?" I asked.

"At your service," he answered, like he'd been waiting for a formal invitation.

"Good enough," I said. "I'll go set it up with Lew."

The arrangements took some discussion. Mama Nez refused to be left behind with strangers, so she climbed aboard with Lew, Fred, and me. The boat wasn't big enough to take the kids with us, and I thought they'd be safer on the beach anyway. Peggy was already getting everyone to sit down on the sand, far enough apart so that they couldn't easily sync up their stories without her hearing them. She wasn't in uniform—and that was an understatement—but she was still a cop.

The other would-be rescue boats were happy to help out by providing supplies. After they unloaded a lot of their water and picnic food, along with sunscreen and soft drinks and bug spray and some boxed wine, she sent them on their way, telling them to stay clear of the smoldering remains of Margolin's boat. She'd keep the rest of the passengers at the scene until more police arrived to take them securely back to town.

Fortunately, Lew's runabout had one hell of a big outboard motor, so we got underway at a good speed. Unfortunately, we were at least an hour behind Kathy. Assuming that she was headed to the marina, I tried to figure out what she'd do once she got there. Abandon the ski boat, maybe? Then what? I tried to put myself in her expensive shoes, and the movie location was where my mind's eye kept seeing her.

Mama Nez sat next to Lew as he steered the boat. Fred took an open-bow seat as far forward as he could get, to keep weight up front. I was left to sit at the back. The ride was almost an hour long. It seemed much longer to me.

As we approached the marina, Lew steered north a half-mile toward the main boat ramp and docks.

"Lew!" I shouted. "There's no phone on that dock! Get us over to Margolin's!"

He swerved toward the dock that I'd left a few hours before, but we couldn't get close to it. It was clogged with Saturday boaters, damn it. He steered back around, cruising slowly to find a place to tie up. I kept scanning the shore for Kathy's ski boat, but the marina was a "Where's Waldo" watercraft puzzle. My heart pounded.

Lew pulled up beside the first available space, so far away from Margolin's docks that I figured it would take at least ten minutes to get to the phone. Lew tied off as quickly as he could, and he jumped up on the dock to help his mother climb slowly out of the runabout.

I slid over to Fred. "We've got to get to the movie site," I whisper-yelled. "If Kathy went out there, God knows what she's going to do."

Fred looked up toward Lew and his mom.

I put my hand on his arm. "Please, Fred. Let's take the boat to the movie location. It won't take long to get there."

He motioned me over to the pilot's seat and unwound the rope from the cleat on the dock.

I reached for the keys, still dangling from the ignition, and shouted, "Lew! Call the police! Call the Park Service! Tell them—"

Mama Nez snapped, "That's not your boat, Naomi," but Lew was already running in the direction of Margolin's phone.

I backed us away from the dock and turned us around at a quiet idle. A hundred feet out, I gave it a little more gas.

Fred sat down next to me and asked, "Did you ever steal a boat before?"

"No, but I've been playing outlaw with Lew this week, so this fits right in." I picked up speed a little and veered to the north along the shore.

"Have we got a plan?" Fred asked.

"The real question is, does Kathy have a plan?"

Fred said, "I've known her long enough to bet that she does." He shook his head. "I can't guess what it is. She's been taking pills—I don't know what."

"Yeah, your boss told me. Well, we can be pretty sure she blew up the boat, so that's a place to start. Maybe she had help, I don't know, but right now she's thinking we're all dead. I think that means we can get a jump on her."

"Maybe. What do you have in mind?"

"I'll beach Lew's boat a few hundred yards away from the movie location," I said. "We'll scope things out. Then we can figure out what to do."

Fred chuckled. "If you ever want a job in New Mexico, we could use you there. Can you shoot?"

"I blew up a boat from more than fifty yards away with a snub-nosed .38," I said. His expression said he thought I was kidding. "Only once, though," I added modestly.

Getting to the movie location by boat took less time than I expected. When I saw the shore of the movie set, I realized that I'd driven too far. I swung eastward and made a big circle back to the south. As soon as I could put a hill between us and the movie site, I beached the boat, running her well up onto the sand so she couldn't drift back out. Fred and I went over the bow onto dry sand.

"I didn't see any boats on the beach back there," Fred said.

"Or between here and the loading ramp," I said, "but Kathy could've gone further north."

"Or she took the ski boat back to the rental place and left it there."

"Or tied up at a temporary visitors' slip," I said. "So, we haven't got a clue."

Fred started walking. He said, "As soon as we can peek over the hill, watch for the car. It's a red Ford sedan."

"I know the car," I said.

Fred was first to spot it. Kathy was not in it, nor was she anywhere in sight. "Well, now we know one thing," he said, "she's here, where no one knows she's a killer." He added, "Well, let's hope not, anyway."

"Yes, let's hope. But I'm afraid she has a gun." I said.

He gave me a grim smile. "Trust me. She has a gun."

I said, "The vest?"

He nodded. "Sometimes she carries it in the vest." He looked back toward the camp. "Or maybe she had one stashed in the car. We'll be lucky if she's got only *one*."

Gulp.

"I want to disable the car," Fred said. "It's closed up, and if I know Kathy, it's locked."

"If she's in her trailer," I said, "she can't see the car."

"Same if she's in the dining tent, I guess," Fred said. "I'll try to get over there and let the air out of her tires."

"No, I'll do it. You've got the gun. Cover me." I'd always wanted to say that. Surprisingly, it wasn't nearly as satisfying as I'd expected, which must have something to do with being in actual peril.

"Okay, you sneak over to the car," he said, agreeing a little more quickly than seemed proper. "I'll yell if I see her, and you hit the ground."

"What do you mean you'll *yell*? Just shoot her!" I said.

"That's against the law unless she pulls a gun," Fred said, and I could hear actual disapproval in his voice. "No, I only need to distract her."

"Shit, Fred! Give *me* the gun. I'm more of a shoot-first person myself, especially with someone who just tried to blow me up."

He laughed. "I won't let her shoot you, Naomi. You want me to go flatten the tires?"

"No," I said reluctantly, "I'll do the tires. You shoot Kathy. I'll lie for you later."

"Spoken like a lawyer," he said.

I crouched down and scooted over the hill to Kathy's car. I'm not sure that the crouching made a lot of sense, considering that there was absolutely no ground cover and the sun was casting long, dramatic shadows. But it seemed like the thing to do at the time.

Letting air out of tires is a slow process. I started with the tires furthest from the movie set. When those two tires were flat, I decided that was enough. I didn't feel like squatting on the other side of the car, with my back to Kathy if she came this way. I looked around and signaled to Fred. He climbed over the hill and walked to meet me.

He said, "Stay out here behind the car. I'll try to find her."

"Hell no," I said. "I'll walk behind you and your gun. Two sets of eyes will be better than one."

"Let's go."

"First, I have a question. Do you think she'll pull her gun and start shooting when she sees us?"

Fred shook his head. "She won't draw on me"

"Why? Because she likes you so much?" I asked.

That got another grim smile. He said, "Here's a fun fact—Kathy doesn't like me at all. But she won't draw on me because she's seen me shoot. She wouldn't have a chance, and she knows it."

I looked at him carefully. "You're serious?"

"Yep."

We headed quietly for the big tent. No one seemed to be around, but Fred stopped so suddenly that I almost ran into him from behind. I could hear Kathy's voice but couldn't make out what she was saying. We walked in to find her standing in front of several actors and crew members who hadn't been invited to the party. They probably didn't even know about it. The only one I recognized was Molly, the script supervisor, who saw me and waved.

Kathy had pages in her hand when she followed Molly's gaze and spotted us. Oh, yeah, I could see her calculating her odds for a split second, but Fred was right. She didn't go for her gun. Instead, she ran out the other end of the tent and went straight for her car. We followed her, ducking behind a big wagon. Peeking around its corner, we saw her jump into the car. We heard the engine start, and we watched the Ford behave very badly in the sand with its two flat tires. The car gave up the struggle, and the engine went off.

We waited. A few long minutes later the driver's window rolled down and a gun came flying out. I took a step forward, but Fred stopped me.

"Could be more than one, remember?" he said. He shouted, "Both hands!"

She swung the car door open. Both of her hands slowly came out first. Finally, she stood up to face Fred as we stepped out from behind the wagon. "I'll call my uncle," she said.

He lowered the gun a little. "Are you shitting me, Kathy?"

She stood still, glaring at him. She didn't seem to notice me at all.

I shouted, "Look at me, damn it!" Her eyes flicked over to me before she glanced back at Fred. Lowering my voice to a growl, I said, "I was on that boat you blew up. My *kids* were on that boat."

She sneered. "Well, you're the one who insisted on bringing them to the party."

Raising the gun again, Fred said, "Shut up. Just shut up and back away from the car. Hands high."

She peered back into the open car door for a few seconds.

"Don't try it, Kathy," Fred said.

"Go for it, Kathy!" I yelled. "Please go for it."

She looked at Fred's extended gun hand and took two dramatic steps back, hands even higher in the air.

I said, "Now take off the vest."

Fred glanced over at me, smiling a little. "Good call." He turned back to Kathy and barked, "You heard her—vest off. Drop it."

She performed a full-body eye-roll that would have done any teenager proud while shrugging off the vest as slowly as she possibly could. It dropped to her feet, where it would neatly trip her if she tried to take off running.

"Hands back up," I said, mostly because telling Kathy Roberson what to do was so satisfying. "And turn around."

Once she had her back to us, Fred said, "Go get that gun, Naomi. Pull out the clip."

I walked over and stooped to pick up the gun. Fred's eyes were fixed on Kathy, so he didn't notice when I slipped the little pistol into my pocket, its clip still firmly in place.

CHAPTER TWENTY-ONE

K AI shook me awake on Sunday morning. "Mom, Mr. Carson is here. Wake up!"

My bedside clock said seven. I threw on a robe and found Carson was the kitchen pouring coffee into two mugs. He looked bone-weary.

"Where've you been, Carson? You're all tuckered out."

"Look who's talking," he said. "I've just come from the police station. Peggy is even worse off than you are, by the way."

"Well, thanks, I guess. I'm sure she got less sleep than either of us," I said. "So, she's speaking to you?"

"Strictly in a professional capacity, it seems, but yes, for now." He sat at our kitchen island with his coffee and leaned down to pet Three-Steps, who gazed up at his face adoringly.

"You're such a charmer," I said as I picked up my coffee from the counter and sat down at the island across from him.

Carson asked the dog, "Is she talking to you or to me?" Hearing no answer, he sat up and shifted his attention to me. "Peggy filled me in about the explosion," he said. "She said you pretty much boatjacked Lew and his mom."

I laughed. "It sounds bad when you put it that way." I hoped that Lew was able to retrieve his boat from impound without too much trouble. His mom was probably dragging him away from Sage Landing at that very moment. She'd seen a little too much holding of my hands for her comfort, so she'd be pushing him to get back to that girl—Anita—in Gallup. Lew might say that Anita wasn't his girlfriend, but I had a feeling that it wasn't entirely up to him. Dating her wouldn't break any rules, and she probably hadn't ever stolen his boat, either. "Did they ever find Benjamin Pressfield?"

Carson nodded. "His body washed ashore about a mile to the south of the explosion." He swirled his coffee for a bit before asking, "What the hell were you thinking, going after Kathy like that?"

I was still trying to figure that out myself, so I said, "Honestly, I don't know. By the time we got to the marina, I was afraid she'd go on a rampage at the movie location. I thought she'd start shooting everyone before we could get the police out there to stop her."

"So, you stormed in to let her shoot at you instead?"

"Don't exaggerate. I didn't storm, I snuck. And I was armed. I mean, Fred was armed, which was even better. And he's really big, too." Like Carson didn't already know how big Fred was.

Carson ignored that, getting up to put his mug in the sink. He leaned back against the counter with his hands resting on its edge, ready to change the subject. "Mike Rodriguez got Dee released as soon as Kathy Roberson started talking."

I said, "Because Kathy killed Shawn Gordon and tried to pin it on Dee."

"Yeah. Mike says Kathy happily laid out the whole story, starting when she put on a disguise that night so she could tail Gordon."

"Don't tell me—she put on a blond wig and big, black sunglasses, didn't she?"

Carson looked surprised. "You saw her?"

"Well, yes, but I had no idea it was her. So that's how hair from a blond wig ended up on the *Deep Inn*?"

"Don't get ahead of the story. Anyway, there she was in Wranglers, watching Shawn Gordon. She saw him tangle with Dee. Later, she saw him get in Dee's truck, so she followed it out to the marina."

I said, "Oh, boy. It couldn't have been more perfect, could it? A perfect set-up with a perfect suspect to pin it on."

Carson gave me a look. "I thought you wanted to hear what happened."

"Sorry, sorry. It kind of falls into place, doesn't it?"

"Kind of. Anyway, after Dee left, Kathy boarded the yacht with a bottle of Shawn's favorite sour-mash bourbon. She told him that Pressfield wanted her to keep Shawn company. She got him drinking—the guy had a serious problem, seems like."

"That's why he had so much alcohol in him?" I asked.

"That's part of why," Carson said. "When he was about to pass out, she told him, quote, 'the truth about what a mistake it was to cast him in the movie' and said he should, quote, 'reconsider the role.'"

I couldn't help myself. I said, "Holy shit. She truly is a monster."

"Well put," Carson said. "She was waving his contract in front of him. Then she started to tear it up, so he stood up and tried to grab it. That was when she picked up my pipe wrench and hit him."

"Giving her a weapon to plant as evidence against Dee later on."

"*Plant*'s the right word. She especially admired her own foresight about that. The news coverage gave her Dee's name, and then all she had to do was look up the address in the phone book."

"So she set the wrench aside to take with her, and then she shot him, to seal the deal?"

"While he was on the floor, yeah."

"Why the knife in the chest?"

"She seemed to think that hiding the bullet in his chest would make it harder to pin down the time of death."

"But it didn't, did it?"

"No, it didn't. But that didn't faze her. She was still very impressed with herself as a take-charge kind of killer."

I shuddered.

He went on, "Anyway, Mike found out that the state police were holding Dee in Winslow. He's already left to pick her up and bring her home."

"She's been cleared, right?"

A quick smile flickered across his face. "Completely. I have it directly from George Bliss—all charges against Dee have been dropped. That's why Mike's driving over instead of letting a state trooper bring her. The college trustees asked him to assure her of their complete support. She's no longer on administrative leave."

"Well, good. And where were you while all this was going on?"

"Eleanor called me yesterday afternoon. She had a tip that Dee was being held at Kingman."

"And you went? But Mike wouldn't—"

"I stopped by the station to let him know I was going unless he arrested me. He said I shouldn't tempt him like that, but he didn't stop me. Anyway, Dee wasn't actually in Kingman. I didn't find that out until I'd driven the four hours over there."

"And it took four more hours to get back here," I said. "Poor guy."

"Six more hours. My truck broke down near Ashfork—it was the ignition coil, so I was lucky that the repair only added another two hours. I got back to Sage Landing around one o'clock this morning and went straight home."

I got up to put my mug in the sink, too, and turned around to lean against the counter next to him. "Yeah, that's about when I got home, too. But at least I didn't have to hang out in Ashfork."

He said, "It was better than being blown up and drowned, I guess."

I nudged him with my elbow. "I don't know, Carson, that drive sounds pretty bad."

Kai and Len were eavesdropping from the living room, and both of them laughed.

Another smile briefly flashed over Carson's face. Then it was gone and he crossed his arms. "Do you have *any* idea what Kathy thought was going to happen after the boat blew up?" he asked.

I shrugged. "She seemed to think she was going to finish making the movie."

He had to think about that for a good long while. "You—you say that as if it makes sense. But I'm finding it very hard to believe."

He wasn't the only one. "I'm not saying it makes sense. She'd been taking who-knows-what drugs. John and Fred both told me about that. She had the crazy eyes out there on the boat yesterday, and before that, too, now that I think about it."

Carson looked up at the ceiling as he mulled it over. "I thought that was just how actors looked," he said. "Anyway, what would blowing up a boatful of people have to do with finishing the movie?"

"I think she was starring in her own private movie called 'Kathy Roberson Makes an Award-Winning Film.' The people she invited to the boat were the ones who hadn't followed the script in her head. They were her bad guys—like, the drunken costar. The producer she'd started to hate. Her uncle's henchmen. The nervous caterer who wanted his investment back. The nosy paralegal. The cop who was smart enough to put two and two together. Crew members who grumbled. The stubborn attorney who wouldn't even keep a pinky promise, though she didn't find that out till later."

"Definitely a capital offense."

"Right," I said. "Now you're getting it. I'm sure she already had another plan to get you out of the way, too. Like you said, Kathy hasn't heard 'no' very often in her life."

"So she set up the party like a special-effects movie climax, getting rid of all the bad guys in one spectacular explosion."

I nodded. "Think about it, Carson. What could be more Hollywood than a spectacular explosion, paving the way for her happy, Oscar-winning ending?"

"And you believe that she was actually that deluded?"

"I don't know for sure, Carson, but I'd be happy to beat the answer out of her."

~ ~ ~

Monday morning felt much more relaxed, more like summer. The kids intended to sleep till nine or ten in the morning, as God intended kids to do in the summer. According to Kai, anyway. So far they were making good on that.

Since they wouldn't be working at the movie location, I'd need to figure out who would supervise them while I was at work all summer. For the next few days, though, I was okay with them taking care of themselves. Len would be busy catching up on the comic books that he and his friends read, swapped, and read again. Kai would be busy, too, writing up a series of articles about her movie set experiences. She wanted to call it "Hollywood Underbelly," but her editor—who was me—gave that a thumbs-down because it sounded sleazy. I liked "On Location." She was still negotiating.

A Desert Place, the movie, would never get made. It had never really gotten started. Maybe there was something to the idea that the production was cursed, the way other *Macbeth* versions had been from time to time. I had no idea who would take charge of the million details that would have to be managed.

Kathy was in the Sage Landing city jail, but she wouldn't be there very long. The explosion happened in the national park, so the FBI got to call the shots. They'd be moving her somewhere else pretty soon. It couldn't happen soon enough to suit me.

There was no word yet on who would prosecute her for killing Shawn Gordon. I was just relieved that the murder wasn't our problem anymore.

My purse was reassuringly heavy as I hefted it up on my shoulder to leave for work. I still had the gun that Kathy threw out her car window. No one had asked for it yet, so it was nestled in my bag. I told myself that since it wasn't the murder weapon, the police could wait for it till they gave mine back. Fair's fair.

When I got to the office, Carson was sitting in a client chair in the front office, ankle on knee, watching the parking lot through the window. He was all cleaned up and wearing the new suit. On his feet were polished shoes and a spiffy pair of argyle socks.

"Are we expecting a client?" I asked as I dropped my purse on the desk. It made a muffled thud as it landed.

"We have clients, and we'll probably see some of them today."

Both of those things were certainly true, but that didn't answer my question. I'd just have to watch how the day unfolded. "Will we get any new business out of the movie production's last gasps?"

Carson smiled. "More likely some Los Angeles entertainment firm will handle those particular issues. But we still represent John Rice and his company."

I thought that the important thing was that we still had most of that retainer in the bank, and I wasn't going to give any of it back to anybody if I could help it. "And there's Dee," I said.

"Well, we haven't been much use to her," Carson said.

"Hold on!" I said, "We were on that from the beginning. You spent the weekend going all over hell for her. Dee's lucky she had us."

"And you don't want to refund her retainer, right?"

"It's business, Carson. Billable hours."

He shook his head, but he was still smiling. He headed for his office. I sat down to turn on the computer. When I thought back over all the crap we'd gone through for Dee, I felt justified in using her retainer to pay office expenses. Especially since those expenses included my wages.

At about eleven o'clock the door opened. It wasn't either of the clients we'd been talking about. It was good old Herman Buckmaster, who seemed very nervous.

"Hello, Ms. Manymules," he said. He cleared his throat. "Good morning. Have you and the children recovered from... from the weekend?"

Here I have to admit that I'd had a hard time letting go of my suspicion that he'd been involved in blowing up the boat. But at the police station Saturday night, Peggy told me that Buckmaster's big coolers drifted to shore after I'd left on Lew's boat. They were empty, and the lids were gone, but they hadn't held any bombs. She'd said, "He's a jerk, but he didn't kill anyone. And he wouldn't know the first thing about how to blow up a boat anyway."

He was still an embezzler. Also a libeler and a complete jerk. But I remembered Carson's warning about what was and was not my business, and, reluctantly, put a friendly expression on my face. "Good morning, Mr. Buckmaster," I said. "We're fine. Thank you for asking."

"That's good. Good." He stopped to clear his throat again and said, "I want to apologize."

This surprised me. "Apologize for what?"

He said, "I should have said something. When we were setting up, I noticed that the gas grill was missing one of its propane tanks. I meant to find it, but I got distracted. And then..." his voice trailed off. He looked miserable.

"Herman," I said, "You were busy. Propane tanks get changed out all the time. And it almost never means that a boat is about to explode."

Buckmaster nodded, but his expression didn't change.

I went on, "Can I assume that your next stop will be Anasazi Community College? The Office of the President, to be specific?"

He seemed to shrink, looking down at the floor and dropping his voice. "I met with Dr. Moreno first thing this morning. What I did was just... well, she was very gracious, especially considering how out of line I was."

Considering how out of line he was, I thought, *maybe Carson will tell her to sue the ever-living daylights out of him.* But I didn't say anything, so he stumbled on. "I also contacted the editor of the Sage Landing Gazette. I'll be giving them an interview, correcting the record, retracting everything ..." He craned his neck, trying to peer into the inner office. "Is Carson in?" he asked.

Carson came to his doorway. "Morning, Buck," he said. "What's up?"

"Maybe we could go into your office?" Buckmaster said.

"No need for that, Buck. My colleague and I share all information in this law firm."

I didn't know whether Carson said that to needle Buckmaster or to compliment me, but it was good to hear either way.

Unusually subdued, Herman didn't argue. He backed up to the closest chair and sat down. "After all that's happened recently, here you both are today, business as usual."

Carson said, "Legal needs don't stop, I guess, because here *you* are, yourself, today."

Frowning down at the surface of my desk, Herman said, "I may have some need of counsel. I'm not sure."

"Well, tell us what you can, Herman," I said, opening the notebook on my desk and picking up a pencil.

Carson walked toward the front window so that we were arranged in a comfortable triangle for conversation.

"I have a matter regarding a rather large loan," Herman said slowly. "Some of the documentation has gone missing. There may be some delays in repayment."

That answered a few questions for me and probably confirmed Lew's suspicions. "Are you the payee?" I asked, as if I didn't know better.

"No. Other way around."

I made a note on my spiral pad. "Have you received a demand for payment?"

"Yes. Well, no. Not from the payee, no. But some other expenses have arisen."

Carson and I looked at each other.

I said, "Expenses related to the loan with missing documentation?"

Buckmaster hesitated. "Not exactly."

"What, then?" Carson asked.

Thoroughly uncomfortable, Buckmaster said, "Business investments. Like, I needed to hire a computer consultant and buy a couple of high-end desktop computers and stuff."

"You hired a computer consultant," Carson said, frowning. "For two fast-food places?"

"Plus two food trucks," Herman said defensively. "It's more complicated than you think, and custom programming doesn't come cheap."

Uh-oh, I thought. Was he saying what I thought he was saying? Feeling a little light-headed, I asked, "Why take on those expenses right now if you're in a financial crunch?"

Carson was a lot more direct, asking quietly, "Herman, is someone pressuring you to make these expenditures now?" He was talking to Buckmaster, but he was glaring at me.

Herman sighed. "No, of course not. I shouldn't have mentioned it. That's not what I'm here for." He waved a dismissive hand in the air before going on, "I have a few legal questions. Hypothetical ones, you understand, about—"

Carson spoke up. "I've heard that you invested in the movie production. Maybe the insurance settlement will resolve your dilemma."

Herman was quiet, and I could almost see the wheels turning as he tried to come up with something to say without admitting to a crime. Eventually, he said, "There could be quite a lengthy delay."

Carson said, "Actually, there's a lot of California money tied up in the film production, Buck. Money that belongs to people who can bring quite a lot of pressure to bear for a speedy payout on the insurance."

Now Herman seemed a little lost. "What?" he said.

Patiently, I clarified, "Mr. Carson is saying that the insurance payout could be in your hands before your 'lender' expects replacement…I mean, repayment."

Tilting his head like a puppy, Herman said, "Oh?"

Carson said, "Keep in mind that the insurance payout may not cover the full investment, whatever that was, but all losses will be prorated among the investors."

I added, "Would you be prepared to make up any remaining shortfall with your own funds?"

Visibly drained by the whole thing, Herman shrugged.

Carson said, "Let's leave it at that for the time being, Buck, and see how it all works out."

The mayor stood up slowly. "Sounds like good advice. All right. Okay. We'll leave it at that."

"Yes, we'll wait and see," I said as he walked past Carson to the door.

After watching Herman cross the parking lot, Carson went back into his office. Through the wall, I heard him laughing.

CHAPTER TWENTY-TWO

N EAR the end of the day, Fred came in without John Rice. He hugged me, and I hugged him right back.

"Kids okay?" he asked.

"Great. They'll be celebrities for a long time on this." My purse was still lying on the desk. I opened it just enough and slid it toward him. "Do I have anything you want, Fred?"

He glanced down into the purse and said, "Nothing we ever want to see again, in fact."

"Thanks," I said. "The cops have mine. I don't know for how long."

"I have no idea what you're talking about," he said, smiling.

Carson came back into the room and shook Fred's hand. He said, "Thanks for coming in. I wanted to be sure we had a chance to talk before you left town. Come on back into my office where the chairs are more comfortable. You too, Naomi."

Carson wanted to talk with Fred? As if Fred were an official client? Was that why he dressed up—he'd made an appointment with *Fred*, the guy who'd thrashed him in the hospital parking lot a few short months before? Stranger things have happened, I guess, but not very many.

After settling behind his desk, Carson said, "What have you found out?"

Fred leaned back in the chair, stretching out his legs and crossing his ankles as if he were still lounging on the sand. "I talked to John like you asked. He said to tell you guys to stay on retainer. Shutting down the movie project is kicking up lots of legal issues."

My boss said, "Thank him for me, and ask him to thank Mr. Deguerra, too. But please be sure that Mr. Deguerra understands that we can't help with Kathy's defense. I'm not qualified for federal court. Is John?"

Fred shook his head. "No, he isn't, but he wouldn't touch it even if he was. Besides, the latest word from Carl was that 'the brat' could do life as far as he was concerned."

"Did he mean it?" I asked. "Isn't he a little concerned that the feds will make her an offer?"

"Nope. She knows better." Fred paused to let that sink in. Then he continued, "I'm thinking he'll stick to what he said about not helping her, at least for a while. But the rumor is that he owes his brother—Kathy's dad—big time, so who knows. It's what I hear. None of my business."

He stood up quickly like he wanted to leave the whole episode behind.

Carson stood up, too. The guys shook hands again and said their good byes.

Turning to Fred, I said, "I'll walk you out."

Carson was a little surprised, but I ignored that. I had something to say to Fred, and it would be easier without an audience.

When we got to Fred's car, he smiled at me and asked, "Need a lift somewhere? Want to go to the beach? Steal a runabout, maybe?"

I shivered involuntarily, smelling again the evil smoke that billowed from the ruined boat as we swam for our lives. "No, not today," I said, "But, Fred,"—here I reached up to put my hands on his impossibly beefy shoulders and examined his craggy face— "Fred, I don't know how to thank you. For everything."

The big guy actually blushed.

I stepped back, looked away, and blinked really fast before asking, "What does John Rice really think about this whole thing?"

Fred opened the car door and sat behind the wheel. "Honestly, I think he was hoping I'd shoot her when we found her." He pulled his sunglasses from behind the visor and put them on. After pulling the door shut, he rolled the window down and added, "But that's not my style."

"I could see that," I said. "But if I'd had the drop on her like you did, I probably would've shot her."

"And *I* could see *that*," Fred said. "She damn near blew up your kids."

~ ~ ~

Sue Gallo was hosting that week's S&B in her lush backyard. Normally I would've walked, but I took my car so that I could swing by the grocery store first. It's poor form to show up at S&B without something to share, and I thought it would be a good idea to pick up some bug spray, too. Mosquitos love me.

I pulled up to the curb in front of Sue's house and parked right behind Dee's brawny pickup truck. Seeing the truck there—knowing that Dee was with the others, wine glass probably in hand already—absolutely made my day. I'd been worried that she might hide out in her house after what she'd been through. I should've known better.

Shoving the car keys into my pocket, I grabbed the grocery bag in one hand and my knitting basket in the other. After quick swivel of the hips to slam the car door shut, I practically sprinted around the house to Sue's back yard.

A mismatched collection of outdoor furniture was spread around the fountain at the edge of the herb garden. The place was full of knitters. Every one of them was laughing. Sure enough, there was Dee, right in the middle of things. Her hair was up in a ponytail, she was wearing a pink tank top over denim shorts, she had old flip flops on her feet, and she looked completely at home.

Sue jumped up from a camp stool near the patio. She grabbed my grocery bag, looked inside, and reached in to grab the mosquito repellent. "You won't need it," she said as she handed it over. "My citronella candles are industrial-strength." She took the tortilla chips and salsa out of the bag, too, and put them on a picnic table already crowded with happy-hour nibbles. "Wine cooler?" she asked.

I nodded, taking the cold pink bottle she held out to me. "What'd I miss?"

She looked out at the group. "Lucille?" she called, raising her voice so she could be heard over the hilarity. "Lucille! Naomi wants to know what she missed."

Lucille stood up to wave me over. "Guys, guys. Hush a minute." After the ruckus quieted down a little, she turned to me. "You're in luck. Dee's just getting started."

"That's right," said Dee cheerfully. "I'm telling stories about the Big House. Life in the clink. Doin' time in the steel chateau as a guest of the state."

More laughter. I threaded my way through the group to sit in a faded plastic lawn chair that I pulled over next to Dee. "Wow," I said. "That's a pretty impressive collection of clichés you have there."

"Thanks," said Dee. "I had a little time on my hands, so I figured I might as well use some of it to expand my inventory of euphemisms for incarceration."

Her face was still sunny, but there was a little tension around her eyes. I could tell that she was determined to make light of the whole being-accused-of-murder thing, not to mention the having-your-reputation-dragged-through-the-mud thing. That attitude was probably for the best, all things considered, and if anyone could pull it off, it would be Dee.

Later, as the sun was setting and everyone packed up to head home, Marybeth and I volunteered to take the trash out to the street on our way. After we chucked the trash bags into the bin at the end of Sue's driveway, Marybeth said, "I'm so glad the movie people are going away. Maybe we can get back to normal—" she laughed softly—"at least, as normal as anything ever gets around here."

I laughed a little, too. "Same here. I'll see you next week." I was about to turn away when I remembered something and added, "Wait, quick question?"

"Sure," she said.

"Was Lew able to rescue those discs for you?"

She looked confused. "Rescue?"

I said, "Didn't you have a bunch of computer discs get fouled up? Covered with something really gummy?"

Shifting her knitting basket to her other hand, she said, "Ugh, yes. Herman Buckmaster is a total klutz. What a mess. I didn't even want to touch them. Lew told me he gave it a good try, but he couldn't recover anything."

I opened my mouth to say something, but no words came out.

Marybeth didn't notice. She went on, "It took me weeks to enter the data on those suckers. Weeks. Lew said he had to throw away every last disc. He couldn't read a thing."

Finding my voice again, I said, "But there were back-ups, weren't there? On the computer?" Lew had said there weren't, but now I was questioning just about everything he'd told me.

She shook her head. "No, and that was my fault. I thought I was saving the data in both places. On the computer and on the floppy. But I must've messed up, because I couldn't find the files on my computer."

"Jeez, Marybeth. Where do you start re-doing something like that?"

"Herman said not to worry about it. He'll dig out the paper records, when he can get around to it, and hire a temp to do the data entry all over again." She glanced at her watch. "Hey, I gotta boogie. Good talking to you!"

"Me too," I said as she hurried to her car. "Good night."

I needed some time to think about what Marybeth had said. Continuing to stand there on the sidewalk in front of Sue's house wasn't an option, so I put my knitting basket in the back seat of the car, got behind the wheel, and drove out toward the lake.

By the time I pulled over next to a bluff overlooking the water, I couldn't even begin to say how angry I was. I'd been able to justify bending the law because I thought I was helping a friend save my town from a crook. But that little adventure looked different now, and I had no idea what to do about it. I was already on edge from dealing with too many people— law-breakers and law-enforcers and everyone in between.

I leaned back against the front bumper of my car, looking across the lake toward distant Navajo Mountain—*Naatsis'áán*, Head of the Earth Woman. A faint breeze came up the canyon, bringing the scent of desert sage on the evening air. It calmed me just enough to start making a mental list of everyone who'd pissed me off. That took quite a while.

~ ~ ~

I got back in the car, but instead of turning toward town, I headed in the other direction. Five minutes later I was walking into the Lunker Room.

After my eyes adjusted to the dim yellow light of the place, I spotted Carson talking to three other guys in a corner booth. When I got close enough for him to notice me, he stopped mid-sentence.

That made the other guys look my way. One of them was Abe Bingham, who smiled broadly and said, "Hi, Naomi. Good to see you."

"Hi yourself, Abe. Does Henrietta know you're here?"

He chuckled. "What do you think?"

I returned his smile. Since we both understood that Henrietta knew pretty much everything that went on near High Creek, I didn't need to answer. Instead, I turned to Carson and said, "Can I borrow you for a sec?"

Abe and the other two guys hastily grabbed their beers and excused themselves. They sat far enough away to make it clear that they wouldn't listen to us, stopping just short of holding their hands over their ears and chanting *lalala*.

I looked down at Carson, who waved his bottle of Miller Lite at the bartender with one hand while raising two fingers on the other. "No thanks," I said.

"What makes you think one of them is for you?" he asked. "I have the feeling that I'll need them both."

"Good call." I sat down across the table from him. "Since when do you drink light beer?"

"Abe ordered it," he said. "This isn't like you."

"What isn't?"

He waited as the bartender set two bottles and two glasses on the table. As the guy walked back to the bar, Carson poured one of the beers into a glass and slid it in front of me. "Coming to a bar at night. At least, that's what you've told me."

I slid the glass of beer back in his direction. "I wouldn't say it isn't like me. It just isn't a habit. I need to run something by you, and I knew you'd be here."

He smiled indulgently. "And it couldn't wait till tomorrow morning?"

"No. It could not—" I looked over my shoulder to confirm that no one had gotten close enough to overhear us "—because first thing in the morning I'm calling Mike Rodriguez to turn Lew in for blackmail."

As agitated as I was, some part of me still enjoyed watching how the patronizing grin instantly left his face.

"Woah, woah, woah." He leaned away from the table with his hands up, like he was fending off some kind of attack. "What the hell are you talking about?"

"You heard what Buckmaster said today. About how he had to buy new computers and pay through the nose for custom programming."

"So Lew's a good salesman. That's business. Where's the blackmail?"

"Well, he told Marybeth that all the data on the discs she asked him to fix was gone. He told her that he'd had to throw all the discs away. She mentioned it when I talked to her tonight."

"I fail to see the connection."

"Jesus, Carson. Do I have to spell it out for you?"

"Yes, Naomi. You have to spell it out for me. Where's the blackmail?"

"Those discs were where he got the numbers that made him suspect Herman Buckmaster. They weren't destroyed. So now I know that whatever he saw in—you know, in the secure room—"

"During your caper?"

"Don't be a smartass." The fire in my eyes could've burned two holes right in his face. I went on, "Whatever he saw in there confirmed his suspicions, which tells me the discs gave him proof."

"Proof of what?"

"Proof that Buckmaster was doing illegal stuff with the city's money. *That* was how Lew forced Herman to spend money he didn't have for computer stuff he didn't need."

"Are you saying that you were an accomplice to blackmail?"

"That's exactly what I am saying, Carson. I'll have to confess."

"Naomi. Take a breath. There's no blackmail for you to be an accomplice to. Who says Herman Buckmaster doesn't need those computer services? He told us that nobody pressured him. We'll take his word for it." He paused to slide the glass of beer in front of me again. "Go ahead and fume about Lew all you want. I don't blame you. But there's no evidence of any crime."

I picked up the glass and took a sip. "What about B & E?"

He shrugged. "Was there a break-and-enter somewhere? I've been in close contact with law enforcement for a couple of weeks now. I'm sure I would've heard if there'd been any breaking and entering."

I searched his face for a long minute. Then I took one more sip of beer and scooted out of the booth. "Sometimes I can't tell the crooks from the heroes."

Carson wrapped both hands around the bottle in front of him. "Me neither," he said, looking up at me with a faint smile. "Fortunately, that isn't our job."

I decided that he might be right.

THE END

Thank you for reading *Bear Witness.* Please rate it and recommend it wherever you can. Written reviews help any book's authors, and they help readers like you find what they are looking for. Do you have a favorite book-review blog, a group of friends on social media, or a large extended family? Tell them all to read Naomi Manymules.

You may wish to visit our web site, jdburges.com.

Thanks again!

The following sample is the first two chapters of *Coyote Alibi,* the first novel in the Naomi Manymules series of lighthearted legal mysteries from the edge of the Navajo Nation. *Coyote Alibi* has won three book awards so far.

CHAPTER ONE OF *Coyote Alibi*

EVERYBODY does good things and bad things—smart things and stupid things.

My law professor, Joseph Shelby, said that once. He said that was the reason we make laws and have courts and attorneys and sentences and settlements. He also said that was why the law was a secure profession that would really pay off for us when we finished our certificates. It was music to my ears. But our little paralegal extension program got canceled when Shelby got caught drinking ninety-proof "milkshakes" for supper during his night classes. It had taken the university three semesters to figure out what I could see in the first week of class.

That's why today found me with only half of a paralegal certificate, sitting on a bench in downtown Sage Landing, waiting for a lawyer. Downtown Sage Landing meant the old shopping mall. Looming over my head was the dusty and faded marquee of what used to be the town's movie theater. I remembered taking my kids to the last movie that played there. That would have been about five years ago, 1980 or '81 maybe. When they were still young enough not to mind being seen at a movie with their mom. Superman II, with adventure for them and Christopher Reeve for me. Now the old theater was an insurance office, but it still used the marquee. A stranger driving down the street would have thought that there were recent movies titled such things as, "Whole life is for loved ones—and for you!" Today's offering was, "Get a Quote for Your Boat."

You might wonder why there are boats needing insurance out here in the middle of the Arizona high desert, if you didn't know about the big lake, or if you didn't call to mind the mighty river on the other side of the dam that had made the big lake. As dry as this mesa is, and as tiny as the town that's perched here is, there are still lots of boats.

Unfortunately, the marquee didn't provide much protection from the midmorning sun that had already started to wilt me. I was as spruced up as anybody ever gets in Sage Landing, wearing a new long-sleeved white blouse with freshly-pressed khaki slacks. One of my more understated turquoise necklaces added just a touch of color. My shoulder-length dark hair was having a good day, and my touch of makeup would add polish if I didn't have to sit out in the sun too much longer. I knew that if I got a chance to talk to this lawyer about a job, my looks would be a plus. With only three paralegal courses behind me, I needed every plus I could get.

Each time a car turned into the largely empty parking lot, I scrutinized the driver to see if it was a man who matched the descriptions I'd heard for Grant Carson. He was reported to be in his late forties, athletic, suntanned, and rugged. He had been described to me by two different women I knew, both of them with a certain dreamy expression on their faces. After I'd spent forty-five minutes sitting on the bench, no such hunk had arrived.

An aging delivery van drove into the lot, and I looked into the side windows with mixed feelings. Seeing my friend Ellen in the passenger seat made me happy, though it reminded me that we hadn't touched base for quite a while. Seeing that the driver was her husband, Willard Highsmith, irritated me. But what made me really angry was seeing that Ellen's two children were in the van on a school day. I watched as everyone climbed out of the van and the two children opened its back doors and began to lift out cardboard boxes.

Before I could muster a cheerful greeting, a small, dilapidated pickup truck drove in and parked at the other end of the parking lot. An older-looking man got out. He didn't fit the mental picture I'd conjured up for the guy I was looking for, but something about him caught my attention. His salt-and-pepper hair was a bit shaggy, and his threadbare green T-shirt stretched over the slight beginnings of a beer belly. Dressed in faded and slightly grubby denims, he didn't warrant much interest, and I didn't look in his direction again until he began to unlock the office that I'd been watching. Then I got up from the bench, picked up the tan blazer that was folded neatly beside me, slipped into it, and smoothed my hair.

As I approached the door, he flipped a switch and flooded the front office with fluorescent light. The office had a large window across which hung the open slats of old-fashioned Venetian blinds—the big, wide metal ones that you don't see any more. The room was furnished with three thinly padded armchairs and a small reception desk that held both a computer and a grungy beige telephone. The computer, though, was state of the art—a brand new IBM 286 that took up almost half of the desk's surface.

He passed through the front room and into an inner office just as I reached his door. I walked in and followed him. His inner room was only slightly less Spartan than the outer one, but its desk was larger and had some genuine wood in its pedigree. Behind it was an inexpensive executive chair. On the other side of the desk sat three comfortable, unmatched armchairs that looked like garage-sale stuff.

He had just turned on the light in this inner room when he turned to see me. I could read the nagging thought he was having—the feeling that he might have forgotten some kind of appointment this morning

I couldn't help but stare at his clothes. His denims looked cleaner than I'd originally thought, but I was surprised that he'd wear an old T-shirt if he was expecting a business meeting. Also, he might have worn a belt, and probably not those sandals. He could have washed his feet.

"Grant Carson?" I said.

"Yes."

"The lawyer?"

"Attorney."

"Pardon me?"

"Attorney at Law," he said. "We call ourselves attorneys. May I help you?" At least he remembered to smile, and when he did, I could see more of the image my friends had described. I mean, he was no Tom Selleck, but he did have a similar moustache, under which gleamed white, even teeth. Like most of the outdoorsy types around Sage Landing, he was deeply tanned. His eyes were looking me over with a definite bit of the devil in them.

"Everybody else calls you lawyers," I said and then regretted it. I looked at his sandals again but tried to put them out of my mind. "On the commercials, too, you guys advertise using the word lawyer. 'Need a lawyer? Call So-and-So.' Then there's TV shows, you know? All those guys call themselves lawyers." I paused only to take a breath.

Then my mouth started up again, seemingly out of control. "Oh. You mean to each other?" I asked. "You call each other attorneys when you're talking to each other, even though everyone else calls you lawyers? What's the point in that?"

The lawyer extended his hand. "I'm Grant Carson, and you are?"

"Naomi Manymules." I barely touched his hand, as is the Navajo custom. "Dr. D. told me to be here at ten o'clock, and I was. I think it's after eleven now. What time do you normally open?"

"Dr. D.?"

"Sorry. Dr. Moreno, the community college president. The sign on her office door says Dr. D. Moreno. Nobody knows what the D. stands for, and everybody thinks it's funny so we usually call her Dr. D." I knew I was babbling again so I shut up. I have a tendency to babble when I'm nervous, which certainly described this situation.

Grant Carson seemed to remember. Dr. D. had already warned me that he had probably had one or two drinks too many when she had talked to him about me a couple of nights before.

"Desiree," he said. "It's Desiree, but she'd kill me if she knew I told anyone. I might be the only one in town who knows her name, and I'm forbidden to use it." He smiled again, and I had to agree with my friends that he was sort of handsome, but not at all in the Adonis way I'd expected. I could see a little of a former Adonis—very little, but still.

For once I kept my mouth shut instead of responding, but I mentally filed this valuable information. Later, I would reflect on its best possible use.

"You said something to Dr. D. about needing office help?" I said, hoping to prod his memory.

I should explain here that what Dr. D. actually said was that this new lawyer Grant Carson had been complaining about the burden of keeping his practice small enough to allow time for fishing but large enough to earn enough income to pay for his boat. His boat, the *Deep Inn,* was already infamous in Sage Landing. During the past few months, its reputation had divided the town's women into two groups—those who were disgusted by its rumored goings-on and those who were curious and would maybe like to see for themselves at least. Most women under seventy fell into the latter group.

Dr. Moreno, with whom I gathered Carson had a special relationship, said that she told him about me and told him I could be just what he was looking for. Grant Carson clearly didn't remember any of that. He had told Dr. Moreno that the student should drop around to see him at ten o'clock, Monday. Today was Monday. That conversation had been on Saturday night.

I tried to keep the exasperation out of my voice. "You weren't expecting me? Dr. D. said that you'd be expecting me this morning at ten o'clock."

I could see him thinking. Buying himself a little time, he walked behind the desk to sit down in the big chair. I leaned against the door frame and waited quietly as he toyed with a pen that was sitting on his desktop.

He cleared his throat and, still looking intently at the pen, resumed the conversation. "Naomi Manymules, you said?"

"That's right."

He finally looked up and said, "That's an unusual name... a unique name."

This seemed rather rude, mostly because it was hard to believe that he'd been here in Sage Landing almost a year without coming across a number of people whose last name was Manymules. So I locked eyes with him in silence for a moment before blandly saying, "Not really. Naomi is actually a very common name on the Eastern Seaboard—there are lots of women named Naomi in New York and New Jersey, not to mention Florida." I maintained eye contact with him, waiting to see if he wanted to continue the "you're so exotic" theme.

He didn't. Instead, smiled faintly and changed conversational direction.

"You're a secretary?"

"Office manager."

"I only need…."

"When you're the only assistant in a small office, you're usually called the office manager. Nobody's a secretary anymore." I walked in and sat down in the closest of the three chairs facing the desk. Normally, I would've awaited an invitation, but I was afraid that none would be forthcoming. I remembered that white businessmen valued getting a foot in the door. He would probably admire my assertiveness. "What type of help do you need, Mr. Carson?"

Without offering an immediate answer, he leaned back in the big chair and appeared to be trying to remember what was said Saturday night when he'd been having a drink or two with friends at the Lunker Room out at the lake. I should point out that I can usually figure out most of what a man is thinking by merely looking at him. Most women can do this pretty well, but I'm especially good at it.

The attorney's face lit up, and I could again see what my friends had said about his looks. When he smiled, he *was* handsome. His face registered some recall and he said, "I was with Abraham Bingham celebrating a pretty damn good day of fishing on Abe's boat when one of his wives—I think it was the younger one—stormed in and raised holy hell and took Abe away. I don't remember what she said, but Abe didn't put up much of a fight." He smiled again and nodded as his memory gradually recovered. "Just after that, Desiree Moreno came into the bar and sat beside me. I had the impression that she'd been looking for me."

He paused, apparently trying to remember just what had happened next. Then he said that Dr. D. had accepted his offer of a drink and had been warm and friendly—quite a surprise to him considering they'd had a recent tiff. Along the way she said that she'd been thinking about his problem of having too much business and too little time. She'd suggested that if he had a *secretary*—he made a point of emphasizing the word "secretary"—he could slough off a lot of the work at a reasonable cost to himself and thus gain additional fishing and drinking time. She had said this as if she approved of fishing and drinking, even though he knew for a fact that she did not much like either one. Now *he* was kind of babbling.

His memory of most of the rest of the conversation had grown fuzzy. He was sure, though, that Desiree had not accepted his invitation to go home with him. She hadn't done that in quite a while, he said.

I thought he had just told me more than I wanted to know, so I interrupted his recollection. "I've had training."

He focused on me and resumed his appraisal. I knew what he was seeing—and thinking. Before him sat an attractive Navajo woman about five-and-a-half feet tall. Minimal makeup; short, rounded fingernails; abundant, shoulder-length dark hair—wavy, no gray. Age was harder for a white man to assess, and I couldn't tell if he pegged me at more or less than my thirty-something years. But I would bet that on an attractiveness scale of one to ten, he'd put me at a seven—maybe an eight.

"In a law office?" he asked, probably proud of himself for replying with a businesslike question instead of some remark laced with innuendo.

"In three courses at the community college, extensions from U of A. They were going to sponsor a paralegal program up here, but they dropped it. I made A's."

That actually seemed to impress him and was probably much more than he expected to find in an office assistant, but I knew he wouldn't want to appear impressed. "I'd only need a few hours a week, Ms. Manymules. I tailor my legal practice to a small clientele."

"Dr D. *said* that you didn't have much business, but that you needed a lot of help anyway. I need a job, Mr. Carson." I remembered that the correct white protocol was to ask directly for what you wanted, though this always struck me as somewhat uncouth. "How many hours a week did you have in mind?"

Carson said, "Maybe fifteen or twenty," but it didn't seem to me that he could have given any organized thought to his needs at all. Immediately, he added, "If things work out. Of course, I don't know your expected rate of pay."

"Twenty hours is good enough for now. Whatever you normally pay a paralegal will be fine, Mr. Carson. When can I start?"

He stalled as if he had no idea what would sound reasonable for pay, and maybe he had no idea what to have me do or when to start doing it. He seemed lost for a moment.

Suppressing a sigh, I gently asked, "What were you going to work on this afternoon?" If he would tell me that, I'd have a better idea about what to suggest.

"Uh, a trust. I was going to make a few notes about a living trust for a client who's coming in tomorrow morning."

I nodded my understanding and decided to try a little legal vocabulary on him. "Revocable or irrevocable? Is it mostly boilerplate, or is it specialized?"

"What? Oh, revocable. Somewhat specialized."

I was glad to have stumbled into a project about which I actually knew something. I'd done a case study on revocable living trusts. "Why don't you just have me plug in the basics and you can concentrate on any specifics. I can start on it this afternoon if the new computer out there is ready to go."

"Uh…" He looked confused.

"Oh, you probably already have the core document prepared since the client is coming in tomorrow."

Grant Carson shook his head, and I could see that he had not yet started on the trust at all. "Actually, I'm a little behind. A lot has come up lately," he said. "I wanted some sample provisions to show him, but we're just in the preliminary stages."

I could tell that he knew I wasn't convinced about his having been too busy. "So shall I get started?"

"We haven't discussed pay yet. I'm afraid that I haven't had an assistant in quite a while…."

"Dr. D. suggested that I start at fifteen dollars per hour," I said. I was pretty sure that Dr. D. would back me up on that. I didn't know what paralegals made, but I got fifteen dollars an hour when I got temp work at the power plant.

"To start?" he asked, sounding surprised.

I continued with a frown. "If you just want someone to answer the phone and file things, you don't really need a legal assistant. I guess Dr. D. got it wrong. Are you just looking for a part-time file clerk? Maybe the high school could help you find a student who could come in after school. You probably wouldn't want to leave them in charge of the office in your absence, but I'm sure you could arrange your schedule to be here for most of that time."

I could almost hear the thoughts running through his head. He was behind on the little work that he actually had. Things were piling up. He wanted to spend less time in the office, not more. I would have bet that he was actually about to hire me when the unmistakable sound of squealing tires and an overpowered and over-revved engine interrupted his train of thought—just my luck.

This racket was followed by a rapid succession of four sharp explosive cracks.

I jumped to my feet and started toward the door. But before I could reach the outer office, a surprisingly nimble Grant Carson had scurried around his desk and grabbed me by the shoulders. He muscled me back into his office and all the way into a space behind his desk where he pressed me downward, and I found myself crouching with him behind it. I knew a few women who might have paid good money to be in my position, and I'll admit that it gave me a little thrill.

"Don't get up, Naomi!" Carson released my shoulders. Still hunched down at an awkward angle, he leaned over me and opened the lower left drawer of his desk. He shuffled blindly around in the papers that littered its interior. I could hear something heavy scraping against the bottom of the drawer. He swore under his breath, coming up empty-handed, and slammed the drawer shut before reaching out to a bag of golf clubs that was leaning in the corner. He tugged on it until it toppled over.

He extracted one of the clubs. "I'll take a look," he said as he slid around the end of the desk. Then he flattened out on the floor and slithered like a reptile toward the doorway and the outer office.

While the sounds in the parking lot had not frightened me, Grant Carson's behavior seemed reason enough to be careful, so I moved slowly as I got up and walked to the doorway. My would-be employer was now crouched beneath his front window and was peering out between the lower slats in his blinds. He held his club's grip firmly in both hands and had the shaft resting on his shoulder.

"Four people are lying in the parking lot," he said without looking away from the window. "I think two of them are children."

Chapter Two of *Coyote Alibi*

"Oh my god," I said as I rushed toward the window. "Are you sure?"

"They're getting up," Carson said. "They weren't hit. They're getting up." He stood too slowly to stop me as I sped across the outer office and opened the front door.

"Ellen, are you okay?" I shouted while sprinting headlong into the parking lot.

Highsmith, the son of a bitch, snapped, "She's fine!" before Ellen could answer me. He had already gotten up and was standing beside his disreputable van. A very good-looking white man in his fifties, he wore a dark suit which was now covered in red sand from the parking lot. Actually, I'm not being fair in saying that Willard Highsmith was merely good-looking. It would be more accurate to say that he was stunning. His dark, wavy hair, with just a touch of silver, was gathered into a foot-long braid that hung down his back. His teeth were so perfect that they would have been right at home in a slick magazine ad. His suntan was carefully maintained, and his dark brown eyes looked honest and sincere, if you didn't know him very well.

Ellen had also gotten quietly to her feet. She was a lot younger than Highsmith. In fact, Ellen and I had graduated from high school together. But today she was dressed like a much older woman, in a conservative gray dress buttoned to the collar. Her children, a boy and a girl in their early teens, stood a few feet away, swatting dust from their clothes. Strewn all around them were paper leaflets. Some had begun to blow away in the light breeze that moved across the parking lot.

I came to a stop in front of Ellen and asked her, "What happened?"

Highsmith again answered for her. "Firecrackers, I think, big ones," he said.

I ignored him and reached out to grip Ellen's shoulders, searching her face and repeating, "What happened?"

She just looked over at the kids, visibly relieved as they moved closer, unhurt but silent.

Grant Carson ambled into my field of vision still holding his golf club like an umbrella over his right shoulder. He seemed to be staring intently at Ellen. When he saw that I had caught him at it, he looked away.

Highsmith said, "No need for weapons, neighbor," gesturing toward the club. "We're not in any danger." Even when making nervous conversation like this, Highsmith's voice was remarkable—deep, resonant, and clear. If he weren't a shopkeeper, he'd have to be a radio announcer. In fact, he sort of was one because he did all of the talking on his own radio ads.

Carson looked down at the club in his hand almost as if he had not been aware that he was carrying it. "Sorry," he said as he let the shaft of the club slide downward and held it as if it were a walking cane. "I thought it was gunfire. When I saw all of you down on the pavement…I thought the worst."

Highsmith continued to try to knock the dust out of his suit. "I thought the same thing. But these were just kids trying to scare us. I guess they succeeded beyond their wildest dreams. I bet they're laughing their asses off somewhere right now."

I turned back to Ellen. Beyond the patches of dust that now covered much of her dress, I saw three distinct bruises along the left side of her face. They'd been covered by makeup, but the shading was slightly wrong for her complexion and the bruises were still visible. I felt an anger that tightened my guts, and I looked momentarily toward the club in Carson's hand. My instinct was to reach for it and to bash Highsmith with it.

Ellen glanced at the club, too, and shook her head slightly. "I'm okay," she said. Then she gestured toward her children by lifting her chin in their direction and pursing her lips. Most anyone raised this far north in Arizona will point like that instead of rudely pointing with a finger, whites as well as Navajos, though the gesture is a Navajo tradition. "We're all okay," she added.

I glared at the man who stood facing Grant Carson and gripped my friend's shoulders tighter. "Come into the office with me, Ellen."

"I can't. I—we have to pick up these leaflets and get reorganized." She reached up and gently removed my hands from her shoulders and turned toward the children. "Pretty scary, huh?" she said, almost cheerfully. "Let's clean this mess up."

Grant Carson leaned over and pick up a leaflet that had blown against his leg. "What's all this?"

"It's part of our latest promotion. I'm Willard Highsmith—you probably know of me as Big Chief on account of the store." He nodded in the direction of the old mall's largest store over which a garish sign read Big Chief's Furniture and Appliances. "This is my family. Today we're trying to get ready for a big sale."

Carson smiled the kind of smile you paste on when you're not feeling friendly—that straight, tight smile that doesn't reach the eyes. "Yes, I've heard of you—heard your commercials," he answered.

Highsmith squinted at Carson's smile. "Is there something funny about them?"

"No," Carson answered. "Well, except that I assume you mean for them to be entertaining." Shifting the golf club / walking stick to his other side, he extended his hand and abruptly changed the subject. "I'm Grant Carson. My office is right over there. My, ah, assistant, Ms. Manymules, and I were startled by the noise."

Highsmith shook hands with Carson. "Thanks for coming to our rescue."

Carson shuffled his feet and put his right hand in his pocket. He looked skyward for a moment and seemed at a loss to know what to say. Finally, he looked at me and said, "We've got to be getting back to work. Naomi and I have a lot to do today."

But Highsmith wasn't finished with us. "If you're in the market for furniture, we've got a hell of a sale starting this weekend."

The children had begun to retrieve the leaflets that had blown farthest away. "These kids should be in school today, Willard," I said. Then I felt Ellen's gentle touch at the small of my back and stopped myself from saying more.

Highsmith ignored me and continued his pitch to Grant Carson. "We've made some special buys. The advertising won't come out until tomorrow. You ought to drop on down and get ahead of the crowds." He glanced toward the law office. "Some nice desks just came in. Walnut—you can't tell them from real wood."

I noticed with some satisfaction that Carson clenched his jaw and shook his head. "We've got to get back to work."

Just then a police cruiser pulled into the lot and drove right up to Highsmith's van. A uniformed cop with captain's bars pinned on his shirt collar got out, leaned against his car, and folded his arms across his chest. The name *Miller* was engraved on a black tag on his chest, but everyone here knew his name. Sage Landing was a small town, and Jack Miller was second-in-command on the town police force. "What's going on here, Highsmith? We got a report of gunshots."

"Firecrackers, Jack, but big ones," Highsmith said. "Kids."

The cop nodded. "Driving a supercharged pickup with oversized tires?"

"That's the one," Highsmith answered.

"Mark Banner's truck—the Ford Phallus?" I said.

Miller chuckled and turned to me. "His truck's a Dodge, actually."

"Yeah, I know, but I didn't want to make the alliteration with Dodge," I said. Miller and I had been in the same English classes in high school and were both just nerdy enough to still be making jokes about alliteration. And we both knew every truck in town.

"Too crude," he acknowledged, "but more people around here would understand it."

Carson looked at us and smiled. "Seems like high-performance cars always have low-performance drivers."

"That's the truth," Miller agreed. "But it wasn't the Banner kid. We already got the little jerks. They ran that short yellow light on their way north toward the lake. The patrolman smelled beer, so he's hauling them in. Just heard him make the call to dispatch." He made eye contact with Ellen, who was standing behind me. "You okay?"

She didn't say anything but must have nodded, because Miller looked at her skeptically before he turned toward Carson. "Did you see this happen, Mr. Carson?"

I realized that Carson's law practice must've brought him into contact with the police officers.

"No, we only heard it," Carson answered.

"Who's *we*?"

"Ms. Manymules and I were in the office when it happened."

Miller looked at me. "Naomi? You didn't see it?"

"No, like my boss said." I figured that calling him "boss" was a good opportunity to confirm my employment status in front of witnesses.

Miller raised an eyebrow and glanced at Carson before continuing. "We'll need a statement later, Highsmith," he said.

I stepped forward and poked Jack Miller in the ribs. When he looked at me, I nodded toward the teenagers. For a moment, he looked perplexed, but I mouthed a word, and he smiled and looked at Highsmith. "Why aren't these kids in school?"

Highsmith scowled. "They're *my* kids, Miller."

The cop shook his head. "They're Ellen's kids, but that isn't the point. The law says they have to be in school today unless they're sick. They don't look sick."

"*Or* on recognized family business," Highsmith answered. "They're on family business."

Miller leaned over and picked up a flier. After looking it over, he said, "Get them in school right after lunch, or I'll charge you. We've had this conversation before."

It was easy to tell that Jack Miller was getting angry, but, for a salesman, Highsmith was remarkably poor at reading people. He raised his voice and slapped his van's fender. "Stay out of my business, Captain! You don't have the right to interfere in family business."

Then Jack lost it. He spun on Highsmith and grabbed up a handful of his shirtfront, shoving the older man back against the van.

Grant Carson turned on his heel and started walking toward the office, saying loudly, "Naomi, we have to get moving if we're going to be ready for that meeting." I stared at him for a split second before my peripheral vision caught sight of Jack reaching for his nightstick, and I turned to watch.

Miller slid the end of his nightstick up under Highsmith's throat, and I don't know what he might have done next if Ellen hadn't reached out and put a hand his shoulder. That stopped him. He lowered the stick and stepped back. Everyone knew he'd gone over the line, but he didn't seem to care at the moment. I'd seen him go too far a couple of times in the past, and I knew that Highsmith had better watch his step.

But Highsmith just didn't know when to keep his mouth shut. "I'll file an assault complaint," he growled.

Well, by then *I'd* had enough so I stepped between the two men and tried to put my face against the Big Chief's. "If you don't shut up, you moron, I'm going to assault you myself." Now picture this: I'm about five-six and weigh about one-thirty, and Willard stood about six-one and probably weighed in at around one-ninety. My nose was approximately at his collar bone.

Captain Miller pulled me back and started to smile. He nodded at Ellen, and for a moment I had a flashback memory of the two of them as our Homecoming king and queen together about half of my lifetime ago. They made just as handsome a pair now as they had then. Jack still had the build of an 18-year-old quarterback, and his chiseled features had only improved with age. His hair was still boyish—not very long, but tousled and sun-bleached—and his blue eyes were as intense as they'd been when he moved to Sage Landing as a kid.

His eyes stayed on Ellen as he said, "Do whatever you want about the complaint, Highsmith, but get those children back in school." Then he got back in his car and drove away slowly.

~ ~ ~

"What was that all about?" Carson asked once he and I had returned to the office and closed the door.

I tried to sound calm and professional, but I felt like screaming. "Willard Highsmith is a crooked son of a bitch with lots of enemies."

"I don't think people take Highsmith seriously enough to try to do him any harm, Naomi. Anyway, didn't he say it was just kids who threw the firecrackers?"

I nodded. "Some of what are called kids around here can be pretty rough little jerks."

"You mentioned Mark Banner. I know that name—where from?"

"His dad's a doctor at the clinic. Both of his parents are big shots. The kid's a wild brat with a mean streak, and he's out of control sometimes."

Carson walked into his office and motioned for me to take a seat. Instead, I detoured back out to the front office where I rummaged around in the desk and found a legal pad and pen. Then I joined him in his office and sat down.

"So you don't like Big Chief Highsmith much." He picked up his golf bag and replaced the club before he sat down.

I scowled. "His wife is an old friend of mine." I paused and then added, "You must be aware that he isn't a Navajo."

"I don't think anyone thinks he is. It's funny, though, that he'd use that business name—Chief. Navajos never had chiefs, did they?"

"No, not really. Outsiders would sometimes label someone as a chief, but that's different." I was actually a little surprised that Carson had learned that much, because it wasn't the sort of thing likely to come up in casual conversation or legal negotiation. "Highsmith is a Texan. Like a lot of Texans, he claims to be part Cherokee. He sells a lot of furniture to Navajos just because he's the only big furniture store out here." I wanted to add that he was a rat-bastard, but I showed some restraint.

Carson's expression darkened and he waited a while before asking, "Do you think he gave her those bruises?"

I was surprised at the question and started to answer but thought better of it. "It's not my place to talk about their business. Let's just say no, I don't like him."

Carson nodded. He let the silence settle for a bit, keeping his eyes on some papers spread across his desk before looking at me. "Is it true that Highsmith cheats on his wife?"

I was surprised again. I hadn't realized that he was in on the local rumor mill. "That's what they say."

"They?"

"It's a pretty consistent topic of conversation." He said nothing, and I saw that he expected more. "I trust the people who say it," I added.

Carson smiled and leaned back in his chair. "I thought for a second that you were going to grab my four-iron and whack him with it."

"You're very observant," I said. "But you were already out of reach by then, hot-footing it out of there—and taking the club with you."

The lawyer—sorry, attorney—grinned. "I wanted to be able to swear that I hadn't seen Jack Miller kill the Big Chief in broad daylight in front of his own stepchildren."

I laughed. "All Jack has to do is wait—someday, I'm going to do it for him." I paused and then changed the subject. "Do you want to tell me a little about the living trust we're doing?"

Carson sat forward and got down to business. This was an important moment for me because it meant that I was actually going to start *working* for the guy.

"Do you know a man named Frank Armstrong?" he asked.

"The trucking company?"

"The owner of the trucking company and other businesses, yes."

"Yes, I do." Then I realized that sounded like I was a personal friend or something. "No, I don't. I mean, everyone sees the trucks and the warehouse. I'd recognize him because he drives a Cadillac with the company name painted on the side." I realized that I may have been babbling again so I shut up.

"He has a daughter named Linda."

"Her I know."

He looked quizzical.

"By reputation," I added.

"She's his only heir."

"Seems pretty simple to me, then. What are the complications?"

Carson started to say something, but paused. Instead of answering me, he asked, "Naomi, in your three paralegal courses, what did you learn about confidentiality?"

The earlier events in the parking lot must've left a bunch of adrenalin still pumping through my system. Usually it takes a while for me to reach full-on fury, but now I immediately felt my face flush. I sat up very straight and dropped my voice barely above a whisper. More like a hiss, actually. "Mr. Carson, I did not need any textbook or professor to tell me that maintaining confidentiality is the most important thing in the practice of law. What? You're worried that I'd gossip about a client's private legal stuff? Discuss his family relationships? Is that what you're getting at? Because if it is…."

Carson had leaned forward, his face alarmed, trying to get a word in. When I finally ran out of breath and paused to inhale, he was saying, "No, no, no," and waving *stop, cancel, do-over* jazz hands through the air between us. I fell silent.

He said, "Of course, of course, I didn't mean to imply…sorry."

Neither of us said anything for a good long while. Then I nodded at him, accepting his apology and maybe making one of my own.

Finally, he cleared his throat and said, "Frank Armstrong has a serious liver disease. He's on a transplant list, and time is running out."

That sort of stunned me. The simple legal-clerical task in front of me suddenly felt personal and sad.

～ ～ ～

Two hours later, I'd made a good start on the basic provisions of a living trust when the office phone rang for the first time that day. The caller asked for Grant Carson and gave his name as Chuck Margolin. I'd never talked to Chuck before, but I knew him by reputation, because boat-owning friends of mine tended to shake a fist at the heavens when paying the bill he'd sent them for working on their watercraft. My hunch was that this call might make Carson unhappy. Reluctantly, I punched the hold button on my phone, got up to poke my head through the door to Carson's inner office and announce the call, and sat back down at my desk. A moment later, Carson closed his door, and right after that I learned that I could hear him just as well through the wall as I could sitting right in front of him. It occurred to me that this unexpected conduit for information would probably be useful in the future.

"How in the hell can it be six hundred dollars, Chuck?" Grant Carson asked as clearly as if he'd been sitting next to me. Actually, he *was* sitting next to me, except that there were two flimsy layers of very cheap paneling —maybe one step up from cardboard—between us.

Carson's remarks were punctuated with brief silences.

"What clutch is that?...Jesus!...That much?...When?...Fuck that! Three weeks?...You said...But you said...I can't afford that...just now. I was expecting a simple adjustment or something....I *know* it's a special engine....I know it's a big boat....I can't, Chuck."

Then there was a longer pause.

"Yeah, I guess we could trade like that.... Right, no money changes... not necessarily any taxes... in theory....I didn't know you needed legal... Okay, I'll probably see you at the Lunker Room tonight....Sure, that will be fine....Order the goddamn parts, Chuck."

I heard Carson's receiver hit the cradle as clearly as if it had been the phone on my own desk. The conversation reminded me that Mr. Carson and I had never concluded our discussion about salary. I'd been right about what kind of mood the call would put him in, so how was I going to bring my salary up again? And how was he going to be able to give me enough work to do if he didn't get enough paying business? Trading legal services for boat repairs didn't sound like the road to success, and I needed for him to be a successful employer.

~ ~ ~

Carson went out for lunch at about 2:30, so naturally the phone rang again. The man on the phone said he was Abe Bingham and he wanted to talk to Grant about getting a divorce. Maybe two divorces, he said. I told him that Mr. Carson was out of the office on business and that I would have him return the call as soon as possible. I asked if there were any details he wanted me to pass along to Mr. Carson. I was disappointed when he just answered, "Grant will know what I'm talking about."

I would have loved to know details about Abraham Bingham and his wives. Lots of white guys around here have multiple wives, but few of them are as powerful and successful as Abe Bingham. It occurred to me to wonder if Mr. Bingham would be a paying client or one who wanted to barter something for legal services. I couldn't see how my new employer was going to pay me by trading favors all over town. But Bingham could certainly afford to pay us. He was a building contractor with projects throughout the region.

When Grant Carson returned at 3:30, he had the faint aroma of beer about him, but he'd gone home and found sneakers and a clean short-sleeved shirt. He hadn't found any socks.

In my most crisp and professional voice, I started to give him Bingham's message. "Mr. Carson, there was..."

He interrupted me. "Grant," he said.

"Most people call you Carson. You prefer Grant?" Up till now, I had avoided the whole issue of how to address my employer by not saying his name at all when talking to him.

"Carson, then. I don't care, just not *Mister* Carson."

"Okay. Got it. Anyway, there was a business call while you were out."

"Someone called here about a legal case?" he asked, as if that never happened in a law office.

"Abraham Bingham."

"That would be about fishing."

"He said he wanted a divorce, or maybe two divorces."

Carson sat down in one of the front office chairs. He appeared to be pondering the information for a moment. "Abe doesn't talk about, uh, domestic things with me."

"He sounded serious, like maybe he really wants a law...an attorney," I said. "He said you should call him back." I hesitated and then plunged ahead. "Maybe we're bringing in some new business."

Carson shook his head. "Abe may *think* he wants a divorce, but he can't have one. Besides, I couldn't help him anyway." He looked up at me, probably enjoying my confusion.

"I thought anyone could get a divorce."

"Only married people," Carson said. "No, actually, people who aren't married *can* get a legal divorce, at least here in Arizona, if there is a presumption of marriage and property or children to be disposed of."

"Dispose of children?" I tried to make a joke and look shocked and disapproving.

He got it. "Right, no, I should have said property or custody issues to be decided." He got up and walked to his office door. "In this case there are no children, but there is a lot of property. In any case, all I can do is refer Abe to someone else because he doesn't live in Arizona."

"And we're not licensed in Utah?"

"Admitted to the Bar," he corrected. "*I'm* not admitted to the Utah Bar. Another way to say it is that I'm not an officer of the court in Utah."

I nodded. "I thought Bingham lived in Sage Landing," I said. "I see his trucks all the time."

"Oh, I guess at least ninety percent of his contracting business is here because we have the larger population, such as it is. Actually, Abe often stays for days at a time on his boat. The marina *is* in Arizona. Maybe I could argue that he's an Arizona citizen. I wonder what residence he declares on his taxes."

I interrupted. "But he's not married? Did you say that?"

"Not in a sense that's recognized by the court."

"Of course he's a *plig* and all, but don't they have some kind of legal standing?" Pligs—short for polygamists—are just another minority around here, especially just across the state line.

Carson raised one eyebrow. "Polygamy is against the law in both Arizona and Utah, so I guess that's more like an *illegal* standing...if it's true."

"It is, isn't it?" I asked, backtracking. I didn't know how well Carson knew Bingham.

"Well, obviously, Naomi, Abe's a plig. But I think the, um, members of the polygamous community consider the word 'plig' to be something like an ethnic slur. I believe the preferred term is 'plurally married.' So let's be a little more circumspect with the language, okay?" He smiled broadly.

~ ~ ~

Coyote Alibi is available in multiple formats in print and as an audiobook. If you haven't read it yet, you should. There are more Naomi Manymules mysteries in progress.

ABOUT THE AUTHOR

J. & D. Burges are a husband-and-wife writing team in Virginia. Having lived for many years on the edge of the Navajo Nation, they write with cheerful authority about open spaces, big lakes, and the unique mix of cultures captured in their Sage Landing stories.

Their mysteries are now hatched in a cottage in the woods near a lake. It's a great place to plot light-hearted homicides. When they're not doing that or working out, they might be dancing. There's also some knitting and woodworking going on.

They can't resist interfering in each other's work. It's often hard for them to remember which story idea originated where and whose words made it into the final draft. Each of them claims that the best lines belong to the other.

Check out their web site at www.jdburges.com

Because reader reviews really help others find good books, please review Coyote Alibi every place you can. It makes a big difference in today's reading world.

Made in the USA
Monee, IL
17 December 2021

86114611R00157